VERACITY

A NOVEL

LAURA BYNUM

POCKET BOOKS

New York   London   Toronto   Sydney

Pocket Books
A Division of Simon & Schuster, Inc.
1230 Avenue of the Americas
New York, NY 10020

First Pocket Books hardcover edition January 2010

POCKET and colophon are registered trademarks of Simon & Schuster, Inc.

For information about special discounts for bulk purchases, please contact Simon & Schuster Special Sales at 1-866-506-1949 or business@simonandschuster.com.

The Simon & Schuster Speakers Bureau can bring authors to your live event. For more information or to book an event contact the Simon & Schuster Speakers Bureau at 1-866-248-3049 or visit our website at www.simonspeakers.com.

Manufactured in the United States of America

10   9   8   7   6   5   4   3   2   1

Library of Congress Cataloging-in-Publication Data

Bynum, Laura, 1968–
   Veracity—1st Pocket Books hardcover ed.
      p.   cm.
   I. Title.
   PS3602.Y57V47 2010
   813'.6—dc22   2009024767

ISBN 978-1-4391-2334-8
ISBN 978-1-4391-5595-0 (ebook)

ACKNOWLEDGMENTS

The day I received the bid on *Veracity*, I'd just had a biopsy on my left breast. Two days later, I received a. confirmation that it was cancer, and b. my contract from Pocket Books. It's been a hell of a ride. What began with a trip to the Maui Writer's Conference (and, while there, winning the Rupert Hughes award for *Veracity*) culminates today in a way-too-brief list of people to whom I am grateful. It is painfully, unforgivably short, considering there are so many of you who were a part of not just helping me heal, but keeping me on track with my work. Were I to list you all, I'd double the size of this book.

Before going right into my acknowledgments, I should mention that surgery and radiation have cured me. I hope *Veracity* can serve as not just a cautionary tale about retaining our words and knowing the difference between fact and opinion, but also about not losing hope.

To my family—my generous husband, Eric Bynum, and our extraordinary daughters, Alex, Téa, and Sammy; my three mothers and three fathers, Trudy and Harold Watson, Bev and Walter Clark, and Sheila and Frank Bynum; my courageous siblings, Christina Olshefsky and Patrick Dill; my siblings-in-law, Paul Olshefsky and Joel, Natasha, and Portia Bynum.

To those of my family who've helped from a little farther

afield—my grandfather, Wilbur Long, Joyce Stover, Don Burch, and Mary (Mom Mom) Bynum.

To my friends—Janet Child, Colleen Cook, Jessica Hall, Barb Johnson, Rhonda and Tony Sinkosky, Carol Ordal, Ronald Rose, Ruth Stoltzfus, Christy Uden, Sonja Wise, Greg Wolf, Tammy and Greg Ziegler, and others too numerous to mention.

To my Illinois and Virginia physicians and caregivers—Dr. Schaap, Dr. Ogan and his bunch of rowdy ladies, Dr. Boyer, Dr. Lander, and Dr. Hendrix and her amazing crew—I was editing throughout my treatment and could not have finished this novel without your support and love.

A special thanks goes out to Dan Conaway who, as Simon so eloquently put it, is my creative beshert. If I could turn your insights into gold, we'd be able to put all our children through college. Also to Simon Lipskar, Sylvie Rabineau, and Jennifer Heddle for their insight into and support of this book.

Most of all, I must acknowledge my Creator who gave me the best diversion of my life on one of its darkest days.

This novel is dedicated to the most spiritually sentient woman I know—my grandmother, Irma Long.

December 23, 1918–July 9, 2009

apostasy

discriminate

ego

fossil

heresy

kindred

obstreperous

offline

veracity

apos-ta-sy: a total desertion of or departure
from one's religion, principles, party, or cause.

CHAPTER

ONE

The deeper I get into the prairie, the more I realize that what I've been told about the wastelands is false. The trees here are green. The crops, tall and heavy with corn. There are no black clouds threatening to drip acid onto my car, no checkpoints full of frothing police ready to execute every onerous code they see fit. I haven't seen a Blue Coat since Wernthal. God willing, it will stay that way.

An old farmer is hitchwalking down a line of corn. I see him in my rearview mirror as a blotch of spoiled yellow. This is how our world considers the inhabitants of this land. Spoiled and decrepit, not useful. But neither are they considered clever enough to pose a threat. So they enjoy the otherwise restricted bounty of nature. A wide-open sky. Grass. Neon-free, unfettered space. I envy them this, but only so much. We live in different prisons, but in prisons nonetheless. Theirs is made up of memories of the beforetime. Mine, of concrete walls and security checkpoints, of no birdsong and no breeze.

Fewer line boards are posted alongside the roads out here. Just one every few dozen miles instead of the standard one per block. Posters of non-sexually attractive housewives blink as I drive by. *Stay Happy*, at mile marker 1. *Stay Healthy*, at mile 32. *Remember the Pandemic*. Mile marker 78.

Used to be something different. *Honor Those Who've Fallen*, to communicate the whole of it. But the word *honor* got too many people thinking. The concept sparked a small fire in those of us not quite doused out, and we began to discuss the *dis*honorable things required of all citizens living here, things that didn't get printed on line boards. And so in small, quiet ceremony, in the ripping down of a hundred thousand posters, *honor* had the honor of being our first Red Listed word. We woke the next morning to *Safety First* and *We Don't Want to Go Back to the Way Things Were, Do We?*

The countryside is more beautiful than I remember, even like this. Bales of trash instead of baled-up hay. Abandoned farmhouses dotting the land like weeping sores. I can't stand to see their burnt or age-worn structures, or their insides seeping out onto the unmowed lawns. I was born in the country, as were my best memories. I won't desecrate them by noticing these shells of civilization zipping past my car windows. In fact, I'll go faster. It's unlikely Blue Coats will pick me up on the way to my break site anyway. They won't be out patrolling in the heat, in the wastelands where nothing happens. They'll come later when the Fatherboard sees I've gone rogue. It will be the most excitement they've had in months.

Maybe they won't be carrying guns. Not all Blue Coats get them. Most guns are reserved for the brigade lined up outside the National House like dominoes. Tin soldiers in tidy rows, they flash weaponry used to guard President and his cabinet of Ministers. Keep people from considering assassination, keep those who try anyway from achieving their goal. Guns also go to police assigned to specific jobs. Hunting down runners and the quick dispatch of terrorists.

Aside from this ignoble guard, the largely gun-free system has flourished. Fists, elbows, knees, mouths, teeth, the fleshy weapons carried by men, the ones used to inflict more intimate punishments—these broadcast an absolute and terrifying power the business end of a pistol doesn't match. When a Blue Coat exacts a punishment, scars are left and people see them.

I try not to think about the Blue Coats and what may happen to me if I'm caught. At least I will have finally stood up.

I've run in what I wore to the office. A white, long-sleeved linen blouse over a white camisole. A pair of gray tweed pants. Soft leather low-heeled shoes. This would have been so much easier in a T-shirt or a tank top. A pair of jeans, sneakers. From my understanding, the clothes I run in, I stay in for the better part of my training. It might prove stupid, not to have changed, but I'm a Monitor who's just gotten off Red Watch. They would have noticed the clothes gone from my closet or sitting in a sloppy pile in the trunk of my car. They can break into anything they want in the name of security. My home, my vehicle, my computer, my neck. It's how they protect us. From whom, I've long since stopped asking.

The sun is in full bloom above the cracked country road. Sweat beads on my brow, drops onto my cheek, runs down past my collar. It stings my slate, the silver identification module embedded in our necks almost as soon as we're out of the womb. It's barely visible above the skin, with just a line of silvery gray to collect Confederation downloads and provide access to where I am, where I've been, what I've said.

The slate is made of a material I don't understand. The first prototypes, like mine, were refitted as an individual grew. Now they grow with us, like my daughter's. Hers was implanted in her eighteenth month. Most children have theirs put in closer to age two, but she started talking early.

My slate has always itched and when I sweat like this, it feels like an infection. For years I've considered cutting it out, but it's wrapped around the carotid in such a way that it's impossible to remove without bleeding to death. Removing one's slate is the number one method of suicide in the Confederation of the Willing. People who are completely sane in the morning are found at their kitchen tables at night, a cup of coffee in their left hand, a paring knife in their right. I can understand this madness. Especially if you're older and have memories of the beforetime, like the farmers.

Most of us are younger than the event that divides our population. A quarter of us, probably fewer are well into our fifties or sixties, the survivors of a bacterial holocaust the likes of which mankind had never before seen. It took out whole continents. Almost half our nation's population. I'm one of a very small percentage of children who made it through the Pandemic. I was alive and aware thirty-three years ago and have small memories of freedom.

I roll down the window and adjust the rearview mirror so I can see my face. My cheeks are flush with blood and my gray eyes look older than the rest of me. I have light brown hair that's too long to be loose. It whips around my face and catches on my eyelashes.

"Goddamnit!" I shout into the wind. We can swear. A small privilege to keep us sane.

I tuck my hair beneath my collar and watch for the green road sign that will tell me I'm almost there. It comes up quick. I almost miss it, just like the note warned:

2050 North Province Rd., three miles southeast of Bond, East Bodland. Look for an old farmhouse, fire took out the barn. One white wall of siding is gone. Looks like your grandparents' place used to with a long rocked drive and a big oak tree bending the road. Don't miss the turn. Sign comes up quick on the backside of a hill.

I memorized each word.

My grandparents' house was thirty-three years ago and a world away. Their front drive was a white river of rock hewn between mounds of wild prairie grass and the entrance to my favorite place in the world. Dim memories show me a dark-haired father who missed the entrance more than he found it and a blonde-headed mother awkwardly smiling back at me from the passenger seat. According to the government, I was four years old when the Pandemic came wheeling down our drive in a big Confederation truck and took us all away. It was the last time I saw the farm, or my family.

I hit a patch of cobbled earth and bounce in my seat. I'm topping a hundred and twenty miles an hour and can no longer see the ugly residue of crops as a set of rows. They're now a haze of brown sludge sliding past my windows. The oak tree is ahead. I hit the brakes and turn the wheel toward the rocked drive, holding tight as the car fishtails on the loose gravel. I'm to the house before the dust trail can catch up. My legs are shaking when they hit the ground.

I'm Off Map now. They'll be sending out a car.

I don't remember making my way through the uneven earth to the screen door. But then I'm there, my hand on the knob, reading a bright yellow piece of paper that's been posted to a broken pane of glass.

No trespassing as posted by the Confederation of the Willing and its representative Province of Bodland. This property has been devalued as a residence or place of business and is Off Map for any citizen. Entrance will be noted via your slate and penalties may include 102A, 102B, 217A, and/or 550.

A 550. I think about the punishment hiding behind that number. *Jesus.* I'd think about getting in my car and lighting out for somewhere less patently dangerous, but this was my assigned place. This was where my recruiter said I'm to meet my trainer. I tear the yellow warning off the door and let it fall out of my hand on the way in. *Fuck 'em.* The false bravado doesn't make me feel better. I feel the false part more than the bravado.

The screen door leads to another that opens easily into a kitchen. There's a round table inside with a couple of chairs, its laminate top barely visible beneath an inch of dust. A gray linoleum counter runs the length of the far wall, separating wooden cabinet doors below and above. Their pine panels have warped and most of them stand ajar, revealing empty interiors. There are no implements. No refrigerator. No glasses to run under the sink that's sitting beneath a window. I can see other farm buildings through the thick panes. An abandoned corncrib made of cement with a rusting ladder running up one side. An old gasoline tank sitting atop a wooden crèche.

Deeper into the house, the air is so thick with the scent of decaying wood and carpet, I can hardly breathe. I pull my shirt over my nose and push aside cobwebs until I find a room with a bed.

"Oh, God."

The comforter looks just like the one I slept under at my grandparents' home, with pink flowers on a striped yellow backing. Except this one is duller, the material browned in large patches by years of unchecked damp. Maybe my recruiter put this here to soften my break. I've met him only once. He held me upright in an alley as I cried. I never saw his face. We didn't speak. I don't know the man's name and he knows what comforter I slept under as a child. This is the way it is between the recruiter and the recruited. They study us for years, review the whole of our lives. By the time we meet, they either love us or hate us and we know nothing about them other than what we permit ourselves to imagine. And I have imagined my recruiter irrationally.

Despite my pragmatic nature, I've allotted him only the best qualities. Kindness. Humor. Honor. A desire to get to know me from the inside out, the same way I want to learn him. It's a spiritual ache Pastor would call pornographic. The State would rather us focus on one another's bodies and forget about the contents of our hearts and minds, but I don't care. If I am a whore for fantasizing about this man's character and desiring a more intimate, less desultory connection, I am a whore. The rest is available on any street corner, anytime, for very few credits per act.

I know, in the long run, such fantasies about my recruiter

won't serve me. But, until I meet him and have to deal with the reality of who and what he actually is, they give me something to hope for.

I dump the contents of my pockets onto the bed, taking stock of the room's small closet. I've brought a picture, a roll of tape, and a handkerchief I tie around the knuckles of one hand. It's completely without function, this red swatch of cotton, save for what it represents and the way it feels. The note suggested bringing something, anything, to help with the pain.

I pull off short segments of the tape and paste the picture to the underside of the closet's doorframe, a good eighteen inches lower than the ceiling. I lie down beneath it, but there's not enough light to see the girl's eyes, so I get up again. Cross the room and yank open the window's shade. A cloud of dust appears, floating for a few seconds in the bedroom air. Through it comes the first sun this room has seen for over thirty years.

I lie back down, faceup, eyes steady on the girl above me, my feet sticking out into the room. Try to calm myself with memories of my daughter. I think of her at age four. A fair-skinned child with wild, honey-colored hair that became a helmet of springs during bath time. I can see her perfectly. Pink-cheeked, chubby hands batting at the bubbles I'd make by pouring in a capful of dishwashing soap. Then, suddenly, she was nine, then ten, then no longer possessed a round belly or light-colored hair. Bath time was spent with me sitting on the floor talking to her through a pulled curtain, as there were now things to hide. Blushes of womanhood to be kept private.

The fear comes back and thoughts of my daughter are replaced with questions: *Will it burn? Will I feel the metal breaking? Will I smell my flesh melting around it?* I work my legs to dislodge these thoughts. Almost begin to scream and feel something cool pressing against my forehead.

Oh, Christ.

A wire hanger. I toss it across the room and feel around the closet for any others. Anything metal grounds the current. Pressed against my body, it would have ended this run here and now. I shake it off. Shut my eyes and pray.

God. Make your truth mine. Even my inner voice wavers. It doesn't sound like the prayer I repeat silently every day. It sounds like something you say when you know you're going to die. And I might. It's a possibility.

Two syllables are all the Confederation needs in order to know if I'm trying to say something on the Red List. Then they stop it from coming, wiping away any other words that start with this sound. Either way, I'll stay physically bound to my slate forever. It will stay put in my neck, working or not. A purposeless organ, like an appendix that shows. If this break works, it will be my daily reminder to be *profound*—a quality of speech considered sinful. These days, the less said, the better.

All regress begins as address, Pastor says. Meaning there is nothing more dangerous than the spoken word. When we try to articulate words that have been Red Listed, a noise cancellation device disintegrates the product of our voices as the slate shocks us into submission. If warranted, Blue Coats are then sent out to make sure the message was clear. This is what the slate does. It regulates our vocabulary. Contains us. Keeps us from harm. That's what Pastor says.

This is what I have to do. Make a Red word audible. Repeat it over and over until one of us short-circuits. Just one word that, to me, means everything.

I look into the eyes above me, young and brown, a doe's eyes in a girl's face. "I love you."

A premature tear slips down my cheek. I open my mouth and begin to scream.

"Vera—." Two syllables escape, then nothing. Nothing but neural fire shooting through my jaws, boiling the fluid in my ears. I keep my eyes on the girl above me.

"   ." The shock is greater, matched by my effort.

My hands have started twitching. I squeeze the one holding the handkerchief. Try again.

"   ."

My head is splitting in two. My face already awash in tears.

"   ."

The feedback splices through my skin and whips down the length of my arms.

"   ."

God help me. I'm getting nowhere. The scent of burning hair is in my nostrils.

"   ."

My eyes blur. My hands have begun to clench and unclench as if I'm convulsing. I may be.

"..." It's something. A tapping sound.

"... ssssssssssssssssssssssssssssssssst-t-t ..." The staccato of consonance. Like at the grocery store, when they're about to announce someone's lost child has been found.

"Sssssssss ... ciiiiiit ... yyyyyy!" The sounds slip through the air and fill the closet. I ignore the blistering heat in my throat and scream louder.

"Ffff ... cccccccc ... t-yyyyyyyy!"

"Fffvvvv ... ccccccccciiii ... t-yyyyyyyy!"

"Vvvvvv ... cccc ... tyyyyyyy!" My voice sounds inhuman, like an android short-circuiting.

"Vrrrreeeee ... rrrrrr ... ccccccciiiiityyy!"

She's smiling at me now from her perch on the ceiling. *Do this, Mommy. Finish this.*

I swallow the last of my fear and scream, "VVEERRAAAC-CIIITYY!" It is my voice in full. Raw and ripped—but mine, a voice combined with a cracking, snapping spark. A flash of orange appears beneath my chin. It buckles beneath my jaw.

"VERACITY!" There is no more pain. I whisper, making sure: "Veracity." It was my daughter's name. My daughter, called by the name they took from her.

The corners of my closet world fold inward. Veracity reaches down and runs her hands over my face. I fall away.

She goes with me. I can smell her, tell how much she's grown and in not so long a time. She's over five feet tall now; I've seen her like this in my dreams. Her hair is long and thick, her body's beginning to curve.

God help her, she's no longer a little girl.

CHAPTER

TWO

Our twelfth-grade teacher, Mr. Coombs, is a hulking, prematurely gray-haired man with an unfortunate face. He's not mean, as his downturned mouth suggests, he's just spent too many years being worried, and as with so many adults in the Confederation, that feeling got stuck on his features. When Mr. Coombs goes to smile at the Sentient Patrol coming through the classroom door, his lips, unused to the practice, form themselves into a scowl.

At the head of the patrol is Sentient Baumfree. She walks directly to Mr. Coombs, who swallows so hard, his glasses lift off his round cheeks. "I apologize for the intrusion," she says, motioning the rest of her group into place around the room. "We won't be long."

Mr. Coombs sputters, finally getting something out that sounds like "Take your time."

Sentient Baumfree is well known. She's a tall woman with bright blue eyes and carrot red hair and has been all over the television. Almost every night, there's a piece on the news about her work with the Tracking and Data group. She and President have been fine-tuning the Monitoring Department, using Sentients she's recruited directly out of schools to lead efforts at finding *runners*—the term used for people who try to leave the system by breaking their slates and disappearing. Where they go is a mystery. We're told nowhere, as they supposedly never complete their runs, but it's obviously not true. Why else would Sentient Baumfree be standing in our classroom, scanning each of us as if we were see-through? Recruiting.

The Blue Coats position themselves at either side of the door and in the corners of the room while the others, all of them women, spread out so there's one every yard around the perimeter. I let my eyes relax and my mind fall into its alternate state and look at these women. Generated from each Sentient is a series of silvery, flickering lines that crisscross the room. *They're making themselves into a net. . . .*

The Sentients look us over. Point and demand names. They are here to do an assessment, to see who might qualify for the highest nonmilitary post in the land. Most of us sit up a little higher in our chairs and put on hopeful smiles. Those of us who don't want to be Monitors sink into our seats and try to focus our thoughts elsewhere. I am one of the latter. I want no part of this program, no matter how great the perks.

"Mary Louise Pembroke." Sentient Baumfree points at the girl seated next to me.

Mary Louise lets out a squeal but is too excited to move.

Mr. Coombs snaps his fingers and motions for the girl to go stand by the door. "Hop to, Miss Pembroke."

With a few more squeals, Mary Louise does as ordered. As she passes my desk, I feel her giddy anticipation like a shower of sparks. As she walks past the girl two seats up— Servina Dobbs—the joy that's turned Mary Louise into a walking firework dissipates. She's too permeable. Too open to the influence of others, especially those who spend a good part of their day breeding the worst colors. Dark red seeded with bits of black. Deep mustard-brown edged in tones of ochre. I've watched Mary Louise's colors sour in the presence of pernicious energy. As she passes Servina Dobbs, Mary Louise turns the color of boiled lettuce.

Servina Dobbs has been poking her head into the aisle every time Sentient Baumfree passes. She smiles and laughs at nothing, does everything but raise her hand and ask to be considered. I never liked Servina Dobbs. Even after she figured out I was sentient and might, therefore, one day be important.

Sentient Patrol began three or four years ago, nearly as soon as we all stepped foot in high school. Those students who passed their tests were plucked out of senior year and fast-tracked into the Monitoring Department. They were treated as valuable members of government and given the best apartments and largest cars. As soon as Servina Dobbs discovered my abilities, she wanted to know everything. How I saw what I saw. Which colors indicate which conditions. How she could learn to do the same. I explained to her that it was either a part of you or it wasn't and not something I could teach her. But to this day, if I so much as sneeze, she brings me a box of tissues.

Sentient Baumfree must see the way Servina's energies have affected Mary Louise. As soon as the quiet girl makes it to the edge of the room, the Sentient makes a beeline for Servina's desk.

"Is there something you want to say, young lady?" she asks.

"Servina Dobbs," Servina introduces herself with a large smile. "Yes, ma'am. I'd like to be tested. Please."

Sentient Baumfree's face is stone. I have no sense of what she's feeling. "How can you be certain you have abilities—"

"Oh, yes, ma'am, I have them!" Servina cuts in, and Mr. Coombs gasps.

"Servina!" he shouts, and the girl goes quiet.

Sentient Baumfree considers her with hooded eyes. "Do you know what happens to young ladies who pretend to be sentient but are not?"

"Yes, ma'am," Servina says, nodding. "I want to be tested."

"You know you don't have to be sentient to become a Monitor, correct?"

"Yes, ma'am. I still want to be tested."

Sentient Baumfree leans down to look Servina dead in the eye. "I'll ask again, are you aware of the punitives assigned to individuals who falsely claim to have sentient abilities?"

Servina's colors fade, but she holds on to her smile. "Yes, ma'am. I want to be tested."

Sentient Baumfree looks at the girl for a long time. Until Servina breaks off and points her eyes across the room at Mary Louise, who backs into the wall.

"Then line up."

Servina walks slowly, proud of what she believes is a victory. But I know different and retreat into my self-created somewhere-else by putting up the thickest wall of energy I can muster. It's dark, the color of wet earth, and, somehow, aqueous. The substance ripples with any wayward thoughts. I have to project myself away from the moment to keep it still. I think about the solitary years of my orphaned youth. About the wastelands, a place rumored to be toxic and the dwelling place of murderers but a place that somehow makes me calm, turns my energy from brown to gold.

I've cut myself off from the world and pray the world is, in kind, cut off from me. But sounds are coming from outside my shell. Voices. Sentient Baumfree is asking Mr. Coombs about the others. Then, about me. *Tell me about Miss Adams.*

Go away. Go away. Go away. Please, go away.

I think about the wastelands as they've been taught to us since childhood. Destitute and quiet. I think of the vast, wide parcels of toxic earth topped with clouds, thick and rotten with waste. The only people sanctioned to be in these rural parts of our country are farmers too old and sick to serve in the cities. Formerly valuable men left to wander around the cancerous earth, poking in seeds and then pulling up the resulting plants, which will require a regimen of cleaning before they're approved for anyone's table. We've been told that time spent in the wastelands can kill us, even short trips. And that the Blue Coats stationed there are the worst kind and worthy of a slow death. These wasteland police have carried out punitives on citizens without having received the authorizing codes. They are men who've raped children or killed and eviscerated old ladies not because the slate directed them to, but because they were bored, or angry. The Blue Coats in the wastelands are supposed to be the worst of the worst—men more hazardous than the polluted earth.

"Miss Adams!" A loud voice punches through the oily slick of my cocoon, creating a hole. *"Miss Adams!"* It's Mr. Coombs's voice. He's slinging it at me from behind his desk. "Are you with us?"

Through a fish-eye view, I see Sentient Baumfree directly in front of me, her lower half bent at a gruesome angle. She's trying to see where I've been and if I've yet returned.

"No hiding from me, Miss Adams," Sentient Baumfree cautions, her voice low. She puts out a hand and, without thinking, I pull away. My fear changes her expression. Makes it soft. "There's nothing to be afraid of," she says, lifting a strand of my dark blonde hair from a shoulder.

I force myself not to jerk away as she leans closer and looks in my face. "Tell me about this one, Mr. Coombs. What's our Miss Adams been like in class?"

"Miss Adams is a good student," Mr. Coombs answers. "She gets good grades, doesn't make any trouble for the others . . ."

"That's not what I meant." Sentient Baumfree looks up. Studies something just above my head, something floating over the part in my hair. "Tell me about the other things."

Mr. Coombs clears his throat. "Yes." He chortles. "Of course. Well, this year we've had one or two . . . uh . . . precognitive moments. I believe that's what you call them."

"Yes." Sentient Baumfree keeps her eyes on the air above and around my head. "That's correct. Can you tell me about these events?"

"Well, once she knew what assignment I was going to give before I had the opportunity to give it. And she knew that Angela Mullins's mother had died before the girl knew herself."

Two aisles over, Angela Mullins shifts in her seat.

"Did she come to you with this information?" the Monitor asks, her eyes still on my colors.

"Yes," Mr. Coombs grunts. "Harper wanted me to know that a Blue Coat was about to enter the classroom and announce it. She wanted me to pull Angela aside and tell her first."

To my surprise, Sentient Baumfree breaks her concentration on me and turns to look at Mr. Coombs. "Did you?"

"I'm sorry? Did I what?"

"Did you pull Angela Mullins aside to tell her that her mother had died before it was announced to her by a Blue Coat?"

Mr. Coombs's cheeks turn red. "Well, no. I mean, I didn't realize it was credible information—"

"Of course you did." Sentient Baumfree stands and walks to the front of the room. "Is there anything else you'd like to share about Miss Adams?"

Mr. Coombs nods ferociously, anxious to find his way back into Sentient Baumfree's good graces. The quick bobbing of his large head seems to knock free some blockage and a torrent of information spills out. "She sees colors. Almost all of the students have told me some story or another . . . it makes them nervous, understandably. I mean, it's understandable in that she's able to see something in them that they themselves aren't able to see . . ."

"Yes. What else?"

"She sees *traces* of things or people, if you follow. Once she thought there was a dead rat in the girls' bathroom but it had been removed days earlier . . . and did I mention that once she knew one of our boys was sick? Appendicitis. She was adamant. Wouldn't shut up about it until we were forced to take him to the nurse. I should also like to mention, he was treated in time." Mr. Coombs smiles, absently patting both arms. "We saved him. We did."

Sentient Baumfree nods at one of the Monitors, and without a word, the woman takes me by the hand and leads me to the line.

LAURA BYNUM

In fifteen minutes, Sentient Baumfree has chosen seven of us as candidates. *Potentials*, as we're called.

"All set, Sentient Baumfree?" Mr. Coombs has brought out his handkerchief and is collecting streams of sweat from his brow.

"Yes, Mr. Coombs."

We're gathered into the middle of the others, then marched out the door and down the hall, Sentient Baumfree at our head. I try to get a good look at her colors as she goes, but she's well veiled. Surrounded in a blue substance I can't breach.

"That's enough, Miss Adams," Sentient Baumfree calls from the front of the line. "None of that until we get to the testing room."

Outside, there are a dozen black vans lined up and waiting at the curb. Their doors slide back and two armed Blue Coats exit and stand on either side of the openings. We're loaded up and driven off. Spend thirty awkward moments trying not to fall off our seats as the vans veer in and out of traffic.

Once at our destination, the doors are again thrown open and we're unloaded into the dark corridors of an underground parking garage. There is an electricity in the air that makes my stomach turn. I look up and down the line created by all us Potentials and see there are others suffering from this barrage of charged atoms. Somewhere beyond the thick concrete walls, there are hundreds, if not thousands, of machines pulsing. I try to get a sense of where they're located but can't. It seems they're everywhere.

I'm in the Geddard Building. The thought must plaster itself all over my body. Other students, the ones who've been watching me, go ashen. The Geddard Building is in downtown Wernthal, in the very heart of President's National House Square. It's home to thousands of Blue Coats and, beneath them, thousands of redactors. Redactors are the machines that collect everything we say and everything we do. These computers talk directly to the slates implanted in our necks. They record everywhere we go and, via the Red word system, regulate our speech. Redactors keep a collective memory of us as individuals. One of these machines contains my entire life's history since age six.

"Ladies and gentlemen," Sentient Baumfree calls from the center point of our line. "I'll be taking you to a series of holding rooms where you will wait to be called. When it's your turn, you'll be taken to a testing room. Testing can take from five minutes to a few hours, depending on the Potential. If a Potential is able to demonstrate his or her ability adequately, he or she is moved directly into the Monitoring program. There will be no returning to school or going home. From this moment onward, there is no return to the life you once knew."

Sentient Baumfree pauses to let the sounds of alarm and surprise pass. None of us knew quite how this worked. Speaking about the Sentient Patrol has always been Red Listed. And since they only recruit from the twelfth grade and no interclass fraternization is allowed, we've never met a Potential personally. None of us. They've been like *The Book of Noah* to us. Known in name only. Revered.

Still, the idea that none of us will be returning from this place hits us like a fist. Our faces go pale. Plumes of frantic red explode up and down the line. Just as the panic is about to erupt in a more physical fashion, with vomiting or passing out, Sentient Baumfree puts two fingers to her mouth and whistles.

"Now that I have your attention, let me ask one final question!" She walks down the line and stops in front of Servina, who's shaking. "If there's anyone here who has misunderstood the nature of this exercise and would like to exit the line and return to class, please say so now . . ." She steps back and waits patiently for Servina to blink.

Christ. I know Servina well enough to know she's not going to back down. No matter how afraid she is, or maybe because of it.

I open my mouth to ask permission to speak and Sentient Baumfree aims a pointed finger my way. "No talking, Miss Adams!"

"I'm not leaving!" Servina shouts into the Sentient's turned ear.

The rest of us are riveted to our spots.

Sentient Baumfree pauses for just a few seconds, then makes a sweeping motion with her arm and the Blue Coats march us forward, hands dangling over their guns. It's rare for police to be armed. There's hardly a need given the government's hold on its citizens. These small cylinders of death don't seem like they're capable of killing anyone, though some of them have retained a unique energy from their utilization. Golden coils of spent friction float off the ones that have been fired. They make a strange trail of O's through which we're to walk.

After piling onto elevators and traveling up a few floors, we exit into an unmarked hall and are taken to the holding rooms. In mine, there are ten girls and two boys. Sentient Baumfree has disappeared and left us in the care of a young woman named Miss Chalk. Young and pretty, the blonde-haired twentysomething flirts with the boys while announcing the rules about time spent in the testing room.

"No talking. No eating. No drugs." Miss Chalk pauses to stare at Andrew Lindman, who turns bright red and begins fiddling with the frayed edge of his collar. "No asking when it's your turn. Your turn comes when Sentient Baumfree comes to collect you." This she says while smiling at Darnell Jones, who rises from his seat as she walks by.

Miss Chalk sachets slowly back to her desk, tossing the final mandates over a shoulder. "If you want to change seats, do so now, as you will be asked to stay in exactly the same ones for however long as soon as the first person is taken back. You won't be able to go to the bathroom without an attendant watching, so you probably want to hold it if you can. Oh . . . and no drinks."

Sentient Baumfree comes for Catherine Bayer first. It's not ten minutes before the Monitor is back and pointing at Darnell. Catherine is nowhere to be seen. The quickness of it throws us. We don't know if it's a good or a bad sign.

"Come on, Mr. Jones," the Monitor urges him impatiently.

But Darnell can't seem to move. Our classmate stumbles getting out of his seat. He's shaken like the rest of us. Wants to know what's happened to Catherine and what's about to happen to him. He's taking too much time to get to Sentient Baumfree, so she comes to him. The Monitor takes Darnell by the arm and the two of them are gone. The rest of us turn and make note of the time on the wall clock: 3:40 p.m.

I feel something strike my back and turn to find Servina's ponytail holder on the floor next to me. I look back. Servina's got her eyes on Miss Chalk, who's not returning her attention.

My classmate points up at the clock, flashes me ten fingers, and shrugs. *Why was Catherine's test only ten minutes?*

Servina has panic scrawled all over her. It's caused her naturally dour colors to bloom into a cloud that envelops the back half of the room. It's moving of its own accord up the holding room aisles, soaking a good third of the others in a pasty pink drizzle.

I don't answer and look away.

Miss Chalk puts down her electronic notepad and sets her big blue eyes on Servina. "And no signing or using gestures, either. Last warning. There won't be another."

6:55 p.m. Sentient Baumfree walks through the door and takes a seat in one of the chairs. She looks from Servina to me then back again, focusing the second time round on our arms and our faces, which are covered in a nervous sweat.

It's been three hours of pure hell. The holding room is nearly bare. Aside from Miss Chalk, Servina and I are the only ones left. We've watched all of our colleagues be called up and disappear. There have been distant shouts and, once, a scream. But no idea of who's made it and who hasn't.

I sneak a look over at Servina, who's gone pale and has a hand full of fingers set against her teeth, then back at Sentient Baumfree. The Monitor seems as desperate for this to be over as Servina. Her eyes go back and forth a few times, as if she's deciding which one of us to deal with first.

"Miss Chalk?" Sentient Baumfree calls.

The girl perks up from her slouch. "Yes, ma'am?"

"I'll be taking Miss Adams back now. You can process Miss Dobbs from here."

The news falls hard on Miss Chalk's face. She opens her mouth to say something and the Monitor holds up a finger.

"Now, please."

Servina tries to stand but can't and falls right back into her seat. "What's happening?" she asks quietly.

Sentient Baumfree motions for me to follow her and begins to leave the room.

"What's happening!" Servina's crying now. She's found her legs. Has made it halfway to the door before stumbling over a chair and landing, facedown, on the floor.

Miss Chalk presses a button affixed to the hallway wall and speaks low into its mesh face: "Removal, please. Holding room B."

"Let's go." Sentient Baumfree takes my arm and pulls me away.

I roll my shoulder and slide out of her grasp. "What's going to happen to Servina?"

Behind us, Servina is making a slight moaning sound. Maybe she's been hurt, cracked a tooth on the floor. Or maybe she finally realizes high school is over and a whole new set of rules now apply.

"Let's go, Miss Adams." Sentient Baumfree is using an

ominous tone. She's giving me a warning not to ask again. So I don't.

Before we can get very far, a group of Blue Coats comes into the holding room. Sentient Baumfree rushes me through a door that leads to a brand-new hall. She gets the door shut just as my schoolmate's screams catch up. The testing room is small. It's just large enough for a desk with one chair on either side. On the left wall is a large television screen, and on the right, a mirrored window nearly as long and wide as the plaster expanse. I'm claustrophobic, don't like any space like this where I can't easily move around, or get out.

"You okay?" Sentient Baumfree looks down at her electronic notepad and makes some notes about my moist face.

"Fine." I wipe myself dry with a sleeve.

The woman makes a signal with one hand and a blinking cursor appears on the large monitor over her head. "Please state your name," she says. On the screen the same words appear almost as fast as she speaks them.

"Harper Adams." *Harper Adams*. I barely get them out before the words appear, already transcribed.

The cursor blinks impatiently over Sentient Baumfree's red hair. It's hard not to watch.

"Miss Adams, at what age did you first notice your abilities?"

I shrug. The cursor continues its pulsing.

"A verbal answer, please."

"I don't remember a time when I didn't see colors."

"So the colors were the first thing you experienced?"

I'm confused. "It's hard to say."

Sentient Baumfree puts two fingers on either side of her temples and rubs. "Try, please. And we're on a clock here, Miss Adams." She looks at the silvered window and the man I feel behind it. He's fatigued, like the Sentient. Wants to hurry it up, add one or two good finds to their roster and get going. The feeling I get from both of them is that they've been at this all day and it's not been a very promising return on their efforts.

"I was always able to see people's colors, though it sometimes comes and goes."

"Why?"

I shrug. "Stress, I guess. Sometimes if I'm too close to a person, I get confused. What I want to see gets in the way of what's there, if you know what I mean."

Sentient Baumfree nearly smiles, then remembers herself. Covers her mouth with a hand. "Auras," she says. "The colors you see are called auras. Moving on, are you able to read people's minds?"

"No."

Sentient Baumfree leans forward and looks at me hard. "Sure?"

"I can sometimes tell what a person is feeling, but I don't know what they're thinking."

"Never?"

I think of Lucille and of our "incident" in Mr. Mitchell's class. "Sometimes I can see things written in their energy. But this seems to happen only with other Sentients."

"How about astral travel—"

"Excuse me," the man's voice erupts over some hidden intercom. "Sentient Baumfree, this Potential wouldn't know that term. A term that's about to be Red Listed, I might add."

Sentient Baumfree leans back and rubs at her eyes. When she leans forward again, her mascara is smeared. "Have you ever felt like you've been out of your body when you were sleeping? Or maybe even when you weren't sleeping? When you were awake."

I think about the one time it did happen. I was out on my grandparents' farm, swinging on the front porch. One minute I was playing with a cattail retrieved from the pond, and the next I was flying over our pastureland. One of our cows had died. I could see her stillborn calf sticking out, half born. When I came back to myself, I ran and got my father. He found the cow with her stillborn calf exactly where I'd said.

"Once," I answer. It never happened again.

The Monitor makes a notation on her notebook and continues. "Have you foretold events before they've happened?"

"Not really."

"Not really? What's that mean?"

I shrug. "I've had nightmares."

"And they come true?"

I look away from the Monitor's makeup-smeared eyes and study the door. "I dreamt that the Pandemic took away my family." *And then it happened*. But I don't need to tell her that. The redactor in the basement, and anyone else with enough clearance, already know.

"Okay, Harper, just a few more questions before we proceed to the tests. Are you able to see traces of a person once they've left?"

"Yes." This isn't uncommon. Sometimes, I'll walk into a room so thick with the residue of someone's colors, I'll forget they're not physically there any longer and ask them some question that never gets answered.

"What about objects? Are you able to see objects as clearly as people?"

"It depends. If they've been used enough. If they're important."

The Monitor thinks about this and nods. "Are you able to hear other people's thoughts? I don't mean reading their minds, now, I mean actually hearing their thoughts. It's called telepathy."

"No. Can others do this?"

To my surprise, the Monitor answers easily, "No. Not a one. But we don't know how these abilities might be shifting over time. So, with an advanced candidate, we add a few lines of inquiry to the mix."

Advanced candidate. My heart sinks.

"May I ask you a question, Sentient Baumfree?"

The woman nods yes.

"Why am I like this? Why are you like this?"

She looks thoughtfully over my face, as if searching for an

answer somewhere on my features. "I don't know, Harper. People like us have been around for a long time. Even the Confederation Bible speaks of people who were given the gift of sentience. In the beforetime, they called us psychics or intuitives . . ."

"Isabella . . ." the man from behind the mirror barks, and the Monitor closes up.

She sets coupled hands on the table between us and proceeds in a more formal tone. "Now, we're going to do a few tests . . ."

They're simple. First Sentient Baumfree asks me the identity of the man behind the clouded mirror. I tell her he's a Manager, is in his midthirties, and has a sore right foot. He's sprained it, or maybe even broken it. I can tell by the pulsing explosions of violet-red that cup the area every time his heart beats. The core of his wound is so tender, the colors there extend right through the wall.

I explain to Sentient Baumfree that this is what I get mostly—a person's position, their age, their physical health. Sometimes feelings, too. The Monitor then asks me if I can tell her what three objects are sitting on the desk in front of the man in the other room. They're easy—a gun, a knife, and a stuffed bunny. Each of the three has been either well used or well loved, and the energy that envelops them creates for me a form made out of color.

Next, people are brought in the room and I'm asked to read their colors, presumably to make sure I'm able to identify them in a standardized way. Then there are card readings and Monitor readings and a set of challenges having to do with audio files and how I'm able to apply my abilities to a nonvisual format.

Having passed those tests, I'm asked to review a real, bona fide Monitoring file. Up on the screen, the dialogue appears as a set of vertical lines. It's a conversation between a man and a woman. The husband is telling the wife that he wants to get out of the city. He's good and goddamned tired of the Confederation of the Willing and believes what he's heard, that *The Book of Noah* is real . . .

I jump out of my seat and back into the wall behind me, my ears covered with both hands. "I'm not supposed to hear this!"

Sentient Baumfree comes after me with softly waving arms. "It's okay, Harper! You've been approved for this part of the test . . ."

Recent events are too fresh in my mind. I shut my eyes and repeat, "I'm not supposed to hear this!"

Tenderly, the Monitor takes hold of my hands.

"I know what you saw," she whispers. "It was an unfortunate event, Harper. But you've been cleared now to have access to such terms as *The Book of Noah*. You will not be punished for witnessing it."

Just six months ago, a few hundred people were lined up against a wide gray building and killed for one of two offenses. The first crime, *Falsely Bearing His Name*, refers to speaking the term *The Book of Noah*. And the second, *Bearing Silent Witness*, to the crime of having heard someone else speak *The Book of Noah* and not turning that person in to the authorities. Those in the second category were largely family members of those who'd actually uttered the Red Listed term. Mothers and fathers, sisters and brothers, husbands and wives. They struggled to hold hands as they were pushed into place. Blew kisses to one another. Stared at one another's faces, no matter how many times they were instructed to watch Press Secretary Johnson. One man broke free from his ordained position and ran full-force toward a woman a few people away. Warnings were called out but the man didn't stop. He was shot in the head and fell into the woman's arms. She was shot just as she caught him.

While these sinners were being ushered into place against the wall, twelve hundred students at my school, aged fifteen to eighteen, were ushered into a gymnasium. Up on the screen, the criminals' confused faces shone pale. We watched them from the bleachers and the gym floors. When Press Secretary read their codes, impossible numbers such as 550 and 917, we turned to one another with question-mark faces. *Murder by being shot? And what about the ones who didn't die from their wounds? Would it really be death by beheading?* We looked around at our teachers, who would not return our stares.

On the screen, Press Secretary Johnson explained that the government had allowed enough loose talk of our founding father. We'd been warned for months, hadn't we? The end of discussion on this topic had been mandated and that date had been tacked up to every free board and wall. Commercials ran morning and night indicating the final day on which loose talk of our founder would result in anything other than a 550. Notes had gone out to each and every mailbox. Schools were asked to hold seminars to educate the youth.

That date had been yesterday. *And today,* Press Secretary Johnson said with a smile, *today is the beginning of a new era. One with no more loose talk.*

That loose talk was fully represented by the term *The Book of Noah. The Book of Noah* referenced a text supposedly written by our founding father but meant to collapse the very government he'd built. I'd heard stories about this book from as long ago as my childhood. Over the years, talk of it came and went but the whispers were always the same. *The Book of Noah* would reveal every lie and every truth. Having read it, we'd be too filled with knowledge to ever again be content with the easier path of ignorance.

"How many more ways are there to educate those who don't want to be educated?" Press Secretary Johnson shouted. "Should we have taken these people's tongues? Should we have taken the frontal lobes of their brains? Think about what's happening here today not as a punitive sentence for the sinners standing here, but, rather, as the final warning for those of you watching! Loose talk of the man who created the slate, through which we learned the fine art of peace, will not be tolerated!" Press Secretary Johnson shakes his bald head in disgust and his loose jowls shook.

I didn't watch the execution. I'd pulled my colors over my eyes and gone away. And now Sentient Baumfree is pulling my hands away from my ears, telling me I'm supposed to be a part of this system.

"Harper, you've passed the tests already. Do you understand?"

"No," I answer. Despite myself, a tear has slipped free. "I don't understand."

"You're a Monitor now. You'll begin as a novice with a heightened clearance, but one of these days, I predict you'll be one of our top Monitors. It will take years, maybe even decades of development, but one day, I think you're going to become something quite unique." Sentient Baumfree smiles and leans in to whisper, "You just might change the world, Harper, if you don't let the world change you first."

CHAPTER

THREE

When I wake up, it's early night. The moon is low in the sky, sitting atop the corn like a single head on a thousand scarecrows. It highlights the smooth edges of the far wall, travels up toward the ceiling, crosses the room, and falls on me, still on the closet floor. I grab hold of the doorknob and pull myself up. It's not the moon. Headlights are coming quick down the drive. Wheels are turning up loose gravel and making gritty, barking sounds that hurt my head. The room twists and bends and I have to lie back down again. Only when I lie flat does my stomach stop pitching.

A car door slams shut. Another car door after. *Two of them.* And me laid out flat, unable to move. They didn't mention this part. I wonder how many of us are caught almost as soon as we've broken just because we have to lie still. If I'd known how incapacitated I'd be, I'd have screamed myself free down by the creek.

"Tore the sign down . . ." It's a man's voice, a Blue Coat. He's standing at the front door, looking at the strips of tape where the notice used to be.

I put my hands up on the closet walls and push myself into the room. The effort makes my head spin.

"You want me to go in?" His voice is shrill in its excitement. He's thinking about a few moments from now when they'll find me. About what numbers he'll get to call and what things he'll get to do. So many Blue Coats are like this.

Deranged. All their humanity lost. Mr. Weigland calls it a hazard of the job, as if there's nothing to be done about it. As if these men aren't responsible for their actions.

"No. You go check out her car." The second man's voice sounds bored. There is no sense of urgency, nothing to tell me he relishes this part of his job.

I use my legs to push myself toward the bed. If I can stand the motion and keep from throwing up, I might be able to make it under the box springs, under the oversize comforter exactly like the one my grandmother let me pick out.

"Come on, Gage. You got the last one."

"Fuck you," the bored man says. He's standing at the screen door. I can hear the whine of the hinge, the squeak it makes when pulled open too quickly.

The men's feet are heavy on the wood floor. Each clunk of their hard-soled shoes, loud. They swallow up the sounds I'm making as I scoot toward the space beneath the old bed. Every exertion brings bile up into my throat, but by the time their feet stop in the kitchen, I'm halfway there.

"Skinner, if I have to tell you to go out to the car one more time . . ."

"What? What are you going to do?" The Blue Coat named Skinner is walking around in circles. "You're not my superior."

"Am until October."

"Fuck October!"

The other man doesn't respond. I imagine him to be tall with a face set in a permanent frown. He scares me more than the petulant one. The quiet ones are usually worse.

Skinner's stomping feet conjure an image of a narrow man with a pointy goatee and an upturned jaw. "You know that was a bullshit call!"

"Doesn't matter." The quiet man is pacing back and forth. I can't tell which way he's going. Maybe into the room above the kitchen, the one hiding behind a door and a set of corner stairs, or maybe toward me.

I lift my head and feel the room tilt violently. I throw up

into my mouth, press my hands to my lips. They're only two rooms away.

"Goddamnit, Gage!" Skinner is yelling up the corner stairwell. "Let me at least check out the bedrooms!"

I can barely make out Gage's response. "You really think she's going to be waiting for you in the bedroom?"

"Oh, she's waiting." Skinner laughs but there's nothing like humor in it.

I stop listening. With great effort, I kick out a leg and wag it back and forth, clearing off as much of the dust as I can before pushing myself under the bed. It's a wasted effort. I've left them a direct trail.

"She's not going to be in the house!" Gage has come down from the room above the kitchen. His voice is much closer, much stronger. "Now get out there and check her goddamned car!" For a big man, he's light on his feet. He's already all the way across the first floor, just outside my door.

"If she's not here, why are we checking the house?" Skinner has moved up next to him. "She broke three hours ago!"

"Exactly my point."

"Exactly *my* point. It was three hours ago, John! *Just* three hours ago!" Skinner is right in front of Gage. I can see the man's shoes from under the bed, five feet beyond my own. As I'd imagined, he has short, narrow feet. "Nobody breaks slate and runs that fast!"

Gage grunts and pushes the man away. "She was a Monitor, Jingo. You think she wouldn't know what's coming?"

"From what I've heard, running isn't high on their priority list for at least twenty-four hours."

Gage's voice shifts, affects disdain. "Why are you so hot for this? What's going on with you?"

Skinner shifts from one foot to the other. Takes a cautious breath. "You think I need help. Don't you? You think I need fucking help!"

"I think all of us need help. It's the nature of the job."

Softer and with the hesitation of embarrassment, Skinner

continues. "I think about it all the time," he says, stepping left foot right, right foot left. "501A. 501B. 458. 482. Christ, man." Skinner is on the verge of crying. *Shift, shift, shift.* I imagine one of his fists knotted up and stuck in his mouth. "I dream about it, even. I wake up and all I want to do is go out and bust somebody just so I can call a number on them, you know?"

"You want my opinion, you were doing exactly what you were supposed to do to that girl. It was a *Book of Noah* infraction, for Christ's sake! What if that kind of talk started up again?" Gage's voice gets louder as his indignation grows. "You were *charged by the Confederation of the Willing* to deliver those numbers! It's what we do to keep the peace! Think about it! What would it be like if the average citizen got the idea that that kind of talk was a possibility? It would be chaos! If bullshit like what happened with that girl didn't happen once in a while . . ." He stops. Shrugs. I can see his trouser cuffs lift. "Who knows?"

Skinner exhales. "Yeah."

"Now, you get what I'm saying?"

"Yeah." Skinner clears his throat. "But how can we do these things during the day and then go home at night and, I don't know . . . be *normal*? You know? How do you turn it off?"

"You get the hell out when you're told. That's how. You listen to the cop on patrol with you." Gage's tone has changed. It's become almost soothing. "Go see that girl you like. Ezra."

"I don't know . . ."

"I got this. Go."

Skinner hovers quietly for a moment, then pushes through the squeaky front door and starts his car. But he doesn't drive away. Instead, he turns off his car and sits there inside. I wonder if the Blue Coat named Gage has even noticed. I doubt it. He's just come into the room.

I can see the toes of the man's shoes ten inches from my hand. Wet bits of mud are caked around the heels. The leather's been scarred in the latticework pattern of someone who climbs through ditches to run people down. He walks toward the closet and stops. He's looking at my daughter's picture taped under the doorframe, has had to bend his knees.

The light begins to flicker. Gage's shoes become black blobs that float toward me from the closet. My foggy mind wants to stretch out a finger and find the curled loop of his shoestring and pull him to me. Maybe he would hold me first before he raped and then killed me. Maybe I'd find it in myself to keep from begging for mercy. The thought of a few seconds of shared humanity is enticing. Maybe for a moment the two of us will remember that we'll be held accountable for each other's welfare when we get to Heaven or wherever it is I'll find God waiting.

The black shoelaces unravel and out slips a long leather tongue. Then the tongue rescinds and a single hand is placed flat on the floor, then the other. Down comes a face. It's in frame and then out.

Time drifts a little. A new face is looking at me. The lips open and deliver a squeaky voice that confirms my suspicion.

"Who do we have here?"

It is not the deep-voiced Blue Coat named Gage anymore. It's his partner. The one with the narrow feet and the trembling voice. Something about him wakes me up, and puts me on edge. He's feral. Reminds me of a fox. His hair is short, a reddish brown, and his fair skin is reddened by thoughts of what he'll be able to do to me. The numbers he'll be able to call. He can use his fists, his teeth, his sex. If he's been granted a Special Use permit, his weapons. A knife. Maybe even a gun.

"Gage!" he shouts, smiling. "We caught her!"

This Blue Coat is anxious. Before he can get to me with his body, his colors crawl beneath the bed and fill up every square inch of space. This man's aura is a cloud of noxious gray and pulsating red. It even has a scent of mold. Of rotting fruit.

"Move out of the way, Junior Partner." Gage kneels down

and the other man's smelly gray cloud rescinds, and, with it, the smelly Blue Coat.

The two argue for a moment about who has dibs. The Blue Coat named Gage appears to be the other's superior and, as such, has rights to me. He reminds the other Blue Coat named Skinner that they share a district and will therefore have to work it out. Or one of them will go to a far worse place, if that can be imagined.

"And it ain't going to be me, partner," Gage says.

They continue to debate in louder voices and then Blue Coat Gage appears under the bed.

Oh, Candace.

There is the stubbled chin and the taut lips. The wide-set dark eyes the color of moist earth. The slightly long, wavy hair.

Oh, Christ, help me. It's the man who killed my best friend.

Gage's face rolls in and out of focus, like a tide. But, even so, I'm sure it's him. He smells the same as I remember from my office. Of musk. Of exertion and fatigue. Even without the scent and the eyes and the too-long hair, I'm doomed to know him forever. Even when he's a corpse, all bones and empty sockets. It's the man who killed Candace. The Blue Coat who shot her a few feet from Mr. Weigland's office on the Murdon Building's hundredth floor.

Gage stares into my wide eyes, and for a moment, there is no discernible expression on his face. Nothing other than the mildest look of surprise. And then, without warning, I'm yanked out from under the bed. Lifted off the floor and slammed against a wall.

"Leave her in one piece, man," Skinner says glibly, not meaning it.

I can't see this man. My face has been taken between Gage's hard fingers. He's turning my head from side to side, studying me. Grunting. He's just another bitter Blue Coat so bored with the gruesome trivialities of his job, he resents the effort it will require to rape and dismember me. As fatigued as I am by my break, I refuse to give in so easily. With all I have left in me, I draw up my knee quickly and catch Gage in the crotch.

"Jesus Christ!" he howls, but doesn't let go.

Success boosts my energy, so I kick at Gage's Achilles' heels according to the instructions provided in one of my recruitment letters. While he's jumping from one foot to the other, I use the blade edge of my hand on his neck.

"You want me to jump in there?" Skinner is laughing from somewhere behind his partner.

Gage shoves me hard against the wall. "She's my collar! My punitives!"

Skinner stops laughing and walks into my peripheral vision. I catch a glimpse of his sharp, darting eyes. "Hey, man! *I* found her! That means you're sharing numbers, goddamnit, and I'm going first!" He walks closer and puts a hand on Gage's shoulder. "I'm not kidding, John! You know good and goddamned well I don't do seconds!"

John Gage is holding my wrists so hard, my hands have gone numb. I turn my head and catch his angry retort in my left ear. "I'm the Senior Officer here, Skinner! That makes her my collar! Deal with sloppy seconds or get the fuck out of here!"

For just a pause, Gage loosens his grip and I'm somehow able to slip away. I make it to the living room and almost to the kitchen. At the threshold, I'm spun around. Caught with his outstretched hand and hung out on the end of his arm the whole way back to the bedroom.

"I'm not going anywhere!" Skinner follows us as we move. Once we're back where we started, he stands at the end of the bed, complaining as I'm pushed down on top of the yellow comforter. "She's my fucking collar! I have rights!"

"Then stand there and watch, but shut the fuck up, will you?"

As Gage rears back to yell something else to his partner, I sit up and begin to struggle against him. He gives me the smallest push and I'm sent an inch into the yellow comforter. Breaking my slate has left me too weak to continue this fight, so I fix my gaze on the ceiling and think about my daughter. It's unimaginable, the things I've given up, and for nothing. For more of the same.

"She's a Monitor, for Christ's sake!" Skinner is yelling.

"Keep it up and I'm going to report you for obstruction of punitives!" Gage shouts. "Get the fuck out, Skinner, or shut the fuck up! It's one of the two!"

Skinner is livid. He's begun to pace back and forth at the end of the bed. The pacing stops only when my trousers are yanked off and flung across the room, followed shortly by my panties. " 'Any and all officers present may take part in punitive actions against a rogue Monitor'!" he quotes. "And seeing as I don't do seconds, you're keeping me from my due service! Maybe I should report you for obstruction of justice!"

Gage ignores the other Blue Coat. He unbuckles his trousers and leans forward, pressing both his hands against my own. "Whatever, asshole." And with that, he makes a surging motion that takes us both an inch or two up the bed. But there is no contact. No penetration. "Stand there and give me a play-by-play if you like." Gage grunts, pretending at a satisfaction he doesn't feel. "It's up to you."

"God*damn*it, Gage!" Skinner shouts.

Gage ignores his partner's frustration, then starts thrusting again in a new way. This time holding on to my legs so I can't avoid the most intimate tangle. We are a mockery but Skinner's been taken in. The other Blue Coat's mind sees what it wants to, but there is no rape here. No violation other than the hot abrasion of John Gage's legs against mine.

Gage turns his full attention to me, reciting my punitives as his thighs scrape against my own. "Harper Adams. You're being served the following Confederation codes: 501A, 93B, and, if I have the strength for it, 878. The hour is roughly 1700 and we're at the farmhouse located at 2050 North Province Road just outside Bond."

Pop. A button comes off my blouse and rolls across the floor. It stops on Skinner's boot, paused in the doorway.

"She's my collar," he whines.

"Then stay. But let me tell you something now." For the first time since my back hit the bed, I turn my face toward my attacker and see Gage's frown. He watches me as he talks to his partner, contrition all over his face. "No cop with an obstruction of punitives charge will be able to keep a partner. Not even out here in the sticks. And no partner, no badge. It's your choice, big mouth."

Gage's eyes are drawn. A line has formed down the center of his forehead and exclamation marks punctuate the outer corners of his lips. It's an expression that says, *Don't be afraid of me.* With it comes another shove, another grunt. Another foot moved up the bed, the two of us locked at the hips. I try to turn my head and he quickly looses a hand and forces my face back to his. *Play along now.*

"Jesus Christ," Skinner pouts. He's about to give up.

I do as told. Struggle. The next jolt is stronger. It hurts my thighs and, for a million reasons, I begin to cry.

"You going to finish up soon, or what?" Skinner's voice is a blend of bitter and sweet. He's somewhere between pouting and needing to mend fences with his superior officer.

"I'll be finished when I'm finished. Now shut up."

"You'll do her, then? Finish her off?"

"Yes, yes," Gage agrees, and without another word, Jingo leaves.

As soon as the front door slams, we stop moving and wait like this, coupled. Hitched at the groin. I can hear Skinner's squad starting through the left-open front-porch door. Then the sound of his tires on the gravel drive.

Gage is staring down at the tears collected in my eyes. I look away and they slide across my cheeks.

"You okay?" he asks.

I don't remember answering. All I know is that a weight lifts off my hips, and then I'm gone.

CHAPTER

FOUR

Every morning I leave Veracity with a neighbor who gets her to the bus stop. I make the drive to work and eat my breakfast of a plain bagel with a cup of black coffee while waiting for the security guards to show up.

From the air, the capital city of Wernthal looks like a fallen moon. A disk smashed flat into the Confederation's east-central hills. Its round outer layer is all road, a ribbon of cement wide enough to keep the surrounding woods at bay. The center is a contrast of spikes and bumps. A cleat made up of diminutive office buildings and skyscraping monuments to President and his Ministers. The largest building in Wernthal is the Geddard Building, headquarters for the nation's Blue Coats.

A massive hunk of cement around which roads have been bent, the Geddard Building doesn't draw the eye or reflect the sun. The windows are small and blacked, the doors made of something metal that can't be broken through or knocked down. It isn't pretty because pretty doesn't communicate the right message. It covers three city blocks and has rooftop vents that belch waves of heat into the oily air. We're made to drive around it as a daily reminder of the hundreds of thousands of policemen working there. Some of them living there. They are ever present because of what's locked up tight in the basement: the redactors. These machines control all uploads and downloads. Gathering everything we say and do, documenting everywhere we go and distributing all freshly Red

Listed words to the slates implanted in our necks. There are tens of thousands of redactors, referred to as slaves, uplinked to the one master. The key to our slates has been stored in a room a third of a mile long by a third of a mile wide forty or fifty feet beneath an infestation of Blue Coats.

President's residence is the National House, the oldest building in the Confederation, boasting the largest patch of domesticated grass. It's retained more of its original character than most buildings are allowed because, as President likes to say, he has a softness for the beforetime. The National House, its adjacent gardens, and the surrounding business district are all considered a part of National House Square. Twelve blocks by twelve blocks, it boasts the most colorful streets in the country. Here, rules about the aesthetic are relaxed. President's gift. A little magenta, a little green, a little purple. Colors rarely found anywhere else.

The tented rooms used by prostitutes are cherry red. There's one on every corner. Inside, male and female prostitutes provide a variety of sexual services for so many credits each. According to the All Equals Law, every citizen aged eighteen and up has equal access to all government-sponsored products and services. It's supposed to mean there's no adult these sex workers can turn away, though files of this nature have crossed my desk a time or two.

The prostitutes are heavily costumed, or sometimes nude, whatever best expresses their sexual style. Each wears a corresponding red sash that runs from one side of the neck to the opposite hip. Customers wait outside for their turns, smoking cigarettes and drinking alcoholic beverages purchased from vending machines. They're unconcerned who sees them queued up between the velvet ropes. It's custom in the Confederation. Men wave as their neighbors pass. Women talk to one another about recipes and cleaning supplies, then disappear through the front door and come back out again, pink-faced and smiling.

In between the prostitutes' quarters are small tents set up

by the state clergy. Purple and green, they serve as coun-
seling offices and Occlusia dispensaries. Inside, one of the
Confederation Pastors delivers the approved word of God
to those needing a little recap between Sundays. If there's an
honest-to-goodness God's man in residence, these movable
churches also dispense compassion, sanity, and hope. As with
any other profession, quality varies. Like with the prostitutes'
quarters, people tend to go where there's a line.

I don't visit either. As far as I'm concerned, both are de-
signed for the same purpose. To sedate us. Or sate us, if just
for a little while. President says it's not his preference, this
safety-driven life we lead. If it weren't for his Ministers and
all their research as to what's healthy for us and what's not,
he'd allow us more to do than drink ourselves blind and
fuck ourselves limp. This campaign has worked. I've grown
less hateful toward President, even knowing what I do. And
harder toward his twelve bug-eyed compatriots, who not so
many years ago had real duties that mapped to real titles.
Minister of Appropriations. Minister of Governmental Affairs. Minister of Tracking and Data. Now they are simply
Minister Thomas. Minister Abbott. Minister Hawthorne.
There is no separation of anything anymore. It is a blend, our
government. A chocolate malt giving ridiculous orders. I'm
amazed we've made it this far.

It's a Tuesday morning. Ten minutes before President's
weekly address. Crowds have already formed at the gates surrounding National House Square. Those outside are squeez-
ing themselves into the security posts. They offer themselves
up half dressed, arms and legs splayed, anything to more
quickly get through. Those crossing toward the gated gardens
from which President will speak are dappled by the moving
shadow of our nation's largest flag. Navy blue with a white
patch in its center in the shape of a wide, cockeyed *F*, it swings
from the nation's tallest pole just fifty feet beyond the gates.

I don't care for President's preening and head straight for
my office. I'm late as it is.

The Murdon Building looks like a giant silver phallus sticking out of downtown Wernthal. The tallest in the nation at twelve hundred feet, it's the center for Tracking and Data, the oldest branch of the Confederation. It was built to sway with the high spring winds and tornadoes that come sideways through the Midwest, and has the largest security system in the country with over two dozen checkpoints. I run to get in line at the nearest one, but President comes out a few minutes early and I'm caught in the crowd running out through my building's front doors.

They flow noisily around me in their standard-issue hard-soled shoes. Rush toward the National House gates open-armed and en masse, their stampede shaking the concrete walk. They ignore the guards who've been trotted out with long, sharp-ended weapons and press themselves, crying, against the fence's steel posts. President is just fifty feet beyond. He's a tall man. White-haired. Eighty years old, though he looks much younger, with taut, shiny skin someone's pulled too tight. It makes the bones of his cheeks appear sharp, like they're about to break through his smiling face. *Children*, he says, as is his way, looking through an opening in his guards' two-line formation. *Let us see what God's got to tell us today.* President's armor of Blue Coats travels slowly, taking small, sliding steps that often land one of them on our High Executive's ample robes. When this happens, President will rock, unjointed, a solid block of plastic, and stop. It's the pause that shows us the potential of his rage. The way he breathes in and out. Slowly and with force.

As the guards see him safely to his raised podium and lock him away inside bullet-proof glass, the crowd grows louder. They're shouting in full voice for President and his Press Secretary to divine our future in the manner set down by the Confederation Bible. One speaks in tongues and the other interprets. President first, then Press Secretary Johnson.

The mood comes on President quickly this morning. He puts up his hands and rolls back his eyes. Unleashes a stream of nonsense words, sounds that mean nothing to the rest of us and everything to the person standing just outside the glass case. Press Secretary Johnson is a heavy, rolling tub of a man who doesn't walk so much as ebb. He nods at President's words and flows toward the microphone to announce the day's good news, gleaned by some mystic knowing from President's gibberish. *There hath been a rash of wrongdoing, mostly in the south and central provinces. We must pray for the unholy among us. Those of wicked hearts and minds who would lead the others to a life of sin* . . . It's the same every time. After the usual lamentations for those who've fallen, usually by destroying their God-given slates, he begins an interpretation of President's predictions. *Lo, but there is to be a mighty technological effort that will still the land. Soon! There will be a new eye in the sky that will end the flight for those who would put themselves first and their fellow citizens last. And, too, there is the program now being tendered by Monitors* . . .

This gets my attention. I turn around to watch the morning spectacle and the woman waiting behind me frowns. She's already got her shoes off. They dangle by their straps from one hand.

. . . *these Sentient Monitors, chosen by God, will be judge and jury* . . .

"Ma'am?" the Security Guard calls to me impatiently. He's new. Young with small, angry eyes and tight, angular jaws. He flips two fingers downward, motioning me into the shoot with a deprecation that makes the others around us cringe. They know who I am. This new young guard does not.

I move ahead as Press Secretary Johnson continues. *There is only one of them now! But she is a prophet to move mountains!*

I can't help myself. Smirk at President's bullshit.

The new guard thinks I'm smirking at him. "Okay. Hold it there." He puts a hand on my jacket. "Remove this garment, ma'am," he says, then yanks it off my shoulders before I can comply, growling when it gets caught on my elbows.

President is still warbling behind us, Press Secretary

interpreting, *This woman and the team of others she will help us find, they shall be the Lord's eyes!*

The guard reaches for my satchel, which contains a dozen confidential files. If even one of them falls out, he'll be fired. Or worse. I drop the handles and off comes my taupe linen jacket into his thick hands. The files stay where they are.

They shall see the corrupt! They will call down the power of God on their heads and these traitors among us will be no more!

The guard flops my things roughly onto a conveyor belt that should have been changed months ago. Its black rubber is pebbled with ink stains and there are long sections where it's been worn down to the white netting. Once my jacket disappears into the scanning chamber, it will be ruined. A Christmas gift from Mr. Weigland, too. Gone.

"Move on through. *Now.*"

Press Secretary Johnson continues behind me. *And with an army of prophets such as these, there will be nowhere for the impure to hide!*

I walk under the archway scanner, noting my temperature and heart rate as I walk by. Ninety-eight degrees. Sixty-eight beats per minute. The information gathered from my slate will be shown on a screen posted to the back side of the machine. If one were to print this two-second grab of downloaded information, the resulting document would be a thousand pages long. Through this band of metal worn in my neck, the Confederation knows where I've been and how long I've been there. Every word I've spoken. In some ways, the most important ways, every thought that's entered my head.

I go to the end of the possessions belt and watch my jacket tumble out its end, one seam torn open. A black spot on the lapel. I stare down at the violated linen, sad to the core of my soul. There are only so many forms of loveliness in this world. My favorite linen jacket was one of them. I would have stopped this were it any other time. But Candace has just been killed. I feel guilty about how much this ruined coat wounds me. Comparatively, it's nothing.

"There a problem?" The guard comes through the archway behind me.

I hold up my jacket, pry open the broken stitches with a fingernail. "It tore."

The guard smiles. He opens his mouth to relieve himself of a little pent-up hostility when another guard vaults over the gate. His name is Jones. He's been here for years and knows who I am.

So will this new guard in about twenty seconds. When my identity is posted on the rear-facing security screen, this sorry young man with his brand-new gun and pristine green suit will go red.

"Can it, Simmons," Security Guard Jones shouts at the young man. Tenderly, he pulls away my ruined coat. "Sorry about this, Alpha Monitor Adams. I'll call Purchasing and get you a replacement." Jones points the other man to the rear-facing monitor. At my image just now coming up. "I think you owe Alpha Monitor Adams an apology."

On the screen's right side is a rotating picture of my face, last updated the day after my divorce. My hair is unbrushed and falls in snarls down my back. My eyes are ringed in in-somnia black. My skin is ashy and broken out. The left side of the screen holds my most vital statistics. Name, address, age. Position. Office. Rank. It's as far as the young guard cares to read. He turns to me, red from the bill of his hat to the bulb in his throat.

Security Guard Jones pulls the young man close. "Apolo-gize to the lady, soon-to-be former security guard Simmons."

A pause. "Alpha Monitor Adams . . . I apologize."

I take back my jacket from Security Guard Jones. Throw it away around the corner.

There are seventy-two High Priority, High Security files in a slumping pile on my desk, none of which I can reissue to other Monitors. I throw my purse into a drawer and take my seat. Kick the drawer shut with a little too much force and it bounces open again. I reach down to push it closed, and when I sit up again, Candace is across the aisle. Just bits of her. Etherlike dissections of her arms and legs, a see-through head bent low over the screen like she's reading a waveform. I put my hand over my mouth and the tears I haven't yet been able to shed roll across my knuckles.

I told Mr. Weigland this might be a problem. And there's her desk, and her chair, and her plastic cubicle walls. These glowing traces of my best friend will be there for days, or weeks. And no one else will be able to see them but me.

I head down the hall toward Mr. Weigland's office. He comes in early, too, but not for the same reasons. His pre-dawn tendencies have more to do with a loveless marriage and no children. Halfway there, he sees me coming and gives me a half turn of his head, performed so slowly, no one else would notice. Mr. Weigland does this if he's in a meeting I'm not supposed to know about, or if he senses I'm about to say something that will adversely affect my position. We never sat down and agreed upon this sign. I'm not sure he's even aware of doing it, but it happens frequently. There are a lot of things I'm not supposed to know, or say.

Watch it. He's nervous today. His eyes float toward the other person in the room, Helen Rumney, the BodySpeak Manager. She's a late-twenties woman with thick blonde hair and sharp, deeply clefted features. Her backside is pressed against the nearest pane, elbows, too, revealing flat rounds of scabby flesh. She's attractive. Knows how to use it. Spends all day posing against all sorts of glass walls.

Helen Rumney's colors are like nothing I've ever seen. When she's in a room, it's an effort to look away. Her insatiable need has its own gravitational pull. Her disregard for humanity has turned her into a slow-turning tornado that feeds on air and light. It's not unusual for her to be obscured by this storm of colors in constant rotation around her. Some days this mass is packed so tight it's more like a cocoon than a cloud. A gray skein of yarn out of which poke arms and legs. Other times, her energy expands into a thick red-brown fog. When it gets like this, I can't even see her for this veil of ambition. She's proud of her resilience and tenacity. Her ability to put emotion away. But she doesn't see what I see—the way it's worked on her like a toxin. On Helen Rumney's worst days, the flesh of her face disappears and all that's left is the pale hue of worn bone.

Mr. Weigland steps past her and opens the door. "I'm running a little late. Give me ten minutes, Harper," he says as if we had a meeting scheduled.

Helen turns her head so I can see the side of her face. One round fish-eye. One half of her A-line jaw. She purses her lips. Says before the office door can be closed, "She's reading my colors again, Richard." Then turns back around.

Ten minutes later, Mr. Weigland is hanging over my cubicle wall, Helen Rumney gone. "She wants to keep going with the program."

I look straight ahead. Don't say a thing.

"You doing okay?"

"You didn't move her desk." I point at Candace's cubicle.

Mr. Weigland bobs his head, contrite. "We're moving somebody else in next week . . ."

"I can still see her!"

"I don't know if I can requisition another office, Harper." He sighs heavily and frowns down at the tips of his shoes. "Manager Rumney's got most of our budget sunk into Body-Speak."

"Then tell her I'm not doing another thing on that program until you move it! The computer, the desk, the walls . . . everything!"

Mr. Weigland opens his mouth to speak, then thinks better of it. He looks at Candace's old space and nods. "I'll have them move it today."

By midafternoon, the scent of fresh plastic is everywhere. They've taken everything away and replaced it with new pieces not yet out of their bags.

I'm elbow-deep in files when I hear a voice over my shoulder. "How are you today, Miss Adams?" It's Evans, our mailman, standing at the edge of my office. His skin is old, pleated, like drapes. It parts over his eyes and mouth as he smiles.

"I'm okay," I say, holding out my hand. "Anything interesting today?"

Evans drops the bundled mail into my palm and leans against my cubicle wall. "I think so."

I flip through the envelopes already torn open by Security. There are reminders from Quality Assurance about our Dispositioning Codes. A dozen terrorist updates from the Geddard Building. And what used to be my favorite piece of mail all year: our annual travel brochure. It's a quarter-inch-thick set of full-color choices as to where we'd like to spend our one free week per year.

"Let me show you." Evans reaches down and slides the brochure onto my desk. His mouth moves silently as he flips through the pages. *Fifty-two, fifty-three, fifty-four . . .* " Here we go." He stops on page fifty-five. Taped to its center is a key, a wallet-size strip of white plastic, coded to fit into one of a thousand-plus lockers. For security purposes, none of them are numbered. "This is where I'd suggest vacationing this year." Evans taps an old yellow fingernail against the letter C that's a part of the featured resort town of Chesney. Then reaches down to the lower right corner and taps against the 5. "What do you think of Chesney?" He taps on the two symbols again: C5. "Ever been down to the southern coast?"

I'm baffled. It takes me a few seconds to respond. "No. What's it like?"

Evans smiles a big yellow smile. "It's wonderful! Warm, I'll say that much. They let you outdoors more than in other regions. Up to three hours a day, if you know someone." He shuffles through the other pieces of mail until he finds a notice I would have thrown away. "It's the best trip I've ever taken. Bar none." Evans is tapping against the notice from Human Resources. It's one of our standard monthlies. A reminder that it's about time to switch out our lockers in the women's gym.

He stands upright. Puts a hand on my shoulder. "My suggestion is to try Chesney this year, Miss Adams. Turned me into a new man. Might turn you into a new woman. And make that reservation fast. Could fill up."

Then Evans is gone. On down the aisle and into the next cubicle. Asking Mary Gibbons about her bum foot.

I gently peel the key away from the page and slip it into my pants pocket.

There are only two women in the gym. One of them is a woman named Margaret who goes through the cardiovascular stations in alphabetical order. The other is a tall, gaunt woman named Flora, who will be on the treadmill for an hour. I nod as I walk past and glance down at the elapsed time flashing red next to her hand. *Twenty minutes down, forty more to go.* I shoulder my purse nonchalantly, put Evans's key between my teeth, and push open the door leading to the lockers.

There are only two places in the Murdon Building with no cameras affixed to the ceilings and walls: the restrooms and the locker rooms. I race down the room's long aisles until I find the one marked C5. My hand shaking, I slip the card into the reader. A small round light above the handle turns green and the tall metal door pops open.

Inside, half hidden by the shadows of overhead lighting, is a piece of paper unlike any I've seen. It's thick and gristled, full of dark dots that blend with the words written on its face. I sit down on the bench. Put the note into the cup of my lap to read.

Harper,

   Should you accept the following invitation, Mr. Evans will be our courier. Read this quickly and commit everything to memory. The paper we use for these communications is made of a special biodegradable material. When you're ready, hold it under running water until it's gone. Do not tear it up and throw it away. Do not shred it. All waste receptacles have decoders to identify key words and soil tracers that will match it to within a mile of our location.

   When you need to respond to a note or want to send a message, set your green coffee mug handle-side out toward the hall. Evans will tell you what to do next. When you're done with a key, place it inside the locker and close the door. Evans will have someone collect it.

   If you're caught in possession of this note, you will be killed and that will be the easy part. Follow these directions exactly. Deviating from them will get you killed, as well as Evans. Possibly more of us.

The letter goes on to describe a resistance. A movement comprised of thousands of citizens hiding in underground bunkers and hundreds of thousands more above it—members clustered throughout the nation and organized for one purpose: to create what it calls a democratic government and overthrow the current regime. This group has spent more years than I can imagine accruing educational tools and books banned by the Confederation. Aboveground, they've infiltrated some of the highest echelons of government. Even our police. Having an intimate knowledge of the atrocities Blue Coats perform every day, I have a hard time imagining that some of them are members of this resistance.

   This group's need of me is simple. I have great knowledge of the monitoring system and I'm a Sentient. There is no emotional plea, not until the last paragraph.

The word freedom *means much more than you've been taught. It's the opposite of restriction. Of how you think, how you pray, how you love, whom you love. For our revolution to work, first you—we—all of us must understand the ways our freedoms are being revoked. There are more than you can comprehend. Come and stand with us on the other side of the looking glass. You have a daughter who can't inherit this kind of world.*

Two additional paragraphs describe exactly what I'll need to do. The when and the how. It's there in black and white, a confirmation of what I've been feeling for years. The sacrifice I've been avoiding equally long. It is an extraordinary request presented in the simplest terms. A perfunctory explanation of the measures required to keep what happened to Candace's daughter from happening to mine.

I shut the key in the locker as instructed and place the note in one of the sinks. It takes no time to dissolve into beads of pulp, then into a thin milky substance. When the note's all gone, I wash the drain with a bit of the soap, splashing some of the water on my face and down my neck. When I go back out into the gym, I don't have to pretend to be too ill to work out. Both women see it. They tell me to forget the weights and the elliptical machine tonight. I should go home, get some rest.

I'm almost off the hundredth floor when Mr. Weigland puts a hand between the silver closing doors. "Hold the elevator, please!"

I press the Open button. It wouldn't have been like me not to.

Mr. Weigland's arms are full. He's carrying one overstuffed satchel and two briefcases, their handles wedged into the palm of one hand. I tuck the travel brochure Evans brought me under an arm and relieve him of one of the briefcases.

"Thanks." He looks down at the brochure jutting out from my side and a fleeting smile crosses his lips. "So. You know yet?"

"I'm sorry?"

"I'm choosing Henley."

Oh. I feel myself visibly relax. He's talking about our vacations.

Mr. Weigland leans against the back wall, trying as best he can to affect casual. "A week in a high-altitude complex. Outdoor hot tub. Warm log fire. Pretty nice, huh?"

I shake my head no. "I'm afraid of heights."

"It's nice up there. Quiet."

"Actually, I was thinking of Chesney. It's down south somewhere. A complex on the coast."

Mr. Weigland considers this news with his tongue pressed firmly in his cheek. "I could use a little sun, come to think of it." The elevator stops and two people get in. Mr. Weigland scoots closer to give them room. "What do you do with Sarah while you're gone? She go to our day care? Or to family somewhere?"

Sarah. I flinch. I never use that name. Ever. "Devon's sister takes her."

Devon was once my husband. A district judge who preferred the company of prostitutes to that of his wife and daughter. His apathy made the divorce easy. I won full custody and a small stipend for expenses. Veracity has no memories of the man who was once her father. She wouldn't recognize him if they were introduced.

Mr. Weigland leans closer to whisper, "Sarah doing okay with the change and all?"

I look at the buttons lighting up as we descend. We're stopping again, at the fifty-second floor. "She's fine," I answer. Get out of the way for the new riders.

Mr. Weigland wants me to use Veracity's new name but

I won't. Over the last twenty-one days, I've managed to go without using it once. Instead, I stick with sweetheart and baby and ignore her pleading eyes. She uses the name herself sometimes, like she's trying to warm me up. Like she's introducing herself. Unlike her mother, she's moved on.

"It's a good name, Harper," Mr. Weigland says.

The trip brochure slides forward, yawns open against my side. Beneath the elevator's overhead lights, the tape is shining, outlining the shape of a locker key. I've thoughtlessly forgotten to tear it off.

I turn toward Mr. Weigland rather than away. "It was my mother's middle name," I offer.

"*Sarah?*" He smiles enthusiastically. "Sarah was your *mother's* name?"

"Yes. Middle."

"Well, that's great. Adds some significance, then."

The elevator doors open and we pour out. I hand Mr. Weigland his bag and wave good night, the brochure curled in my hand. My heart beating hard enough to drown out his farewell.

Oh, Mr. Weigland. I find myself taking a step toward his retreating form. He smiles at me. Squints at the ungainly way my feet are moving toward him of their own accord. It takes him two tries before his shoulders will correct themselves and point forward, toward the exit. Then I am alone with the blue and green swirls of color he's left in his wake. They resemble contrails. Or the long banners flown over the National House when something bad has happened and President wants us to know everything will be all right.

I watch him walk past the windows. There's no one to talk to anymore, now that Candace is gone.

Mr. Weigland, I want to shout. *Come and help me.*

He doesn't look over.

HAPTER
FIVE

I am dreaming of my daughter. Of soft brown hair springing wildly around her face and huge brown eyes focused on my own. She's beautiful, even happy, but this will change soon enough when she's down on the floor, flailing. I've been having this dream ever since Chalmers, since the night I was put on Red Watch. As much as I want it to be, this isn't a nightmare. It's a glimpse of the future.

Veracity's sitting in someone else's house. Behind her is a floor lamp, the kind with a neck that extends. To her left, a small table with curved, old-fashioned legs. Soft light is flooding in through the window to her right. It turns the room butter yellow, Veracity's favorite color. Through the panes I see the pickled brown bark of trees and, beyond them, green earth and blue sky. There are no buildings to disrupt the view. No white sidewalk or gray road. My daughter has been placed in the countryside, as promised. Somewhere far away from Wernthal.

"Mom," she calls me. Not so long ago, I was Mommy. "I understand now."

I call to her, but she can't hear me. She's staring straight at me but can't see me. It's all for naught, finding her like this, happily living in someone else's house, unable to warn her. In the first few seconds of this dream, when her image pops up on the screen of my night, I'm overwhelmed with joy. Then I remember what happens in the rest of it and would die first if I could.

"I'm sorry I didn't visit you in Chalmers. And I'm sorry I didn't take your call," she says, eyes brimming. "I know you were just trying to keep what happened to Hannah from happening to me."

I'm screaming impotently. Pounding my fists against something hard, though when I look down there's nothing there but my lap and my trousered legs wedged against the arms of a chair.

Veracity sits back to pull a tissue from a pants pocket, and static draws one of her long locks toward the light's metal stand. Inside my transparently walled cell, I begin to flail.

"I understand what you're doing." Her head is resting against the metal pole—hair, scalp, bone, brains. "I don't have to go by Sarah anymore."

I scream, *Don't say it!* Get up out of my seat and hurl it against the transparent wall separating us, but nothing shatters. The chair disappears right through.

Veracity looks at me, head to pole. "You were trying to give me back my name . . . Vera—"

My daughter's voice is stillborn. Only the first two syllables come, then an ending I won't allow. She thought her slate had been turned off and was speaking a Red Listed word.

God help me.

I can feel my legs flexing, working to wake me up before the rest of it comes. I open my eyes and the present rushes in like a sickness.

Have I been killed?

I almost cry out but then feel the bed beneath me. I'm alive. In one piece. May or may not be alone. I turn my head and look down at the floor. There is no Blue Coat at the side of my bed. For whatever reason, he's left me alive, and not so long ago. I can see shining traces of him on the dusty floor, though the colors suggest something the opposite of rage. Iridescent green and robin's egg blue. They must have been left by someone else. Most likely me.

Have I been raped?

I'm on the bed, not under it. Wedged under covers that smell of mold and feel like burlap. When I try to kick them off, they don't budge. Someone has squared the corners so tight, my toes are bent at right angles to my feet.

Bare legs. Someone's taken off my clothes.

I lift up the sheet and look down at myself. I'm in my bra and panties. My nicest pair of trousers, my most comfortable eggshell chemise, the white silk blouse Mr. Weigland issued me as a bonus for the last three months of overtime. All are gone. My slurring mind doesn't comprehend it. *What's happened to me?* Maybe I've had a stroke.

The ceiling is moving above me and every muscle in my body aches. I put my arms over my head and bring together the thumb and forefinger of each hand. They all work. No stroke. No pain between my legs. No rape.

I try to get up and stumble, throw out my arm to rebalance, and it connects with something soft and warm. It's a woman's hand come forward from the shadows, small but thickly muscled.

"Congratulations, Adams. You're officially offline."

Offline. It's a recently Red Listed word meaning no longer connected to the Fatherboard.

"I laid your clothes out to dry on the porch. You sweat them through. Now lie down." I'm thrust back onto the bed and the hand withdraws.

The woman's only given me three short sentences and a silhouette as she moves past the window, but it's enough. She's in her midthirties. Either a Confederation prostitute or someone who bounces from one Food Service position to another. The other thing I know about this woman is that she's a lifetime smoker. We get this breed in Monitoring on a daily basis. They're people who wind up committing suicide or being executed. People who can't find the middle ground required by the government.

Her face appears over my own. "No, you didn't have a stroke and, no, you're not dead. Yet." She manages to sound annoyed and bored at the same time. I wish I could see her features but the moon is over her shoulder. All I can see is coarse yellow hair.

"Who are you?" My postbreak voice sounds cracked and torn. Just exactly how it feels. It will be a couple of days before it's back to normal.

A small orb of orange light travels up to the woman's mouth. She inhales deeply and spits the smoke down at my face. "Ezra."

Ezra. The one the Blue Coat named Skinner was going to call.

I cough and start to fall sideways off the bed. Ezra catches me. "Jesus." She rolls me back into my original position and battens me down with the blunt ends of her fingers. "I said keep your ass in bed! Are you deaf or just stupid?"

She lets out a sigh and returns to a chair that's been pulled up next to me. I can finally see her face. Makeup has been applied liberally. A mask of black and brown shadow highlights the white orbs of her eyes, drawing attention to their green centers. Her lips are painted a metallic yellow and her medium-length blonde hair is twisted into multiple braids that have been banded away from her white face by a wide ribbon. She's pretty. Very. And she's small. Small body, small waist, small hands. I'm surprised about the small breasts. Most prostitutes opt to augment, whether or not they need to.

The recommended appearance for a prostitute is white base applied to the whole face, red lipstick, and razor-thin brows drawn higher than the natural line and always in black. Ezra's makeup is garish and feral. Her perfume is something like lavender, a floral. Most prostitutes smell like musk. Instead of wearing the signifying red sash over one shoulder, this woman has it tied around her neck, a box of menthols hanging from its end.

"You can't smoke yet." She sees me looking.

"I don't want to."

There are a dozen cigarette butts jackknifed into the surface of a side table. Ezra adds another while looking me up and down. "So, you're the bigwig." She frowns.

"Harper Adams." It comes out sounding like a croak.

She rolls her eyes at the introduction. "And here I might have been in the wrong house."

"There were two men here before." My eyes wander up to the ceiling and over to the closet. *Where's my picture?* One of them must have taken it. "There were Blue Coats . . ."

"Don't worry about them."

"I was almost raped."

"You call that rape?"

"By the man who murdered my best friend!"

"Get over yourself, Adams. You got saved is what you got."

"Her name was Candace!"

Ezra steps forward, allowing me a look at the ease of her features and how little she cares. "I have about two minutes to waste here and that's about a two-*hour* conversation. I said you don't need to worry about them and that's as much as you'll be getting out of me. Got it?"

I push myself up, just to my elbows. Want to move on with my mission and away from her. "I'm meeting my trainer."

Ezra pushes me back down, this time with enough force to hurt. "Oh, really? Right now you're not doing anything but keeping your ass in that bed." She's bitter. Doesn't like me.

"What are you doing here?"

"If I could be somewhere else, believe me, I would be."

I'm too tired for this repartee.

"Should move." I'm parched. The words get stuck on my tongue.

"Should do what I tell you."

Ezra gets up and walks to the door. "There are some

vitamin packets over there." She motions toward a small box on the floor. "Take one when you wake up tomorrow and then another one before you go back to sleep. There's food in the room above the kitchen."

My mind is taking its time to formulate thoughts. When they come out, it's all at once: "My trainer? When . . . where do I . . ."

"You do nothing! You wait, is what you do!" Ezra shakes her head, but she's smiling like the cat that just caught the canary. "Seems you're not all that bright, Adams. Can't seem to catch up to things. There are going to be some pretty disappointed people where you're headed." She taps short, lacquer-free fingers against her mouth and adds in a whisper, "Jesus Christ, he better not have made a mistake with you."

I can see Ezra's slate, shining on her neck just above her prostitute's sash, and feel for my own. It doesn't feel any different than before. Won't look any different either.

"When did you break?" I ask.

"A long time ago. Now listen up, bigwig, were you lucid when I explained your instructions? Or do I need to repeat them?"

Her escalating voice is making the air vibrate. I shut my eyes and focus on not throwing up. "Where's my car?"

"Towed."

"Towed?"

"You didn't think they were going to leave it here?"

"How far is Bond?"

"Three miles. Why?"

"Which way?" The answer is north. I just want her to stop sounding so superior.

"What do you care?"

I don't answer.

Ezra takes a couple of steps toward the bed. She's checking to see if my eyes are still shut. "Take a right at the end of the drive, go three miles, take another right at Route 54. Stay straight and you'll drive right through it. Oh, but you'd be walking, huh?" she sounds pleased to add.

I'd like to spar with her, use my newly expanded freedom of speech to tell her what I think of her *help*, but the room has resumed spinning so I keep it brief. "You don't like me."

Ezra doesn't respond like I thought. She leans down and whispers in my ear, "You want to know why? Because you're the worst kind of whore. You and your kind make me and mine look like Mary Fucking Poppins." Whoever that is.

She turns to leave and I hold out a hand. "Is Veracity safe?"

Ezra pauses at the threshold. "Yes."

"Where is she?"

"Not in Wernthal. That's all you need to know."

"They haven't gone after her?"

"No."

"Are we watching her?"

Ezra sighs. "What happened to Hannah is not going to happen to Veracity. Enough with the questions. Go to sleep."

The room is going away along with Ezra and her invective. I lie back down and close my eyes. Behind them, I find an image of Candace's daughter waiting. It's the *before* picture when Hannah was a long, dangling girl, feet swinging beneath her mother's desk. In this image, she was exuberant. Full of questions. Never able to hold still. Then comes the *after*. The picture channel 4 broadcast toward the end showing a stick figure in a hospital bed, the skin of her face and arms gray and patchy. Her copper-colored eyes hollowed out. The Confederation went after her, Candace's daughter. She was used as bait to lure back the errant mother.

HAPTER
SIX

JUNE 18, 2045.

Maybe I'm being vain. I don't take up a knife and puncture my carotid, flicking out my slate along with a bit of that vital artery. I don't open that juncture where arm meets hand, or bruise the most lovely part of the body, the crease where neck meets head. I work death upon my body from the inside out. I choose pills. Seventeen Occlusia. Medication the government provides to keep us happy. It was the first method in a brief list. The *how,* my only decision. The Confederation would have used my daughter to flush me out. They would have brought her to Wernthal Central Hospital and tortured her until I came running, like they did with Hannah.

I have to sever ties to my child in such a way the government will classify her as *Unloved By Her Mother.* As *Not Likely to Produce a Return,* no matter what they do to her. I have to get her reassigned to new parents. The recruitment letter assured me that the resistance had enough people on the inside to make sure Veracity's new home would be far away. Beyond the easy reach of the Confederation.

Veracity, or *Sarah* as called by her court-appointed name, has been sent off to spend a week with my ex-husband's sister and brother-in-law on the East Coast. Anne is the kind, quiet, motherly type with no children of her own. She was my first choice. Her husband, David, has a quick smile and a good sense of humor. He works as an engineer and provides them a Class III house. Three thousand square feet. Five bedrooms, two and a half baths. Too much room for a couple that desperately wants kids. They were my first choice. Both of them. But they're family and, therefore, too obvious. My recruiter has promised to find Veracity new parents who will be like Anne and David. Kind, if not familiar. A different home the Confederation can't remove her from.

Anne has flown out to get Veracity so she won't have to fly back to their house alone. I say my good-bye as dispassionately as possible, as if it's meant to last just the span of a long weekend and not a lifetime. I make it all the way through the main terminal doors and out to the taxi stand before collapsing onto the cement. A man asks if I need help. I can't answer. Don't remember hobbling to my car. Getting in. Finding the key, all the other actions required to get me from the airport back home.

What happens next is like a scene from someone else's life. A woman with long blonde-brown hair sits down at her kitchen table with a bottle of Occlusia. She removes seventeen pills with crystalline precision and lays them out on her table-top like a swarm of bees. Black and yellow, they buzz and flutter. She produces a glass of water, downs the swarm. It's that simple.

The woman goes to the front hall and sits down on the cool tile to watch the door. Fifteen minutes in, as planned, she calls for help. There's no blacking out, just tremendous vomiting and spasms. She rocks back and forth in front of the toilet, side to side, while being hoisted into the ambulance. She vomits off the side of the gurney while being rushed down the slick white hospital corridors. Ruins her second-favorite blouse.

Of the rest, there is no memory. For a few sour moments, she simply isn't. She lets her sound waves go flat. No activity on the machine. No signals, no prescience. Then, a pulse. A beat. My words, *my* words, *my words* . . . *dum-dum*, dum-*dum*, dum-dum. Back to being monitored, back to being here.

For three days, Chalmers Hospital keeps me on suicide

watch. When the officials come to do the standard interview, my eyes are swollen shut by a continuous stream of tears. I can't see the men. They're dark shapes explaining in monotone voices what will happen to my daughter. She's being reassigned to a new family. It's best for all concerned. I don't disagree.

I'm released. Go home and languish on my sofa.

The skin beneath my eyes is still black, my hair forgotten. Most days I pull it up into a ponytail to exempt me from the process of running a brush through the long, uneven strands. I wear whatever clothes I manage to lay out the night before. Eat only if my path takes me past the refrigerator. I'm a mess. Forgetful in the most basic ways.

Mornings are the worst. I arrive to the conscious world, my life unremembered. I'm given a few seconds of blissful ignorance before the memories come rushing in. And then I drown. Every single day.

The Confederation doctors and Mr. Weigland all tell me the same thing. I am to eat. To bathe. To go on with my life as if nothing's happened. I feel it as yet another abandonment. To live without Veracity seems crass. What will she think of me, continuing on without her? Haven't I always said it would be impossible? *Keep on goin', Harper.* Bullshit. I've lost my child. What else can matter?

A week later, Mr. Weigland comes to my apartment. He walks in behind a bouquet of yellow daisies, his eyes everywhere but on me. He puts his hand on my arm, asks why I haven't come to him. Do I know my job is still there? It is. It's waiting for me. I'm to come back the following Monday, resume my duties. Just the same as before.

"It'll do you good to get back into a schedule," he says. And he's right. He leans in, presses a paper napkin into my hand. Kisses me, barely, on the top of my head and leaves.

The napkin contains one poorly handwritten line. *Fake it 'til you make it.*

It's an act of trust. I can't return such kindness with

anything but the same and burn the soft swatch of paper immediately over a gas burner.

Fake it 'til you make it.

It's good advice. I need to do the small things, the daily things that will help me forget what I won't be coming home to. I rearrange the furniture. Go back to work.

At first, the office feels completely the same. On the surface, not much has changed except for a pile of top clearance files that's grown precariously high in one corner. I delve into the work that's familiar and distracting and more soothing than I'd anticipated. It's not until late morning of my first day back that I begin to notice the Monitors passing by. They're being tender with me. Furtive. They walk by in groups. Up and down the center aisle until the moment feels right and then they begin stopping at my cubicle door. Asking me how I am, expressing their remorse for my loss. Some mean it and some are there strictly to see if I'm staying or leaving.

I've just been sprung from Chalmers Hospital. For the next six to twelve months I'll be on Red Watch. My home, my car, my work will be monitored. A special set of Monitors back at the hospital will review my schedule, my diet, and my words—all of it, every day. They'll then report back to Mr. Weigland, who'll report back to his superiors. If I say I need a break, this is the one time in my life I'll get one. All because I'm important.

When I'm gone, others will be forced into BodySpeak early. About half of my first-day-back visitors are scared to death their number will get called. Their worry is fatiguing. Eventually, I tell them so. Ask them to go away.

It's the end of the day. I know it by the masses of people who're queuing up at the elevators, ready to leave. I go to turn off my computer and feel someone behind me.

It's Evans, the mailman. The man who delivered my recruitment letter. "Hello, Miss Adams."

"Hi, Evans."

Seventy years old, Evans has a back rounded by arthritis and long yellow teeth that make him look slightly feral, the exact opposite of who he is. He's polite and thoughtful. Is always asking questions about Veracity. Wanting to know how I'm acclimating to the litany of bumps in the road of life. He knows more about the people working here than our Human Resources Department. How and why, I never think to ask.

"You've had a lot of visitors today," he says. "I hope you don't mind one more."

I unplug my earphones. Turn off my computer. For kind Evans, I lie, "I don't mind."

He puts a hand on my shoulder. Wants me to look at him when he talks. "Miss Adams, I've come to make sure you're still planning that trip we talked about earlier this summer. The one to Chesney." He's shrouded in an uncharacteristic yellow-gold today, a color that turns his liver-spotted skin green. "I noticed you haven't let Human Resources know about it yet." He's worried I'll forget myself. Say something that will net me a punitive or blow his cover. He's right to be worried. My mind is elsewhere.

I pat Evans's hand, still on my shoulder. His skin is loose. It slides over the bones as if not attached. "I'm sorry. I've changed my mind about a vacation this year."

Vacation. Evans smiles sorrowfully at our use of such a term. What we're discussing is just the opposite. "Oh, Miss Adams."

I shake my head. "I don't think I could enjoy it."

"That's not always why someone takes a *vacation*, is it? Some of the best things I've done in my life have been done on vacation."

I grab my purse, my keys that are already out on my desk. "Good night, Evans." I leave without looking back. "Thank you anyway."

I drive to the grocery store and go straight to the liquor aisle. It's become my routine. The choice of alcohol is inconsequential. Whatever comes into contact with my outstretched hand comes into contact with my bloodstream. White wine. Red wine. Brandy. Whiskey. Never anything cold. Nothing that requires me to so much as open the cooler door.

I have my fist bound tightly around a bottle of pinot noir when someone grabs me and pulls me away toward the back door. I'm removed from the liquor aisle and the few customers sober enough to notice. Wine still in tow, I'm taken out into the rear alley and pushed up against a wall. The arms binding mine loosen to perform whatever punitive has come up in my file, and I'm glad for it. This is how it will end. Not with me joining the resistance but being raped and murdered out here with rain coming down in hard, cold drops. I stand quietly, complicitly, with my arms bent painfully behind me. I smile for the first time in weeks. The hurt will finally end. To me, it's a miracle.

The man's hand fumbles across the muscle of my thigh. Searches until it finds the bottle of wine and pulls it free.

No.

He's not here to rape me. Murder me. Take away the pain. I close my eyes.

"No." It is a plea.

This man isn't a Blue Coat come to call out the worst numbers. This is a man I've met maybe without realizing it. Someone who could have walked past my desk, or ridden with me on the elevator just once, maybe twice. I have the smallest memory of his scent. And a familiarity with the warm blue at the heart of his colors. He doesn't work at the Murdon Building where I would have felt him, even floors away, or caught his iridescent prints left behind here and there. Still, I'm sure that's where we must have met. It's the only place I ever go besides home. How I recognize him, I don't know. Right now, it's enough that he recognizes me.

"You're my recruiter. Aren't you?" I whisper.

His jaw against my head, the man nods in confirmation. He holds me as the grief begins to flow, and I let him.

My recruiter knows to lean in so I can clutch and sob against the wall, so no one walking by can see me beneath him. Knows to stroke the skin of my hands so I can retch up everything I've been keeping locked away. Knows to put his cheek against the top of my skull. Softly, imperceptibly, press his lips to the top of my head.

He says nothing to me. Doesn't ask if I've been restored to my mission, to my recruitment into the resistance. He holds me until I'm all cried out, and then he goes. My recruiter is the only person today who's provided me assurances, requiring no assurances in return.

I don't know what color his eyes are, or the color or cut of his hair. I don't know how young or old he might be and will have to erase from my memory the green-blue aura his hands left on the brick wall. I don't want to know him the next time we meet. Anonymity is what I've chosen because I need him as a blank slate. The fantasies I hold about my recruiter are as important to me as the man himself. There may come a day when I'll want to know who he is and what he does. But not until I'm ready and not unless I'm ready. Right now, I need him to be perfect. And, in this world, there's not one chance he could be even slightly close.

When my tears have finally been spent, I push away from the wall and he leaves. I stand for a moment, shivering. Keeping my eyes off the trail of turquoise footprints that leads away into the street.

HAPTER
SEVEN

I am eating my breakfast outside the Murdon Building. Standing in one of the numerous security gate lines that are backed up for half a block each. They're training new guards, or maybe there's been another disruption in the system, as has happened frequently of late. I don't mind. It gives me time to watch the impressive sunrise crowds collected around the prostitutes' quarters for an early morning session.

The most popular prostitute on National House Square is a small woman who calls herself Jezebel. She likes to come outside between clients. Strut her boy's frame up and down the street, makeup still smeared from her last session. It's a testament to her style, her who-gives-a-fuck attitude. She never fixes it. Goes the whole day with lipstick on her chin and mascara leaked into the half-moons beneath her eyes. Queues at Jezebel's are always the longest.

Jezebel sees me leaning against the security arch. "Beta!" she shouts. *"Beta!"*

This woman already knows. How fast news travels. Candace was made the Alpha. Our BodySpeak test was just yesterday. I came in second.

Jezebel struts the half block over, shushing those she's left behind—men and women who're tapping their watches. Reminding her of their schedules. They're everyone. Managers. Monitors. Blue Coats. People who should have nothing in common, least of all her.

The prostitute waves one end of her sash in the air. Pulls down her shirt and flashes me a flat, almost nipple-free breast. "How come you never visit me, Beta?"

It would be legal if I did. Sex however the customer wants it. A threesome, two men and one woman, two women and one man. Or simply two women. Two men. Gender, number of partners, whatever other variables might be considered, it's of no matter. Sex any way you like it is as common as ordering a pizza. But go and fall in love with someone of the same sex and you're classified a *Cultural Terrorist*. The government doesn't extend such an open mind to the less sexual aspects of a relationship. The *falling in love* parts. The wanting to share a family and a life. The government says this prejudice has a purpose. They need to maintain a healthy population, and two people of the same sex can't reproduce. They say there is no danger in setting such a precedent. But just as soon as they find a way to replace workers with robots and don't need heterosexual couples for the purposes of procreation, marriage itself will be at risk. President has become fearful of what even two people, united, could do.

"Come on, hotshot!" Jezebel calls, one finger beckoning.

My wristwatch beeps 7:00 a.m. and guards begin flowing out through the Murdon Building's front doors. Security Guard Jones is the first one out. He waves a hand at the small prostitute, her bare tit still on display. "You get on now," he says without meaning it. He likes her all-day energy. Her carelessness that's the opposite of his job.

Jezebel blows him a kiss and sashays back to her office. I'm cleared to go on to mine.

Candace Hillard is tall, six feet without shoes. She has long blue-black hair and toffee-colored skin, the kind our physical profiles would define as Medium-Black. Her eyes are hazel, meaning they change. Brown if she's calm, green if she's angry. She was torn from her mother's arms when she was seven. Listed under the not-too-old file, like me, in exchange for God knows what. She was given to new parents who didn't want her. Married the wrong man. Had a beautiful baby girl who's now a ten-year-old named Hannah. Got divorced and became a single mother. Pursued the wrong career. *Pursue*, the wrong verb, because it suggests choice. But the one she'd prefer to use, like me. I'm four inches shorter, seven months younger, my hair ten shades lighter. My skin falls into the checkbox category of Medium-White. If it weren't for our bodies, we'd be sisters.

Candace has been holding up the line with crossed arms and long planted legs. A huge gap's formed behind her but no one's asked her to get out of the way.

"Late?" she shouts. *"Today?"*

I don't answer.

Candace takes me by the hand and drags me past the other Monitors who've been queued up for an hour. They aren't angry at our small abuse of power, going to the front of the line. They know what we do, what we see. They move aside easily, smiling as we pass. None of them are jealous of our positions. Just the opposite.

Once inside the conference room, we're escorted down the long center aisle to our seats in the front row. A Manager is standing behind an elevated podium at the head of the room. He's young as Managers go. Forty, with a full head of dark brown hair. He's angry he's had to wait for us but doesn't dare let it show. I see it in the sparkling brown clouds that appear around his head. They swirl and drift as if on a breeze, then evaporate beneath the mask of a forced smile. In a booming voice, he begins. "Good morning, everyone!"

Candace bumps my knee. *Watch.* I'm to look up at the young Manager standing on the stage before us. Smile.

"Welcome to the twenty-fifth meeting of the East-Central Monitoring Division," he says.

We clap as expected.

"Today's guest host will be none other than our own Manager Strauss."

Candace leans forward in her seat as a sparkling red corona forms over her head. Manager Strauss runs a group of Monitors on the ninety-ninth floor. He demands too much of them. Time and energy. If they're pretty, more. Years ago, Candace worked under Manager Strauss. Then something happened, an event even I don't know about, and she was transferred out of his department and put in the office across from me. I was lucky. I went straight to Mr. Weigland, for whom such an abuse of power isn't a thought in his head.

The young Manager steps away from the podium and Manager Strauss takes his place. By comparison, this Manager looks as old as Methuselah. He has a narrow, skeletal face and wisps of feathery white hairs scattered over a freckled scalp. He wraps bony hands around the lectern's edge and speaks with his black eyes pointed over our heads. He tells us today he'll be covering the ins and outs of the new and upcoming technological programs. SKEYE, then BodySpeak.

"But first," he adds in a ponderous tone, "we're going to discuss the recent resuscitation of that unfortunate and painful old artifact. That bit of nonsense born of the chronically unhappy and subversive . . . *The Book of Noah.*"

A few hundred Monitors suck in their breath and the long room goes quiet. Though, as Monitors, we're allowed to bear witness to this with impunity, it's still a class one Red word term and earns anyone who says it an immediate 550. There have been an unusual number of *Noah* incidents passing through Monitoring lately. We'd all hoped management would let it go.

"We're going to be handing out pamphlets we'd like you to read," Manager Strauss announces, and a line of assistants appears from the outer aisles.

Candace and I receive ours first.

"Take a moment and flip to the inside of the front page, please," Manager Strauss instructs.

On a flap inside the front cover, a list of Noah's accomplishments has been neatly bulleted for easy reference. Our founding father is credited with developing the coded methods of torture and murder used today by our police, drawing up the boundaries of our world, and, most important, developing the slate. None of these are news.

On the inside flap of the pamphlet's back cover is another list. All the things *The Book of Noah* is not. This fictitious book is *not* a guide to finding and joining a secret society whose sole intent is to stop progress and take down all technology. It is *not* a weapon to be used against the Confederation, or a new Bible, or a thing at all. *The Book of Noah* is nothing more than a terrorist campaign. A lie to discredit the government and all the good work they do. In between the two covers, there is a prodigious amount of information about Noah. I scan a few of the ten pages. It's all trivia. Details about Noah's likes and biology. He owned a black labrador named Duke. Was thirty-three when the Pandemic hit. Never married, having given the new country his whole life. The last few pages are a long-winded repetition of what's inside the front and back covers, repeated over and over so those basic facts stick.

"Now, I want you to take these home and read them, cover to cover," Manager Strauss says. "You're to return them by tomorrow afternoon, no later than four o'clock. It's imperative you bring them back in exactly the same condition as they are now." The old man leans down and lets his shriveled lips dangle over the microphone as he explains the ramifications of noncompliance.

Tomorrow afternoon, whole groups of us will be called up at once and placed single-file in the middle of our floors. Our names will be checked off long lists as the returned copies are sent through high alert security checks. The pamphlets will be scanned for more than one set of fingerprints per pamphlet, for ghostlike grid marks that will indicate copies have been made, and for flash marks—the result of a pamphlet having been photographed. All violations will gain the owner an on-the-spot 550.

I slide the pamphlet gently inside my purse, taking care not to dog-ear the corners.

The yellow pamphlets disappear as we collectively hurry to relegate *The Book of Noah* to the closet of our memories. At least until tomorrow. In the history of the Confederation, *The Book of Noah* has been responsible for the deaths of thousands of people. All those years ago, the public execution of *Noah* offenders was damage control meant for the masses. It seems today's efforts have been tailored with Monitors in mind. Perhaps we're the new targets of the infamous resistance. Maybe there is a resistance out there right now, wanting to recruit me.

Manager Strauss holds up his hands to recapture our attention. "Why don't we move on now to the SKEYE and Body-Speak programs."

He takes them in order. SKEYE is a compressed term for the Eye in the Sky program. For the first time in the Confederation's technology, automobiles are to be surveilled. Satellites will monitor our cars in an effort to protect citizens from rogues who've broken their slates and are traveling to some unknown locale. All large vehicles, anything seating more than eight people, will be requisitioned. Too many cars traveling in the same direction at the same time will raise a flag. When the satellite's global positioning system notes an infraction, Blue Coats will be sent out to investigate and be given full authority to handle situations as they see fit. Manager Strauss tells us they're aware there will be unnecessary fatalities. Innocents paying a price for a greater good. *It is the way of things,* he says. All those inadvertently killed on the path to progress will be memorialized. Their names etched in stone on a few of President's pavers out in the National House gardens, where no one's allowed to go and where there will never be enough stone to hold them all.

Candace's hand shoots up. When Manager Strauss ignores it, she stands. "Why now?" she asks.

Manager Strauss smiles at the crowd. "Ladies and gentlemen, our Alpha Monitor Candace J. Hill—"

Candace cuts him off. "Are you finding that more people are running?"

Manager Strauss's neck swells over his collar. He clears his throat and answers slowly. "Well, yes. As a matter of fact. We're finding there's an . . . an illness of the mind cropping up. Not in all areas. Certainly not in most people. But just in those sad, sorry few who don't know how to be happy with a world that's given them everything they could possibly want. What can I say? It is an illness. And we need to catch these people so they can be cured of it." Happy with his improvised answer, Manager Strauss smiles. "Do you have any other questions, Candace?"

"Yes," Candace answers. "How many people are running?"

The old man coughs into a hand and wraps the sticky palm around his lectern. "Too many. But not enough for you and your friends to worry about. The heart and soul of it is that this new program will cut down on personnel and systems maintenance. On hours of needless monitoring. Anyone who attempts to drive into the wastelands without permission or without a working slate will be stopped. This ensures that no cohesive group of radicals could possibly form. This program will take the legs out from under those among us who are considering a run. Think about it a moment. How would they move? How would they get food and water? If they got sick, how would they receive medical care or get medicine? When this program is brought online, everything in our world will be monitored. We are closing the final gap."

Candace nods as if this has answered her question and sits down. Manager Strauss continues.

The details of SKEYE roll on for nearly an hour before a long, wide screen drops from the ceiling behind Manager Strauss and he moves on to the next topic. Using a long black cane, he taps against the black tarp and words appear. *The. BodySpeak. Program.*

"Ladies and gentlemen, we've reached a new age regarding the business of Security and Monitoring. BodySpeak promises a brand-new way of identifying and handling previously established terrorists and individuals trending that way." Manager Strauss walks back and forth in front of the screen, tapping on dots that bloom into pictures. A woman at her kitchen sink making a homemade bomb. A man driving down some National House avenue with a gun lying on his front seat. Our speaker enjoys the oohs and aahs. Reactions to his excess.

Next to me, Candace is glowing. I can see her aura from the corner of my eye. It pulses red, then chartreuse. Anger and concern.

Manager Strauss walks to the very edge of the stage. "Let me ask you this, friends. How would it be if you never had to read another data set again? How about we just find these people who are out there leaking poison into society? And just . . . get them out of harm's way?"

Some of us clap, turned just like that. Most are skeptical and keep their hands in their laps. Monitors would give up anything to skip the process of verifying codes. It is a tremendous burden, the things to which we bear witness. The daily effort to save the innocent has hollowed us out. But to skip the review process would mean no judge and no jury. No due process. It's a fast pass to murder. No one knows that better than Candace and I.

Manager Strauss taps the screen and a picture of Candace and me comes up. It's footage of yesterday's field test. The two of us are in the long Quonset hut, standing on a high platform. The space beyond us is dark, stretching out into an optic infinity. Our eyes are half open. Our bodies locked in the position of reading, hands out, heads up. We look like terrorists about to be shot.

I'm outraged at the mistruths worked so deftly into this display. They're making us out to be deities. We've just barely been named the top two Sentients in the whole Monitoring

Department—and now everyone's acting as if we've changed. As if the things they want us to do are things to be admired.

Suddenly I'm the one out of my seat and down the aisle. Away from Manager Strauss and his magic wand. I'm in the holding room before Candace can catch up.

"It's a good goddamned thing you're so important!" she says, green eyes sparkling. "Now let's go sit back down and be through with this thing!"

I ignore Candace's anger, her ability to forget her own indiscretions and see only mine. This is the way her love comes out. As irritation and worry.

"I'm not important," I respond, pushing away the hand of a young Manager who's come pleasantly through the door to march me right back to my seat.

apostasy

discriminate

ego

fossil

heresy

kindred

obstreperous

offline

veracity

dis·crim·i·nate: to make a distinction in favor of or against a person or thing on the basis of the group, class, or category to which the person belongs rather than according to actual merit.

C HAPTER

EIGHT

I'm up with the sun, ready to eat and drink. Breaking one's slate feels like the equivalent of running the length of Wernthal. My muscles ache, starved for protein and fluids. My head hurts. It protests each step until I'm in the room above the kitchen, staring at Ezra's promised box, heavy with canned food.

"Thank you, God."

The box has been marked *Girls Room* in poorly made cursive writing. It smells of rot and in places is wilted through. When I go to move it, sections crumble and fall away. It's amazing Ezra got it up here in the first place. I'd throw it out were it not for the imperfect writing on its side. Blue-black ink scribbled with haste and without thought, as if it wasn't a privilege. I trace the letters with a finger, trying to imagine what it must have been like to write and, further, to have produced such ugly little wonderful words on the side of a box. I would find it exhilarating. The person who wrote *Girls Room* found it an irritation. It's there in her loops, the way the last letters fade away.

I look around the room before eating. Its old beams must be over a hundred years old. They're nonregulation, like the windows with their thick, warping panes that are much too wide and much too high, letting in too much light. There's something familiar in the sun heating my shoulders, in the early morning chirping of birds. In the landscape of trees and fields just outside. They make up some kind of code I can't crack but am happy to know is there. Set into the world and calling me out of doors to study. *The unnecessary distraction of nature*, the government calls it. They're right to be concerned. Had I been more exposed to it, I might have broken my slate earlier.

My stomach is rumbling, so I abandon that which feeds my soul for that which will feed the rest of me and line up the cans of food in a row on the hardwood floor. Perfect little Confederation words have been affixed to each one: *Green Beans, Butter Beans, Processed Ham,* and so on. I haven't eaten for almost two days and my anxious hands are clumsy with the beaked opener. One letter suggested salty foods to fight the nausea, so I eat the can of green beans first, then turn to the processed ham that tastes better than it looks. I eat until my hunger's sated and ignore the clanging thirst that takes its place.

I look around. Grow frantic. Is it possible Ezra hasn't left me any water?

I dismiss the immediate panic and resolve to search for anything that can be turned into fire. I'll find matches and kindling. I'll break the goddamned legs off the chairs if I have to and whittle them against each other until I get a spark. I'll boil the brown water coming out of the tap or go down to the promised stream, boil out the pesticides and strychnine there. Creek water will be more polluted, will require more time over a fire. But it will be clear. It will taste better because I won't see the dirt.

I begin a search for anything that will further my cause.

There are some old empty boxes stacked up in the center of the room, the kind used to move people from one house to another. I pull free the one on top and examine it for any traces of relocation left inside. Find a stick of gum wrapped in strange-looking aluminum wrapping that breaks when I try to bend it. In the third box down I find a flat, round piece of metal. On one side is the head of a man with the words *In God We Trust*. On the other side, a building that looks like a part of the National House. Above and then below this structure are the words *United States of America* and *One Cent.* Inside the box on the very bottom, I find a single playing card—the jack of diamonds—and my heart falls into my feet.

Card games are allowed in the Confederation of the Willing. Veracity and I would sit up each weekend night, drinking soda and eating popcorn, playing Chase the Ace, poker, and rummy. My daughter treated the cards as if they were holy. She kept them close to her. In the drawer of her bedside table along with a flashlight—should the power go out—and some sand collected from our only vacation to the ocean. We'd play until the decks would become worn and need to be floured to slide correctly across the kitchen table. We never played to win.

Veracity was strangely good at cards. There were times my daughter seemed to know exactly which ones I was holding or what card was next to be drawn off the top of the pile. Upon questioning, she confided that she was sometimes able to get up out of her seat and walk around behind my chair to see my hand. Just the see-through parts of her moved, she explained. Not her real body. On those evenings when Veracity did particularly well, I went to bed distraught. Praying, despite the obvious, that my daughter hadn't inherited my abilities.

I lift the jack of diamonds into the morning light and run a finger over its cracked edge. Start to put it in my pocket, then stop. Instead, I put the card back inside the box and stack all the others on top, Ezra's voice from the night before in my head. *No baggage.*

There's a rolled-up old rug propped in the corner. It's bent at the waist and looks longingly down at the floor. I lay it out flat and discover a handful of dusty old books hidden in its center. *The Grapes of Wrath, The Story of Old Jeremiah, Frog and Toad*, two books called *Reader's Digest*—one with a green cover, one red. Nothing I can use for a fire, but each a treasure nonetheless. A cursory glance tells me these books are full of words I don't know. Words I'm not supposed to say. I go to line them up on the floor, and from the center of the thick one—*The Grapes of Wrath*—a dark yellow pamphlet falls out. It's something I haven't seen for months, *The Myth Behind "The Book of Noah."*

I flip it open to the first page, where someone's written a note.

> *Now you know in part, then shall you know in full, even as you are known. Then can be now. You don't have to die to see clearly. All you need to do is open your eyes.*

It's one of the pamphlets passed out by Manager Strauss. How it got out here, I can't imagine. I slip the pamphlet back into the old knotted rug and push it back into the corner, but the inscription stays with me.

Downstairs, the kitchen has been stripped of everything but a table and two chairs, a broom, some clothesline lassoed around the top of a door, and an old stainless steel pot that's turned a dull gray. I forage the rest of the rooms like a rodent. Am now a harvester of thrown-away bounty, things that will heat me, feed me, protect and hydrate me. Isolation is more dangerous than I'd anticipated. There are too many must-haves I don't have, and by midafternoon my tongue is so swollen, it protrudes slightly through my lips.

I could die of thirst before I get the chance to fight. I shake off the thought. It's time to go outside. See about the creek that, from the window, splits the far crops in two.

The creek is a couple hundred feet from the house. Burrowed into a tree line left over from the old days when such landmarks were used to demarcate property. Back when people, not the government, owned the land. Most places like this are wired. Some wires signal movement, some distribute voltage. According to my recruiter, any found on this property will do neither. Still, I keep an eye out for dead squirrels killed by the electricity. Proceed slowly, tossing ahead sticks and rocks. Waiting for any sparks.

As I predicted, the water I collect from the creek is deceptively clear. It sits in the base of the steel pot, baiting me. *Screw waiting for Ezra! Drink me!* I have to throw it back in the stream and find a spot farther away. Somewhere I can make a fire without the distraction of unclean water over my shoulder. A place where I can remember terms like *parasites, poison,* and *dysentery.*

By early afternoon, I've worn myself out trying to produce a spark from two chair legs I've peeled with a piece of broken glass. An hour later, I consider drinking my own urine. Another hour ticks by and I'm so mad at Ezra for not leaving me water I could strangle her with my bare hands. By late afternoon, I've cried out all the moisture left in my body and can't even pee.

I march to the bathroom located on the first floor and look at myself in the mirror. Dirt is smeared over every angle and crease of my face, arms, and torso. Pockets of dust have formed in the loose waves of my hair. I'll have to clean up.

I retrieve a pot of brown water from the kitchen and pour it into the bathroom's yellowed tub. My face and hair are fixed easy enough. But my clothes are torn at every joint and muddied in places I won't be able to conceal. They're beyond the repair of brown water from the sink or even clear water from the creek. But there's not much of a choice. If Ezra doesn't come soon, I'll have to walk into Bond.

HAPTER
NINE

JUNE 1, 2045. AFTERNOON.

I've done this job since I was eighteen. Have lasted longer than anyone save for Candace. For this, I've earned an ergonomic chair with a built-in massager for my lower back. They offered me the component that would massage my calves but I said no and Mr. Weigland took it instead. My calves are where I store the things I see. When I get a difficult file, I flex them beneath my desk. *Left, right, left, right* until I've typed up any required notes and dispositioned the file. Those things—screams, desecrations, sins I still don't have the words for—will go with me to the grave. Mr. Weigland thinks I'm a stone but I'm really a mother confessor. I'm God's mathematician, counting the violations of humanity. It's how I do what I do.

I have twenty-four hours to evaluate a data file. To see how well the slate has cataloged the infraction and determine how appropriately assigned was the punishment. People create these data files by speaking Red Listed words or phrases. Sometimes the shock delivered by the slate is payment in full. Other times, Blue Coats are dispatched to deliver a correlating punishment that requires hands, feet, knees, teeth. More. Punishments a slate can't affect. Often, Blue Coats will improvise. Go off script and add interrogation, mutilation, rape, or murder. Something that better fits their mood.

Recordings of Red List infractions, and any subsequent Blue Coat visits, come to me as pieces of audio we call *waveforms*—acoustic data we can watch as well as hear. Each sound creates a series of red spikes that travel across my screen from left to right. The same way a seismograph articulates an earthquake.

The chronology of events following a Red List infraction that will require a Blue Coat's visit is far from perfect. For example, if someone uses a class one Red Listed word, the first person to be notified by the offender's slate isn't a Monitor who can verify such a life-threatening blunder of speech, but the Blue Coat who will be sent immediately and with great prejudice to kill the person who's said it. In this case, it's only after the punitive action has been carried out that I will be allowed to review the waveform and verify the diction. It's not often that an infraction requires an immediate 550. But it happens.

If I think an infraction was false or accidental, I write notes suggesting a different punishment than the one assigned by the computer. For this, I use our book of codes, a guide that maps to a few hundred different punishments, all parsed out according to the severity of the action and how large a threat it is to the Confederation. The computer isn't always able to discern who's a child stumbling onto just the right combination of sounds, or a new mother gone days without sleep. I am the human element. Like the computer, sometimes I make mistakes. Unlike my digital counterparts, I feel them all.

Mr. Weigland is watching me from behind his desk. His small brown eyes are wrinkled and worried. "You taking your Occlusia?"

"No, sir. Most Monitors do."

"Harper . . ." He drops off, but I know what this is about anyway.

"Should I . . ." To my surprise, my voice breaks. I clear my throat and look up at the ceiling. I'm afraid to cry in Mr. Weigland's office. He wouldn't know what to do. "Should I send some flowers to the family?"

"What?" Mr. Weigland repositions in his chair.

I look at the pictures on his desk. At his wife, who's too pretty for him. His dog, Mabel. A vase with some dirty water growing mold.

"The Alberty case. Should I send the family flowers?" My report was late. I'd cracked a tooth, gone to a dentist whose office was all the way across Wernthal. It took me all day.

"God, no!" Mr. Weigland laughs. "Are you talking about the man? The husband?"

"Yes."

"There wasn't anything to be done differently." He laughs again. I want to jump over his desk and make him drink that poison mold water.

"My Disparity Report was late," I say, my voice chilly. As a result, the man died. Was *killed*. By what means, I don't yet know. It will filter through the grapevine sooner or later.

"You think that's why I called you in? To talk about the Alberty file? We can't save everyone, Harper. You want to stay around the clock? That's what it would take. Don't beat yourself up about this! We do what we can do."

Something in Mr. Weigland's tone makes me nervous. He's placating me and he never does that.

I look up at his red, freckled face. "What did you want to talk to me about, sir?" This meeting is for a purpose he's trying to keep hidden. He's so bad at this. Putting up a thin screen of deception anyone, even a non-Sentient, could see.

Mr. Weigland adjusts his tie. "It's nothing big, really. Not in the scheme of things. Nothing *bad*." Which means it's exactly that. Bad. Hard for him to say and harder for me to hear.

I shift my focus. Relax the muscles of my eyes until I can see each grain of air zipping by. Mr. Weigland is an open manual. *This way to hopes and dreams. This way to secrets.* Information gleaned from people like this arrives in my head independent of their colors, a sudden and intimate knowledge delivered without visible transport. I focus on whatever truth

Mr. Weigland is trying to hide with his courtesies, but all that comes back is the image of a tall brick wall.

"Stop it, Harper." Mr. Weigland has noticed my drifting eyes.

"I'm sorry, sir."

Mr. Weigland leans back and puts his hands together, just the tips so they make an arch. He sits quietly debating what to say next as the ever-present scroll of Confederation news rolls across the television behind me. It shines off his forehead. I can read the temperature off his skull: eighty-seven degrees. Above that is a floating nimbus of yellow worry.

"We're going to start your field training for BodySpeak this week," he says. "You've met Manager Rumney, yes?"

I nod. "Sure."

Manager Rumney's first meeting with me and Candace was all questions and no introductions. *How has the Pandemic impacted our lives? How often do we dream? Were we like this before the Pandemic?* These things are in our files, if she'd take the time to look them up. We know she won't, so we never tell her the whole truth.

"Sir?" I ask.

Mr. Weigland doesn't move his eyes from the screen. "Yes?"

"What do you need to talk to me about, sir? It's not about Helen Rumney."

Mr. Weigland gets up, brown eyes swinging from the screen to my own. He walks around his desk and turns my chair so I'm facing the television and the addition of new words to the Red List appearing on the screen. "Watch."

"What am I looking for?"

"Just watch." One of Mr. Weigland's feet taps against the floor. "You watching?"

It's a ridiculous question. "Yes." Of course I'm watching. It's required.

Citizens have twenty-four hours to commit each word to memory. I pull out my electronic notepad and steady the tip of my stylus over the blank screen, one eye on the monitor. This is another thing that adds to my misery. To me, each lost word is a small death.

The announcement reads, "Please note for future purposes the following Red Listed words: Apostasy . . ."

Apostasy is a word, like many words, I don't recognize. Probably something a high-ranking government official blurted out in the company of slated people.

". . . Discriminate . . . Ego . . . Fossil . . ."

"You getting all this?" Mr. Weigland is looking at the computer in my lap. I haven't written anything down yet.

"Yeah." I hold the stylus over my electronic notepad and write out cursive words that appear on the screen in size 12 Courier font. Writing anywhere but on your electronic notepad, a computer the length and width of a piece of paper and not that much thicker, is a violation of law that can get you a 550. It's how they keep people from scribbling down notes the Confederation can't review.

The list continues. *Heresy . . . Kindred . . .*

It's short this time. Usually, we get eight or ten words before we're all the way to the *K*'s. I'm wondering what Mr. Weigland is so worried about when the last few words come rolling out the left side of the monitor.

Obstreperous.

Offline.

I freeze. Blink. Watch the next word cross the screen, then disappear.

Veracity.

I don't know how long Mr. Weigland has been speaking. Eventually, I hear him.

"Harper, are you okay?"

I look up at the man who's been my boss in Monitoring for more than half my lifetime and don't answer.

Mr. Weigland clears his throat. "Is this going to be any kind of problem?"

This is why he's brought me in for this meeting. He's judging my response to this new list. To the one word that's so profoundly personal. *Veracity.*

I set my face in stone, the way he likes it. Flex my calves. "No problem at all, sir."

Mr. Weigland clears his throat and the small wattle above his slate shakes. "If you'd like to take an hour or two, go talk to your daughter . . ."

"Yes, sir."

My daughter is in school. The same news screen here is also there in her classroom. She already knows. "May I have the rest of the day, sir?" So quickly, I'm ready to forget poor Mr. Alberty and take off a whole afternoon. But it's the way of things when you're a parent. You are cleaved in two the moment your child is born.

Mr. Weigland nods and walks back around his desk. He rifles through his drawers and produces a piece of paper marked with an authorization. He removes a tool from his top drawer, a pen containing real blue ink, and writes out an excuse that reminds me of the ones my mother sometimes gave me for first grade. For chicken pox. The death of my paternal grandfather. A deceased dog.

"Here." His handwriting is sloppy, worse than mine when I was a child.

I take the note as if it were sacred, gently between my thumb and forefinger. I've only seen handwriting a few times, mostly behind glass in the Government Archives wing of the Confederation museum. It's his gift to me, this artifact of freedom. Something to keep me in line now that my child has just lost her name.

"And something else!" Happy, Mr. Weigland raises his eyebrows and opens another drawer. *Another gift!* He smiles, wiggling another piece of paper in the air. *More handwriting!* "Here you go."

It isn't a whole sheet, just a half piece of paper that he

probably tore over the hard edge of his desk like I've seen him do a thousand times. Trees haven't done well in the heated climes. We conserve everything we can. "Thank you." It's a list of names. Suggestions.

"You're welcome." Mr. Weigland reaches across the desk and taps my arm, keeping his nail-bitten fingertips on my skin. "It's a good list, Harper. They'll accept one of these at your daughter's name hearing."

Ruth. Mary. Rebekkah. Sarah. And so on. All taken from the Confederation Bible, as are most names anymore.

On the day of Veracity's hearing, I ask for another name. One not provided as a suggestion. *Victoria.* Maybe it won't be such a drastic shift. They each have four syllables, each starts with a *V.* The judge tells me he's a senior member on the Board of Words Ministry and he knows radical when he sees it, intimating that radical is me. A crazy mother not content with a biblical name, too high on her own delusions for something from the Good Book. *And while we're at it,* he says, *where'd you come up with Veracity in the first place?* He asks where I could possibly have seen such a preposterous word. A word that means absolutely nothing of note and should have been Red Listed years back.

I tell him. I'd seen it under glass. In an Antique Handwriting exhibit in the Confederation Museum, at the bottom of some old postcard. It had meant something to me when I'd read it. I couldn't discern the word's meaning from the context, so it became for me a feeling instead. I don't tell this part to the judge, who doesn't care and doesn't let me continue anyway. He's on to other threats.

"Should we turn this hearing into a custody trial?" he asks, leaning forward. His hair is gray, the flesh of his face heavy. It falls beneath his eyes, around his jowls, beneath his chin. Makes him look wiser than he really is. "Are you even a Christian, ma'am? I see we've allowed you a divorce?" He rolls his eyes. Doesn't agree with the splitting up of those whom the Confederation has brought together. Especially considering my ex-husband is also a district judge, now serving in Hollister on the West Coast.

"Yes, sir."

"Yes, sir to what? Yes, sir, you're a Christian or yes, sir, you're divorced?"

"Yes to both. Sir." Veracity is in tears next to me. She has both hands up to her face, not looking, afraid of this man and his power. I turn back to the judge. *Goddamn you,* I think as hard as I can. As if it will mark him.

"Are you a good Christian?" he asks.

"Yes, sir."

"And yet, you feel that a non-Christian name would better reflect the nature of your daughter? As the record already shows this to have been your sole purpose in requesting the name *Victoria* . . ." he says, wobbling his voice, ". . . then I must draw the only logical conclusion left to me and assume you do not intend to raise her in the Christian faith. Should I also gather from your request that maybe, just maybe, you will be teaching her something other than the one true religion behind closed doors?"

"I am a good Christian." I don't add "sir" or "Your Honor" and continue on before he stops me. This is the one question I'm capable of answering without a lie. "I believe with all my heart and all my soul that we're supposed to love one another and stop judging and hating one another. And I would have it no other way for my daughter. I will teach her Christianity. Sir." *My kind, not yours.*

The judge goes sour. His whole face turns inside out. "I know who you are, Monitor Adams. And let me tell you something, your status will have no bearing on this court's decision. Your daughter's name will be Sarah. Sarah Adams. Pick up your new registry on the way out." He bangs his gavel and we're pushed away, through the turnstile gates and into the next government line.

This is how my daughter's name was stolen. In a courtroom wired to broadcast such goings-on via a program on channel 4. In the light of day with millions of people watching.

apostasy

discriminate

ego

fossil

heresy

kindred

obstreperous

offline

veracity

ego: The "I" or self of any person; a person as thinking, feeling, willing, and distinguishing itself from the selves of others.

HAPTER
TEN

The walk nearly kills me. *Just three miles,* as Ezra put it. Three miles with no water left in my skin and my tongue swollen inside my mouth. By the time I get to the green sign announcing *Bond, Pop. 356,* I feel dizzy. My face is as white as my blouse. I know from the few passing people who turn to watch me walk by.

I see no houses, only a handful of businesses surrounding the town square: a small convenience store, a bar, and a funeral home. The rest have signs posted in their windows that read *Redistributed by the Confederation.* Smack in the center of this square is a flat cement slab just one step up from the surrounding grass. It's a dozen feet wide by the same long and cracked in a few places with weeds peeking through. It has the same bronze flagpole growing up from its center that every small town has. The kind posted since forever, most of it turned copper-green. The Confederation flag hangs limply from its top. There is no breeze to wake it up. The white middle sleeps, sunk back into its blue folds.

I pause to let a few kids walk in front of me. They cross right to left, from the chalky sidewalk to the street, daring me with their slow, speculative gaits to look at them, or talk to them. They're teenagers trying as best they can to be teenagers in such a tightly controlled environment. Their tops are worn inside out. Pants low on their hips. Some have found extra material and tied it around their heads. One, the boy who comes closest, has an earring in one ear. It's a bold move.

Mixing gender-appropriate anything is an on-the-spot 488. I envy him. To be so deliciously unaware of one's own mortality. So true to one's self, damn the consequences.

I nod. "Hello."

He doesn't acknowledge me until he's crossed to the square and is seated on a rotting bench that faces the street. "You looking for something?" he asks.

His young cheeks are stubbled with pimples, his chin with sparse bits of facial hair. He's structured himself to look angry, this boy barely sixteen years old and not as big around as my thigh. It's an attempt that leaves me feeling sad.

"You know where I can get some water?" My lips are cracked and my pants are torn. I've shown my hand, so I add, "Fruit? . . . Bread? Groceries?"

The boy squints into the setting sun. "Store's right behind you."

I turn. The sign on the window says *Produce/Bond*, the way all places of business announce their product or service. First by what they sell, then by their location.

"Thanks."

As the front door opens, I catch my appearance in the reflective surface. I look like I'm about to fall down, so I stand taller. Square my shoulders. Pretend I have the energy for good posture. The door closes and I see the boy on the bench get up. He bolts back across the square, skinny legs kicking up grass.

Shit. I put my hand on the door again, ready to run back to the farm, to the creek, to the bottom of the old concrete grain bin I saw on the perimeter where I could hide. But a voice stops me.

"You okay there, miss?"

I turn. An old man is standing just behind me, holding out a pint of strawberries. They're pink, more round than heart-shaped. Too young. "Picked these this morning off some pots I keep in the greenhouse. They're a little early off the vine but still good. Just set 'em out on your counter for a day or two."

He smiles a little too big. As if we were discussing something tawdry, something other than strawberries.

I have to walk around him to get farther into the store. "No, thank you." Long windowed coolers are humming in the back. It's an effort to conceal my thirst.

The man follows me to the blue bottles of cold filtered water that line the whole of the first door. I turn left, walk past them, stop at the third one down. At the amber bottles of beer.

The man stops next to me. I can see his slate beneath the stays of his collar, flesh bagging around it like cooling lava. "Not used to us old folks, huh?"

I don't answer. Edge past him back to the appropriate cooler, where I retrieve two sodas and, casually, not even looking, one bottle of water.

I live in Wernthal, the seat of our government. I see old folks every day. In rich black suits striding between rows of Blue Coats. In red robes making speeches from their front lawn.

"Well, I probably wouldn't know what to say, either." It's false, his deprecation of self. It comes out with a low barking laugh, the result of too many cigarettes.

The shop keep has been sent out here as some form of punishment. He was once a Manager in some bigger city. I can tell by his haughty air and jaunty shoes. They were expensive once. Made of the best leather and cut just so. There's a buildup of polish around the heel. Too many sweeps of the brush have dulled the leather's roundest parts. I bet he wears them every day, these vestiges of his life elsewhere.

I walk to the checkout, ignoring the droplets of condensation the bottles leave in my hands. But he's in no hurry to help me.

"What happened to you?" The old man is looking at my torn trousers.

"Gardening."

"Gardening?"

"Pulling weeds." I wave my pay card.

"Must have been some weeds!" the old man says loudly, drawing the attention of the other shoppers. They wander over slowly to look at my pants.

I put the bottles on the counter. "Can I check out now? Please?" *It was a mistake, coming here.* The thought makes me dizzy. I have to steady myself on the counter.

"No need to get all riled up, sweetheart—" he begins.

Ezra's voice stops him. "Ed!" she shouts, storming through the front door on platform shoes. "Back off!"

The shop keep looks from Ezra to me, his countenance now a little less desultory, a lot more unsavory. "You two friends? You in the business, honey?" He leans down. Wiggles his eyebrows. Turns back to Ezra. "You teaching her some special tricks?"

Ezra's green eyes swing over to me as she proceeds down the main aisle. "Next time, tell me when you need something, yes?" She retrieves a bottle of water from the cooler, unscrews the plastic top, and takes a long, thirsty drink, some of the liquid running down her chin. It's everything I can do not to rip the bottle from her hand.

Ezra turns back to the shop keep. "What she does for a living isn't any of your business."

"It's business, right? Could be mine."

"Forget it."

The remnants of any kind-old-man features dissolve. Ed throws back his shoulders and heads for the register. "You don't make the rules, Ezra."

She waits for him to walk by before giving me a scowl. "You couldn't wait?"

"You paying, then?" Ed calls out to her. He has one hand flopped indiscreetly over the register, beckoning.

Ezra retrieves her pay card from a small purse carried around her waist like a belt and throws it on the counter.

"You think too much of yourself!" the shop keep snarls. He runs the card through the reader, a trenched piece of oblong plastic sitting atop the register like a malformed head. "Too good for the local clientele, huh? Unless they happen to wear a badge, maybe?" He looks up, soliciting approval from the other shoppers, but they turn away or hunker into the shelves.

"I'd like a bag for my beverages, please." Ezra studies her nails, ignoring Ed, who's come back around the counter.

"The church allows it!"

"Plastic, not paper."

The old man reaches over the desktop and yanks a plain white bag from the underside. "You just like a little pork with your pork, is that it? Those of us without the blue suits, we don't meet your standards." He laughs, throaty and wet.

"My card?" Ezra puts out her hand, palm up. Fingers waving.

Ed throws it at her. "It's my right as a Confederation citizen to partake of that particular social service and there's no shame in it! Nobody's going to make Ed Saunders feel anything but satisfaction for having chosen *to release my loins to better service my soul*! Eh? That's how the Pastor puts it! And I know my rights, Ezra James! You can't turn me away unless I have a record and I don't have a record! The rule of All Equals applies! Even to you!"

Ezra is cool. She follows me to the front of the store. Shoves a bottle of water into my hands.

The woman next in line walks over to the shop keep. Whispers something in his ear while nodding at us.

"Come on." I hold open the door for Ezra.

But Ed's been pressed into action. He runs a hand through his thinning hair. Starts toward us in long, dragging steps. "Hold up, Ezra," he says. "I know you're providing society a service, honey. You think I don't know that? I'm a widower! I'm the best kind of customer you gals got! A man with straightforward, no-nonsense needs! We're all placed according to our individual strengths. This just happens to be yours."

Next to me Ezra is tensing. I can see each vertebra of her neck extend as the muscles of her shoulders compress. "Excuse me?"

Good Christ. I twist the top off my water. Drink half the bottle in one gulp.

Having caught Ezra's attention, the old man goes back to the woman waiting at the register. Scans her items as he explains, "When somebody turns eighteen they're given tests to determine their best placement, right? We all take these tests and then the government officials tell us what our strengths are, what are weaknesses are, and so on." He looks up at us. "They're very accurate tests, Ezra. If you'd been better suited for other work, you would have been assigned other work. Think of it this way. If you weren't so pretty, they'd have made you a day laborer." This makes Ed happy with himself. He smiles at Ezra. Gives me a wink. *You, too, honey.*

Ezra retrieves a pair of sunglasses from a trouser pocket and slips them over the bridge of her nose. "Thanks for the water, Ed," she says, smooth. Then looks at the others, who turn immediately away. "Have a nice day, ya'll." And is gone.

By the time I get through the front door, Ezra's already halfway across the street. I have to jog to catch up with her. We walk together for two blocks, not talking. I'm torn between anger that Ezra's put me in this position and guilt that I've acted on it. Ezra's thoughts are impenetrable.

"Well?" I'm the first to break the silence.

"Well, what?"

"You have something you want to say?"

"What do you want, Adams? You want me to grill you?" Ezra looks back at me with hooded eyes. "Okay. What were you fucking thinking? Walking into town. Are you fucking stupid? Is this your version of hiding? How's that?"

"You didn't leave me anything to drink! Or any matches so I could at least boil creek water!"

Ezra turns the corner and we're suddenly in a residential area. On a road lined with old-fashioned, pre-Pandemic houses. She jogs ahead, onto the sidewalk. "You're not my only problem, Adams."

She moves along quickly past the old homes. Most are two stories with front yards and porches, some of them screened in. They'd look nice if it weren't for the boards used to patch up the missing strips of yellowed plastic—some material from the past that's no longer used. No replacement parts available.

Ezra turns up the drive to a large, pretty house, all its cream-colored siding intact. The grass is neatly trimmed. Boxes of purple and orange flowers line the windows. It's domestic. The kind of home my grandparents had, without the crops.

"You coming in or what?" she asks.

"This is your place?"

Ezra frowns at my disbelief and disappears into the screened porch. Her voice trails back through the open door. "Don't let the cat out."

I'm halfway in when she releases the screen. It bangs me in the nose.

"You own a cat?" I ask. It's a stretch to imagine Ezra caring about anything long enough to keep it alive.

She ignores my questions. "Wipe your feet."

I do as I'm told. Shoo away the ugly gray cat that appears and rubs itself against my shins. Drag the soles of my shoes across her Welcome mat. Once inside the kitchen, I stop and look around. It's not a home with sterile white walls and gray floors. It's the house I wanted to grow up in. There's a loaf of bread resting on the counter, fresh-baked, breathing out the heady scent of yeast. There are spices in a rack and dishes upside down on a towel, perspiring. The kitchen is well used. Loved. I'd have done anything to live in a place like this.

I imagine Veracity here. Imagine her bursting through the porch door after hours spent playing in the autumn leaves. She kicks off her boots, struggles out of her coat. Steals a soda from the refrigerator. Not the government-issued kind.

A *Coca-Cola,* the kind my father used to drink out of a bright red can. I imagine us—a family—and maybe a few friends playing cards at the large round table. *We see you over there, Veracity. Come here, darlin'. We'll deal you in.* A roast cooking in the oven, a pie cooling on the windowsill, all foods we could separate into parts and eat together as a whole. This should have been Veracity's life. This should have been my kitchen.

"Harper!" Ezra is in front of me, snapping her fingers in my face. "Hey!"

It takes a moment to shake off such powerful longing. "What?"

"Shut the door," she says, disappearing through a side hall.

I follow Ezra around the corner to a plain bedroom. A wide, nine-drawer bureau and an equally long mirror line one wall. Her bed is made, covered with a white comforter sporting pink flowers, the corners tucked in. There's not much else to see. She walks through an arched doorway and enters a room with a sofa and a chair and a mirror the length of its closet door.

Ezra is waiting for me with her evening wear in one hand and her prostitute's sash in the other. She needs to change. The bare skin of her face and forearms is paler than I'd thought. White as snow, and thin enough that the veins show through.

"You're going to have to stop taking things so goddamned personally," she says. Then, somehow, shoves a glass into my hand, though I don't remember seeing her move.

I look down into the clear water. "You left me alone. With nothing to drink."

"I was being watched, Adams! What did you want me to do? Compromise the whole fucking bunker for you!"

No. I blink. Time elapses. When I look up, Ezra's already changed into her evening wear. A short black skirt and a shirt made of see-through plastic with bits of black material sewn on.

"What's this really about?" she asks. "It's not about you getting *dehydrated.*"

The room is wobbling. Jostling the thoughts in my head until one spills out. "I left my daughter for this! I let her be *taken away* for this!" *Oh.* I've said it.

Ezra turns and looks into the mirror. "You have to let go of that shit, Adams. It's not helping you or your daughter."

I feel the last vestiges of my strength drain away. Sit down, quickly, on her recliner. "What do I do?"

"You don't die." Across the room, my blinking eyes get snapshots of Ezra dabbing at her mouth with a tube of bright red lipstick. "Don't die and someday you'll be able to tell her you didn't leave her."

My mind is drifting away and my eyes start to go with it. Ezra's arms become wispy bits of poplar. White and black branches caught in a breeze. They change, become long ropes of flesh tubing that have no children at their ends. Umbilici.

It would be so easy to shut my eyes and drift off. I'm so thirsty. My lips taste like salt. My body is a pool with the plug pulled out.

"Hey. Bigwig." Ezra is right next to me. I've nodded off again. Lost more time. "You have to let it go. Got it?"

HAPTER
ELEVEN

AUGUST 2012.

A woman has passed out in the checkout lane. The things in her wire basket are strewn all over the floor: tins of government food covered with white labels full of black words, a tall bottle of hairspray like my mother's, a pouch of beef jerky, and, peeking out from between her thighs, a jar of green olives. While everyone else checks for a pulse, I worry about what's going to happen when she's taken to the hospital. Then after, when she doesn't come home.

"Mommy," I say. But my mother is watching the woman and doesn't hear.

Two other customers put down their wire baskets and adjust their masks with jerky fingers. They split the woman up, one arm and one leg each, and carry her to an office in the back where she'll be given some juice and the officials will be called.

We aren't to worry, the Store Manager assures us. *Happens all the time.*

When it's our turn to upend our basket onto the black conveyor belt, my mother asks the checkout girl *why* it happens all the time.

"Them announcements." The girl points to the latest yellow note with a covered hand. Her name is Lindsay. She lives on the spread of land across from my grandparents' farm. Doesn't seem too worried about the box of latex gloves now posted at every checkout. They make me nervous. Remind me of visits to the doctor. Of shots.

We follow Lindsay's finger to the racks that used to be full of magazines showing pouty-mouthed women. They've been gone for a while now, just like the blue metal boxes out on the sidewalk that used to yawn when fed a quarter, spit up a copy of the daily news. Now there's nothing left to read. Just these bright yellow pieces of paper delivered by men in blue suits.

Today's message is briefer than usual. Mostly numbers. A five followed by a long series of others.

"How many dead to date," Lindsay explains, looking down at me with her empty blue eyes. They're spectacular above the white paper mask everyone's supposed to wear over their mouths. Cerulean. "How you doin', sport?"

My mother collects her bag and walks me roughly through the automatic front doors. Misplaced rage. She thinks I'm clueless about what's happening and that the checkout girl let the cat out of the bag, even though, for months, things have been changing. The television has been losing its stations. We used to have ninety-nine and now there's just one—channel 4. The only thing channel 4 shows anymore is news that turns my parents pale. It makes them drink more. Huddle around the kitchen counter and whisper. A woman with gold hair tells us, *Everything's fine. Don't risk your lives with so many questions. Go get your shots. Do what you're told. Blah-blah-blah.* My parents won't keep it on. Call it gibberish.

It's not just the television. My favorite brands of cereal and soda have been disappearing, too. Kindergarten. Play dates. The yellow bus that used to pick me up at the end of my grandparents' drive a few months after we left the city. Belly laughs. Pats on the back. *See ya'll laters*, *Good to see you agains. Good to* anything. The Pandemic isn't here yet and most people have already died, their important parts anyway. My mother thinks I'm too young to understand this. In some ways, I understand better than she does. What's happening. What's already been allowed.

There's an old fire burning in the middle of the square.

It's been there for weeks. My mother is so angry, she walks us back to the car the wrong way round. Through the gray smoke that smells like must and makes me cough. Past other men in blue uniforms posted one at each corner. *One, two, three, four.* All of them with guns.

I look past them into the red and orange center of the fire, my heart racing. I've been told not to look. On any other day my mother would have put a hand over my eyes. Or picked me up and forced my head into her shoulder. But today she's forgotten and I'm free to see what it is they're burning. I prepare myself as my head begins to turn. It could be anything. Puppies with their eyes gouged out. Kittens with legs like four blackened sticks. *What if they're burning people?* The idea almost stops me, but there's something even more awful and exciting about that.

Ahead of me, my mother is rounding the last corner. We're almost back to the car. Quickly, I turn my head. Feel the heat of the fire on my cheeks.

Nothing exciting. No dead kittens or people. Just a set of sloping red hills come up from layers of black ash. No bones or teeth or feet or paws sticking out. Just books. Words I can't read shining through the hills' flaming tops. Most of the pages are gone or going quickly. Plastic covers are dissolving. The hardback ones have held out the longest and cut the fire into seesaw angles.

When my mother turns around to hoist me into my child's seat, she catches me looking and frowns.

"Do you want to know why they're burning those books?"

I nod yes because she wants to tell me. I sit quietly as she buckles me in.

"Because the government thinks there's the possibility this flu might be passed through the oil in our skin." My mother's voice is low, like it gets just before she starts to cry.

She sits back on her heels and looks down at the sidewalk between her feet. "It's nothing you need to worry about, okay?"

"Okay."

I put my hand on hers. We link fingers.

The man in the blue suit nearest glances over. My mother feels him watching and stands up. She kisses me on the forehead and shuts my car door. Starts driving back to my grandparents' farm. I know what will happen when we get there.

She'll pull my father aside and tell him about the whole thing. She'll say Lindsay mentioned the Pandemic in front of me. And all those people dying. She'll tell my dad I've seen them burning books. My father will tell my mother, *She's a smart kid. She's been dreaming about it, hasn't she? Must have leaked into her head somehow.* He's not going to march over to Lindsay's house and tell off her parents. Besides which, *We've got bigger fish to fry, don't we? Damned right we do.* My mother will end the conversation with the same thing she always says. She thought things would be different out here in the country with Grandma and Grandpa. But it's not. And she misses our home.

My father's right. I have been dreaming about it.

The dream starts like this. I'm outside on the front lawn with my mother and father and grandparents playing a game of Wiffle ball. Above their heads, a big tan cloud is hanging low in the sky. Nobody sees it but me. It crawls quickly onto the corner of the farm. Moves toward us like a wide brown mouth. Before we can move, the cloud of earth explodes into a million tiny pieces that fly around and between us, pulling my hand from my mother's and hers from my father's. Reducing my grandparents into kneeling sculptures of sand. The air is thick and I can't breathe, or see my family, or my hand before my face. Then, as suddenly as it came, it's gone. Any left-behind sand drops to the earth and I see my family come up out of the fresh brown hills. The horror of it never fades.

Holes have been bored into their bodies, starting at the top of their skulls. Their features and joints have been smashed flat by what looks like a head-to-toe bandage pulled too tight.

Cheeks, noses, foreheads, chins, all the parts of them I recognized are gone. These tube people have no eyes, just holes where they should be, no tongues in their open mouths, not even teeth. When they tip down their heads, I can see straight through to the sandy ground. But they can still move. They are still alive.

These tube people walk around like they don't know where they are. They bump into me on their way to somewhere else. Don't know me. But I don't know them either. They've become empty, hungry monsters with so many places needing to be filled, I worry they might try to eat me. Pick me up and stuff me whole into their toothless mouths. I try to run but the hard ground has become soft with sand. Behind me, they have their arms stuck out, feeling for my small body, which won't be enough for even one of them.

It feels like I'm the only one unchanged by the storm, but I have no mirror. No way to see if there's a hole in my head, too.

Almost every night for the last few months, I've had this dream. Some nights, I find my mother at the side of my bed wrapping a cool towel around my neck, hurrying to get a bowl under my mouth. She never asks me any questions and I understand why. I can see it in her eyes and in the colors swirling around her. The purplish blue cloud she usually wears like a poncho, the one only I can see, has changed colors. It's now sickly brown, spiked with lines of vibrant, terrified red. She doesn't ask me about my dreams because she's having them herself. Calls me an acorn fallen not so far from the tree.

Our car is barreling down the country road way too fast. It makes the car vibrate like we're on a ride at the county fair.

"Mom?" I ask.

"Yeah, honey?"

I'm thinking about the woman from the grocery store. About her soft knees on display, the jar of olives buried halfway up her privates. "Is that woman going to be okay?"

"Yes, honey."

"Will they take her to the doctor?"

My mother finds me with her rearview mirror. "I'm sure they will."

"Someone's going to have to go to her house."

"Why?"

It's a sore subject between us, me knowing things I'm not supposed to, though I've heard Grandma talk. Know my mother did the same things, too. "Just somebody needs to go out there."

"*Why*, honey?"

I look out at the fields where I won't see her furrowed brow. "Somebody needs to feed her cat."

My mother doesn't ask how I know the woman has a cat. She tips back the rearview mirror so I can no longer see her and quietly drives us home.

Two weeks later, we're out on the front lawn playing Wiffle ball when a long white truck comes tearing up the drive.

There is a cutoff age, the man tells us. *Four.* I'm two years older than that but don't look it. Could pass for four. My mother says this is a blessing. And the Confederation has lost my records or they'd have known about my special abilities, too. Another blessing.

I know things I'm not supposed to. Mostly through colors people wear around them like their own personal clouds. Each color tells me something different. Bright pink can mean love. Yellow can mean happiness. Blue most times means a person is some kind of teacher—not the kind standing in front of a chalkboard who passes out books and homework, but the kind who makes you feel better just by talking to you. No one's ever just one color, but this doesn't make it any harder. All I have to do is look at them and I know the insides of their hearts. I used to like it until the Pandemic came along and everyone got scared.

When people are upset, their clouds get dark and can take up a whole room. All the time now, mostly down at the square, I see big blobs of dark color where people should be. Outside Mr. Caldwell's pharmacy, in front of the tavern, in the grocery store where we saw the woman fall, the one with the starving cat. Wherever the bright yellow notices are posted. Sometimes, these red-black clouds turn a light moldy brown while their owners are standing in our little town square, looking up at our new flag. This one is all blue with a big white splotch in the center that's supposed to be the new shape of our country. The man standing here in Grandma's kitchen is wearing a suit of the same blue color. Just-after-the-sun-goes-all-the-way-down blue. The color of the sky after all the light is gone.

My mother pulls me behind her and pushes me down with the palm of her hand. I'm skinny and have the wide eyes of youth, but I'm not short. I'm quick but don't have a child's desire to ask too many questions. *Stoic,* my mother calls it. A good way for a child to have been born these days.

Atop this man's blue suit is a cloak made of ugly purple mist shot through with pulsing bits of red. It tells me he's giddy with his new authority. High on it. This official with his shock of white-blond hair has been told to take what he wants. What he wants right now is my mother. It's in the red parts all around him, like a hundred eyes blinking.

There are more men like him out in the yard, standing around the van where my grandparents and father have already been taken.

"Mommy." I take her hand. Try to pull her away. She won't come, is pretending to listen.

I am here for . . . I have been sent here by . . . I am planning to . . . This man is all about his mission. He's become the same as the men stationed around the square, marching and barking orders through large white tubes. They all have a single stripe on each sleeve and a red handkerchief tied around one arm. Have all become their new suits.

"You're Abigail Sarah Adams, is that correct?" The man's curious blue eyes are fixed on my mother's dress. At the place it tore when they removed my father.

"Yes, sir." My mother is using a foreign tone. *Careful,* she'd whispered when the other men took away my grandparents. This new voice is soft and quick. All tone and no words. *He could hurt us, baby.* I hold stock-still, bending in such a way that my calves cramp.

The man is holding a small black machine with a window on its top. He taps a pen with no ink against its surface while asking her questions.

"And she's . . . ?"

"Harper Abigail Adams."

"And she's *four*?"

"Yes, sir."

"What's her birthday?" The man shuts his mouth as if his questions are over.

"September the thirteenth, 2008," my mother answers without pause. So quick and even, I wonder if I've had it wrong all this time.

"She's awful big for four." He doesn't look down at me. Instead, he puts a finger through the ruined material of my mother's dress. My mother stifles a sob.

She nods and the man withdraws his hand.

"You got a secure room down here? One with a lock?" He motions to me.

I can't see my mother's face. She takes me by the hand and steers me to the long closet behind the bathroom, the one with the washer and dryer and yesterday's clothes still piled on the floor. With her face turned away, she squeezes my palm hard. *Don't you say a word with that deep voice.* Then lets me go. The swing lock my father attached to the outside of the door scrapes against the wood; hook falls into eye. I turn around too late to catch any trace of my mother or the man just behind her, but I hear them out in the hallway. Up against the wall.

The man's voice begins to rise and fall until my mother asks if he wouldn't please mind being quieter. If he wouldn't mind, *please*. His voice goes away but the scraping sounds continue. So I count the scratches our old dog Vixen has left during her numerous closet lockups. Count louder as a banging starts up against the plaster hall, *eight, nine, ten . . .* I put my finger on the wood and trace its scars. Think of my torn jeans that were new a day ago, the one leg peeking out of the trash. Of my favorite movie that was taken away because I didn't clean my room and how, just a week ago, that was the worst thing that could have happened to me. I think of anything that's other than now until now ends and the door reopens.

My mother is crying when she comes back in. No longer cares if I see her smeared mascara. "Come on, honey." Before I can take a step, she picks me up and carries me, baby-style, to the waiting van.

We're taken to the local community center, a flat, wide building shaped like the sheet cakes they sell at fund-raisers. My mother thought we'd be put in the same line but I'm pulled out of her arms as soon as we come through the front door. She's swallowed up by a bunch of blue suits and somehow disappears. Or maybe I'm the one who goes away. All I remember is we're together and then we're not. We're at the community center and then I'm in the hospital, a strange nurse holding my hand and a bandage on my neck. The lights above me make me want to throw up. My throat stings as if I've swallowed glass.

"Hush now." The nurse has kind eyes with bags of excess flesh beneath. They swing as she whispers, "It'll be active in an hour. Best not to talk until you've had time to learn what not to say." I'm being moved down a hall with bright bulbs every few feet. They blink at me as we go. Tell me something bad is coming. Something worse than my neck.

I'm moved into a room with a tiled ceiling where the sad-eyed nurse tells me I'm going to be traveling to a nice big building full of children. Then after a while I'll be traveling again to a nice new family that will make sure I want for nothing. *Traveling,* she says. As if it were a vacation. I give her credit for trying not to tell me the *why* behind all this traveling. But I have to hear the words. Stare at her until they come. *They reacted poorly to the injections,* the nurse says. *It was a flaw in the serum. A venom hiding behind the cure.* People over and under a certain age often couldn't process something in the yellow fluid. But the older ones got their shots anyway because, *What was the other choice? To get sick? Become contagious? Put all you kids at risk?*

"The shots are mandatory, darlin'. That means your family didn't have a choice." The old nurse takes my hand. Wipes at her running nose with the back of a sleeve. "You just keep quiet for a year or two and you'll be just fine."

I don't remember much of what happened next. I cried. The old nurse stayed long past her shift. I traveled to an adoption center. Traveled on to a new life with new parents. Traveled on until I wasn't me anymore. Somehow on my way to somewhere else, I lost my abilities. Couldn't see colors anymore. Thought maybe the doctors had cut out this special part of me when they'd put in my slate.

Contagious becomes a word I hear every day for the next few years, wrapped tightly around places the Confederation doesn't want us to go. Like a barbed-wire fence.

apostasy

discriminate

ego

fossil

heresy

kindred

obstreperous

offline

veracity

fos-sil: any remains, impression, or trace of a living thing of a former geologic age, such as a skeleton, footprint, etc.

HAPTER

TWELVE

I wake up in Ezra's easy chair, spittle leaking down my chin. Casually, I stretch my arms overhead, clean my face with the back of one hand. Ezra has been watching. She puts down her hairbrush and frowns.

"Finally."

Ezra's eyes are bright green beneath a mask of indigo shadow painted across her lids. The rest of her face has been dusted with pink sparkles. The effect is ethereal. Even beautiful. But I don't know how a man could make love to a woman who looks so alien. Maybe it's what they like.

Through her dining room window, I see the sun is down. "What time is it?"

"Late."

I lick my lips and push myself upright. "Can I have some water?"

Ezra answers slowly, in time with the application of her light silver mascara. It looks like snow caught in her lashes. "Can . . . I . . . have . . . some . . . water . . . what?"

"Can I have some water, *now*?"

The retort makes Ezra smile. I catch her biting her lips in the mirror. "In a minute." She zips closed her makeup bag and adjusts her red sash between petite breasts. "How were you going to pay earlier?"

"Pay for what?"

"The water." She sits down on the sofa and begins working a pair of thigh-high stockings up each leg. "Were you going to use your pay card?"

"I'm not a complete idiot. I have someone else's."

Ezra stops pulling at her panty hose and looks up. "Whose?"

"Nobody you know . . ."

"Whose! Candace Hillard's?" She springs off the sofa, her nylons a tether between her ankles. She stumbles, righting herself on my chair. "Have you used it before? Did you pay for anything with it on the way to the break site?"

She knows Candace?

"It's not Candace's!" I shout, then add, "I was assigned to monitor a woman who died during her punitives. She was poor. If there are no real funds to pilfer, they don't even bother to close their accounts."

Ezra pulls up her hose, then goes back to the couch and grabs her brush. She yanks at her hair, spraying each strand away from her face like the petals of a sunflower, as if nothing's been said. She's avoiding something. It's all over her. A cherry-colored cape floating down her back and around her shoulders. I'm afraid I know what it is.

"Did Candace and I have the same recruiter?"

Ezra stops spraying her hair. She turns away from the mirror to look me in the eyes. "Yes."

"If Candace had survived, would you have recruited me?"

"Candace was your beta, Harper. We wanted you."

"What do you mean, she was my *Beta*?"

"She was your understudy. Your tester . . ."

"She was . . . what?" I stumble. Can't find the words. "Testing my break for me?"

"Yes," Ezra says. "We'd never recruited someone under such scrutiny before."

"But Candace was the Alpha Monitor . . ."

"Candace wasn't the one we needed. You were."

Before I can stop it, out comes a new question. One whose answer I want even less. "You know the man who killed Candace, don't you? The Blue Coat I saw out at the farm."

"You really want to get into that now?" Ezra grinds. *"Now?"*

No. It's too much. Too many answers leading to more questions and all of them making me dizzy.

"I'm thirsty. Is it safe to use the tap?" I push out of my seat and go to the kitchen, where Ezra won't see my flushed cheeks.

"There's a pitcher of water in the fridge. Use that." Ezra's voice is loud. I turn around and find her standing in the doorway, watching me.

I clear my face and push past Ezra toward the refrigerator. Inside, I find more food than I've ever seen in one place. Bacon. Tomatoes. Gallons of milk. Clear, lidded containers packed tight. Each shelf is full. Perishables are lined up in rows, back to front to maximize space. I pull out the only clear pitcher. Hold it over my empty glass and pour.

"Did Candace know she was the Beta?" I ask.

"Jesus, Adams. Why this sudden need for hard answers?"

I don't know, Ezra. Maybe it's because I've lived so much of my life hiding from the truth. Or maybe it's just because I'm good and goddamned sick of being afraid. But I don't say either of these things.

Ask again, "Did Candace know she was the Beta? Did she know she was testing the process?"

"Yes. And she was happy to do it."

Spilled water hits the counter. "And what about her daughter? What about Hannah?"

Ezra walks across the room. She picks up the pitcher and pours the water for me. "No one could have anticipated that. Now, that's enough. No more."

I lean against the table and stare at the full glass. "Who's my recruiter?"

"Goddamnit, Adams . . ."

"Is he a Manager? Does he work in Tracking and Data?"

Ezra lights a cigarette and answers on a stream of smoke, "You've already met him. You tell me."

She knows about the one encounter we had in the alley. The thought makes me blush. "It was raining. I never saw his face."

"Uh-huh." Ezra opens her mouth to say something else, but doesn't.

Her silence infuriates me. I'm not going to beg her for answers.

"Where are the matches?" I walk to the counter and begin opening drawers. "Just in case you never come back, I'll need to boil water. Right?"

Ezra nods at the far drawers. "Last one down."

I rifle through a mess of pens, batteries, little scraps of paper containing handwritten phone numbers. Come up with no matches.

"All the way back." Ezra points.

I push deeper until my fingers come into contact with a rectangular box. It's black with an image of a brick building and a phone number on its cover. One of her johns. His grubby hands have left a shining bit of color on the slick black cover. A glowing sludge brown. Nobody I'd want to meet, much less screw. I push back the cover and look at the red-tipped sticks lined up inside. They look fresh enough, will keep me from such dependence on her.

We get into Ezra's car, don't speak on the way back to the farm. Once there, she throws the car into Park and turns around in her seat. Something about her face is different. It's less enraged than usual.

"Adams . . ."

"What?" I don't want her to be soft with me. To apologize for telling me about Candace and not my recruiter. Or for telling me I was effectively the reason Hannah was killed. And Candace. "What!" I shout.

Ezra turns and looks through the front windshield. "I'll be back in the morning."

I tell her I won't hold my breath.

Ezra doesn't come at first light. Or by noon when the sun is straight overhead and I no longer cast a shadow. So I decide to build my first fire.

I set a ring of stones next to the creek where the ground is hard, yards away from anything that might too easily catch fire. With one strike of the match, the kindling is lit and the smoke is filtered through the canopy of trees above. Making the fire was easy. All I needed was the match.

I collect creek water in my iron pot and set it over the embers, then bring down the remaining jars of food. Breakfast is warmed vegetables eaten right off my fingers and hot, germfree water. It's a too-short task that leaves the sun still hovering just over the horizon. Leaves me with pulpy, idle hands and an active mind.

What if Ezra doesn't come? How will I find my trainer, and the others? Will they be able to come get me? What if Ezra is the only one who can transport me?

Fear like this infects the quiet. Makes every rustle and bump something else in my mind. I go back to the house, to the room above the kitchen. Spend the afternoon reading chapters from each of the books. At least a third of the words are new to me. They frustrate and tantalize like a door opened slightly, a slice of universe revealed on the other side. They come in nearly every sentence, often two or three per line. A man couldn't *liberate* himself from his wife. A woman who became paralyzed lost her ability to *sculpt,* to *paint portraits,* to make *art.* The list is small at first. Then, in a piece about the necessity of *investigative reporting,* it grows a hundredfold. *Solitude. Culture. Fulfill. Fulfillment. Democracy. Lifestyle.* And so on. The list of words I don't know is infinite and I become what the government expected an educated me to become. Angry.

What about these words is so dangerous? Would they have allowed us a glimpse into our own form of poverty? Revealed different boundaries existing between the possible and the impossible, the moral and the immoral, the decent and the unconscionable? Allowed us to discover we've been living according to someone else's definition of joy? The truth of it rushes up on me. I put the books back in the box. *The Grapes of Wrath*. The *Reader's Digest* with the red cover.

I've followed the sun around the room, enjoying the feel of it on my face. And now the moon's up in the low sky and I'm sitting in the near dark. And Ezra's still not here.

Again. It shouldn't surprise me. I'm surprised to find it does.

I bring the books downstairs and stack them on the table. I'll start reading *Old Jeremiah* when I get back from the creek, if my eyes can adjust to the poor light. Tomorrow, I'll walk into town, find the boy with the pockmarked face. I'll ask him to take me to the resistance. Screw Ezra. She's not the alpha and the omega. I'll find other ways to get to my trainer. I'm no good to them dead on this green prairie. They've chosen me for a reason. Even if I was chosen second.

The sun is still bobbing above the far horizon. I have just enough time to boil a fresh pot of water before the fire becomes brighter than the fading air. I run to the creek. Gather wood and the grass I've laid out to dry. Stack them in the ash-filled pit. Then realize I've left Ezra's matches in the kitchen.

"Damn it." I won't have time to boil anything. I pick up a small branch and throw it hard into the rows of corn. It means a bad night's coming. Nothing to drink means no sleep. Dehydration is like that. Like a gnat stuck in your ear, buzzing.

Halfway back to the farmhouse, a trail of gray smoke appears over the tall grass. I rise up on my toes. *Not over the grass, over the road*. It's a car. I start to run. I've left the books out on the table . . . and the matches . . .

My legs bend and punch, stamp down the uneven earth. It's always the small things that trip people up. I see it all the time. If it's the Blue Coats, they'll see the things I've left out and the fresh pleat I'm leaving in the field. If I get to the kitchen in time and manage to grab the matches, I won't get far enough away. Even if I get back to the creek, the other side of the waterline is steep. It's a hundred feet of no cover before I'd find the skirt of the neighboring crops. And I'll only be able to run as fast as my water-starved muscles will go.

If it is the Blue Coats, I'm dead. I run faster.

The car is taking the curve around the tree too quickly. The tires bark as they fall off the shoulder. I pick up speed, clear the grass, leap onto the rocked drive. I fumble my way through the porch door, run to the next, the one leading to the kitchen . . . the car is on the drive. I burst in. Rocks are pinging against the car's undercarriage. It's halfway to the house.

"Where are . . ." *The matches.*

The car slides past the window just above the sink. If I leave right now, *right now,* I can make it out the front door and head the other way.

God help me. I see the the matchbox on the counter. Fly across the room, tuck it into the hollow of my hand.

A car door closes.

I race back through the kitchen entrance and push open the rusting porch door. That goddamned squeaky hinge. *It's too late.* Whoever's come is already out of his car and would have heard me. Before I can clear the porch, someone steps around the corner. I bolt off the concrete slab and run toward the crops. Behind me, the person is yelling. It is a man's voice, repeating my name over and over.

In the faded light, the stalks resemble people. I thrust myself into the crowd of them, pushing aside their sharp limbs as I stumble forward. With no light to guide me, I misjudge the placement of each row and crash into one bristling bunch of ears after another. They tear my pants, my shirt, my skin. Pull out chunks of my hair as I pass.

I've gone a good way before I hear the man behind me. The sound of him running quickly down the trail I've created interrupts my focus. I turn my head just in time to catch him coming up at me through the crops. His fists wrap themselves in my clothes and I'm pulled toward him, then slammed to the ground. He places either knee on my thighs and either hand on my wrists, then leans down into the shadowed trough and speaks to my turned cheek.

"Harper . . ." It's the Blue Coat who pretended to rape me. John Gage.

I shake my head, trying to catch some part of his face with my upturned chin.

"Harper! Hold still!"

I continue flailing back and forth until his nose is hit hard and something warm spills onto my shoulder.

"Stop it, goddamnit!"

Gage removes one hand to attend his bleeding nose and it's all the opening I need. Up goes one knee into his groin and down goes the man onto his belly. He falls onto the space I've made warm as I begin running back toward the house.

It's easier going in this direction via the path the two of us have cleaved into the harvest. I erupt onto the farmhouse lawn and make it only two or three strides when my feet suddenly find no earth. I'm hauled up onto the man's shoulder and thrown hard to the ground. I lay blinking dumbly at the stars while working to get air back into my shocked lungs.

Still bleeding, the Blue Coat paces back and forth at my feet. "Now just *lie there* for Christ's sake!" he shouts, removing a cloth from a trouser pocket and pressing it to his nose. "My name is John Gage." He stops pacing and comes over, leans down so I can see his face. "I'm your recruiter."

No. I take in his wide eyes. The slightly too long, curling hair. The same chin, same lips. Same look. *So this is why Ezra didn't want to tell me.* It's the Blue Coat who killed Candace.

The man who shot her in the head. And the man who comforted me in the alley.

I turn away so he can't see the tears stacked up behind my lashes.

"Harper," he says quietly. "I'm safe. I'm with the resistance."

"You killed Candace! You tried to rape me!"

A pause. "I saved both of you from far worse things."

Intuitively, I know it's true. All I can think to say is, "You're a Blue Coat."

"How else did you think I'd be able to get to you?"

My heart is beating so hard in my chest, I want to throw up. "What are you here for?"

Gage repositions himself so I'll have to see him or turn my head. It's an effort not to look away. "I'm here to take you to the bunker," he answers with his eyes on mine. He's worried. About me or my abdication from the movement, I'm not sure. The concern softens him, turns him momentarily into the man I'd envisioned.

I have to sit up.

Gage puts out an assisting hand I don't take. I roll myself off the grass and stumble away. Past his State car. On through the line of tall grass that leads to my creek sanctuary. I want out of this fear that's always with me, away from this moment and the joy-filled future that can no longer be. I've romanticized my recruiter. Turned a Blue Coat into a good man. A savior. A soul mate. The idea of such ebullient self-deceit is like a kick in the gut.

I sit by the creek for a few long moments, absorbing as much of this nocturnal peace as I can. Hoot owls help me reassemble my thoughts. They call to me from the wireless trees. Fly out and swing down toward my head like bats.

Gage never comes to find me or starts his car to leave.

When I'm as full up as I can get, I wind my way back to the house. Find the Blue Coat sitting in the kitchen, *Frog and Toad* spread between his large hands.

"Where'd you get this?" he asks, voice dim.

"Upstairs."

I try not to notice, but this man's colors have begun to turn. His natural blue-green aura becomes a deep violet with small cores of amber, the colors of a bruise.

John Gage sees me watching and pushes away from the table. "Let's go."

I follow him to the car and, without protest, get in.

HAPTER

THIRTEEN

Helen Rumney has sharp knees. They peek out in turns beneath her skirt as she drives, left then right. Gas then brake. She's a two-footed driver, and on an automatic. A woman like this, with more lust for power than any human I've ever met, and she can't manage the road. Candace and I are floored.

"How are you this morning, Harper?" Helen asks. She's aware of my eyes on her legs, the one foot always hovering over the brakes. A rabbit runs across the road in front of us and down goes Rumney's pointed black boot.

"Fine, ma'am."

"Nervous?" She smiles, producing slightly long white teeth.

Next to me, Candace lets out a soft grunt. I shift on the leather seat, press into her side with a hand. *Don't.*

"No, ma'am," I say, speaking over Candace's muttered *Don't what?*

"Good," Rumney responds. "I'm confident in your capabilities." She shifts her eyes left in the rearview mirror and gives Candace her obligatory attention. "And you, Candace? You doing okay?"

Candace leans forward. Shows Manager Rumney a few of her own teeth, mostly the lower ones. "Never better."

Candace and Helen Rumney do not like each other.

Today's test will determine which of us will be the Alpha Monitor and which of us will be the Beta. To Candace and I, it doesn't matter. But to everyone in the Murdon Building, to President, and especially to his beady-eyed, potbellied Press Secretary, it will mean a great deal. In addition to handling files requiring the very highest clearance, the Alpha Monitor will act as the Chief Operating Officer of the BodySpeak program and be its liaison to the public. Who it will be after today's test, neither of us know. Our abilities are very nearly the same. I'm slightly better at reading scenes, while Candace has superior powers of prognostication. We both see auras with the same clarity and come away with the same textual analyses of these scenes. Our abilities to see residual energy seem to last for roughly the same amount of time. Which of these abilities will come into play during our testing is yet to be seen.

Next to me, Candace has her eyes locked on a pair of buzzards circling so close we can see the red skin of their hairless heads. "What happens today?" she asks.

Manager Rumney shrugs. "You'll do what you did last time, just without the pulse box. It won't be that different."

Without the pulse box? I don't understand.

A pulse box is a small black computer the size of a fist. It's programmed with a specific identity, someone we can find. It even throws off electronic pulses—the closest thing Body-Speak programmers could get to an artificial aura. Candace and I have never worked with live targets before. Something about it makes my stomach ache.

"We're not going to inject you with anything," Helen says. "If that's what you're thinking, don't. It's not an issue." It isn't what Candace or I are thinking, but Rumney's immediate turn to this denial tells me it's on the schedule. Someday we're going to get a veinful of modifier. Something that will enhance our perception or reduce our guilt.

Candace turns away from the circling birds and leans over the front seat. "So we'll be hunting real, live people now?"

Helen Rumney disapproves of the question. And of Candace. "Monitor Hillard, you know I can't answer that. And you also know better than to ask." It's a part of our Disassociation Protocol. If it doesn't begin with a *How do I*, *When do I*, *Where do I*, the question's not allowed.

We stop at a checkpoint a half mile outside the compound. Helen smiles through the driver's-side window, rolled halfway down. "Morning, Carl."

"Morning, Manager Rumney." Carl is wearing military blues with two guns strapped across his back. Behind him, there are four more just like him. He flashes a reader over Helen's slate and clears us to go through. "Have a nice day, ma'am."

We drive another mile to the hut where we train. It's hidden and huge. Extends forever alongside an artificially straight creek bordered on each side by tall oaks. All you'd see from the air are their wide arms stretching.

We nod at the guards piled ten deep behind the front doors. Then follow Manager Rumney down a corridor to a changing room, where we take off our clothes and put on the regulation testing suit. A white jumper with a high neck worn rolled up over our slates, even though, for the duration of these tests, they've been turned off.

"This way." Manager Rumney motions us toward the far end of the building, where men and women have come out of their offices to watch us pass.

Some of them wave, as if we know them. Most of them stare blankly, voiding themselves of thought. They worry we might try to break into their heads and read their secrets. See the things they're guilty of. The same things we struggle each visit not to see.

For the last few weeks, we've worked out of a small twenty-by-twenty-foot room barely large enough to hold two desks and two terminals. As of this week, we have our own place. The whole southern half of the building.

"Watch your step," Helen says. "We're running dark until after." She opens up the single door and disappears inside. Tells us to follow the white of her blouse.

We're on a long cement landing that, twenty feet in, cascades away into nothing. There's a post every foot with a chain strung between, a railing meant to keep us from falling over. The soft glaze of reflection is on every link, showing me the outline of a football field–size hole. Our platform sweeps down into it, extending out for a long way. I can tell by the echo of Helen Rumney's clicking heels. Each step takes long seconds to come back.

There are people out there. I can feel them in the dark, buzzing. Humming for me without a sound. The waves coming off of them make me dizzy. They know exactly what we're here to do. Some of them are terrified.

Jesus Christ. I turn to Candace, who's already turned to me.

Can you feel them? she's asking me with her green eyes.

I nod just barely. Helen Rumney's watching.

"Murphy!" she shouts to a woman standing near the rail. "Start the clock now! We need to get this prepped better for next time, people. They've already begun!"

The blackness is interrupted by dozens of staff members scrambling to attention. These people are here to take notes, control the atmosphere, God knows what else. I can see them moving in the dark as waves of dull pink, beneath which are suddenly wide blue lights dimmed by black shielding hoods. These covers are meant to harness the luminescence of their electronic notepads. Keep it off those others meant to serve as our subjects.

Before we can ask questions, Candace and I are ushered into place on a makeshift podium of uneven boards that have been secured on the prow of the landing. We face outward, toward the hollow space. It gives the feeling of being about to step off a cliff.

"Ladies, what we're doing today is *not* remote viewing. Today, we're working on a more proximal stage. Before you is a bunker thirty yards wide by seventy deep. And directly in front of you is a schematic. Murphy, light it up."

I see Rumney's assistant move and a piece of floating

plastic blooms into view. It separates into two pieces, each traveling on invisible cords toward us. Mine stops a foot in front of where I stand. It's been angled like the top of an old-fashioned school desk and shows the room before us in miniature. More than two hundred boxes have been drawn in luminescent blue ink. Someone steps forward and puts a stylus of the same color in my hand. When brought close to this map, the working end catches light.

Helen Rumney clears her throat, drawing our attention back to her. "Before you are two hundred and eight spaces and, in them, one hundred and ninety-eight targets. Some have volunteered. Some have been drafted, thus the Blue Coats you noticed coming in. We'll be keeping the lights off and you'll be wearing earphones to prevent any attempts at echo-location." Rumney pauses as a black drape is lowered between Candace and me. She continues with her pale face dipping in and out of view. "You have ten minutes to put a mark over each square of space you determine as occupied. If it's a woman, we'd like you to use an O. If it's a man, an X. If you have trouble finding the spaces, you can ask your assistants for a correct location and they'll direct you. But you are to make your own marks and to never speak about them out loud."

Helen moves closer until her nose is almost touching the black drape. "If you pick up any colors of interest to the Confederation, anything that may represent a potential terrorist within this group, you are to forgo the use of an O or an X and put down a number. The number one represents a minimal threat and ten represents a certain and aggressive threat. Your time begins now."

I startle as headphones are clamped over my ears. I thought there'd be time for questions, of which I have many. Time to meet my assistant, a woman already here to my left. She's featureless in the dark, an outline wearing an oversize watch that ticks down the seconds. The assistant moves nearer, scoops away my hair, and adjusts the headphones so they're tight against my skin, and taps a short-nailed finger against the time. *Ten minutes*. I'm flashed so many fingers to confirm. She steps toward my shining map and her uniform comes into view. She's a Blue Coat. *Shit*. I focus on Candace and her beautiful blue-purple aura already beginning to grow. On how pleasant the air-conditioning feels on my skin, the perfect temperature of the room. Anything to help me put away this woman's profession and the distaste that will color my results.

Tap, tap, tap, my assistant prods. *Hurry it up.*

Candace is thinking what I'm thinking. I can feel it through the drape. *Helen Rumney's crazy if she thinks we can be timed.* Time isn't a part of the process when we're out of our bodies, looking for whomever they've prescribed. But how to explain? There are no words for what we do.

I breathe in and breathe out. Soften the muscles of my eyes so no one thing is in my sights. It's pitch-black out where the people are standing. There is no ambient light to differentiate them from one another. The first thing we have to do is stop trying to see. To stop placing the matrix of expectation over ovals of black wanting to be faces or figures. Even under bright lights, we never get it right anyway. We see in two dimensions and use conjecture to bridge the gap. The biggest part of letting go is remembering this. That most of what we consume as truth skips sight and sound and goes right to becoming what we just know.

I breathe in and out until my palms grow hot. *There is no building. No cement landing. No us and no them.* We are an atomic family, these people and I. Things circling things circling things. I ignore an itch on the back of my shoulder. The pull of the headphones on a few strands of hair. Next to me, my assistant glares hard at her watch. Her impatience is distracting.

Each ball of light begins small. Not anything bigger than the glow of a cigarette. Each inhalation makes them brighter. Their breaths or mine, I don't know, an insignificance. How suddenly these sparks become observable clouds of energy always surprises me.

The room is glowing. Blinking like a Christmas tree. Blobs of color are everywhere, of nearly every hue. Dull red fear and deep red anger. Mustard-yellow self-concern. Dull blue arrogance. Light pink guilt. The prolific mold-brown of confusion. There is a woman in the front row drawing my attention. She wears a veil of black. Throws up contrails of smoky puce as she fidgets in her space. She's afraid of what we'll see. And she should be. We can both read her like a Confederation manual.

This woman is a Manager, maybe of Blue Coats. The things she's done are marked on her body like open sores. They leak patches of burgundy into the roiling black storm that surrounds her, mapping the unthinkable things she's done. She's killed people. *Kills* people, present tense. So often, it's become a chore. The ubiquity of it bores her, so she tortures them first. And she'll keep doing this forever until she's locked up. Candace and I have been empowered to stop her. All we need to do is write down the number ten on her square and she'll be put away. It would be easy. Good for the people she works with, best for her future victims. But it would also be bad and for far more people. Really, for everyone. The program would receive too many funds, too many green recruits anxious for too much power. It would be straight to the gallows for anyone standing at the end of a pointed finger. So the question becomes, *Should we?*

Tap, tap, tap. Five minutes left. Next to me, the assistant flares.

I step toward the floating map and begin with the back row.

I don't fill in all the spaces correctly. Helen Rumney doesn't need to know the depth of my abilities, or how far into a person's mind I could reach if so inclined. I don't write down a ten where the Manager stands, either.

Our time ends and the lights are turned up. Candace and I

are allowed to sit down on the edge of the landing with our feet dangling into the abyss while we wait for our answers to be tallied. We're exhausted. Drink glasses of juice and nibble on protein bars. Rumney has learned the hard way to let us recuperate. Used to be she'd put us in her fancy car, anxious to get to the office, and one of our weak stomachs would ruin her fine cloth upholstery on the way back.

With the lights brought up, we can see the people lined up in the sunken room. Some of them are putting on a show for us. Looking bored when they should be scared. Calm when they should be nervous. Like the guilty woman in the front row. She is a well-practiced stone. No one will come to get her because I've kept her little secret. Better to have her on the streets than the government any further into our heads.

Helen Rumney marches over. "Excellent results," she says. "Candace. You're our Alpha." Copies of our answers are dropped onto the floor. My chart has a couple dozen markings. Red circles placed around the squares I've thrown. Candace's answers are nearly identical, save for one—the awful woman from the front row. Instead of an O, she's put down a ten to show them a terrorist. *A ten*, meaning absolute threat.

Candace! I try to look in her face, but Helen Rumney steps between us.

"This effort has proven very helpful to our argument, ladies. I can guarantee that within the year, you two will be the heads of a brand-new department! You have no idea what BodySpeak means for Tracking and Data! We'll be bringing in bad guys without the drag of judicial input. Monitoring as we know it will become obsolete. No more post-event, after-the-crime processes of justice. It will become a new, proactive approach to handling terrorism. That's how we're going to roll out the campaign. What do you think?" She kneels down and picks up Candace's chart and I'm able to see my friend's face. She's calm. Almost happy.

She knew what she was doing. But why?

Helen Rumney shows the chart to both our assistants, then

motions to the guilty woman standing just below. "Row one, space two. Take her into custody, please."

The woman shrieks and flails all the way out of the room, glaring up at us whenever she can. She's indignant, stunned to have been caught. Next to me, Candace has her eyes glued to the piece of paper in Rumney's hands. She won't look at me, our new Alpha Monitor.

Two weeks have passed since the test and the conference led by Manager Strauss. Candace and I are barely speaking. We are busy. We are avoiding each other. It's both, in equal parts.

I feel as if I don't know her anymore. Worry I might have been best friends for all these years with an illusion and not the real Candace Hillard. The thought makes me leave the women's gym when she comes in to run. Keeps me falsely preoccupied with files all day long.

"Harper." Candace has stopped at the door to my cubicle. She speaks while rifling through her mail. "I'm going out of town for a while . . ."

I push away from my monitor. Pull off my headphones. "Where?"

Candace shrugs, her eyes glued to a pink notice from Quality Assurance, nothing she cares about. "It's one of Rumney's projects. I'm sending Hannah to stay with Mrs. Cutchins for a while. Could you water my ficus while I'm gone?" An ugly plant that's been molting brown leaves onto her floor ever since she got it.

"Sure."

"And would you stop by sometimes to check on Hannah? You know how Mrs. Cutchins can be."

I look at Candace's face but her eyes are still averted. It's a strange request. Emily Cutchins, Hannah's housekeeping assistant, is as organized a woman as I've ever met. "Sure."

"Thanks."

Candace goes to her office and grabs her purse. She begins

to walk down the aisle leading to the elevators without anything further.

I jump out of my seat and follow her halfway down. "Candace!"

She stops but doesn't turn around. "Yeah?"

I cross the final few feet between us and put a hand on her shoulder. "Are you okay?"

She reaches up and puts her hand on mine. "I'm great." But it's a lie. She's radiating worry and pain. Is virtually blinking with it.

"Hey." I try to turn her around, but the hand on mine squeezes and then lets go. And off she runs to catch the elevator.

Once there, Candace never turns around. Not even when I shout an *I love you* and the silver doors close.

I go back to my cubicle and immediately call Mrs. Cutchins, who tells me in a very strange tone that everything is fine. I'm not to worry. I can come over to see Hannah in a week, maybe two. In the meantime, she's thinking of going to the ocean for a while. She'll be pulling Hannah out of school. I'm not to bother coming over until she calls. They won't be home. They'll be gone. She has to go. They're packing.

A couple of days later, I go to the break room for a cup of coffee and find it filled with Monitors. They look back at me with pale faces. Knit themselves into a barrier through which I won't be able to see whatever it is they're watching.

"What's going on?" I ask.

No one answers.

In the silence, I hear a man's voice coming from the television. "We've always suspected a dormant strain might have survived. Now we know."

Another, deeper voice follows. "Dr. Priory, how might this illness progress? Do we have a trajectory on the symptoms and, well, how they may play out?"

I strain to hear the doctor's answer over the Monitors, who are shooing me away. "Well, yes and no. When we have the mother here, we'll be able to do more testing on her and then, well, we'll see . . ."

"For God's sake, Becky!" a Monitor named Ann shouts at the woman nearest the set. "Turn it off!"

Becky looks over as I thread myself toward her. "Harper, you're not going to want to see this . . ."

"Don't you turn off that television!" I clear the crowd just in time to find an image of Hannah up on the screen.

Becky puts plump fingers over her face. "Oh, Harper!"

Oh, God. There is my vivacious goddaughter, now a scared, skinny girl lying in a hospital bed, eyes big, tubes running into both arms.

A doctor with bad skin and thick glasses stands next to her, his face trained on the near camera. In a cool voice he says, "This young lady has contracted a resurgent strain of the Pandemic. Look there, on her arms." He points and stands back so the camera can zoom in on an array of crusting red sores. They're as large as bottle caps, maybe a few dozen on either arm. The doctor adds from offscreen, "She's also got them on her torso and upper thighs."

"Harper." It's a whisper in my ear. Someone has taken my arm. They lead me away from the screen to a chair someone else has pulled out. "Sit."

"Look at her eyes," the doctor clucks. "Such immediate loss of fatty tissue . . ."

I'm pushed into the seat as the doctor is replaced by a Manager with black eyes and white hair. He tells us that masks will be distributed and symptoms will be posted on the Confederation website. Adds while walking to the mouth of the hallway, "We're attempting to contact Alpha Monitor Hillard, who's been sent on a highly classified mission." He motions for the camera to pan back toward Hannah as he finishes his comments. "Candace, we hope you're able to see this." The camera closes in on my goddaughter's face. Finds a tear starting at the outer corner of one eye and follows it down to the splotched and scabbing skin of her neck. "Time to come home, Alpha Monitor. Time to come be with your daughter."

The man finishes by saying that anyone other than Candace shouldn't bother going to the hospital. No one else is being permitted entrance for obvious quarantine reasons.

All around me, it's pandemonium.

The early morning traffic is light, as it has been for the last few days. People are staying in where possible. Most of those on the streets are wearing the protective blue masks. I catch them watching me at stoplights. Peeking at me through the windows of their cars. Perhaps it's that I'm godmother to the dying girl and best friend of the absent Alpha mother. Or maybe they're surprised to see me without a mask, breathing the polluted air. It's not bravado, or stupidity. I simply know there is no threat of infection. How I know, I can't explain.

I park my car in the underground garage and walk the few blocks to the Murdon Building. When I make it to National House Square, I notice there are no people waiting outside the prostitutes' quarters and many queued up at the prayer tents.

"Morning, Monitor Adams." Security Guard Jones smiles as I pass through the gate.

"Good morning."

He picks up my satchel and purse from the conveyor belt and slides them over each of my arms, taking his time to adjust them on my shoulders. Head lowered, lips close to my ear, he asks, "Heard anything from Monitor Hillard?"

I shake my head no and he nods, lips rolling back into a frown.

At my office, I put down my things and turn to find my desk covered with dozens of new folders. I pick up the top one and stare at the two words stamped on its front: *Urgent* and *Confidential*. Slowly, I turn it over, holding my breath. Praying not to see what is indeed stamped there in bright red ink. *Security Class Alpha*.

I put a hand over my mouth. *Jesus, no.*

Something has happened. Last night, sometime after I left, someone left these Alpha class files in a long, sliding pile on top of all my others. I close my eyes. *Have they already killed her? Without any formal notice, have I already become the Alpha?*

Quickly, hands shaking, I gather up a few of the beige folders to take down to Mr. Weigland. I go to push out of my seat and am grabbed by the arm. Before I can see who it is, the files are knocked to the floor and I'm pulled through my cubicle door. Candace is marching us down the rear aisle, her stride long and fast. She doesn't look over as we pass Mr. Weigland's office, but I see him there. His head turns quickly, conveniently, away.

As soon as we're through the door to the women's restroom, Candace pushes me against the marble counter and begins turning on all the hot water taps. I watch her as she works. Her hair is loose and kinked. Not styled as she usually has it, every curl pristine and in its place. Her long nails have been cut and her hands look chafed. She's not wearing a suit. Isn't even wearing her own clothes. I can tell by the way they fit. Her dark blue trousers are too short, ending at the top of black lace-up boots. The straw-colored jacket is a man's, and beneath it there's a beige cotton shirt stretched tight across her chest.

"Sssshhhh." She holds a finger to her lips and points at the fogging mirror. As I watch my reflection thicken and fade, she backs up toward the door and sets a foot along its base.

Letters are forming, condensing on the mirror. Cursive writing that's hard to make out because I've rarely seen it like that, full of loops and connected. With the oil of her skin, Candace has written something inside the obscuring steam.

There is a resistance. There is such a thing as The Book of Noah. *Inside it are all the answers to all our questions, how we'll win back our lives. It's worth fighting for. Even at this cost . . .*

I look immediately back at Candace, who nods. *Yes.* She was recruited by this resistance. *Yes.* She tried to run.

"Hello!" A woman is banging against the closed door.

There's more writing but no time to read it. The door moves toward us an inch, then recedes. Candace repositions her foot and spreads her arms against the threshold for leverage.

"Just a minute," I say, turning off the hot water and turning on the cold.

I dip some paper towels into the basin and begin wiping at the mirror.

"Hello! *Hello!* Let me in, please!"

"Spilled some water . . . just a minute." I throw away the towel. Use my forearm against the mirror, like a blade.

"Hey!" One heavy push and Candace is knocked sideways.

I quickly ease down from the sink's marble shelf and turn just in time to see the woman come in. It's a Monitor from the south wing. A rustling, broad woman who wears thick glasses that are currently hanging by a string around her neck. She stops when she sees Candace. Her expression of annoyance turns into one of pity. With a nod and a quick turn of her head, the woman trudges down the line of toilets, taking the one at the very far end. She doesn't see the smudged mirror.

Quickly, Candace and I finish wiping away the words. I've barely tossed the last of the paper towels into the trash when, again, the door's pushed inward, this time producing a dark cloud of men. Most of them surround Candace, trapping her inside the tight circle of their bodies. The rest make themselves into a fence neither I nor the heavy Monitor can breach.

"Alpha Sentient Monitor Candace Hillard!" One of the men begins calling her numbers. There are so many, they run together. "501. 505. 637, 688, 881 . . ." All the worst ones are there. Rape and torture. Numbers reserved for people needing to be made an example of.

I can't see Candace through the blue-clad bodies between us, but I can feel her. The fear and rage that had marked her for all the weeks surrounding BodySpeak is gone. What's left is peace, the fragrant deep purple of forgiveness and finality. Clouds of it are rising off of her. They collect above her like waves of heat and impale her captors with soft, potent tendrils. Some of them are changed by it. Confused, they step away, leaving an opening through which I see a part of her face. Her green-brown eyes. Half a smile. She's ready to go.

At first, I think Candace is being escorted by gunpoint to the bank of elevators. I expect the Blue Coats to take her out of the building and down to the Geddard Building, where the torture will begin. But when the silver elevator doors open, a new group of policemen appear—three of them short and one tall, even taller than Candace. The shorter men are folded into the waiting group as the tall one takes the lead. He walks directly toward Mr. Weigland, who's been trying to penetrate the wall erected around Candace with no success. The tall Blue Coat takes Mr. Weigland by the arm and heads the whole bunch of them down the hall toward the large conference room. I watch from the middle of my group, captive or onlooker, I'm not yet sure.

Candace flashes me a backward glance and my composure is lost.

"No!" I'm screaming. "Stop! Stop this!" I know where they're going, what they're about to do, and cup my hands around my mouth to scream. "Candace! Candace! Candace!"

Just before turning into the meeting conference room, the one we visit Mondays and Wednesdays to go through the latest Red Listed words, she turns around.

"My baby paid for this!" she shouts. Candace has stopped moving of her own accord and is now being dragged along the other way. "Make it worth it!" She's producing tears that run in perfect lines down both cheeks. "Make it worth it! Make it worth what happened to my baby!"

A Blue Coat begins toward me. He asks, "What was that supposed to mean?" That thing Candace just said. *Does it make sense to me? Is there something he should know?*

All I can see of this man are his colors. He's obscured by a cloud of brick-red lust and dark brown self-loathing. I'm stunned when an arm comes through this fog and grabs me by the arm. Like the lens of a camera adjusting, the Blue Coat comes into view. He's short, with scratches scarred into his cheeks and neck. One of his earlobes has been bitten off. These are the signatures of his victims. Wounds he probably considers trophies. It produces in me a rage I'm able to use as cover for my lies.

"I don't know what she was talking about!" *You asshole!* "And I don't have anything else to tell you, so fuck off!"

The man is confused by my seeming lack of fear. He lets go of my arm and steps back. Pulls out a cigarette for our wait.

The other Blue Coats are going through the women's restroom. I hear a summation of their efforts as they pour back out. The only thing found was a spill mopped up with a basketful of wet towels. No sign of messages. No remnants or codes. No utensils that would've been used in their production.

I'm taken to Mr. Weigland's office, where another group of Blue Coats are waiting to question me. Then I'm pushed into a chair and made to regurgitate into a recording device answers that mean nothing. Lies I know damned well will set off alarms upon even the most casual review. But what are my options? Anyone with any sense will see right through me. It's absurd to think that the thing to kill me may very well be my ineffectual ability to lie.

The sound of a gun firing startles us, even the Blue Coats who've been shouting over one another to make sure they each get in their questions.

Someone shot Candace. I can't believe it. From the deflated looks on the other Blue Coats' faces, neither can they.

"No." I stand up and nobody stops me.

I step toward the hallway and am pushed back by the tall Blue Coat coming through the door. He's disheveled. His brown eyes full of what he's just done.

This is the Blue Coat who just killed my best friend.

This man is all business. He pushes me roughly back into my seat and goes directly to Mr. Weigland. Without asking, the Blue Coat frees the handkerchief my Manager keeps neatly tucked in his vest pocket and uses it to wipe off some blood caught on the ridge of his hand. Candace's blood.

"No." It's such a simple recalcitrance, I don't recognize it as being me. "No," I repeat so low, no one even hears.

Mr. Weigland can't meet the man in the eye. He takes back his ruined handkerchief and folds it perfectly between his hands. Tucks it back into the lapel of his suit.

Is this what we've become? I am lost. This is, finally, beyond what I can comprehend. We now stand for formality over the murder of our loved ones. *Is that who we are? Is that who I am?* This can no longer be the place I live, the place I work, the place I raise my child. *Where am I to go. Where am I to go. Where am I to take Veracity.*

"Harper," someone is saying.

I ignore them. *Candace is dead. Killed by a Blue Coat. Worn in Mr. Weigland's right front pocket.*

Sharper, spoken in a concerned whisper, "Harper."

Mr. Weigland has come over to look directly in my eyes. In his I see panic. In his voice, I hear stern command. "Harper! Sit down! Now!"

I'm out of my seat, though I don't remember standing.

"Sit down, Harper. Now." Mr. Weigland is acting all business but there are large red veins starting in his eyes. *Play along now.* He's putting on a good show but, like me, is ruined inside.

The tall Blue Coat concurs. "Sit her down, boys," he says, and I'm shoved into my seat.

Mr. Weigland puts both hands on my shoulders and gives me a pointed look. *Stay calm. Stay put. Don't do anything rash.*

The tall Blue Coat goes straight to the terminal that's been gathering my answers and inserts a flash drive into a port. After my answers have been dumped onto the fingernail-size chip, he couples the disk to a palm-size machine both he and Mr. Weigland can read. They huddle themselves into a corner, watching and listening as the other men gather around me. I try to catch glimpses of the red waveforms shining from the tall man's hand, but the other Blue Coats fill in the holes between us. I can't see a thing.

Mr. Weigland whispers something into the tall Blue Coat's ear, and that quickly, it's over. The group of men leave. I've been deemed innocent.

I watch them go out the door, then get up and follow them all the way to the elevators, daring them with my proximity and large, questioning eyes. Down buttons are pressed and the tall Blue Coat waits for the elevators with his head bowed over rounded shoulders. Just as the silver doors open, he peeks covertly over a shoulder and looks at me as the other men flow around him. I can't process the nature of his stare. It appears as if he might change his mind. Come back and gather me up. Drag me along with them.

The next day, channel 4 declares a reprieve from panic. The Pandemic has not returned and the threat is over. The blue masks disappear. Lines at the prostitutes' tents reappear.

I go to the hospital, sure they'll finally let me in to visit Hannah, but am too late. I'm told by a pale nurse with wandering eyes that my goddaughter has passed away. Her body is already in transit to some research facility in the south. I can't see her. I should stop shouting.

But I don't stop. I scream the simplest questions until I'm hoisted away. *How? When? Why?* Monosyllabic, ultimately answerable questions. But the pale-skinned nurse and the three Blue Coats who bear me away from her station can't answer a one.

HAPTER

FOURTEEN

With me hidden on the floorboards of his passenger seat, John Gage drives to the far edge of Bond. To the southern expanse where the square brick homes give up their geometry to the flat terrain of the wastelands. We don't speak on the way. When we're to our destination, Gage stops his car and reaches over to unbuckle my seat belt.

"Ezra has to take you in."

The belt slips off my lap and is sucked back into the car. I watch it go, wincing as the metal head slaps against the passenger window.

"Take those to Lilly," Gage says, motioning to the books I found at the farm currently spread over my lap.

"I will."

We sit for a couple dozen breaths, night sounds piping through the open door. Ezra's car is just ahead and facing this way. I can see her inside, inhaling smoke and blowing it out the open window.

"I'll give them to Lilly," I say again, and for no reason. Then get out of the car and watch John Gage drive off without a good-bye.

Ezra comes over to collect me, her cigarette a small moon hovering over the dark road. "Ready?" She doesn't wait for an answer and walks back to her car. "Let's go meet Lazarus."

"Who's Lazarus?" I ask, hurrying to take my seat. Ezra's already behind the wheel.

She takes off before I can close my door. "The head of the resistance."

We aren't a half mile down the road when Ezra turns and frowns at my head wobbling against the rest. She bangs the end of a finger against the glass-covered fields. "We'll be driving back this direction someday. Better get your bearings now."

The "someday" bothers me. I look through my window but there's nothing to see. This is, by the Confederation's definition, a wasteland. A rural area devoid of mountains, water, canyons, anything to stop the eye. Anywhere a person can't hide, making it the worst possible place for us to be.

"Why out here?" I ask. The flat earth goes on for miles. "It's not safe. They could have planes looking for us."

"Have you ever seen a plane? I mean, outside the National Museum." Ezra laughs at the suggestion.

I don't answer. The only usable plane I've ever even heard of is President's, though its whereabouts are so secret, some people suggest it, too, might have been lost in the Pandemic.

"There's no cover."

"There's cover out here, Adams." Ezra takes a hit off a new cigarette. "Have you ever heard the term 'hiding in plain sight'?"

"No."

Ezra sighs. "There's cover."

None I can see. "How are we going to move? When it's time to fight, how will we mobilize?"

"You don't need to worry about it."

I look at the trees a hundred feet back. Maybe the wires strung between their trunks and through their arms have been turned off, like those at the farm. "Is that tree line safe?"

"This is Skinner's stomping grounds. He's got every god-damned one of them wired. I told you, moving out isn't what you need to be worried about," she says.

She's wrong. Right now, these roads aren't censored. But soon enough the satellites will be brought online and anything larger than a bison will be stopped. Any vehicle carrying unslated people blown up. Unless we move quickly, we'll be stuck out here.

Ezra looks at her face in the rearview mirror as the car pitches over dirt hills and mud valleys. "So, now you know about John," she says, plucking at her bangs.

We hit a deep hole and I have to steady myself on the roof. "All I know is that he recruited me. That's not much."

Ezra swings her muddy eyes over to where I'm trying to look calm. They're done in browns tonight with coffee-colored shadow on the lower lids and topaz across the brow. "I'm giving you three free answers about Gage just to stop this bullshit from going down into the bunker with us. And you'd better hurry it up. Only one more mile before we get there."

"He says he's one of ours . . ."

"Yes. He's one of ours. Next?"

I didn't mean it as a question but let it go. "How long has Gage been with the resistance?"

"Sixteen years. Now hurry it up, Adams." Ezra turns the wheel sharply and we careen onto a muddy drive. "We're almost home."

"John Gage killed Candace. Why?"

Ezra parks the car in a clearing hidden from the road by a line of trees. She leans forward and rests her chin on the wheel. "*Your recruiter* put a bullet in Candace's head before a line could form between her legs. He saved her from a fate far worse than a bullet. It is what it is." She glances in my direction. "We can't afford your naïveté, you understand? Not all Blue Coats are what you've experienced."

Ezra goes to open the door and I put a hand on her arm.

"Do you have any idea what I've seen Blue Coats do? To little girls, I'm talking. To *babies*!"

Ezra pushes away my hand. "Gage is an important member of the resistance *and* your recruiter. And he saved Candace, whether you like it or not. Now I have three questions for you. How many people died on your watch up top? And do you really think a Blue Coat is any less a part of President's justice system than a Monitor? Guess I didn't need three questions to say fuck you, Adams. You're no better than anyone else here, including John Gage."

Ezra swings one leg over the threshold of the car and I see where her beige tights have been torn. It draws my attention to her other clothes. To a sleeve where a seam has been loosened. A trace of blood smeared against her skirt and just a dab more on the inside of a thigh. It's cranberry colored. Fresh.

Someone's been rough with her. I should hate her. There are so many reasons. But I find myself angry on her behalf.

"What are you looking at?" Ezra asks, voice sharp.

"You tore your outfit."

Outfit. She makes a face. "Let's go."

This is why she's always late. Rough johns. The Blue Coat named Jingo. Men who control her time and abuse her body.

I hurry and follow. "Are you all right?"

"I'll tell you what. You just worry about you," Ezra says, her back turned. She's walking toward a hole between the trees and a house hidden behind. "Now just follow me and don't say anything stupid. Got it?"

We're flanked by a line of thin, poorly kept firs. Most are dead halfway up, their top branches gone or turned brown. Their remaining pipe cleaner arms are strung with cigarette butts and bits of yellow paper that were once official notices of some kind. When the house beyond them comes into view, my heart sinks. It's a misshapen box. A beige square with missing strips of siding and boards over almost every window. Suddenly, I don't want to walk the path to this front door, knock on it, and meet the people who live here. Who live like this.

"There are procedures. You do what I tell you." Ezra takes the books from my arms and arranges them so *The Grapes of Wrath* is on top. "You need a minute?"

I almost laugh. To what? Take in the natural beauty? The dead trees and rotting house? Or maybe she's asking me to pick up the yard. "No."

"Okay, then. Watch where you're walking. We have a dog."

There's an enormous clump of tan, cracked feces just a few strides away. I step around it and find myself in a sea of discarded bottles, wrappers, and bits of partially eaten food. It's disgusting, the way these people have ruined such a generous patch of land. Having lived my entire life in the city, I've never seen such filth. Whatever else the government may be, they are efficient landlords. These people have managed to make nature unattractive.

"Buck!" Ezra shouts as she walks, craning her head from side to side. "Buck! Come here, boy!" Buck fails to appear and we make it to the front door without an introduction.

Ezra rings the bell and we wait a whole minute before a shadow fills the space behind the peephole. It's enough time to notice the door's wounds. Dents and holes, some round and small that go straight through. Others, scratches with mold growing in their centers.

"Yeah?" It's an older woman. Her voice is thin and grating. A reed in high wind.

"Hello, Lilly." Ezra slides the books into one arm. "Let us in, please."

The door opens and there stands a woman in her sixties. She's short with a slightly rounded spine. Her hair is dark gray and curly, hanging just below the line of her jaw. Barrettes hold the fray away from a face obscured by a pair of enormous glasses. Her eyes, magnified by the lenses, have turned a milky cornflower blue.

"My sight's going," she says, reaching out to feel the muscle of my arm. "Not too shabby. A little too tall. Talking to you will wear out my neck." She turns and smiles at Ezra. "How you doing, honey?"

"Fine, Lilly. Let's go on down."

The woman nods. "They're all waiting."

I try not to stare, but with her thin lips pulled upward into a smile, the transformation is remarkable. The cheeks drooping over Lilly's jaw become wide and high. The blue eyes bright. Certainly, this woman was beautiful before the hardness of her hidden life. In the right light, she still is.

Ezra takes me by the elbow and leads me farther into the house. The stench is awful, worse than outside. Flies are everywhere, collected on half-eaten, spoiled bits of food. Reproducing themselves in the foam of the decaying couch. Cans that contained soda or beer litter the floor, their contents spilled on the unfinished wood. Rude or not, I have to pinch my nose.

"I don't think she likes it here." Lilly nods at me. Shakes her head.

Ezra nudges me forward with an elbow, puts up a hand to cover her nose, too. "Introduce yourself."

"Harper Adams, ma'am."

"Lilly Bartlett. How do you like my house?" Lilly waves at the ceiling that appears to be caving in. "It's been in my family for generations."

I go to step away from the reeking sofa and my foot sticks to the floor. "I don't have a very good eye, ma'am."

"Uh-huh. Well, she's honest, anyway. That's good." Lilly waves a hand in front of her face. "Christ, I can't stand it up here anymore. Let's go meet the family."

I follow Lilly and Ezra to the rear of the house. To the kitchen with its empty, open cupboards and all the dishes in the sink. Lilly grabs a small basket already full of small paperback books and Ezra dumps mine in without ceremony. All save one.

"This is for you." She hands Lilly the book on top.

Lilly's eyes grow pink. *The Grapes of Wrath.* She puts the volume up to her lips and whispers quietly, "One of my favorites."

In the kitchen's dimmed light, the older woman's face spreads and contracts, threatening to break into tears. It is a large thing to her, this book. I'd like to open its covers and read until I understand the impact that can be brought on by a collection of words. But out of respect, I give Lilly her space and look away.

"I'm going on down." Ezra disappears into the adjacent pantry.

Lilly slides the book tenderly into the crook of an arm. "You're not going to introduce her?"

"I have to talk to Lazarus." Ezra's bodiless voice floats up from somewhere beneath us. "Bring her down yourself."

"Yes, yes." Lilly rolls her eyes and motions me away from a table covered by bottles of noxious-smelling liquids. "Watch yourself. Don't knock anything over. Most of these are for show but some of them will set you on fire."

"What are they?" I step away.

"Molotov cocktails." She sees the blank look on my face and explains, "Liquid explosives. Jingo almost drank one last week. Wouldn't that have been something?" She laughs, turning to the dark of the closet.

"Jingo? Skinner?" I follow her in.

"Ummm-hummm." Lilly is moving her free arm around in the dark. Looking for something. "What'd you do to Ezra?"

"I'm sorry?"

"What'd you do to Ezra?"

"Nothing. You say you know Jingo?"

Lilly squints up at the ceiling. "Of course, but you're not listening, Harper. You have to learn to *listen*! You have a tendency to get caught up in your own thoughts and don't listen to what the people around you are saying. For a Monitor of your stature, of your *abilities*, it's a bit of a dichotomy, don't you think? Maybe you'll discover you don't like Ezra for exactly the same reason she doesn't like you. Whatever it is, you two need to resolve it soon. Before you go into a war together."

It's strange to be so intimately known by someone you've just met. It occurs to me that she's probably been watching me for years.

Lilly pulls on an overhead string and dim light spreads through the cramped space. "You ever had cashew butter and pickle on a bagel? I could make you one before we go down. It's past dinnertime. And the best stuff's up here, never mind the stench."

Lilly's going a hundred miles an hour. I can't catch up. "No, ma'am."

"Don't call me ma'am. It's Lilly. You sure? The salt of the cashew and the sour of the pickle . . ." She rubs her belly. "Umm-ummm."

"No, thank you, Lilly."

She shrugs. Puts her hand deep into a hole on the closet's right side and fumbles with something at its end. A loud *paawwpp* noise escapes and the back panel moves slightly forward, exposing the pretend wall for the door it happens to be.

"Now, you have to give the password whenever the portal keep gets around to asking for it." Lilly leans in to add, "You have to make sure no Blue Coats tailed you. If you suspect something, you stay at least thirty minutes upstairs, just in case . . ." *Thirty minutes.* Considering the smell, I don't know if I could. "Then you have to press the button there in that hole, wait to be asked, and call out the password. If you're right, they release the safety and the door pops all the way open. Right now, it's only open an inch or two. Just enough to alert the underground somebody's trying to get in."

"And if you use the wrong password?"

"Then you'd best be moving on." Lilly smiles up into the overhead light and I can see where decay has taken all her back teeth. "We shoot mustard gas through a pipe in the ceiling." She looks back down at my face. "Good things to know, just in case."

Mustard gas. I have no idea what that is. But I like the idea of passwords. They mean I'll be coming and going. Needing to be let in because I've needed to be let out.

"What do you do if you're followed?"

"Well, then we call Jingo. But that wouldn't work for you, of course. He knows who you are."

"Jingo?" I don't understand.

"You know about all that," Lilly says as if I actually do. "We tell Jingo another Blue Coat's harassing us and he gets them off the property. Are you telling me Ezra hasn't told you anything about Jingo?"

I shake my head. "Nothing."

Lilly presses her lips together and clucks disapprovingly. "Ezra is keeping Jingo in line, if you follow." She leans in to whisper, "It's the most selfless act, you have no idea." *Ezra* and *selfless* are two concepts I've not considered putting in the same sentence. It's an effort to control my expression. "Jingo is in love with Ezra. He thinks I'm her mother. He takes care of me. It's that simple."

"So he knows she's broken her slate?"

Lilly shoots me a speculative look. "Good Lord, yes. Lots of prostitutes go AWOL, Harper. It's the oldest relationship in the book, hookers and politicians. And of course, these days, anybody working for the Confederation, anybody with any *power*, is a politician. Oh, don't give me that look. You know what I mean. The girls provide them a certain service in exchange for protection."

"I've never heard about this." And as a Monitor, there's nothing I haven't heard.

"Come on, darling. They're not going to send you those data files. Don't be so naïve."

"It's just . . ." *I thought I knew what went on.*

Lilly laughs as if I've said something extremely funny. "Oh, I forget how pleasant it can be to talk to you freshly broken people. You always think you know everything! It's delightful!"

Embarrassed, I clear my throat. "So Ezra is Jingo's *girl*."

Lilly's laughter subsides. She nods. "If he ever got wind of what's happening right here beneath him, we'd have to have

Ezra relocated. And you, for that matter." She puts a hand on my face. "You don't have any idea how important you are, do you?"

I shake my head. "No." The wastelands had me worried about our worth. About mine. I smile and Lilly joins me.

"In the beginning was what? Come on, now, they've made sure you know your Confederation Bible. Tell me what it says in the Book of John, chapter one, verse one."

"'In the beginning was the Word.'"

"'And the Word was with God, and the Word was God.' It's with the revocation of the word that we lost our country. And, by God, it's with the word we're going to get it back!" She pats my arm. "We're the linguists! The language people, the cultural intercessors! This is the Holy Grail of critical thinking right here beneath your feet! We're the ones who'll be able to explain the nature of this country's imprisonment to its prisoners! Seeing as a good number of the people we're fighting to free will be fighting us, it's a pretty important post, don't you think?"

I blink. "Yes."

"Do you know what number we are on the government's most-wanted list? Two! Right here in Bond sits the number two most-wanted group, after the Streator crew. And that's just because they're a bunch of techno-geeks that have already hacked into the system."

"Two," I repeat. I had no idea.

We're that important, and unbeknownst to Jingo Skinner. Amazing.

"Lilly, what is it we're going to do? I mean, what is it we're going to be?" I ask quickly. Before we get buzzed down to wherever.

Lilly's smile shines in the dim light. She's been waiting for this question. "We're going to form a new government. One with elections and checks and balances. Those who represent us will be of us, see? We're going to yank out those goddamned plutocrats, theocrats, and autocrats and reestablish a democracy where the government is only so large to serve the needs of the least of our people and only so personal to allow for freedoms as outlined by the Constitution. I'm talking about the old Constitution, now. The one with a Bill of Rights!"

We're going to be the next government. And I'm going to be a part of it. The news distracts me. I lose some of what Lilly's saying.

"Oh, and Jingo shot Ezra's dog." Lilly shakes her head, whispering, "Don't tell Ezra. She loved that dog no matter what she likes to say."

There's a piping of static overhead. Ezra's voice is filtered through the noise. "Protocol, please."

"Sojourner," Lilly says. "Now open the door!"

Sojourner. It's a word I've never heard before. It sounds like a spice. Something one sprinkles over soup.

Lilly steps down and I follow thoughtlessly. Like a child, without a backward glance. Just below me is the shiny edge of a step that falls off into an abyss. I hadn't anticipated the absolute blackness. The portal door closes behind me and even the step's white edge disappears. My foot dangles over eternity. I could make one false move and be dead on a concrete floor. The thought prompts another—I could survive these stairs and be down here indefinitely. I forgot to look back, savor the small bits of sunlight coming through the kitchen blinds. And now it's gone, until.

Down goes one foot, finds a board, then comes the other. It's pitch-black. Like stepping into a hole. I could close my eyes and it would make no difference.

"Watch your step, now." Lilly's taking the stairs fast. She knows each and every one of them. "There's a turn to the left down here. Follow the handrail."

I put out my hand, swallow loudly. *Thank you, Jesus.* There's the cold metal bar she promised.

Lilly hears. "You okay?"

"Fine," I lie. Step onto a new surface, this one concrete. We're down thirty feet, maybe forty.

The stairs end in a cavernous dark. It collects my breaths and echoes them back to me, providing no hint at its depth of field. Lilly has moved on ahead so I wait. I can sense people out there I can't see. They're watching me and seeing me. Hearing me in my breathy panic. It's like standing on a stage, the audience beyond a black maw. I wait for someone to collect me and set me on mark. To introduce me. Attach a microphone to my shirt. Point me toward the camera's red light.

"Ladies!" A black form is coming toward me. By the look of the stride, it's a man. Without meaning to, I back up, thinking he's going to run me down. But he moves deftly past. Heads for a panel of television monitors behind me, stacked beneath the stairs. "Did we secure the front door?"

Lilly answers from somewhere out in the blackness, "Yes, Noam."

"You know why I'm asking?" He turns around and I see his features in the blue light of the screens. He's around Lilly's age, in his sixties, has a long nose and no hair to speak of, although on him, the two qualities are attractive. He's my height, five feet eight inches, and is built like a bull with rounded shoulders that pull at the seams of his sleeves.

His eyes catch me in the act of staring at his arms. I can't imagine how he's stayed so fit while living underground. "Who are you, again?" he asks.

"Harper Adams!" Lilly answers, suddenly next to me. She takes me by the hand and pulls me over to where the man stands. "She's our Monitor! Don't you recognize her?"

"Sorry." He smiles apologetically and turns back to Lilly. "Did we get the door shut?"

"Yes, Noam! *I* got the door shut!"

He talks to Lilly while thrusting a large palm my way. "You know why I'm asking. We can't have another incident like last week with Jingo just wandering in." He turns back to me and smiles over our shaking hands. "Nice to meet you . . ."

"Harper!" Lilly supplies.

"Harper! Yes! Nice to meet you, *Harper.*" He gives me a smile and I accept his firm shake.

"Nice to meet you, sir."

"Noam Feingold." He reaches out and wraps a hand around my bicep, measuring, grunting. "You've been training?" he questions.

I grow red, thankful for the dark. "Yes."

Noam crosses his arms in the physical act of study. Taps a finger thoughtfully against his lips. "No recent illness? You've had your shots?"

Before I can respond, Lilly answers as if she'd been with me at all my appointments, "She's up to date on her immunizations but does tend to get run down easily. She had appendicitis last year. Gets sinus infections and flu bugs." I must make a noise, some small protest. Lilly looks over and pats me on the shoulder. "It's okay, dear. We're not going to kick you out for being puny." She turns back to Noam. "Now, I've already talked to Patsy. She'll have a full panel done when we've been seated in Wernthal, but Harper will have to be shipped to Marietta." She says this as if I were a parcel.

"To the CDC?" Noam seems mollified, like myself. "Jesus, Lilly! She doesn't have the plague!"

"The Centers for Disease Control is the only modernized facility we'll have functional for at least six months!" Lilly replies. "I'll need her for at least two full days of testing so you'd better make sure the council knows!"

"Testing?" I interrupt their back-and-forth.

Lilly nods. "Allergy testing, a full thyroid panel, the basic heart regime, not that I anticipate anything. I'm sorry you couldn't have had this done earlier, darling. You were watched too closely. Tests like these would have seemed suspect. You're too important to go without a checkup."

You're too important to go without a checkup. What Lilly means by this is, *You're too important to go and die on us.* It makes me smile. I like this woman immediately, with her light blue veil of honesty and even the sporadic sparks of impatient orange. She's absolutely without guile. Someone I can trust.

"What about her headaches?" Noam asks.

My headaches? I've only been to the physician once for headaches that are really migraines. I vomit. Lose portions of my vision.

"I'm quite sure they're hormonal. She's tremendously irregular." Lilly nods.

How do they know about that?

Lilly puts a hand up to my face. Strokes my cheek. "I believe you're polycystic, dear. It's why you don't ovulate regularly. It's too bad I couldn't have gotten you that little bit of information from here. Those bastard doctors out there now . . ." She leaves off. Shakes her head. "We'd have had you pregnant again in no time." I realize with a shock that she's talking about the few years after Devon and I had Veracity when a second conception eluded us.

"Were you a doctor, Lilly?"

She blinks at my question. "I'm an anthropological linguist! But down here, it's not like it is up there. We're too few in number to be pigeonholed in one field of study. Underground, we all wear multiple hats. I can deliver babies, hotwire a car, and teach you the English language. It's different for each collective. It depends on what textbooks and other training materials we find. We keep all of them."

"We have a sort of interlibrary loan system." Noam smiles like a proud father. "We digitize our books. Send them out on flash drives. The whole resistance participates."

The whole resistance. I wonder about the number, how many separates constitute a whole. Turn to Lilly and ask instead, "How many babies have you delivered down here?"

She smiles. "Twenty-four. But we don't have the facilities we need. Seventeen survived. Twenty of the mothers." The smile fades for a moment. But then Lilly sets her eyes across the room, on a woman standing with a young man, and it returns. "Ben and Mary Dean. She's our first pregnancy in seven years." I can see a moderate bulge beneath the woman's high-worn skirt. She's five or six months along. And in love with her husband, who's in love with her. Every time they touch, the air between them ignites.

"What do they do?"

Noam answers, "Mary is our seamstress, and in charge of keeping an inventory of our living supplies. Ben is a computer technician and a backup runner."

Lilly takes me by the arm and walks me toward a crowd of waiting people while she talks. "We smuggle families with children over to Springfield, where we have physicians who can provide them immunizations and better health care. You should see it there! It's ten times as big as this bunker and just full of kids. Wonderful! They're like little generators of hope."

Noam turns me toward the crowd. "Sorry to interrupt, but we have a few people waiting to meet you."

Forty or fifty sets of eyes stare back at me from the near and far ends of the long space. Men and women, young and old, with every color skin and every color hair. All are watching me intently. Not one of them has said a word since I've been here. And with a room this size, anything, a whisper, would have echoed.

This basement world must run eighty feet long and be the width of the house and surrounding fields above it. The floor tells the tale of its progression: the portion closest to the pantry is poured concrete, the next a composite of paving stones and brick, the next tamped down earth. Zigzag posts have been erected to support the low ceiling that runs forever. If I were to wake here in the middle of the night, I'd think they were apparitions. Women and men set on posts, stooped in the act of holding up this underground world.

Lilly prods me with a finger. "Introduce yourself."

I swallow. "Hello. I'm Harper. Adams."

Lilly leans in to whisper. "Not everyone's been following your recruitment, dear. Tell them a little something about yourself."

I straighten up. Start again. "I've been a Monitor for over two decades. I'm divorced. I have a daughter, Veracity. She'd be eleven years old now. She's the reason I'm here."

The audience is watching me intently. Soaking in my every word. They're staring at my clothes. My dirty hair. Some of them slide forward to touch my hands. Some thank me for making this choice.

"Protocol requires us to give you a formal introduction, but there are forty-seven of us," Noam says. "And within the next few weeks, there will be hundreds. Try to remember first names and areas of expertise only."

Lilly interrupts. "There's more to it than that!"

"She's not going to remember more than that!"

"She should at least know field numbers!"

Noam acquiesces. "Okay," he says, turning to me. "Let me give you an example. I'm Noam Feingold. I was a college professor of American history in the town you know as Roslyn. History, by the way, is the word that means a record of important events . . . of all the things that have come before. America is what this part of the world used to be called . . ."

America?

". . . and those of us living in America were referred to as Americans."

Americans. I cringe. Another name taken away.

"Now," Noam continues. "I'm married to Lilly Bartlett here and have been slate-free for sixty-two years." He pulls down the collar of his shirt and shows me his bare neck as proof. "I hid out here in Bond after the Pandemic and happened to meet Lazarus. He brought me down here. Saved me, really."

I can't take my eyes off Noam's sixty-two-year-old skin, marbled by time and youthful sun, but without a slate or even a scar. Beautiful.

"You forgot the field number," Lilly says.

Noam rolls his eyes. "I'm ranked seventy-second on the field list. I'm going to be a senior judge on the Checks and Balances Board."

Most of this means nothing to me. I ask the question I hope will be easiest. "What's a field number?"

It might have been the easiest question but, from their faces, I see it's not the easiest answer.

"The field list ranks our most important people into the hundreds of thousands," Noam says. "The closer you are to number one, the more guards you get when it's time to take the field."

Lilly slips her hand into her husband's. "Everyone on this list will have a role in the new government. We'll be serving in it, creating it, teaching our new world about it. Your number on the field list directly correlates to how integral your role will be to the new government's success."

It's a scary thing to consider. I wonder what number I've been assigned and Lilly can tell.

"You'll have plenty of guards." She smiles, uncoupling herself from her husband. "I'm Lilly Bartlett. I was a linguist at a university in Joad and am married to Noam Feingold. I broke my slate thirty years ago and rank sixty-eighth on the field list. I am to serve on the Board of Expression and the First Amendment Council and will focus on reconstituting language. I'll be working closely with you, Harper."

"Adams!" Ezra yells from somewhere farther back. I turn to find her patting the empty seat of an aluminum chair that's been dragged out into the middle of the space. Behind it, walls just high enough to provide the barest privacy create separate rooms. They remind me of the cubicles that fill the Murdon Building and aren't much bigger. In place of doors, dowel rods have been stretched across the openings and sheets of canvas hang to the floor. They're tiny spaces in which to live and work. About a fiftieth the size of my home.

I take a seat on the aluminum chair and face my audience.

"Name, rank, position. That's all," Ezra whispers, giving me the same advice as did Noam, then disappears.

The people queue up in a single line, become a vein that runs all the way to the stairs and halfway back again. Most of their skin, regardless of color, is ashy and pale. Lilly tells me that despite supplements, they're all suffering from vitamin deficiencies. It explains the purple bands beneath their eyes. The sallow skin.

Those at the head of the line are older. The younger set has fallen back to give their elders first go. I listen to their ranks, from number two to the hundreds, and note the tasks they're to perform in the new world. Chief Counsel of the Health Advisory Board. Chief Architect of something called the Internet. Lead Researcher on the Semantics and Symbiotics Council. Principal Advisor to the Board of Economic Recovery. *Chief, Principal, Lead, Head.* Titles that come up with rhythmic regularity. All suggesting important roles I've never heard of.

Their pre-Pandemic jobs are varied. I don't bother to commit them to memory. Lilly tells me it's been like living inside a university. That some of the smartest people in the world are standing in line waiting to meet me. And I'm the only one sitting. I'm glad Ezra isn't here to watch them shake my hand and shuffle by. It's a strange relief when the younger set begins their introductions and the field numbers climb well into the thousands.

This community is split almost evenly between those who do and those who don't have slates. Some necks reflect the dim light like sand, some like water. Some were brought here to hide years ago when the Confederation began killing nonconformists. Others were late additions, having been slated against their will and having chosen to run. Each person is a revelation. The things they've given up astounding. I'm overwhelmed and without the proper words. Need to know what this is I'm sensing in these people, need the words so I can tell them what I admire before they walk away.

"Lilly, what makes them do this? What's the word?"

Lilly looks at me. "What do you mean? What makes who do what?"

"What makes people give up what's easy for what's right?" There's no word in the Confederation of the Willing that fits.

"Courage," Lilly says, her face turned toward the crowd. The word has to wind its way around her turned body to reach me. "It's called *courage*."

I use this descriptor for every person thereafter. Each time, my eyes water, my voice breaks. It's insufficient. Like using the word *bright* to mean *the sun*.

After so long, Lilly cuts in. "Let's stop for a while. You need to use the restroom?"

I nod.

I'm escorted to the farthest corner of the bunker, to a room made up of three walls and a canvas door. The toilet is a hole in the ground with a place marked for one's feet.

"You know where to find us when you're done." Lilly motions me in, then leaves.

I put my hands against one wall and bend over until my upper body is horizontal. I want the tears to fall straight off my face so they don't leave a trail.

These people have lived too much of their lives in a squalid basement masked by the stench of filth. I stand there, bent, leaking onto the soil for only a few moments. I won't keep these people waiting. They've been waiting long enough.

When I come back to the main room, the line has dwindled to ten or fifteen people. Gangly twenty-year-olds standing idly, scratching their elbows and hands. Softly, they give me their name, rank, jobs—past and future, their palms that feel like they've been crafted out of sandpaper.

"It's the work," Lilly whispers, holding up the line with her explanation. She says these kids with no parents, no concept of freedom, no memories to buoy them up, get the worst duties. Tearing down trees with their bare hands. Tending gardens hidden between rows of tall thistle.

"We give them the words, too, and that helps some. Most times, you need to be able to say a thing to feel it," Lilly concludes with a frown. Then, just as quickly, she smiles. "You should see the zucchini we got this year! And the tomatoes! Oh, they were delicious! If we can get in some cheese at the same time, we make pizza!" Lilly is a sprite in her sixty-year-old body. She morphs from rage to joy like a child, exuberant over zucchini and pizza. Maybe I'll feel the same soon enough, when I've been deprived of color and taste, textures that suggest a sunny somewhere else.

"Why do the younger ones get the hard chores?" I don't understand.

Lilly rolls her eyes. *Such an obvious answer.* "Because they want to stay mad! They want to remember their mother committing suicide on the dinner table. Their sisters and brothers taken away. They sweat and bleed to keep those old wounds good and open. And they need the sun more than the rest of us." She leans in to add, "Of course, there are some kids we can't let go up top. Flight risks." She holds out her hand and motions to the next person in line.

It's a young woman with long brown hair that shields dark, recessed eyes. She's been watching us talk from beneath her bangs. Has a vertical furrow at the top of her nose and a pink slash in place of a mouth. She's showing me some of the things that have happened to her. In her features, in her fisted hands and thrust-out neck. Maybe she's been raped or lost her parents. Maybe she came home to them, like so many. I give her a look of too much softness and she hardens. *Fuck your pity.* She's a girl when she's not fighting, a woman when she is. It's the schizophrenic nature of young adulthood in the Confederation. Be water, be stone.

She sticks out her hand, ready to cut mine with her rubbled skin. "Rita Ramirez." She shakes my soft palm hard.

"Harper Adams. Nice to meet you."

Rita steps forward. "What do you want to hear?"

I look at Lilly, who offers me no help. "Whatever you want to tell me."

In short, quick sentences, Rita gives me the basics. Her field number is 12,062. She'll be a guard when we mobilize. Will stand at the front of our line, carry a weapon. Stop bullets if she has to. She's had training and experience. Knows where to point. How to shoot. She's seventeen with a mother who died before she could form sticking memories and a father who drank too much. She fell in love at the oh so tender age of eleven. With a boy who knew how to break slates and help girls run away. He taught her to hunt, to track, to live off the land until he grew tired of her. Then he beat her and left her out in the woods. She was found by one of our runners and brought back to the bunker. The council hadn't wanted to let a left-for-dead girl stay, but Lazarus argued her case and won.

Rita doesn't seem all that pleased with her rescue. She's mottled with resentment, her skin splotched with little patches of blushing blood. She'd leave here if she could. I catch it in her eyes. She'd go back to living off the land if given the chance. As long as it meant dying there, too. *Some people come down thinking it will be one way when it's another,* my first letter had read. But Rita hadn't been recruited. She never got the fine print. Or the choice.

Rita doesn't say good-bye. Just stops talking and marches away. She's not that much older than Veracity. I wonder if my girl's coming up like that somewhere, bruised and hard. A seed pod instead of a daisy.

"That one's angry but harmless," Lilly says. "It's the ones who don't show their anger we have the most trouble with. Too quiet usually means something's brewing underneath."

I continue my introductions. Most people seem happy to have me down here. Some seem almost reverent. I attribute this to my newness. I've brought down a memory of the soil and the air. And fresh hope. They try to wipe it, like silt, off my skin. I see it in the way they rub their palms together as they walk away. In how they listen for some bit of profundity in the things I say, stopping all speech if I so much as open my mouth. They're hungry for fresh things to hear, so I find myself insinuating color into my responses. Using too many adjectives or adverbs. Bigger ones than required in small attempts to paint them moments of a life that isn't theirs. Such misplaced faith might wither some if they knew how afraid I am of small, skyless places. How afraid I am of failing them.

I'm finishing my last introduction when a voice that sounds like gravel comes from the back of the room. "Excuse me, please." It's a man's voice, doubled. As if his vocal chords have been split and are working separately. "Yes, thank you, Nancy. We'll have to discuss that later. Hello, James. How's Celia?" The words come out with two distinct tones, one rich and deep, the other strained. It sounds like two people speaking at once. This is a slate injury. I've heard it a couple times before.

The man puts cupped hands to his mouth and shouts over the crowd. "Lilly!"

I can see his full face now, towering above the people who're collecting around him. They remind me of the moths that flock to electric lights put out in summer and spring. Eager to be in his presence, they close in tight. Flutter their arms to get his attention.

"Lilly!"

Lilly has been waiting impatiently through my last introduction, picking at a callus that's developed on her heel. She stands and puts her hands up to her mouth to shout, "What, Lazarus?"

"You clear the training room?" I can see his eyes moving, assessing the number of bodies between us. The number of people he'll have to talk to between there and here.

Lilly turns to Noam, who's leaning against the wall too nonchalantly. "What's he talking about?"

Noam looks down at the floor, then pleadingly up at her. "Just one more time?"

Lilly now understands this request. She turns back to Lazarus and shouts with a finger pointed at me. "I'm not doing it!"

"There's no more time!" Lazarus's twin voices bark, then

buckle. He grimaces, just slightly. Most people wouldn't notice but to a Monitor, it's obvious. It hurts him to talk. And yet he yells.

"Yes! There's no more time! That's exactly why I'm not doing it!" Lilly has read his lips. She points her bent finger to three men who've lined up in front of Lazarus on his slow way to me. "Edward! Daniel! Nabile! Leave him alone! You have time scheduled tomorrow night!"

The men shuffle away and the place goes silent. Like Moses through the Red Sea, Lazarus passes through the parted crowd. He walks like he talks, with great difficulty. Hands go out, assist him over a broken piece of concrete. When he loses his footing they reach out to catch him. And he does so often. These people love his every contorted joint, his softball knees, his long hands with marbles in the bending parts. It's as if he carries their collective pain. I imagine, were it more accessible, anyone here would gladly suffer his daily agony and my throat closes. Fills with emotions I haven't yet defined.

Lazarus smiles as he draws near and, immediately, I feel warm. He's seen my life, has been watching my every move, and embraces me without judgment. I feel loved, and by such a man as this. A man who makes the air bow before him. *Can I help you walk? Maybe if I take one arm, position myself beneath your weight* . . . I can see why people want to help him. He helps every one of us back.

Lazarus extends a malformed hand. "Hello, Harper. Lazarus Cobb." I take it, squeeze gently. Down here he hasn't had adequate care. In this moist hell with no sun.

"Hello," I say. "So nice to meet you."

Lazarus smiles, allows me to shake his hand long past the collapse of social grace. "You're exactly as I'd imagined."

I drop my hand. Gaze down at my feet. In addition to being a man of some presence, Lazarus is still handsome. I find myself flustered. "Harper Adams," I say again. Everyone laughs. Lazarus smiles.

He must be seventy years old. His skin is pale brown and

freckled across the nose and upper cheeks. He has a mustache and beard. Has gray and white hair tufted around his head. His eyes are dark and sharp. They watch everything I do and betray nothing, not his thoughts, not the tremendous pain the rest of his body is much quicker to impart. For my sake, he is pleasantly comfortable. Infinitely kind.

Lazarus turns to Lilly and puts a hand on her shoulder. "I've requisitioned the guest room for her training." He looks over at Noam, who blushes.

"I never got around to telling her."

"I'm not doing it!" Lilly shouts. "I have to digitize the entire library, Lazarus! The entire thing! And I've got what? A month until the war?"

A month. Christ, help me. I feel myself falling. Put out a hand.

Noam catches it. Gives it a squeeze. "Sorry we're so unorganized. It's the war." He hasn't noticed the sweat on my forehead. I nod. Wipe it quickly away.

Lilly is pacing back and forth. "We should have been making copies years ago! Why can't we just do it the way they're doing it on the West Coast? Their retention rates are acceptable! They're able to train *hundreds* of people with that electronic course!"

"Because we're the government. The source from which all information will flow. We know what happens when the source is polluted." Lazarus leans closer to Lilly, whispers, "People will find a way to give up everything for another car in the driveway and a little less thinking to tax their minds. The code must be kept, Lilly."

She shakes her head. "I can't cram thirty years' worth of data into someone's brain in a month, and that's assuming she'll actually stay! It's a waste of time that I don't have! Not now! Not with those goddamned programs ready to go live any moment!"

Lazarus nods. "I understand. But it's necessary."

"You don't understand!" Lilly pushes her huge frames

farther back on her nose. Sniffling, she launches into a long explanation about the difficulties of teaching language, not to mention all the topics that come thereafter. So much work for so little return. The majority of recruits bolt, can't handle the barren quarters, the lack of light, personal items, personal space, bad food, bad plumbing, the constant threat of being discovered. More.

Noam turns me away from his wife's cracking voice and her litany of reasons to leave. Quietly, he gives me something else to listen to. "Core training usually takes twelve weeks. It includes about a dozen topics: critical thinking skills first, then politics, history, technology, linguistics, psychology, art. You don't know half of those words yet so that's the first thing we'll cover. Language, so you can keep up." Noam continues but I can't concentrate. Lilly's drawing my attention with her plaintive voice.

"There's no time! I'm not doing it!"

"There's time, Lilly. We don't even know when our crew in Wernthal will be ready."

"They'd better be ready!" Shaking, Lilly points at the stairs leading to the house above us. To the sky beyond. "It's the end of summer, Lazarus! You can't put us through another year down here!"

I take Noam's hand. "What happens in Wernthal?"

Noam turns me around. Away from the other two. "We have to get into the Geddard Building. That's where the redactors are stored. The network is daisy-chained in such a way we don't know which one is the master. Thousands of slaves are linked to that one. We take out the master and the others follow. But which one . . . ?" He smiles lightly. Shrugs. *No big deal.*

But I know how big a deal it is. Noam's talking about the Geddard Building. The one three city blocks long constantly venting hot air. They have yet to find a way in. Then the bigger job of finding the right redactor and turning it off, all before getting caught.

They don't know how to take down the slates. To a Monitor, the need is obvious. This is how we win the war. If the slates aren't turned off, there's no chance. No way to teach others to follow us. I think of my dream. In it, Veracity believes we've successfully taken down the slates. She'll try to speak a Red Listed word sometime after we go to battle and that show of faith will kill her. All because we don't know which big black processor to turn off first.

Behind us, Lazarus is trying to put his arms around Lilly. "You're right. I misspoke," he says.

I turn and catch her shouldering him away. "Any more than four weeks and it will turn cold! We could get another blizzard and then we won't be able to move! And what about that goddamned SKEYE program? If we don't move out before the satellite goes live, we'll be trapped here!"

With a quick glance over at me, Lazarus interrupts. "I'll do the training." He sees me, pale and sweating. Misunderstands my fear. "We'll get you trained. No worries, young lady."

"I don't know," Lilly says to no one, and everyone. She expected something else. Maybe to be pushed into my training. Or maybe she's still thinking about frozen earth. "This isn't going to work. Is it?" She looks up.

Lazarus steps closer. Answers low, so the others won't so easily hear. "We're going to war, Lilly. Before these programs go live and with or without the slates having come down. We're going to war. Don't you worry."

Lilly thinks about this for a moment, then turns and leaves, shouting over her shoulder, "I have vaccinations to give. Then I'll be in the library." She sways under the weight of such a heavy thought. *Another year without sun or sky.*

I want to find the aluminum chair and sit down. But someone's already moved it.

"You okay?" Lazarus is looking at me. He shifts his weight and for a tortured second, his mask of calm slips. His face goes slack, eyes all but roll up in his head.

Noam strides quickly across the room and retrieves a bag

from a hook on the wall. "When was your last pill?" he asks.

"Two hours ago."

Noam rifles through the bag's contents and pulls out a large amber vial.

"Next one isn't scheduled for two more hours," Lazarus protests.

"Let's say we don't worry about that." Noam twists off the vial's top and holds out a long white tablet. "Pain is not our friend today, Lazarus. And Davies isn't going anywhere. He'll be there tomorrow and the next day and next week for our med run. And then, yes, even after we win this war, he'll *still* be there. You're covered, Lazarus. Take the pill."

Lazarus pauses, then swallows the capsule without the aid of water.

Noam turns to me. "Davies is our pharmacist. Once a month we arrange a transfer. Davies gets us the medicines we need in exchange for banned items. Books mostly. Movies. A thing you're not familiar with called music." He yanks a thumb toward the bag he's put back on its hook. "Without those medications, Lazarus is bedbound. Same's true for about a quarter of us."

I peek around at the people who are covertly looking back at me. Most of them are older than the average citizen. I don't know how they've done it, living with nothing and doing it underground. Suffering their bodies for the cause.

"We're an old collective," Noam says, following my eyes. "We have people with diabetes, emphysema, arthritis . . . worse. Davies is as important as our contacts for food, water, and intelligence. He's our ambassador to tolerable living, if you will."

The number of words I haven't understood since I've been down here could fill the bunker. There's no good time to start asking for definitions so I choose now. "What does ambassador mean?"

"Ambassador?" Noam looks surprised. "What other words haven't you understood?"

There are so many. "I know what courage means." It's meant to be funny but both men frown.

"Come on, Harper. We better get started now." Lazarus disappears into the mouth of a hallway leading toward the back. I hurry and follow.

"Rest when you can, Lazarus," Noam calls after us.

I follow Lazarus's voice past the first few rooms, through a canvas door that's been marked with a large X. "I'll rest after we've won," he calls back.

The room is nearly empty with just a round table, two high-backed chairs, and a tall stack of books in the corner. They're one atop another, a rickety ladder that leads up and up.

Lazarus begins speaking before we sit down. "Never less than the whole will be told, regardless of how it might serve or hinder our purpose. The same information will be made available to everyone at all times. Last and most important, critical thinking is mandatory. This is the code." He collapses into a chair. Sighs. "This is the part where I'm supposed to tell you about who goes up and who stays down. Not to be late for meals, to keep track of the one blanket you'll be provided. To sign out your toothpaste and your toilet paper. Why we'll be coming up out of the ground and how we're going to win the war. Not with bullets, but with something greater.

"I could tell you all these things, Harper. But I'm going to ask you for one more sacrifice. I'm going to ask that you trust me. We go to war as soon as time and nature allow. It could be a few short weeks. It could be longer. But too much talk about how to live down here puts the focus on exactly that. And I need you focused elsewhere."

He's rolling me over with those big knowing eyes. Is seeing my dilated pupils blinking an SOS.

"I know how you like control, Harper. But there is method to what might appear to you as madness. A fancy way of saying you're going to have to trust me."

It's humiliating. To walk into a group of people who know

every aspect of my life. All my mistakes and defects of character. I nod. "Okay."

Lazarus is amused by my pink cheeks. He crosses his arms and leans back in his seat. "You know what I enjoyed the most, watching you all these years?"

I shake my head no and catch sight of a crack in the ceiling. Immediately I'm wondering if chunks of it occasionally fall down and knock people in the head. If at any moment, we'll be sandwiched between it and the floor.

"You never became addicted to comfort. The niceties, the security. You never fell for their usual tricks. You were motivated by other things entirely."

I look away from the ceiling to Lazarus, who's restoring my mood with his words and the integrity of the structure with his gentle tone.

"You okay now? The claustrophobia pass?"

I nod, my cheeks pink. *Breathing in, breathing out.* "Yes."

"Think of Veracity when you get afraid. Think of what you're doing. To give your child, *any* child, a world better than the one you came into . . . there is no greater gift. You're showing her what courage is. Inspiring her to be the same. Incorruptible. A woman of honor."

I know I should nod, smile and agree. But I can't imagine this for my child. A life beyond the sun. A world made up of mud and straw.

apostasy

discriminate

ego

fossil

heresy

kindred

obstreperous

offline

veracity

her-e-sy: opinion or doctrine at variance with
the orthodox or accepted doctrine of a church
or religious system.

CHAPTER
FIFTEEN

I'm in the tenth grade. In a medium-size school that houses first through twelfth. We are a dozen to a class, if that, and have one teacher for all subjects as there aren't enough of us for them to specialize.

Our teacher, Mr. Mitchell, is young. He has a thick head of dark oily hair and a forehead full of pimples that show beneath long bangs. He's angry about his height, his hairless chin, and slight muscles. Doesn't know what to do with a class of taller, stronger teenage kids.

"Today's test will be oral," Mr. Mitchell says, and the room goes cold.

Each one of us turns inward, stampedes toward the knowledge tucked hastily in the backs of our minds. We repeat them out loud, sounding like a swarm of buzzing insects, *the answers, the answers, the answers*. Memorized last night in our beds, in the bathrooms just before class. We're fifteen years old now. Expected to perform or considerable punishments will apply.

"I'm going to give you five minutes," Mr. Mitchell says.

The girl in front of me turns around. "Help me," she whispers, a piece of hair clamped between her teeth.

Her name is Lucille. People think she's not smart but her problem isn't that. She's sentient, like me. Gets her realities confused. I both like Lucille and resent her. Somewhere along the way she became my problem; I'm supposed to protect her from people like Mr. Mitchell. From herself.

Someday, when Lucille doesn't have someone to help keep her on track, something will come out reeking of too much truth in too public a place and the Confederation will kill her for it.

I pull the strand of hair from her mouth. Whisper harshly, "Stop that!" Mr. Mitchell has a corner of the room reserved specifically for hair-eating Lucille.

She leans over the back of her chair. Whispers, "Help me, Harper!" through huge pink lips that are forever chapped. She sucks them into her mouth when nervous. Dries them out with her voracious fear.

"We studied last night," I say. "Don't worry so much."

"I can't remember any of it!" Lucille's fear is making her spit. Little droplets spray across the corner of my desk and for a moment, I hate her. *What did she expect?* Eating her hair. Walking around with bright red, cracked lips. She does this one thing right, excels at making herself a target.

Before I can say another thing, Mr. Mitchell claps his hands together. "Okay. Materials away, please! We're going to start *right now!*"

"Harper!" Lucille reaches out to me, as if I can physically save her. Scoop her up in my arms and carry her out of the school.

But Mr. Mitchell is already there, next to her desk. Shouting into her hair, "Miss Campbell!"

She startles. Turns quickly around. "Yes, sir?" She dips her head. Offers him her blushing scalp.

"Let's begin with an easy one. How many continents are there?"

Lucille shakes her head. I can feel the heat coming off of her from here. "I know the answer, Mr. Mitchell . . ."

"Then give it to me, please!"

Lucille swallows. "Seven?"

The Pandemic had taken out every other country and human on the planet. There were pictures on the national website showing a world now only partially blue and green. Most of it had turned gray. Most of the sea a chalky brown.

I don't know why the government has lied to us about the number of people killed during the Pandemic or the number of continents swimming between the two poles of the earth. I'm not even sure how I know it's a lie. I just do, in the same way I know I have two eyes, two hands, two feet. I don't care what particular bit of power they're attempting to keep. I just want Mr. Mitchell to leave Lucille alone. Her mind has never been able to keep up with her sentient abilities and one day it will kill her.

Mr. Mitchell pulls on his chin. Wheels around and points at a red-haired boy in the front row. "Russell?"

The boy shoots to his feet. "Yes, sir! Five is the right answer, Mr. Mitchell!"

"That's correct. And what do most of these continents have in common, Russell?"

"They're dead, sir. They're uninhabitable."

Mr. Mitchell smiles big and turns back to where Lucille is almost crying. "Let's end our mutual misery, Miss Campbell. You get the next question right and I'll leave you alone, how's that? I'll let you stay here and squander away my time. But if you get it wrong, it's a transfer."

A *transfer* is no such thing. It's a *removal*. From class, hope, society, family. Kids who can't learn for whatever reason are yanked out of school. They're given jobs, the basest work. Made to leave their families and disappear.

Mr. Mitchell clears his throat. "How many people were lost in the Pandemic? Round up to the nearest hundred thousand."

Something's forming over Lucille's face and upper body. As I watch, she's covered by a morass of storm clouds, gray and silver and white. They rotate around her, obscuring her arms and chest, most of her face. I can see nothing but her eyes and the sharp knob of her chin. Out of these clouds, an answer rises.

150,000,000. The numbers are somehow recumbent on the twisting heave of Lucille's colors. I watch as the first few digits proceed out of sight.

One hundred fifty million. One-half of our former population. It is a pure energetic truth that's going to get Lucille sent away. A real number, but not the answer Mr. Mitchell is looking for.

"Lucille." I say her name and she turns, blinking. The numbers floating around her drop away.

"That's enough, Miss Adams!" Mr. Mitchell shouts. He reaches out and yanks Lucille back to attention. "The answer, please!"

Lucille opens her mouth to provide the number her body has already produced, but I beat her to it.

"Ten million," I say. It's the official answer. A figure sanitized for our easy consumption. Too late, I realize I'm out of my chair. Taller than our teacher by three or four inches, I find myself looking down at the top of Mr. Mitchell's head.

"Out of my classroom, Miss Adams!" He points a finger at the hallway. Takes me hard by the elbow and leads me to the door.

I look back and see Lucille crying. But this time, it's for me. Her face breaks. Stumbles headfirst into a smile, then into something else, like joy or relief. Her colors have changed. A patch of bright blue has bloomed just over her heart. It's a good sign. Tells me I just might have taken away a little of her fear for self, having done something she might remember. Maybe she'll be better now, having seen good things from somebody. Anybody. Maybe she'll stop being so afraid.

Lucille waves the tips of her fingers. Some of the other students wave, too. I've followed that internal voice and it's the best feeling of my young life. And then my back hits a hallway locker as the hard ridges of Mr. Mitchell's fist unhinge my jaw. Pain like I've never imagined shoots through my head and into my ears and his voice becomes a high-pitched note. He's hitting me in places the other students will see. And I'm sobbing. Begging for him to stop.

Mr. Mitchell takes away my beautiful, giving feeling and makes me walk back into the room bruised and bloodied. Anything I've provided the other students is also taken away. They've learned the price for stepping up and the better choice that is compliance.

The next day, Lucille is gone.

HAPTER

SIXTEEN

Noam has built us a gym. We walk past it on our way to training. There are weights here, or things to be used as weights. Canned tomatoes, thirty-two and sixty-four ounces. Irons, the kinds used for pressing wrinkles out of clothes. Some have been strung to the ends of pulleys, some sit in duos on mats. Some of them have been conjoined to a bar, the weights at either end. Noam tells me he built this place long ago, which explains his well-muscled physique.

We turn into a small, clean room. Cool air is being piped in through a footboard grate. The walls are painted light blue. In the center of the room is one long wooden bench on which is one computer. Next to it, an empty chair. Sitting at this desk is a young woman with white-blonde hair and pale blue eyes. She gets up when I come in. Curtsies, as if I were President.

"This is Amy." Noam nods at the girl. "She'll be assisting with your training."

"My training? On BodySpeak?" I ask. I both dread and resent this.

"We call it sight training," Noam says. "To keep you well tuned, if you'll forgive the expression. What we're going to do first is get a base line on your current abilities." He looks at Amy, who writes something on her clipboard. She messes with her computer and something bright comes up on her screen. It lights up her face.

"Now, you need to relax your body . . ." Noam is reading

from a script. It's a premature gesture, as I've already closed my eyes and begun my way out.

I hold a finger to my lips and shush him gently. As soon as my eyes go soft, I can open them again. Or keep them closed. It doesn't matter. If I can make everything else fade away and get to that one plane of awareness, the colors come. The rest of it is all filtering. Who's who and what's what. There may be a day when I'll need Noam's guidance to find my way into this calm, but I hope not.

"Harper," Noam says. I look over at him. A spot of color the size of a kiwi has started just over his neck. He walks to the far corner and the color trails with him. It paints the whole end of the room a curious pale green. "What we're going to have you focus on is the following. In the back gathering room, we've asked two of our members to sit on the floor. Amy has pulled them up on our monitor so we can watch this with you. Is that okay?"

I nod yes. It doesn't matter.

"Can you identify those two people, please?"

I breathe in and out. Loosen my gaze until Noam dissolves and I move through him, too. I advance myself through the wall and into the hallway, where there are four tall dark blobs of people waiting just outside the door. They wonder how I'm doing, are abloom with anxiety. Their mud-brown worry expands down the hall toward Noam's gym, where others are working out. A woman wound in an aura of light yellow senses the long, twinkling bank of clouds as they approach. She turns around, looks to see what's there, and absorbs a bit of the brown into her color. Her beautiful butter yellow turns to a sickly orange. She sets down her weights, suddenly tired. Tells her friend she might go back to her room. Rest.

"Where are you now?" I hear Noam asking, but I'm not in a position to answer.

Sssshhhh.

I'm moving through our sleeping quarters, aware of people below me, some of them in the middle of varying intimacies.

These acts and their creators toss up streaking red arcs that tickle as I pass, fireworks of passion that startle me with their warmth.

I see the back hall long before I get there. It's shaped like a barrel, and brightly lit. The source of this light is a rectangular book sitting between two people. A hundred years and thousands of hands have left their mark on it. Fingerprints, soul prints, whatever the leftover of faith should be called, it's been painted onto this book like so many coats of iridescent lacquer. It's so full of shine, the base of the surrounding walls are thick with its cast-off whorls. Separate, self-contained units of color swept into the corners by movement. Next to this light source, the two people are dull. Sixty-watt bulbs. Forty.

One male, one female. They don't seem to understand this book's great glow. They sit upright, unaware of the white-hot glare between them that should have them bending away, their sides at an outward arc. The male energy on the right is that of a young man. Pale yellow, telling me he's kind, with a good heart and good intentions. There is a patch of dark orange over his belly, indicating a tendency toward sickness. Fevers and stomach trouble from another tendency to overdo. I like him. Would prefer to spend time with this man than with his partner. The woman sitting on the left is pulsing an all-the-time, red-hot rage. Her youth has given her reserves of heat she uses to fuel this fire. I know her name, but more than this I can't tell. She's hidden herself away behind a thick band of puce that keeps me from looking any deeper. It bothers me. People who hide usually have a reason.

I take one last look around the room, blow out my breath, and am recoiled.

Harper?

Amy is there with a cool cloth. I put it around my neck as Noam leads me to a seat. He paces back and forth while I collect myself. It takes a few moments to readopt a perception based on sight and sound. Until then, I'm not good for much. Speech is slurred, my words put together wrong.

"Okay," I say, and Noam starts his questions.

"Can you tell me who you saw?"

"A man. And a woman."

Noam beams, happy with such parochial things. Behind me, Amy squeals.

"Can you tell me anything about them?"

I put the cool cloth down on the table. It's now hot. "I think the man is . . . what do you call people who go up top for supplies?"

"A runner. Yes!" Noam nods at me through clasped hands.

"His name is Eric. I think he's sick."

"Could be, I suppose." Noam's hands fall back down to his sides. "I'll ask Lilly to give him a checkup. Anything about the woman? Do you know her name?"

This part's easy. "Rita Ramirez." The thousand-year-old teenage girl.

Noam smiles. "We didn't think you'd be able to identify people this early."

I wish he wasn't so easily impressed. Down here, it's a small pool to choose from.

"Anything you noticed in the room?"

"There was a book between them."

Noam practically leaps in the air. "This is wonderful, Harper! We weren't absolutely sure you could read inanimate things. Do you know the name of this book?"

It's simple. *"The Confederation Bible."*

Noam's smile falls slightly. Behind us, Amy's fingers have gone silent on the computer keys. She's having a hard time typing up my response to Noam's last question. *F.A.I.L.E.D.*

I nod good-bye to Amy and step into the hall. Noam follows so we can talk alone.

"You did a good job," he says.

I try to keep my voice light. "So, it wasn't the Bible."

"Stop it now," Noam whispers into my ear so the others around us won't hear. "We've got plenty of time." It's something he truly believes.

Noam is full of hope. It floats off him like a broadcast, pink and sparkling. Bumps into the waiting crowd, who's happy to accept Noam's faith. They open up for it. Turn their heads into it. Absorb his optimism like rays coming off the sun.

Lazarus is walking around the edges of his room. He waves me in. "Good morning, Harper. Sit down. Have something to eat."

On the table is a tray. And on the tray a pitcher of water, a plate piled high with biscuits, a jar of honey, and long, peppered slices of bacon. I consume the food quickly, barely bothering to chew as Lazarus completes his laps. Every time I look up he's smiling at my bulging cheeks. He enjoys watching me eat. Or rather, watching me become full.

"Try the honey." Lazarus falls into his seat.

The jar has been marked with a photograph and some strange labeling. It was made in a place called Toronto and shows a picture of a brown bear playing with a hive. Circling bees have printed the honey's name in dotted lines, *Dunbar's Best*. In the Confederation of the Willing, all labels are the same: product, date of packaging, ingredients. We have nothing like this inviting little bear I'm assuming is supposed to be Dunbar.

I turn the label toward Lazarus. "What's this?"

"Advertising." Lazarus removes the top and pours a few drops of the honey onto his halved biscuit. "Before the Confederation took over, citizens owned and operated their own businesses. Because they had to compete with one another, they created brands people could identify with. That little bear is an example of marketing. He's the face of the brand and, therefore, the face of the company."

No doubt Lazarus has just imparted nuggets of intellectual gold. But all I get is a sprinkling of recognizable words between strings of others I've never heard.

"So this picture is the brand?"

"Not entirely. A brand is a business identity that can be re-peated by something like this character. But it could also be a song, a phrase, the colors they use in their advertising, even the font used in the company's name. Repetition is the key."

"Repetition?"

"In a world where critical thinking skills are almost wholly absent, repetition effectively leapfrogs the cognitive portion of the brain. It helps something get processed as truth. We used to call it unsubstantiated buy-in. Belief without evi-dence. It only works in a society where thinking for one's self is discouraged. That's how we lost our country. And why it's stayed lost for so long."

Almost none of this registers. I pick something at random. "I'm sorry. What's evidence?"

Lazarus sits back and wraps his hands behind his head. "Where to begin." He gets up and goes to the stack of books. Pulls from its top a notepad made of actual paper and a yel-low pen with a strange-looking tip. "Here. Write down any-thing you don't understand."

I take the writing utensil in my hand. Settle it in the crook between my fingers. It's slicker than the tool I use. Slips in my sweaty grasp. It must be a pen, though the exposed end looks different. It tapers into a dark gray point.

"It's called a pencil," Lazarus says.

Those of us who aren't Managers or President or high-ranking Blue Coats use a thing called a stylus. A long piece of plastic shaped the same but with nothing at its end but a plas-tic tip. I turn the pencil upside down. Point at the soft pink helmet on its other end.

"What's this?"

"An eraser. If you need to change something, rub that over the part you want to get rid of and it disappears."

It sounds like magic. I open the notepad. Write the letter *A*, upend my instrument, erase. The letter is gone, replaced by particles of pink waste. Lazarus doesn't find this an occasion for pause. I, however, am amazed. I'm examining this miracle of current science when Lazarus's hands find mine. My palms are squeezed until I look up. He's leaning over the table. Sad for the things he has yet to tell me.

"The first thing you need to know about the Pandemic you experienced as a six-year-old girl is that it never happened."

"I'm sorry?" The pencil slips in my hand. Produces a jagged line on the paper.

"There was no Pandemic. All you saw about it, all you heard about it . . . it wasn't real. It was marketing. *Spin*. A way of scaring the public into doing whatever the government wanted. And it worked."

"Marketing?"

"Yes."

"Like the honey?"

"Yes."

I let go of the pencil. Sit back in my chair. My parents died as a result of the Pandemic, which was not a plague. That was a marketing campaign. "There wasn't a virus?"

"That's what I'm saying."

"There was no Pandemic."

"It was fabrication. All of it."

I can't believe this. The whole of my life, the death of my parents, the death of so many . . .

"I have to go." I'm out of my seat. Out through Lazarus's door and down the hall.

"Harper!" I hear him call from behind me, but can't stop my feet.

They're taking me up and down halls, into rooms, through tunnels that end in locked doors. Then I'm back where I started, standing outside Lazarus's office, my back against the mud wall. I'm sitting, legs splayed, dropping tears of fear and incredulity on the dirt floor.

I can't stay down here with this big truth. It will crush me.

My breathing is out of order. I can't figure out when to inhale and when to exhale. Lilly is here now. And Noam.

Their hands are on my shoulders. Lazarus is speaking from behind them. He's telling them to leave me be. I have to deal with this on my own. But he doesn't know that I'm not strong enough. I want to stand up and grab our leader by his lovely face and tell him that I'm not the person he thinks I am. Despite the way I've been treated up top, I'm human, and flawed. And I can't stay down here with this big, huge truth in this crowded place that feels so much like a grave . . .

"Harper!"

I look up. Lilly and Noam have been pushed back behind Lazarus.

"Harper Adams!" His voice is stern.

I wipe away the sweat now pouring down my face and flick it on the floor. It makes a dotted pattern there, like a star.

"We're not done with our lesson," he says.

"Lazarus!" Lilly scolds. "She's just found out that the one event that ruined her life was a lie!"

"Yes, and she'll have time to process that later. But right now, I need her to be aware of all relevant information. And if it makes her angry . . . perhaps all the better."

No one says anything further. I wipe my face dry on the hem of my shirt and get up. When Noam goes to help me, Lazarus stays his effort with an arm.

Again, I'm sitting across from our leader, trying to listen to what he's telling me. But his voice floats in and out like a poorly tuned channel. I'm full to the brim, yet Lazarus is trying to cram more inside my aching head.

He tells me the Pandemic began as with any great shift of power. With fear. Fear of infection and the loss of security. Fear of loss. This led to a centralization of power Lazarus refers to as a Military State in which President and his Ministers were able to use the militia to control the masses. There were many members of the armed forces who wouldn't comply. *Holdouts,* Lazarus calls them. Men and women in uniform willing to die to preserve *democracy*. These troops bombed supplies and blew up planes. Some drove rigged trucks into hangars and stores of ammunitions. President lost most airborne capabilities but still managed to take hold of the nation. When the time for rebuilding came, he and his cabinet saw no reason to resurrect an air patrol meant for monitoring. People were doing a good enough job of that themselves.

Only now, with a rebellion grown several hundred thousand strong, does President long for an aerial strike force. Thus, his development of BodySpeak and SKEYE. Satellites and Sentient Monitors to fill up the gap. Candace and I and whomever else we found during our own form of Sentient Patrol were to be President's aerial weapons.

Lazarus tells me that once the vans came down your drive, there were two choices: swear fealty to the new government and choose the slate, or die by an injection of the so-called vaccine. But by then, the Pandemic had become a series of images. Pictures of infants with their eyes bleeding. Women and men vomiting up their own entrails. So when Blue Coats came calling, there was really only one option if a person got an option at all. Those who were too old or infirm were given the amber-colored vaccine they'd been shown on television. But this serum wasn't for curing. It was for killing. For getting the less productive and the potentially troublesome out of the way.

My hands have begun to hurt. I look down and find eight half-moons cut into the flesh of my palms with my nails. "Tell me how."

"They planned it out, just like any other campaign. Members of the former government studded international news with false reports of outbreaks. They even started a few themselves in small countries in Africa and South America. Then they started pitching it here."

"Africa?"

Lazarus nods. "There are other countries out there."

I think of the Confederation website. The satellite feed showing an earth all brown and gray.

As a Sentient, I must have known this. Another truth I've spent my life ducking to make time spent in the Confederation tolerable. "How many other countries?"

"Hundreds."

I can hardly speak.

"What do you remember of the Pandemic?" Lazarus asks.

"Just a little."

I remember television and radio broadcasts. Commercials with busty, yellow-haired nurses holding syringes filled with gold liquid. Line boards telling us to go to our doctor appointments. Do as we're told.

"As I said, not everyone got a choice," Lazarus says. "Children four and under were automatically slated. The government didn't think they'd developed enough memories of the beforetime to pose a threat. If you had a specialty, if the government thought you were of value, you were given the option."

I set down the pencil. Pull my hands back into my lap.

"There was no pain," Lazarus says.

"How do you know?"

"We know what was in the injections."

I look around for a window. I need to open it wide, lean out, and inhale some fresh air.

"Harper?"

But it's all brown earth and dark sky. Everywhere I look.

"Harper!"

"Yes?" For a moment, I'd forgotten where I was.

Lazarus tries to smile but the effort fails and leaves him looking surprised. "There was nothing to be done differently. And there's a very good reason you survived. I tell you this as a friend and compatriot: guilt is something you can't afford. Not now."

I nod. He's right. "It's unimaginable."

"Yes. But only because what we can imagine is so often a

product of what we need to be true. Our past is littered with things like this."

Lazarus cites examples of neighbor turning on neighbor. He speaks of populations that have been killed en masse. Whole continents of indigenous peoples, wiped away. One and a half million. Two million. Six million. Buddhist. Muslim. Jew. Places, numbers, and rationales for hate I don't begin to understand. They are what Lazarus calls genocides. Horrors committed by humankind that have been conveniently left out of our studies.

Lazarus continues in full double-voice and immediately I'm writing out phonetic interpretations of words I've never heard and struggling to keep up. He explains the world of the beforetime. How pay cards used to be credit cards. How before credit cards, there was money—specially printed paper that could be traded for products and services and wasn't tied to a mainframe; therefore people could roam freely. Travel where they wanted. Buy what they wanted. Nobody had to know. *Paper*. I can't imagine it. Getting people to concede great worth to what was then such a ubiquitous thing. I wonder if they had to market it, put cute little bears on each bill.

Lazarus tells me of the other countries beyond our borders. He says in actuality, we represent only a small portion of the world. That the geography we were taught in school was shit and someday we'll be using Confederation maps to wipe our asses. He tells me stories about faraway lands that catch me off guard because they represent the extent to which I don't know my own world. *Australia. Asia. Mauritius. Madagascar.* Beautiful words used to represent places with other languages and other religions. Places where women can teach in church and speak during services. Places where women are leaders. Where people can choose partners of the same sex, can live as they wish. Can marry, have or adopt children as their hearts direct, and not as the government prefers.

I don't want him to stop but am utterly lost. "You used a word . . ."

Lazarus looks down at my notepad. He's been so caught up in this potent history, he hasn't seen me writing all the words I don't understand. He flips through the pages full of long, poorly written words, eyes wide. "How many have you taken down here?"

"Two hundred, maybe. What does alternative mean?"

"Two hundred?" Lazarus blows out a breath. It takes him a moment to answer, "The word alternative is a lot like the word option. It means there are other decisions that can be made regarding some issue. Alternative routes that can be taken." He looks at me with an expression of forced calm, though I can see his thoughts. They're painted in broad strokes across his face.

Lilly was right. This training can't be done in a month.

I swallow so loud it fills the room.

Lazarus pats my hand. "Okay. I can see there's no point in proceeding until you've had a chance to study." With a grunt, he's up and scratching his way across the dirt floor, through the canvas, and out into the hall. "Lilly!" he shouts. Pauses for a moment, then yells again. The drape is caught on his shoulder, providing me a look at his face and the discomfort with which he waits.

Eventually, Lilly comes down the hall and stops in front of him, hands on hips. "What, Lazarus?"

"We need to cede rights to Harper, temporarily."

Lilly looks through the open canvas door. She studies my height, my hair, the width of my shoulders, as if she's measuring me for a State bridal gown. Then retreats until all I see is a pointed finger jabbing at Lazarus's chest. "Not for at least four weeks!"

"We've spent years watching Harper. We recruited her, for God's sake . . ."

Lilly steps forward. She's forgotten I'm watching or no longer cares. "I'm the current keeper and I'm telling you even a four-week watch period is too little time!"

"We're about to go to war, Lilly. We've got to cede Harper

all rights and we've got to do it now! She needs *Reading Rights* . . ."

"You're making my point for me!"

"*Copy* Rights."

"A four-week watch period is *especially* ill-advised considering the war! She could be a spy! She could take it from us! Use it like they've used everything else about *Noah* . . ."

"*International* Rights."

"As if we're going to be needing them! She might lose it, Lazarus! You've seen how panicked she gets down here! What if she leaves it lying out somewhere? Or drops it down the toilet? It's the last copy in the nation!"

"We've scanned it. We have a digital version."

"Yes, and it's sealed by your own orders! You want her to go changing definitions? We need the original! Now listen, I'm the keeper and I say no! You want the council to turn over your own law, take it up with them! But until you do, don't come to me with this nonsense again!" Lilly marches off down the hall, Lazarus yelling after her.

"What do I do in the meantime? How am I supposed to train her?"

Lilly's voice comes back softened by distance. "You see now? I told you there wasn't time!"

Lazarus comes back into the room and sits gently down at the table. But his mind is elsewhere. Maybe on how I'm to be trained while he's strategizing a war. "I need to end today's session early. We'll work on history and tackle your language skills tomorrow. Do you have any questions before I go?"

I pause. "What am I here to do? Please, just tell me that much."

"The answers I have for you will just leave you with more questions. Why don't you just process this much for now—"

"Please," I interrupt.

Lazarus sighs. "You're here to give us hope. To help us on media watch. To oversee the deconstruction of Tracking and Data when we're in office."

"Do you know how people are looking at me?" I ask. "They're looking at me like I'm supposed to save the world. Please tell me what I'm supposed to do, Lazarus. Please."

Lazarus clasps together his large, knobbed hands. Looks thoughtfully down into the cross-hatched digits, steepled like a church. "You know the Geddard Building."

"Yes, but what's that got to do with this?"

"At any given time there are thousands of Blue Coats sitting at their desks, doing whatever it is they do when they're not out on patrol. Their real duty is to watch what's in the basement. You know what's in the basement, yes?"

"The redactors."

"Fifty thousand of them, all set up on a docking tree and slaved to one master. We turn off a slave and we take out a hundred thousand slates at odd places throughout the Confederation. If we turn off the master, we take them all down at once."

"So I'm supposed to find the master."

"Yes."

"And if I identify the wrong redactor, a slave instead of the master, an alarm goes off?"

Lazarus nods. "Yes."

"And?"

"And Blue Coats will rush in and our man will be gunned down."

"And who is our man?"

Lazarus sighs. He doesn't want to tell me what I, somehow, already know. "John Gage."

"How long do I have to find it?"

"How long do you need?"

I blink. "I'm serious. How long do I have?"

Lazarus puts a hand on my cheek. "I know you want me to give you a date. But that's not how your gift works, is it? I could tell you exactly when we plan to go to war if I, in fact, had that information, which I do not. But what good would that do, Harper? You know what we need and you know that we'd like to have it before wartime, so just . . . find it as you're able."

I'm frustrated. Even though, if I were Lazarus, it's the same answer I'd be giving me, too. "What if I can't do it, Lazarus?"

"*What if*, nothing. What you can't do is start thinking like that."

"People won't join us if their slates aren't turned off."

"They'll join us. It'll take longer, and cost more, but they'll stand with us. We don't plan on leaving the other guys an option."

Lazarus is trying to diminish the impact. *Lives* is what it will cost if I can't produce the redactor. "People will get killed trying to follow us. Just trying to *speak* like us." People like my daughter.

"Harper, stop this." Lazarus has his hands over his face, fingers drumming against his forehead. He slides them down slowly. I'm expecting worry and disappointment. Instead, he's smiling. "You're going to find the master. I'm sure of it."

"How can you be so sure?"

"The same way I know the sun's going to rise in the morning. When you know a thing, you just know it. You don't need evidence." He nods over to the door, where Lilly is waiting. "Now, Lilly's going to show you latrine duties. We each take a turn and today just happens to be yours."

HAPTER

SEVENTEEN

MAY 29, 2045. AFTERNOON.

Mr. Weigland is rushing me. Sweaty palms on my back, he pushes me without knowing, his mind elsewhere.

"You ready for this?" he asks.

I nod. "Sure." But I'm nauseated and sweating. Praying I won't lose my cool or pass out.

Every few years, it's another go. Another test to see if we're ready. If we've been able to put aside our emotions, like computers, and read a scene *properly*, without the filter of compassion. With our eyes as well as our ears, in real time, and without the crutch of playback. Last time, a Sentient Monitor named Martha was chosen to take this test program out for a drive. She came back a wreck. Took a seat at her desk and didn't move for twelve straight hours. Not to go home. Not to go to the bathroom. We never knew what happened. She was there the next day. The day after, gone.

And now it's my turn up to bat for the Monitoring team. Management and the Executive Elite want me to knock it out of the park. They'll be bringing the suspect into an interrogation room so I can watch through a mirrored window as the Blue Coats do their thing. If I perform well, we'll be doing this kind of Monitoring from now on. Really, it's a prelude to the BodySpeak program. A way to see how viable it will be to turn Sentient Monitors into investigative police.

"You doing okay?" Mr. Weigland asks from next to me. He's looking at our reflection in the closed elevator doors.

Watching the floor buttons blink as we move down. *97, 93, 89, 86 . . .*

"Fine."

We get off at the Murdon Building's basement level and trek through a tunnel that stretches for blocks beneath the city streets. We walk until the bright lights of an underground foyer come into view and, behind them, a different set of elevator doors. This is a hidden entrance to the Geddard Building. Somewhere beyond are all the redactors in the Confederation of the Willing. I can feel the heat of them from here.

Mr. Weigland nods at the Security Guard. "Good afternoon."

"Good afternoon, sir." The young man runs a mobile scanner over our necks. Opens the elevator doors and pokes in his arm. He hits the button marked 88 without looking. "Have a good day, sir."

The room to which we're directed is medium-size. Large enough to comfortably hold Mr. Weigland, myself, and the two men in black suits who crowd us toward a long table. Their hands are odd-looking. Long and thin, the knuckles too large. Their faces are white and have slipped some over the bones. They don't look human, and not just because they're the oldest men I've seen aside from President and his Ministers. It's their colors. Red-brown through their centers. Charred black around the edges. The clouds wrapped around these two men look like fallout from a bomb.

"She the Alpha?" one asks. He's frowning at my dove blue tunic with mother-of-pearl buttons. The shoes Mr. Weigland gave me for Christmas.

Candace is the Alpha but she couldn't come. There was some kind of conflict, a meeting somewhere she couldn't miss. I was there when she told Mr. Weigland. To my amazement, instead of chastising her, he'd walked across his office and taken her into his arms. I was asked to leave, *please*. To close the door on my way out. Mr. Weigland would be by in a few moments to discuss my files, or whatever I'd come to discuss. He never stopped by that afternoon three days ago, or made himself available when I stopped in to ask why I hadn't seen Candace since.

"No, sir," Mr. Weigland answers. "She's not the Alpha Sentient, but she's damned close. Damned close." He pumps a fist in the air for emphasis. Chortles nervously.

The old men huddle, speaking to each other in an indistinguishable hum. A moment later, they look up again. Nod at Mr. Weigland and disappear through the door. I've been approved for the task.

"What do I do?" I ask.

Mr. Weigland points to the opaque window behind me. "Watch."

He flips a switch and the fuzz clears. On the other side, four people appear. Three men and one woman. Already, there's blood on the floor. Hers.

"Oh, God."

In the other room, cameras are mounted to the walls. Their toggles are here, on a control panel before me. I move one until a close-up of the woman appears on a screen. She's sitting on the floor. Her head is down, showing me dark roots with the barest hint of gray starting. She's in her thirties. Around my age and a little too thin.

"Is she a known terrorist?" I ask.

"Unknown."

The woman opens her mouth and I see where a tooth has been knocked free. I pan down with the camera. See the pale edge of it in the cup of her right hand. It shines white off her dirty palm.

"What do we have on her?" I ask Mr. Weigland. He's messing with some papers and hasn't yet seen the blood or the woman.

"You're supposed to be watching," he whispers. "Not asking questions." He points at a fan on the ceiling and the round outline of a lens farther up. I'm being monitored. Recorded for later review.

It's a sickening feeling, to know that later, people will be checking this recording to validate the authenticity of my effort. Going over every single peak and line, sorting me out. Deciding what to do with me if I've thrown the test.

"Harper!" Mr. Weigland is looking at me. He jabs a thumb toward the window. Mouths, *Watch!*

"Watch with me." I wait for him to put down the page and come over. Together, we look at the assemblage on the wall's other side.

"Oh, God." Mr. Weigland hadn't anticipated the woman and her lost tooth. And, really, this much is nothing.

Mr. Weigland puts a hand to his mouth. He's made his days about the numbers and the words and not the people and events behind them because he doesn't want to acknowledge the violence. This woman in the other room is evidence of what he's chosen to ignore. It compresses him like a coil. I watch his small, knobby shoulders roll forward as he backs away, *whist, whist, whist.* He moves until his shoes hit the closed hall door and I can no longer see his red face without turning.

"Watch the screen, puh-lease." His voice is thick, breaks the one syllable into two.

I turn away from Mr. Weigland and do as I'm told.

The lead Blue Coat is on the far right side of the room. He has white hair and a full belly. Is sitting atop a desk. The other two defer to him. They keep their heads slightly bowed while asking permission to lift the woman from the floor and give her a little what for, just to make things go a little faster.

"You ready?" the older Blue Coat asks. He's looking at the wall between us. They see it as a mirror.

Mr. Weigland leans over a small cluster of holes drilled into the panel. Depresses some button or throws some hidden switch. "Yes, sir."

The old man nods at his men. They pick the woman off the floor and stretch her arms away from her body. She doesn't complain or lift her head. She stays chin on chest. Knows someone's watching and doesn't want me to see.

"Subject is thirty-eight and single," the older man says. "We started watching her ten months ago when she got flagged for too many Red List violations." He slides down from his table seat. Walks slowly to the trio on the other side of the room. "She's Maintenance, level one. A garbage collector. Not too damned bright but smart enough for them, I guess."

I turn to ask Mr. Weigland, *Them? Who's them?* But he's already scrambling. Trying to press the intercom before the old Blue Coat can say anything else. "Sir? Sir!"

"Yes, Weigland. What is it?"

"She's not cleared yet, sir!"

"Not cleared?" The man rumbles over to the mirrored window. Puts up his fat hands so I can see the hollows of his palms. "What in the hell are we doing here if she's not cleared? She's the goddamned Alpha, for Christ's sake!"

"She's the Beta, sir."

The old man chews on this for a moment, then turns and goes back to the table. "Fine, then. We think the subject is a trafficker. Running books. Just the one, if you get what I'm saying. Am I allowed to say that. *The one book?*"

Flushed, Mr. Weigland nods. I have to point him to the intercom. "Yes, sir. *The one book's* fine, sir."

He's talking about *The Book of Noah*. A week ago, the phrase was again placed on the restricted list. This time, even for me, the Beta.

The old man continues. "We pulled a kill pill out of her mouth just in time. You know what kinda pill I'm talking about, right?" They're talking about a poison pill. Terrorists call it a *kill pill*. Something to keep their people from being tortured for information.

"Yes, sir." Mr. Weigland is glowing in his discomfort.

The old Blue Coat loosens his collar. "What I'm trying to say in this goddamned moronic way is that the suspect isn't stable! We need to get on with this interrogation, with or without your uncleared Monitor, *before* this suspect gets another chance to take herself out! Are we good, Mr. Weigland? Our department's not taking any shit because you people couldn't get your Alpha to come." The old man smiles coyly up at the mirrored window.

Mr. Weigland is sweating profusely. "Yes, sir. Just proceed as you need to. I'll, uh . . . I'll write a note."

"Your girl want to start first or what?" the old man asks.

Mr. Weigland looks at me and I nod.

He answers for me, "Yes, sir."

"What do you need us to do, then? We need to move the subject or something? You want us to get her face up for you?" The old Blue Coat doesn't wait for my response and shouts at the woman, "Look into the camera or I'll have my boys do it for you!"

The Blue Coat nearest her marches over. He grabs the woman by the hair and yanks back until all her features are clear under the lights, save for her eyes, which are pressed shut.

Oh, God. I put out a hand that lands on the window. There are the same long brown lashes. The full lips, no longer chapped. It's Lucille, the girl from Mr. Mitchell's class.

"Harper?" Mr. Weigland comes over. Puts his big eyes all over me. "What is it?"

"Make them stop."

On the other side of the wall, the old man is shouting. He wants the subject's eyes open. Doesn't matter how.

"This isn't helping!" I rush past Mr. Weigland toward the intercom but don't know which button to push. "How do I talk?" I flip buttons and levers, shouting as if the old man can hear me. "Hello! Hello! Stop it! It's not helping!"

"Harper!" Mr. Weigland wraps his wrists around mine. Pulls me away while whispering in my ear, "What are you doing?"

"I know her," I whisper back. "Help me, please."

Mr. Weigland looks through the window toward the men who're pulling at the woman, extending her. He grits his teeth and reaches under the panel. "Sergeant, our Monitor would prefer the subject be left . . ." He can't think of the right word and frowns over at me. ". . . unadulterated. If you don't mind."

The Sergeant motions his men off the suspect. Immediately, she ducks her head. "Okay. You've got two minutes. What next?"

"Sergeant, sir . . . Monitor Adams is a part of BodySpeak."

The old man's look of skepticism subsides. He sighs. Scratches his head. "So she can *see* this suspect's answers? Is that right?"

"Something like that, sir."

"Something like that or exactly that?" The Sergeant pushes off the wall. Comes closer so he can frown right into one of the cameras. "We don't have time for bullshit, Manager."

Mr. Weigland looks at me. "Ask your questions, sir. My Monitor will read the woman's answers." He shrugs. *Is this right?*

I nod vigorously.

The old Blue Coat motions to the others, who come sulking back over to his side of the room. "We're to shout out our questions first, boys, and give this Monitor here a little time. We'll get to doing it our way soon enough."

The two men are eager. Their questions come out tangled, one on the tail of another.

Do you have a copy?

Fuck that. We know you have a copy! Tell us where you got it!

Is it whole?

Is there only one?

Is it being carried into the war?

They really talking about going to war, or what?

Lucille has pulled something over her head, a drape of camouflaging energy. It deflects everything. The dark and mirrored walls, the men and their red-black hate. It's a good bit of cover but I'm able to project my way through it anyway. It's as simple as touching the substance with the thought of a finger. It's aqueous. Ripples outward like the disrupted surface of water. Lucille jolts and the substance splits. *Sentient Lucille.* She recognizes me easily and for a few seconds, we're safe and away from all this death and torture. Then Sergeant starts barking and I'm sucked back into the observing space.

"Does she have the goddamned book or doesn't she?" Sergeant looks into the camera and smiles. "Does she have *The Book of Noah*?"

Mr. Weigland glares at me. *Well?*

I'm too fuzzy to speak quite yet. It's too early.

Sergeant yells, *"Goddamnit, Weigland! How long are we going to do this?"*

"Harper?" Mr. Weigland is asking gently. Behind him, Sergeant is shouting the same question through the speaker.

I'm sad to the core. Ask thickly, "Can you bring her closer to the camera, please?"

It's what Lucille wants.

Mr. Weigland steps to the speaker and relates the information. In the other room, Sergeant has the two Blue Coats deliver Lucille closer to camera one. She smiles up at me. I've done right.

"Does she have a copy of *The Book of Noah* in her possession?" the Sergeant asks.

I answer, "No."

"Has she read *The Book of Noah*?"

I nod yes. Mr. Weigland relays my answer.

"Does she know where to get a copy of *The Book of Noah*?"

Yes.

"Is she a part of the resistance?"

Lucille answers this time. "Yes."

"All right, Manager Weigland . . ." I hear Sergeant saying.

But I'm watching Lucille. A ball of electric blue has begun in her chest. It expands past her other colors, envelops them.

I put my hand on the screen where her face is barely visible beneath it. She reaches up and touches the bare metal of the camera's arm. There's a terrible beauty to what she's doing. I wish Mr. Weigland could see it. And these men.

Mr. Weigland has a hand covering the microphone. *Harper?*

In the other room, all three Blue Coats are in the far corner, conferring.

Lucille's hand is firmly on the camera's metal joist. She begins, smiling, " 'Two roads diverged in a wood, and I—I took the one less traveled by, and that has made all the difference.'" She smiles at exactly the place I'm standing, "It's called a po-e . . ."

Poem. I don't know this word, have never heard it before. But it's there, like those long-ago numbers from Mr. Mitchell's class, suddenly stamped on her energy. *P-O-E-M* has appeared over the territory of her bosom, even before she can get out the final syllable that will set fire to her slate.

The silver explodes, becomes a spark of orange-red, and back goes Lucille's head. The Red Listed word has become a surge of electricity eradicating her voice and rolling up her eyes. It shoots through the camera's metal arm and explodes the bulb, and the fuse beyond. The lights go out and all that's left in the other room are voices.

Goddamnit! Goddamnit! Goddamnit! Walker, why the fuck weren't you over there!

You told us to give her space!

Motherfucker!

Sarge, maybe we can still read her. Have that Monitor brought in . . .

Too fucking late! It's too fucking late! How's she supposed to read a corpse!

Mr. Weigland and I sit together in the dark on the floor, not moving. We listen over the open microphone to the people coming and going in the interrogation room. There is the scraping sound of Lucille's body being removed. A hose unwound. Water forced through. The high-pitched hiss of blood being washed off the concrete. Then the gurgling sound of it being sucked down the drain. Sergeant says there's no fucking way they're going to do this again. No. Fucking. Way.

The announcement of the program's termination is a small relief. Salve on a terminal wound.

"Harper. You okay?" Mr. Weigland asks.

"Sure," I answer. Look what Lucille became. So much more than me.

HAPTER
EIGHTEEN

"Get up." Ezra shoves me on the back. She's standing at the side of my cot wearing garb different from her norm. She's in all earth colors. A beige cotton T-shirt. Canvas pants cow-pattied in greens and browns. "Here." She tosses me a handful of clothes like her own. "Get dressed. Meet me in the back room. Training starts in five minutes."

I'm about to meet my trainer.

I roll out of the cot. Shuck myself like an ear of corn. "Who's training me?" I ask simply. As if I don't care.

Ezra rolls her eyes. "*I'm* your trainer, Adams. Jesus, I'd have thought you'd figured that out by now." She disappears back through the canvas door before I can close my mouth.

I sit limply on my bed. Pull on my socks. The right boot slides on without a fight. The left one needs to have the laces pulled out some, but I don't want to slip it off, go to all the goddamned hassle of working them loose again. So I jam in my foot, yanking on the heel with both hands until my fingers turn white, but it won't go. I pull it off. Slam the boot into the near wall.

"Motherfucker."

When I get to the back room, Ezra's already moved the tables and chairs out of the way. She's sitting on the floor, stretching and smoking a cigarette.

I drop the too-small boot on the floor. Sit down and try again to yank it on. "Are we allowed to smoke down here?"

"*I'm* allowed." Ezra blows a smoke ring my way. "Now listen up. We're going to run through self-defense and ground skills."

"What about weapons?" I ask, taking too much time with the laces. The way Veracity used to do when she didn't want to go anywhere.

"We don't hand out guns to every new recruit." Ezra gives me a long-suffering look. Stubs her cigarette out on a dish brought in from the kitchen. "Have you ever even *seen* a gun?"

"*Yes.*" I work in the country's capital, drive past the National House all the time. I see guns every day. Hear them as long, tall blips on dead peoples' files. "I don't want one. I was just asking."

"Good." Ezra takes her plate of ashes and sets it on a corner chair. "You know why most Blue Coats don't carry guns?"

"I don't know, Ezra. Tell me." I can't focus on this woman and her sour mood. A haze has begun to rise up from the floor, like heat coming off hot pavement. I watch it float toward the ceiling and try not to notice the walls and how they shake as Ezra talks. This is how my claustrophobia begins. The room falls apart first, then me.

Not now. Not with her.

Ezra drones on but I'm lost to her voice.

"Hey! Adams! Have you heard a thing I've said?"

I've been staring vacantly past her. Move my eyes over and nod. "Cops don't like guns because there are more of us than there are of them. Because they can fall into the wrong hands. Because they prefer to torture people. I heard you." It never ceases to amaze me, this other brain I've developed. It keeps me prescient when my first one wants to wander. "Do we have *any* guns?" I've started to sweat. Wipe my head on the hem of my shirt.

"A few. But any weapons you'll be bringing onto the field, you're already wearing. Now put your hands up."

A few people have come out to watch. They stand propped up against the walls. Sit sideways in the chairs.

Ezra moves to the center of the room. Frowns at my stance, my curled-up fingers, my thumbs sticking out over the knuckles. "Did you actually *practice*?"

One delivery from my recruiter was two sheets of dissolving paper showing sixteen basic fighting stances. It took me two hours in the women's locker room to learn just over half of them. By the end of that time, my sweating palms had disintegrated a good part of the edge.

"Yes." *Some*. I didn't have anyone to practice with.

She leans down and takes hold of one of my hamstrings. Digs in with the tip of her thumb.

"What are you doing?" I step away and she pulls me back.

"Hold still." She pokes me on the back. Tricep. Bicep. Delt. Hard. Quick. Punishing.

"Ouch!"

Ezra smiles, just barely. I see the corners of her mouth go up. "I need to know what I'm working with. Take off your shirt."

I've done my time on the wood floor of my bedroom. In my closet doing pull-ups on a bar I installed as if it was just there to hold clothes. Am happy to pull my T-shirt over my head, show off the muscle I've spent months of countless hours making. I throw out my chest. Subtly squeeze my fists to pump a little extra blood into my arms. I'm excited to see how Ezra will react.

She circles me with a frown. Unimpressed, underwhelmed, unhappy with my meager tithe. She shakes her head. "You've been doing *all* your exercises?"

"Yes."

She crosses her arms, looks more closely at my torso. "For how long?"

"Since I decided to break."

A sigh. "Christ, we have some work to do."

"I'm not that bad." I hate that I say it. Wrap my arms one over the other, covering up.

"Uh-huh." Ezra pulls her T-shirt over her head and I'm abashed.

She's all muscle. Every ounce. Abdomen, arms, chest, nothing but shadowed clefts and bundled sinew. Her shoulders are broad, distended away from her collarbone, showing their knobby ends. A line marks the division between her breasts, or where her breasts would be if she had any. Most of her wardrobe is slight of material. It's amazing such physicality doesn't show.

Before I can process it, Ezra's running toward me, her tight white body a blur against the dark walls. She knocks me off center but I don't lose my footing. As I right myself, she uses the backward momentum to spin into a perfect fighting stance. I sidestep so I won't fall. Ball up my hands and raise them in front of my face. There's not going to be a warm-up.

Ezra throws a fist that catches my forearm. The pain is immediate.

"Jesus Christ!" I jerk away, expecting she'll give me leave to nurse my injury, but she doesn't.

Ezra uses the distraction of my pain to punch me repeatedly. Three more crisp, potent jabs. Kidneys. Back. Side. *Christ*.

"Come on, Adams! Fight me!" She doesn't even sound winded.

Ezra steps forward again, drives a fist into my shoulder, twice into my ribs. *God. What if they snap?*

I twist away. Offer up my back. She lands more blows on my shoulder, a few close to my spine. One tags me on the hip, right on the bone, and the pain is like fire on an exposed nerve. I step back and gather myself. Sufficiently pissed to finally get in the game.

"Come on!" Ezra shouts, bouncing on the balls of her feet.

I mimic her position. Turn my body sideways to narrow her field of contact and lash out with my left fist. It lands solidly in the cup of her hand. She pitches it away like it was nothing.

"Come on! I don't have all fucking day!"

"I'm trying!" I shout back.

"Bullshit! Hit me!"

I throw out my right. She's fast and is long gone by the time my shoulder is jarred by the effort of finding no resistance. Her next punch lands on my side, letting me know all the ones that came before were giveaways. She turns her knuckles against my ribs and the pain of nerves being rubbed against bone drives me to my knees.

"Stop it!" I wrench away. Curl up into a ball and wait for her to start beating me on the neck and head, the only places left for her to bruise. But she doesn't.

"Get up." Ezra sounds like I've let her down. The others standing against the walls are the same. Deflated. Disappointed. Some wander away.

I expected Ezra to be pleased at having given me such a beating. But she has one hand on the back of her neck and both eyes on her feet. *Worry.* Ezra's worried. She thinks I'm not ready. Or just not strong enough. It makes me want to start over. To land a few blows and remove the wind and the worry from her person. But standing is easier than it sounds. When I go to push upright, the pain in my ribs gets sharp and I have to stay hunched.

"If you stand up quick it'll go away faster."

Hesitant, I try it her way and find Ezra is right. A flash of pain passes and is gone. She walks over and I instinctively move.

"Hold still!"

I do as I'm told and she puts the flat of her hand over my ribs. On the place she's just brutalized.

"Now pay attention. Location's the key. If a Blue Coat's thin you can usually get them with that twisting move. But you have to be right on the boniest part. If they're fat, forget it. There's too much padding." She moves to my side and we focus on the far wall. "Do what I do without looking at me. You need to get used to following movements with your peripheral vision."

We practice this for a while. Ezra bending her knees and Ezra rising. Ezra's arms moving gently up, Ezra's hands floating back down again. I follow her with some difficulty until I learn to trust what I can't quite see. After a while it becomes normal. Following Ezra, feeling which way she's going to go.

"Women need this skill more than men," she says. This knowing what's around us. Finding the flow and jumping in. She says we're more likely to be in closer proximity to Blue Coats than men are. Beneath them, faceup or facedown, half dressed or nude. We'll have to learn different mechanisms of escape, an alternate set of distances between our bodies and theirs. In certain ways, such intimacy gives us an advantage, like biting off appendages. Twisting, knuckling, elbowing areas of particular vulnerability, some less obvious than others. Like the wrists. Not the targets I'd have first considered.

"Go for what's offered," Ezra suggests.

She shows me how to break a choke hold, break an arm, dislocate a shoulder, dislocate a knee, smash a windpipe, shove the nasal bone up into the brain, and, if need be, rip off a penis. She assures me this last trick will work if done correctly, with a twisting, snapping motion.

"Even if it doesn't work *entirely*," she adds, "it will make you his second priority instead of his first." I don't ask how she knows.

Next, Ezra shows me a set of rigorous exercises, each of which I'm to perform one hundred times while she stands at the head of the room, smoking. We do this for four hours until she's out of cigarettes and I'm out of oxygen and have been given leave to collapse on the dirty floor. I'm covered in the slime of filth, sweat, and blood, all of it my own.

"We'll start with these exercises every morning," Ezra says from above me.

Her bra has been pulled out of place and I'm able to see a rounded row of small, purplish bruises above one breast. Fingers that have squeezed too hard, left their identity in the prints.

Goddamned Jingo.

I nod okay and Ezra stands up. She rolls back her shoulders and stretches out her neck, turning the little purple ovals pink.

I don't want to ask, but have to. I'm not in this alone. "Ezra." I point and she looks down. Sees what everyone else is seeing, having followed the extension of my hand.

The remaining onlookers shuffle away, but she doesn't look up. Won't give them notice of their leave, won't reach up and haul her bra back into place.

"It's nothing you need to worry about." She grabs her shirt off the floor and starts down the hallway. "I'm taking care of Skinner."

"Yeah? Who's taking care of you?"

Ezra stops and turns around. "What about those walls, Adams? They stopped closing in yet?" She pulls out a cigarette and disappears.

apostasy

discriminate

ego

fossil

heresy

kindred

obstreperous

offline

veracity

kin-dred: a person's relatives collectively; kin-folk; kin; having the same belief, attitude, or feeling.

HAPTER

NINETEEN

After going rounds with Ezra first thing in the morning, training with Noam, and studying with Lazarus, I'm to work in the library until almost midnight. Watching the government feeds.

"It's a little of the up top to keep you sane," Lazarus says, but he's a bad salesperson. It's the worst part of the up top. I'm supposed to cull through the Confederation's regurgitated truths. See if I can't separate the wheat from the chaff.

I sit in front of a screen for five hours every night, watch the Confederation's bullshit government line presented in two radio feeds and one television station. Lazarus doesn't tell me about these duties until he's buttered me up with the art. It starts like this.

After my morning session with Noam, he takes me to the kitchen for a quick bite. We fill up one tray with both of our meals and eat on our way back to the main hall. There isn't even time to sit down. It's a few bland spoonfuls of oatmeal and two pieces of toast and then our tray is slid onto a table— *Betsy, can you take that back for us?*—and we're back out in the long hall again, my fingers greasy from the buttered toast.

At the mouth of the rear hall, I'm passed off like a baton. Lazarus swoops out of the darkness to take my hand and nods at Noam, who falls back, waving. Lazarus knows about my failure in yesterday's test. In today's test, too. But he's not fazed.

We walk down the back tunnel for a good half mile. Stop in

front of another solid wood door. This one is more elegantly adorned than the one hung in my training room. It has a lever for a handle and has been piped all around with weather stripping. It's the wood that catches my eye. Hard years for this tree have produced in it beautiful, layered eyes of orange and amber.

"This is our library. Two full levels." Lazarus punches in a number on an access panel affixed to the wall and wraps his hand tightly around the door's lever. A blue light comes out through the handle's upper lip. It rolls over his thumb and the four tips of his fingers that have been pressed with some difficulty along its underside. The light blinks and goes out and, with a loud whooshing sound, the door moves inward. The heat of the hallway is sucked into the library as cooled air rushes past.

We are in a foyer sandwiched by tall-backed seats. We sit down, remove our shoes, and put on bright blue footies with white plastic stripes sewn into the soles. I look around while waiting for Lazarus, who performs this chore slowly. Beyond this small foyer are two floors. They travel well beyond the boundaries of what would have been any natural part of Lilly's property. Here, every bit of floor space is carpeted. Each wall surface covered with paint. It's finished, meticulous. Necessary for the machines that would choke on the dust so prevalent in the rest of our bunker.

The lower level is filled with humming computers and work spaces that remind me of the Murdon Building. The upper level appears to be made up of shelves. Tall and co-lumnar, they run the length of the space, save for the absolute center, which is dotted with rectangles of color hung against the wall. On the shelves are books. Thousands of them. I imagine their pages leached with age. Yellow and brittle, dripping flakes of story onto the floor below.

Lazarus is trying to push his second shoe off with toes from the opposite foot. I kneel down and help him and, in doing so, see a large gap in the hard sole that's been replaced with an old box top.

"Someday, the things in this room will be a part of the first library this country has seen in over three decades," he says. "A library, by the way, is a place you can go to find books, reference materials, and works of every type of art."

I stand up and offer Lazarus a hand. Follow him up the stairs, looking down on the first floor as we go. There are a dozen heads bent over their screens. Some people are out of their seats. They're collecting books from a stack and laying them, flattened, on a scanner. The machine blinks and the page is turned. The process is repeated. They're digitizing books. A flash drive the size of a fingernail could hold thousands of them. We could carry this library in our pockets if we needed to. I suspect it is their intention.

All we have up top are *What to Do* books. Or *What Not to Do* books. Or the Confederation Bible, which is both, and the longest at 288 pages. I can't quite grasp why Lazarus and Lilly are so fond of what they call *fiction novels*—books about things that aren't true. Maybe once I read one, I'll understand.

Lazarus steps onto the second-floor landing. He points past the voluminous shelves toward the clearing in the middle. "Over there." He's worn out from the climb. Waves me ahead with a flapping hand.

Past the shelves are tall, wide patches of color pressed against the wall. They're pictures that aren't photographs, or maps, or images *to be used for*. The first one is a woman drawn in ridiculous lines with her heart broken and her face bowed. I've never seen anything like this before. Shadows and valleys making a neck, lips, and eyes.

Lazarus has caught up with me. He puts a hand on my shoulder. "It's called a painting."

I move to the next canvas. This one is a picture of a man. Gold and cream whorls stand in for his features. Up close, they look like scales. A few steps back, they form a nose, a chin, the curve of a cheek. A smile. I go to put my finger on the paint, tipped up like a wave, and Lazarus stops me. *No touching*.

I follow the movement of this man's body with my eyes. "How would a person know to do that?"

"An artist," Lazarus says. "And if I could answer your question, we'd all be this good."

I look closer, mystified. To have painted on his face a peach. A piece of fruit to imply the cheek. And his hair. In segments, it's blue. *Blue* to show me a spiral where the rest is straight. It's nothing but paint, yet my mind is deceived. Happy to be taken in. It's as if we're sharing a private moment, this artist and me. As if he or she painted this man for us to discuss all these years later.

The next few paintings are nonsensical. Combinations of flowers and skulls. Childlike drawings of squares and triangles. Then we're on to photographs unlike any I've ever seen. The Confederation of the Willing uses photographs for informational or identification purposes only. So the Human Resources person knows our names in the hallway. So Blue Coats can yank us out of crowds. In these, something mystical is happening. Bits of light have been captured, the secret insides of people and places are showing.

Lazarus taps me on the shoulder. "Come on," he says, walking to a desk pushed against the wall. He pulls open a drawer and comes back with a heavy, oversize book, already flipped open. "Here."

The presenting page is upside down. But it's obviously a picture of a man being tortured. Shot through with pipes or knives, blood is everywhere, leaking from his face, hands, and feet.

"Who's that supposed to be?" I give Lazarus my hardest stare.

"Jesus Christ," he says.

"Jesus Christ?"

"Yes."

He turns round his book and I see the irrefutable halo of light. The large, understanding eyes. But the other aspects of this Christ would never be sanctioned by the Confederation. Our Lord and Savior died a clean, painless death. Had short, clean hair, a wide-shouldered, muscular physique, and a freshly pressed blue suit. The Confederation savior climbed up onto a cross and kicked away the ladder. On the third day, God waved his hand and the ground shook, opened wide, and swallowed the tongue of our world—birdsong, the whistle of wind through well-canopied trees, *words*—then all was brought forth anew. To that end, our only image of Christ, inserted in the center of each Confederation Bible, is of a glowing man in a blue suit, always after the event, on its glorious other side. Our resurrection was all rapture and no pain—a thing reserved for the wicked. Our lord was born under a shining star. He came into the world recognized and was ceded all power. No struggle required.

"The cross you know, the one used as a symbol of the church, is also a symbol of something called crucifixion." Lazarus taps a finger on the picture. "Criminals would hang suspended by their wrists and ankles and sometimes their more intimate parts until dead. It was an excruciating way to die. Had Christ been born into the Confederation of the Willing, he would have met the same fate. Only this government would have known better than to provide his followers a public execution."

I look back down at the picture. There's a halo of gold around this Jesus's head, much like the colors I see. And a crown of thorns. His hands and feet have been punctured by nails.

Lazarus has already begun down the stairs. He stops in the foyer and sits down to peel off his footies. "They kept this Christ out of Sunday school because he wasn't good press. 'Love one another' and 'Stand up for your beliefs' don't do the Confederation much good. The machine that is this country runs on prejudice and censorship."

Before I can ask what *censorship* means, Lazarus disappears through the door in his ruined shoes.

Lilly's been waiting her turn on the first floor. She motions me toward a chair with worn armrests, above which is a computer with a screen as wide as the table on which it sits. Immediately, she begins pointing out the buttons I'm to push and the notes I'm to take on what I hear and see. I'm to listen and watch for developments. For mentions of BodySpeak and SKEYE. Anything having to do with us.

We're referred to by a number of terms. *Members of the resistance. Terrorists. Recruiters of the young and innocent.* If any television or radio feed says there have been *developments*, I'm to find Lilly and Noam. Then they'll go alert Lazarus.

I watch Lilly's skinny arms poke and jab as they connect three pairs of headphones to my terminal. Somehow, I'm supposed to listen to all three media feeds at the same time. Lilly flips a switch and the television screen lights up.

"Watch now!" She jabs me in the arm. "They shouldn't be broadcasting them this late, but just in case you see any Red Listed words come round, you write them down, then come find us fast." Lilly turns and pads off on blue footies. Doesn't ask if I have any questions.

Hours later, a young woman taps me softly on the back. She's young with bright blue eyes. "I'm the night shift," she says, scooping up my notes. "Let's take these to Gene."

My first shift has been uneventful and there are only two pages. Daily updates provided by Tracking and Data regarding their progress on the SKEYE and BodySpeak programs. But nothing we didn't already know. Nothing that sends up any red flags.

The girl walks me around the room to Gene, my pass-off partner. He'll type up my notes and enter them into the system, checking them as he goes. Like the young lady, this young man looks fresh. They must sleep all day to work all night. Down here, it doesn't make much difference.

I go back to my station and clean up an empty package that contained cookies someone brought me earlier in the night. Retrieve a mug containing the sludge of my last cup of coffee.

The night-shift girl has followed me. "I can take care of those." She pulls the mug out of my hand. Even the garbage I was about to tuck inside a pocket.

"Thank you." I turn and start toward my shoes. "Good night."

I'm halfway there when she stops me.

"Harper!" she calls nervously.

I wait as she jogs across the room, her moonshine eyes as big as stars.

"Can I ask you something?"

"Sure."

Her chin wobbles some. It dimples her white cheeks. "Are you really . . ." She can't think of the word. Is hoping I know it.

"What?"

The girl looks around at the others who're watching from behind their desks. "Are you our Sentient?" she asks. All big eyes and quivering lips. "You know . . . the one here to help us?"

I have no idea what she's talking about. "What?"

The girl smiles up at me, unfazed by my confusion. She leans closer, whispers, "I think you are." Then says good-bye and goes back to her station.

I nod my farewell and go to my room. Hold up the ceiling for a few hours with a concentrated stare, ruined for sleep.

The cot I've been given is lumpy. I turn from side to side but a comfortable position eludes me. So I get up and pace around the edges of the room. *I'll walk myself into tired,* I think. But just a couple laps passing the canvas door, and I'm pushing through it. Out into the hallway that's lit exactly like it was this afternoon, even though now it's deep night. It's an expectation I've brought down with me, that the light will change. But it won't. Come morning, it will be as dark as it is now.

There appears to be no one else up so I take a turn around the front hall, letting my outer shoulder drag against the wood planks that have been put up on the north and south walls. I pause. Look more closely at these odd vertical beams. They're grooved, thick as my hand. Starting at my knees, they run up the walls six feet, all the way to the top. There are seven on this side and another seven on its opposite. Fourteen total. They are our tables. Built to be tucked away inside the walls when not in use.

I reach down, trace the worn strip of plastic at its base, and accidentally press. There is a loud metallic click, then release. The beams come snapping out bottom ends first, a zigzag of boards and hinges that straighten as they're lowered. *Click, click.* Too loudly, aluminum rods pop out of the far ends to catch their fall. *Boom!* They land, silver legs shaking.

Oh, God.

I duck behind my hands as if this action will stop the noise from leaking into the ears of my underground comrades, who are all fast asleep. No such luck. I hear them before I see them. The canvas doors come open and the people behind them, tired and sullen, spill out.

"Harper!" Noam is running down the hall. I can see his bald head fading in and out beneath the lights. Other people are following. Lilly, Rita, Ben Dean, and his pregnant wife, Mary. A dozen others with names I don't remember. Lazarus brings up the end of this wave. All of them are peaked and frowning. They probably thought it was an alarm of some kind. A bust.

"I'm sorry." I'm whispering. As if there's anyone left to wake.

Noam makes it to me first. He puts one hand on my

shoulder, the other on the table. "What are you doing?" He's not quite awake. Keeps looking from the table to my face as if there's any sense to be made of us.

"I'm sorry," I say to no one in particular and everyone in general. "Sorry!" I repeat to Lilly, who marches up next. Again to Lazarus, who's trying very hard not to look mad. He'd obviously just gotten to sleep, having finally found a position to quiet his bones. "I barely touched it." I point at the place on the wall where the lever should be. Where now there's a dull brown table in the way.

Lilly turns and waves her arms at the people still coming up the hall. "False alarm! Harper put down a table!" I cringe at the sound of my name bouncing off the walls.

Noam pats me on the back. "I'll put this up in the morning." He follows the others down the hall and off to their rooms.

Lazarus takes me by the hand. "Follow me."

I'm escorted past the stairs that lead up to Lilly's house and on to a solid brick wall original to the foundation. The door leading through it isn't made of canvas. It's black velvet, or velour, and heavy, as if its base has been hemmed with sand.

"It's weighted," Lazarus confirms, stopping to show me a thick quilted backing. "Noise absorption." He looks up. Points at the acoustic tiles that run down a wide main hall. "Helps keep the generator noise from leaking out."

I roll the material between my fingers. "Why not use regular doors down here?"

"Two reasons." He turns and looks down at me. "The noise. And because people become interested in locking them."

Lazarus motions me into the kitchen, padding his way across its dark floor. There's the soft issue of a pulled string and then light. Just one bulb's worth, but it's enough to illuminate the small space. There's a refrigerator packed into the corner and a sad, squat microwave atop the round table in its center. The kitchen is barely larger than my room.

Lazarus opens an overhead cabinet and I see columns of

silver cans and thick, wide-handled mugs stacked neatly inside. I'm given the rules Noam already provided as he boils some water.

"Never use a plate when you can eat directly from the container. Eat all of whatever you open. Don't use too much water. And don't leave on any unnecessary lights. Too many people and places have been taken down by utilities disproportionate to the number of citizens on file." Thus this hidden generator. The single-bulb, low-wattage lights.

"We have cocoa if you don't mind a mix." Lazarus positions a package over my coffee mug and I bob my head enthusiastically.

"Yes, please."

"Any questions I can answer?"

I didn't think such an offer would be extended. Try not to sound surprised. "When it's time, how will we be moving out?"

Lazarus looks up from his stirring. The mug in his hand looks like it's full of muddy water with a twirling island of dirt in its center. "We have a contact in Antioch. When it's time to move out, we have T-Units lined up to take us to a rendezvous point." He hands me the drink handle-side out, so he's the one touching the hot part.

T-Units. Huge buslike vehicles with wings off the front. These manned vehicles are used by the Confederation to mobilize large numbers of Blue Coats. They're partially armored and carry gunner stations off a T-beam that rides above the vehicle. Each T-Unit carries fifty people and there are only forty-eight of us. "Do we need more than one?"

"We will by then. We're the central spoke in our region. Other groups will gather here in waves a few days before the war. We'll mobilize together."

Lazarus shouldn't have asked if I had questions. I'm like a plugged-up hose, finally sprouted a hole. *How are we going to get people to join us? What freedoms do we have to show them? If the SKEYE program goes up, we'll be seen in those T-Units. How will we get anywhere?*

Lazarus smiles. "Then I guess we'll walk."

I look down at the floor. "Veracity . . ."

"Is safe. Candace knew what she was getting herself into. And Hannah . . . what happened to Hannah is exactly why it's time to go to war." Lazarus's voice is as sad as I've ever heard it. I won't come near these questions with him again. "Now." He claps his hands. "It's time for bed. We have a big day tomorrow."

I watch as he sets his empty mug in the sink.

"Lazarus, people are thinking of me as being way more important than I am."

His hand goes still on the faucet but he says nothing.

So I ask, "What does it mean?"

Lazarus turns the knob. Pours out enough water to rinse the basin. "How many people have been referring to you this way?"

"A couple of people. My relief in the library."

"Christine." He turns around. "She doesn't mean to gossip. She's just young."

I look down at my muddy cocoa. Most of the mix is still floating on the surface, clumped together. Doesn't matter as I'm no longer thirsty. "What does she mean?"

"Nothing. It's just superstitious hope to get us through the days."

"She thinks I'm some kind of savior, Lazarus. I don't want anybody being misled." The stress of it rushes up on me. The fear I've been cultivating is a black mass in my chest. It keeps me from breathing. Melts my shirt against the hot skin beneath.

"We're all somebody's savior." Lazarus is unaware of my spinning, can't see past my still body. "I'm asking you to trust me, Harper."

"I need this one answer, Lazarus."

"You need something you can control." He takes my full mug and frowns down into its middle. "You didn't like it?"

I take hold of his hand. Squeeze until he can surely feel my pulse racing along beneath my skin. "I wasn't thirsty."

Lazarus sighs. Sets my mug on the kitchen table, where it's fair game for whoever comes in next. "Lucille told us about you, your friend from Mr. Mitchell's class. She said she recognized you." He's talking about hair-eating, lip-sucking Lucille who got thrown out of class. The needy girl who grew up to be so much more than me. Lucille, whom I watched die through an interrogation room window.

"Lucille was a part of this group?"

"Came down here at age sixteen." Lazarus nods. "She was one of our best runners."

I pause before asking, "What did she say about me?"

"That we should keep our eye on you, bring you down when it was time. She believed that, someday, you'd be the one to save us."

"Lucille . . ." I have a hard time telling Lazarus. He's going to be so hurt. "Lucille was confused."

Lazarus looks fatigued. He goes back to the table. Pours himself into a seat. "Why does it bother you? Lucille believing you're the one."

I turn my head, dabbing at my eyes with a sleeve. "Because I know why she thought it."

"You're talking about the time you stood up for her." Lazarus laughs, strong and hard. Both voices buckle and snap until he starts to cough and I have to bring him some water. "It wasn't that, Harper. It was something she *saw* in you. You're not the only Sentient in the world. Yes?"

I sit down across from him. Glum. "I didn't save her."

"What do you mean, you didn't save her? You saved her not once, but twice. And in the most important way a person can be saved. From hopelessness." He reaches across the table and taps a finger on my palm. "It may not seem like much to you. But it's everything to us. Hope is how any war is won. It makes us fight better. Makes us stronger. I know in my heart that you're going to get us what we need to take down that one redactor when the time comes. But what you need to hear is something different."

Lazarus repositions, scooting onto one hip. "With or without the master, we've already won, you see? Because, for the first time in years, there is the feeling that we just might. Let people believe in you, Harper. Maybe some of it will start to rub off. Deal?"

I nod, pensive. "Deal."

Lazarus picks up a towel and dabs at my moist head and flushed face. "This is why I didn't want to tell you. You think you need that worry and pain. You think it serves you. You think it *saves* you, but it doesn't. Try keeping those walls in place with a little faith for a while. Now." He slaps his knee. "It's late."

Lazarus gets up from the table and leads me back to the main hall. He says we could both use the next five hours' sleep. I'm to go straight back to my room and lie down. Ezra will be waiting for me in the morning, six o'clock sharp.

He won't let me talk. Shushes me, good-naturedly, every time I start to ask another question.

HAPTER
TWENTY

Lazarus comes in with a jar of honey and a plate of cut lemon to go with his tea. Things I've seen Lilly bring in to soothe his voice. Means he'll be talking awhile.

"How are you doing today?" he asks.

Lazarus's eyes are drawn. It's the pain in his joints. Moist days like this, when the rain up top swells the beams of our underground home, are his worst.

"Fine," I answer. "How are you?"

Lazarus waves a hand. "Yesterday's training with Noam go all right?"

A shrug. "Yeah."

It was another of our daily sessions in which Amy was taking notes behind her computer and Noam was at my side, guiding me farther and farther out. He hasn't come right out and told me so, but each day's *training* is obviously an actual attempt to find the main redactor. With Noam's soothing voice in my ear, I'm guided as far as my mind will go. We're making progress toward the fields of redactors that lie in the Geddard Building's basement, but it's often one step forward and two steps back. Yesterday, I was able to approach National House Square and even get close to some of the people walking the streets. But then I couldn't find my way around a city I know like the back of my hand. Travel via the mind doesn't work the way it does with the body. It's not *Turn left here. Take a sharp right there.* It's *Imagine a room you've never been in and think yourself there.* The process can be so disorienting that today, I wound up in an entirely different city.

"It's going okay," I offer.

Lazarus doesn't buy my answer, but he lets it go. "I have a tight schedule so we need to get right to it. I'm going to tell you about the beforetime," he says, then proceeds without pause.

Before the Pandemic, our country was governed by a central text known as the Constitution. A doctrine that established a government by the people and for the people, meant to keep us from becoming what we are now—a tyranny. Slowly, the freedoms it provided were rolled back. Plucked away only as quickly as people could adjust. So when the Pandemic hit, there was some precedent for the exchange of rights for security. It had become natural, this forfeiture. Expected.

The first few were small. People handed them over as if they were old clothes. Things they never got out of the closet anyway. Warrants. Trials. Privacy. All last year's fashions. By the time Blue Coats came calling for the real finery, people were already beginning to lose their good taste. Out came the big-ticket items, the ones they kept stored in clear zippered bags. Personal beliefs. Personal possessions. Personal anything. It was no longer in vogue to be an individual. It became more about *not* standing out. *Not* standing up.

The Pandemic was coming across the water. On the backs of birds, in their waste. Sometimes the story changed. The birds became fish that would pollute every lake, stream, and ocean. The disease became a flu and then a fever that went up and up. They were all variations on the same theme. What the Pandemic brought was the fertile seed of fear. It was planted and took root, choked out all reason. Allegiance became servitude. Servitude became acquiescence. You either lined up for the silver shackle worn in the front of your neck or you were proved a traitor. Taken away to the unknown elsewhere or shot loudly and on the spot because that had become the right way to serve your country. To hold still and die when you're told. To take aim and, on command, fire.

The Pandemic coincided with an election year.

In the beforetime, our government was different. People voted for *a* president. A man or woman subject to the title, willing to submit himself or herself to an article such as *a* or *the*. If they proved themselves not equal to the task, they were removed or replaced. So passionate was the respect for the title of President, the man or woman holding it melted away. They became their role. The role did not become them.

A month before the vote, the government announced the election was being postponed. The Pandemic was coming. It would be too dangerous for citizens to leave their homes. People were to stay inside. Protect themselves with blue masks worn over their mouths. They could leave their homes to buy groceries, to go to church, and for medical emergencies only. December passed, and January. In February, small pockets of resistance formed. A few troops were attacked outside the National House.

One died.

It was the opening those in office had been waiting for. They could remove all remaining liberties in the name of safety and defense. People were turning on one another. Riots would ensue and morph into civil war unless we gave them everything they asked. They couldn't help us without our compliance.

"Compliance became another word for patriotism," Lazarus says.

If a citizen so much as questioned a command, they weren't good Americans, weren't fit to keep company with other, better citizens. One word might spread their restlessness, so such toxicity was protected against. The murders of these freethinkers and the eradication of their poison was deemed *preemptive self-defense*. A beautifully marketed term for Confederation-sanctioned genocide.

Lazarus takes a sip of his coffee and sets his mug too hard

on the table. Some sloshes out. "We lost our capacity for tolerance when we lost our freedom. Or maybe it was the other way around. I'm not sure which one I miss more." He's angry, one finger banging against the table.

"The trouble comes when we forget we're family! You, me, the people living halfway around the world! The problem is this ridiculous idea that there is an *us* and then an *other*! A *them* to which the rules of humanity don't apply! If I could put one word on that goddamned Red List, that's the one I'd choose! *Them!* There is never a *them*, Harper! There's only *us*! If we could get that learned, we might just figure out how to stop killing ourselves!" Lazarus sits back. Pours out a glass of lemon water, rubs some of the butter melting in a small dish over his chapped lips and into the gray, crusting skin of his palms. It is his rite of composure, moisturizing. Putting back in some of the soft that's been leeched out.

People began to sorely miss those giveaway rights. They were detained with no charges levied against them and no appointed time set to go before the judge in their Sunday best. Detentions could go on for as long as the government felt necessary. Families didn't warrant notice or information. Those that grew too loud or drew too much attention disappeared. A person, many persons, could fall off the face of the earth and no one would have to know. All government records were closed to the public. The policy became *Don't ask*.

A new kind of military took over. They took down the old flags and replaced them with their own. Those too loyal to their former cause, too honorable to serve under this new flag, were lined up against a wall. Made to go away. Those who were left, and others who were recruited, were to collect data and record any potential threats. Renting a book on world religions, purchasing the wrong ingredients at the grocery store, saying the wrong thing could get a citizen hauled away. Killed outright or imprisoned without trial.

Families gathered around their kitchen tables and prayed. They stayed indoors until Sunday, then went clambering off to church in record numbers, even before it became mandatory. The new church was so successful an advocate for the new government, it became an extension of it and was given reign over media, communications, and social programs—anything endemic to the human condition.

Lazarus has been talking for two hours. Lilly's come in three times to fill up the water pitcher and pout over his bleak countenance. She's asked him to take a break. Go lie down, settle his voice. The first was a request, the second a demand. Lazarus responded to neither and out she went. If he was going to keep this up, he wasn't going to see the new world. She had other, more important things to do. A whole library to turn digital while he was pushing himself, compromising the whole thing. Lilly continues her tirade out into the hall. Off to wherever she works night and day, fingers spent down to the bone.

Lazarus brushes away the books between us and takes my hands. "This is a lot to consider. Are you okay?"

I nod. "Yes." But there's so much.

He turns over my hands, rubs the skin of my palms. "We had the numbers to take them all those years ago, Harper, and we have the numbers now. What we lack is a way to talk to one another. A way to wrestle away the technological advantage from a surprisingly small group of old men. Now is the time for us to come together. What we're doing isn't surviving. We're dying, slowly and quietly." Lazarus is whispering. It makes one of his voices lift while the other dips. "Your family died with their integrity intact. Integrity means living life according to one's own measure. Doing the right thing as it's defined by just you and God and nobody else." Lazarus grimaces. He's been twisting in his seat for a few minutes, trying to stretch his back.

I go to his medicine bag hung up on the wall and dig into

the slouching front. I bring him the largest vial. Pour him some water as he unscrews the top.

"Thank you." He swallows two tablets between large gulps. "Do you have any questions?"

I nod. "What was it like for you back then?"

Lazarus rubs thoughtfully at the stubble on his chin. "I had an important position at the time so I was recruited, which means I was taken by force to one of their vetting centers and handed a packet of materials that outlined everything. The new governmental structure. The surgery I'd be having to implant my slate. My new position. It was a press kit. There was even a DVD that explained all the benefits of living and working in the Confederation."

He smiles at some memory. "If you were a man of some consequence, you got a beautiful young woman as an assistant. If you were a woman, you got a beautiful young man. They handled chores, served as nurses. If you wanted something more, they were lovers. It was a strange introduction to life in the Confederation of the Willing. Here comes this stunning woman with legs up to her neck. She pours me a glass of wine, asks what kind of carpet I'd like installed in my new home, then tells me there won't be any more traveling or music or free self-expression. They'd be replacing those with nicer things. It worked for a while. With me and the rest of the country. But then we got to remembering what it had been like before."

Clusters of insurgents formed. They killed Blue Coats, spray-painted government buildings with the Red Words coming out on daily lists. These groups thrived for short bursts of time. But without a glue stronger than rage to bind them, without a leader, resisters grew disenchanted. They quit. Or took their lives.

"So the government put together a team of social scientists," Lazarus says. "They came up with the antidepressant you know as Occlusia, doubled the number of bars, provided free sex. Their goal was to anesthetize the public and it worked. People stopped killing themselves, but they were so high on their antidepressants they couldn't remember the Red Words. Before Confederation scientists found the right dosage, it wasn't uncommon to see people walking around with scorch marks on their necks. And the smell . . ." He grimaces. Leaves off.

Lazarus doesn't like this topic of conversation. I can see it in the way he turns his head, offering me an ear instead of a voice. So I ask something else. "I've heard it was Noah who developed the slates. But who discovered how to break them?"

The ponderous, world-weary look leaves Lazarus's face. He turns to me with fresh eyes, laughing. "Noah didn't develop the slates."

"Who did?"

"Scientists, neurosurgeons, linguists. Twelve of us, in total. I was second generation to the project. The first model had already been developed but it didn't always spark correctly. Too many infractions and a person could catch fire. So I was asked to be lead on the optimization team. While working out the misfiring issues, I studied the way slates were implanted."

My eyes fall to the scar running above and below Lazarus's slate. The skin there is dull and shriveled. A mottled purplish pink. "How did you break?"

"Every morning at eight o'clock, the pretty, young assistant I'd been assigned would come in and hand me a needle full of Occlusia. She was supposed to watch me so I wouldn't stick it in the dog they let me keep, or take it to the bathroom and flush it down the toilet. One day she came in, gave my dose to the sofa, and threw a schematic on the table. It was the last piece of the puzzle. The insertion points. Precise measurements of how the slate's extensions are placed around the carotid. The risks were obvious and the process, well, you know the process. And the possibilities for harm."

They'd been clearly written, taking up the whole second page in one of my many recruitment letters. *Breaking one's slate has and could result in death, stroke, heart attack, infection, long-term damage to the voice box.* And so on. The ways in which you could be maimed or killed were mind-boggling.

"Where'd you break?"

"Right there in my apartment with my new assistant, who by then had become something a little more. I went first. It was a bad one. But I was off the grid immediately. We had no trouble getting out."

Lilly pokes her frowning face around the canvas door. "We have news from Dover."

Lazarus looks up. Nods. "I'll be out in a few minutes."

"It's Dover!" she shouts.

"Another few moments, please." Lazarus is calm with his answer.

It's a quality that infuriates Lilly. She grunts, then disappears.

I have two or three minutes, tops. "What about the assistant?"

"We had to get her off the map as quickly as possible, so she pulled over on old Interstate 55 and broke right there in the backseat. Thankfully, hers went better than mine. She knew a doctor who stitched me up a new pair of voices, then we came here."

"What happened to her?"

Lazarus points to the hall. "That assistant was Lilly. She'd been a world-famous linguist before the Pandemic. Before they turned her into a nurse." He shrugs. "Lilly and I, ours was not a real-world passion. We knew each other too well by the end of the first week to keep confusing excitement with love. Then along came Noam."

Lilly clears her throat from the door. She's been listening. Is glowing red beneath her gray hair and large plastic eyes. "It's time to go."

Lazarus smiles. "Just telling our novitiate about old times."

Lilly pulls back the canvas to reveal the empty hall. "Now *Wernthal* is calling."

Wernthal is the magic word. Lazarus gets up. Almost leaves without a good-bye, but then stops to give me his most attentive look. "Losing your perspective happens faster than you think, Harper. I expect you to be paying attention."

Lazarus kisses Lilly on the top of her head and scoots past. The old girl turns her face toward the wall as he goes. Sniffs.

"Dinner's at six." When she looks over, I see that times past have clouded her eyes. I can read the secret on Lilly's body as if she's written it there in ink. She's still in love with Lazarus.

"Lilly," I call out before she can walk away.

"Yeah?"

I motion her into the room, far back, away from the canvas door. "Can I ask you something about John?"

Lilly looks at me hard from behind her thick glasses. She's protective of their Blue Coat. "You can ask."

"There was a book he was looking at when we were out at the farm. A child's book."

Lilly frowns. "I'm waiting for the question."

"Did John lose a child?" Such a loss imprints itself very specifically on a person's energy. A son, a young son, is what I saw imprinted on his that day at the farm.

Lilly puts a hand to her mouth and taps her lips, thinking how best to answer. "That man's loss is equal to your own, if that answers your question. Now, if you'll excuse me, Harper . . ."

"Is he a good man, Lilly?" I blurt out. "I know he's a Blue Coat, but his colors are so . . . the opposite of that."

"John Gage is a good man," Lilly says sharply, then walks to the door.

Her approach causes the canvas to swing. Standing there behind it is a woman named Elsbeth. She's huddled against the cloth door, one ear proffered up. She and her husband are always doing this, skulking around the bunker. Listening in on conversations. Lilly sees her and makes a sound of indignation, then pulls the canvas door as closed as it gets.

"What does it matter if John is a Blue Coat? Or that he's

lost a child?" Lilly says. "You find someone in this world who makes you feel right about yourself, you'd better hang on tight. It's not unusual to find the right person, Harper. It's recognizing them before they're already gone that's rare."

With that, Lilly leaves.

I can't imagine the burden of it. Living a whole life with the man you love but can't have. Down here, stuck with the everyday reminder of what might have been up above.

CHAPTER

TWENTY-ONE

It's eleven o'clock at night and I'm in the library, at my post on media watch for another hour. Just when a filler program called *How to Spend One's Off Time* is supposed to begin, up comes an image of the National House, its white facade turned yellow by the lights. A special press conference has been called on President's front lawn but President isn't there. Instead, it's a handful of his Managers, a legion of Blue Coats, Helen Rumney in a new off-white suit, and Mr. Weigland.

Helen Rumney is smiling into the camera. Next to her, Mr. Weigland looks bloated, his eyes swollen from lack of sleep. His gaze settles on the nearest camera and his head moves just so. Just the way he used to do when signaling me. *Watch out, Harper. Something's coming.*

I grab my notepad and ready my pencil.

With no prelude, Helen Rumney begins the announcement of a new set of Red Words. They're shown on the screen as she speaks, scrolling left to right beneath her feet so the viewer can get the full benefit of her matching off-white shoes.

. . . Insurrection. Rebellion. Revolt. Revolution . . .

These are words I don't recognize. They're from the beforetime and no longer in use. There's only one reason the government adds pre-Confederation words and that's when they're doing what Monitors call a *Themed Sweep*—the extraction of an idea from society by revoking all associated terms. I jot down the words without looking at my notepad, watching the small scroll at the bottom of the screen as others are announced.

. . . *Riot. Sedition. Uprising* . . .

Finally, some with which I'm familiar. And all of them pertinent to us, a group of resisters grown large enough to warrant a little defensive action.

Helen Rumney finishes the list and smiles into the camera. She's giving me a *We know you're out there*. Though, really, a list like this—one that threatens to reveal their purpose—is more. It's a declaration of war.

I take down the rest of the Red words while keeping my eye on the list that continues to scroll across the bottom of the screen. Between the words Helen Rumney has announced are three she has not. *Car. Drive. Gas.* They are ubiquitous words, the kind that will keep Monitors busy for weeks. Trick words, each one a net.

I pull off my blue footies and sprint out of the library barefoot. Halfway to Noam and Lilly's room, I start shouting their names. By the time I turn the corner, they're already standing at their door, sleep thick on their wrinkled faces.

"What is it?" Lilly rasps.

"Helen Rumney just gave a Red List update from the National House lawn." I'm winded. Steady myself against the wall.

"Just now? At eleven o'clock at night?" Noam asks.

Lilly pushes him aside. "How many words?"

"Eleven."

"Anything unusual about them?"

"Most of them have to do with the resistance. But then there are these three. Car, drive, and gas. Also, I saw them in the list they run on the television, but Rumney didn't announce them. Anybody not watching wouldn't have heard them."

Noam and Lilly turn to each other.

"Good Lord," Lilly whispers.

"Did we send out a runner?" I ask.

"We sent out Eric," Noam answers. "It was a run to Antioch. For medicine. That's eighty miles away. He'll need to stop for gas."

Eric was the man sitting next to Rita in Noam's viewing test. The man with the sore, yellow stomach.

"No, Noam." Lilly blinks up at him. She can hardly get it out. "He came down sick. We sent Ben instead."

Ben. The man with the pregnant wife.

Tonight, anyone who missed this announcement and stops to get gas is at risk for stumbling onto a Red Listed word. Which, of course, is the whole point. *Car*, *gas*, and *drive* are three words so endemic to the process of refueling, a few thousand Confederation citizens will pop their slates tonight. Any runners out there, their slates already broken, will be able to say these words just fine. And that's how they'll get caught. By *not* getting zapped.

I put a hand on Noam's arm. "If this is a trap, they'll have warned the Service Managers at every station."

Noam nods and takes off like a shot, gone to tell Lazarus. Lilly slips back into their room. All I see are white limbs dipping in and out of clothes.

"Lilly, someone must have told them we were sending out a runner."

She steps back into the hall, head shaking. "Impossible."

I bite my lip. Don't want to be the one telling her this. "Helen Rumney wouldn't go to this kind of trouble without knowing there was somebody worth catching out there."

"Why not?" Lilly asks harshly. "They've never been loath to harm the innocent."

Noam and Lazarus are hurrying down the aisle toward me. They've probably heard most of what's been said.

"Whatever else they may be, Lilly, they don't like snarls in their system. Even right now, I can guarantee you Tracking and Data has already been jammed with data files and disparity reports that will set them behind at least a week. It's why we don't issue Red words at night or on weekends." I pause. "Why *they* don't issue Red words, I mean. I'm sorry."

Noam puts a hand on my shoulder. "Nothing to be sorry for."

Lilly is unmoved. "Impossible! The only people who go up top, outside of Ezra and me, are the runners! Those people risk their lives to bring us the things we need to live, so don't tell me you think it's one of them! There are no leaks in my media room and there are no leaks in our group! The last thing we need to be worried about is each other. You understand?"

She marches away down the hall and Noam motions for me to let her go. He tells me anything more will be wasted on Lilly, resident matriarch to all us children.

I grab hold of Noam's arm before he and Lazarus can follow her. "What if Ben's caught close to Antioch?"

"Then we'll be lucky. We have Blue Coats in Antioch who can get him out of the field."

"What if he's caught closer to Bond?"

"John was sent to Grange this morning. That means Jingo's the only Blue Coat on patrol in the area," Noam says, following Lazarus down the hall. "Try and get some rest, Harper. We'll call you if we need you."

A woman named Tabitha is coming down the hall, stopping at each room to inform us of what's going on. I know her from media watch. She sits three rows behind me, has a naturally deep voice. It ebbs in and out as she sticks her head into rooms to announce the event.

"Hello?" she says, then knocks twice on the earthen wall. Before I can answer, she's popped her head through my canvas door. "Harper, we have a Code Black. That means we have a potential medical emergency and essential personnel only are being permitted in the trauma area."

Tabitha's fair-skinned face disappears before I can ask her any questions. I have to follow her out.

"Wait . . ."

She frowns. "Yeah?"

Our walls are thin and our doors inconsequential. Les, the resident of the next, and last, room down, has come out into the hall rather than wait for Tabitha to come in. He's a nice man. Sixty or sixty-five, another professor. He leans against the wall to listen.

"Where's the trauma area?" I ask Tabitha.

"At the mouth of the back tunnel. In Noam's gym."

"Am I essential personnel?"

"Maybe." She shrugs. "We'll find out if and when Ben gets brought in."

Tabitha looks at Les, who waves her along. He's already got the message.

"If you don't want to wait in your room, a group of people have gone to the kitchen to make bandages," Les offers, then disappears back through his canvas door.

By the time I make it to the kitchen, everything's done. The bandage-making crew have torn up the few scraps of clothing they could find and dispersed. All the dishes have been washed, the counter has been cleared. Potatoes are already soaking for the morning breakfast. There's nothing left to do.

In the main hall, a group of women are sitting with Mary, Ben's wife. They take turns rocking her. Holding her head on their shoulders, their bodies moving in unison like a pump. It's ritualized. A thing they've done before. Her belly is the only thing I can see of her as I pass by.

I'm on my way back to my room when I hear people talking in the area by the back tunnel. I veer off course. Don't take the hallway leading to the sleeping quarters, but slip onto a side path that empties into Noam's gym. I nod at the few people shuttling quickly past and keep going until I'm standing in what's become a trauma area.

The stumps used as seats have been pushed together in the shape of a long, narrow table. Next to it is a cart someone's wheeled in from somewhere near the kitchen. The caster tracks are still visible in the dirt floor. On this cart is a collection of needles and vials. I don't study the contents too long. Noam and Lazarus are coming toward me from the dark rear tunnel. I can hear them discussing supplies and the forecast for the next week's weather. Like everyone else, they're trying to kill time.

"Harper!" Lazarus calls to me while coming into the room. He's in pain. I can see a rosy-red corona floating over his joints.

"Yeah?" I jog over.

"I need you to be here in about fifteen minutes," he says. "They're bringing in Ben." It's a bad sign. Means he's been caught by Jingo.

"Is he hurt?"

"We don't know." Lazarus leans down so I have to look into his face. "Harper, they're also bringing in John."

My face falls. *Is he hurt, too?*

Lazarus is kind and doesn't make me use the words. "We don't know anything about John's condition, either."

Noam interrupts with a hand on my other shoulder. "Could you do me a favor? Could you go to Lazarus's room and get his medicine satchel?"

Despite my desire to stay, I agree and head off toward the sleeping quarters. I pray silently beneath my breath, taking turns: Each step on the left foot, I pray for Ben. Each step on the right, for John.

I've just turned the corner when a man runs past. He's come from behind me—from the vicinity of Noam's gym— his head forward, legs like a wheel beneath him. Were someone to step into his path, he'd never be able to stop. I open my mouth to shout a warning when I'm nearly hit by another man, also running. They're headed for the main hall.

Almost immediately, I hear Tabitha's voice. She's running up and down the halls, shouting names, presumably of those of us cleared to proceed to the back. Her voice is still hanging in the air when the place explodes. Canvas doors blow open and the occupants rush out, each with a set direction. It's practiced. No one bounces into anyone. No one is panicked. Everyone is graceful. They are one body with many arms.

Ben Dean is here. And John.

I race to collect the medicine satchel, then turn and run back to the gym, which is now filled with a third of us. Lazarus and Noam are standing at the mouth of the rear entrance, waiting for a procession of people who look like black shadows in the dimly lit hall. It feels like eternity before Ben Dean and his group of rescuers appear in parts as they enter the trauma area, their bodies dissected by the dark.

The light announces them as they proceed into the gym. A thin white arm and ruffled brown hair become a woman named Sally, her head bent over the top of the carried board. A pair of thick legs becomes a sentry, one of two people I've seen carrying guns. I don't know the woman backing toward me. Or the other three men on the team's far side, their arms stretched out, just a finger each on Ben's transport board as there's no helping room left. A skirt showing powerful legs below with a silver blouse on top becomes Ezra, no surprise. Laid out on the board, all dangling fingers and shining clothes, is Ben Dean. So far, John is nowhere in sight.

Arms, shoulders, and heads sidestep into the gym. They stop and lower Ben Dean onto the board. Their faces are all business, as if Ben Dean is already dead. Then one of his arms moves.

Lilly shoots forward and takes hold of Ben's wrist. "Where'd you find him?"

The woman at Ben's head opens her mouth to answer but is stayed by a voice proceeding out of the dark tunnel.

"Four miles north of Bond."

We all turn and watch as John Gage is led in by one of Lilly's young nurses. Despite efforts to take cool, even steps, he's limping. His arm finds the girl's every other footfall and she slumps under the sudden and sporadic weight of him.

As John advances, I log those bits of him revealed by the

lights. *Unedited face, head, arms, chest . . . No.* One side of his shirt has been pulled free of the hem and the loose dart is stained with blood.

Lilly leaves Ben to examine our Blue Coat, who's trying to lower himself casually into the seat. But he fails to look unaffected and lands with some pain on the hard plastic seat. John's jacket gapes upon impact and there, on his lower left flank, is the hole.

"Good God, John!" Lilly pushes him forward and pulls at his sleeves until the coat is free and she can poke at another hole, presumably on his other side. "At least it's gone through. You were lucky this time."

I take a step toward him. *John!*

I don't think I've said this out loud but suddenly there's a quiet around me. Noam has put out his hand and stopped me on my way to our Blue Coat.

"Harper," Noam says. Then, slowly, the way Mr. Weigland used to, he inclines his head ever so slightly while looking at the others. *They're watching, Harper.*

"He's hurt . . ."

"Harper." Noam again tries to draw me back. *No. Not now.* Or maybe, *Not in front of everyone.*

But I don't move. Can't make my legs or my eyes turn away.

Noam reaches up and slides a finger beneath the satchel's strap, still wrapped over my shoulder. "Thank you, Harper," he says, ever so gently pushing me back into my original position while taking Lazarus's medicine bag with him.

Behind him, John begins talking. He's giving Lilly a briefing.

"Jingo couldn't have been with Ben for more than a few minutes," John says, grimacing as Lilly's fingers move on his lower back. "He'd been cut by the time I arrived." His eyes are swinging beneath a sweating brow, looking for someone. "He's lost too much blood, Lilly," John tries to whisper, but can't modulate such hard truth. When he finally finds Mary, Ben's widow, she's heard her husband's prognosis. Down go her arms to cover her round belly.

Lilly leaves John, who's going to live, to attend Ben Dean, who is not. The others standing there part like a drape and allow her entrance.

Lazarus puts a hand on my arm while whispering into my ear, "Harper, we need you to read Ben. Find out whatever you can."

I'm rushed to the board by a collection of hands, my eyes turned backward. Behind me, John's shirt has been removed to allow Lilly's assistant better access to his wound. I can see it from here. A small round bullet hole distal from the spine and just beneath the ribs. The young woman pokes at the plum-colored lesion with a long swab while someone places my hands on Ben Dean's body. The abilities I'm supposed to be using on Ben, I use first on John. I won't be able to focus on our runner until I know he's safe.

A diffuse, purplish pink light has collected around John's wound and spiraling out of its center is a core of brownish green. Nowhere do I see the thick ash of irreversible damage. Or the fine red lines of death that so often rise out of bullet wounds, spreading and swelling to paint the victim a burgundy-striped, gunmetal gray. *Thank you, God.* Around John's head, I see a yellow green, the color of worry. But his eyes aren't set on his friend and compatriot who's nearly dead on the table, or even on Mary, the pending widow. They're set squarely on the couple's unborn baby. On the child who will be born into a war and without a father.

Lazarus clears his throat and I turn my head back to Ben. My eyes don't need to see what my hands already feel. Our runner is sheathed in the colors of death. I have to wave away the roiling clouds of it in order to see his face.

Another of Lilly's assistants opens a tear already well begun in the fabric of Ben's trousers. She looks up without moving her body and delivers the news with large eyes. "The femoral artery's been cut."

"What have you done to stop the bleeding?" Lilly calls out to John, who's gritting his teeth. A mix of rubbing alcohol and gin has been applied to his open wound. It foams upon contact.

"I tried to get a tourniquet above the artery, but he's lost at least three pints of blood . . ." John leaves off. He can see Mary, Ben's wife, now huddled in the corner of the room, listening. The skin around Mary's eyes is streaked with the mascara of tears and dirt, but she's no longer crying.

Lilly motions for the young woman to come over, if she wants. But Mary shakes her head no. That red, bleeding form on the table isn't her husband. She sinks into the friends still circled around her and Lilly turns back to me.

"Go ahead."

I ignore the activity going on around us and watch as Ben Dean's dark colors float up off the board on which he's been laid. They're tinged with green, a burnt sage. It is the color of waste going bad. Of compost, resurrection. These strands of color have almost separated from the young man. They seem attached at his joints by very thin threads.

God help me. It's too late. I don't know how to pull answers from this man and it's these people's assumption I do. I'm about to disappoint them. All the lucid parts of Ben Dean are already dead.

The board where Ben's lying has become a blur of hands that pass along cutlery and thread and homemade bandages used to blot Ben's continuously leaking blood. Ben's only job is to breathe, and twice he quits and a pair of round paddles are pressed to his chest. They shock him so that, for a fraction of a second, he's up on his head and his hips, then down again. Twice brought back. But it's never permanent. Ben flickers in and out like a wet candle. His colors change as he dies. Now they're all pastels. Pale versions of others.

"Are we safe, Ben?" I whisper into his ear, knowing it's too late. He's no longer here to answer. He wasn't available for questioning when they got here.

Ezra leaves her station at Ben's side and runs up the hall toward the sleeping quarters. Elsbeth takes her place. She tells Ben she's going to take over and ask him a few questions of her own. For a yes, he's to wiggle a finger or a toe. For a no, he's to lie absolutely still. Ben's begun to shudder, is losing control of his body. If he moves, it will be an autonomic response.

"What are you doing?" I ask, and the whole room looks over.

Elsbeth draws herself up and stares at me with her small button eyes. "What somebody else should have already done!"

Immediately, she leans down and asks her questions. *Has our medical contact been compromised? Does Jingo know anything about us? God bless you, we'll love you anyway, but did Jingo get anything out of you? Did you throw out your kill pill? We didn't find it in your pockets, and we know you didn't swallow it. Did Skinner knock it out of your hand before you could take it? We know you'd never compromise us, would you? We haven't been compromised, have we, Ben? Or the war?*

Ben doesn't move and Elsbeth comes up beaming.

I begin to interject, but Ezra does it for me. Already she's back, now wearing a clean black skirt and green tube top. "Move it!" she shouts, pushing Elsbeth out of the way. "Harper!" She turns to me. "What did you find out?"

"He's gone," I say. And, as if he needed it spoken, there is the smallest trembling of release from Ben. A sigh, like a tire punctured. And he's dead, so simply. As if there was no pain in the going, just the staying.

"Too late," Lilly announces. "We didn't have time to debrief." She undoes the blood-staunching pliers set tight against Ben's leg and throws them haphazardly into the dark hall.

I don't have to turn my head to see John Gage's expression of grief. It's coming across the room like a storm. Next to me, Ben's eyes are rolled up in his head. Large purple poppies have begun blooming beneath his skin. Stagnant pools of blood with nowhere else to go.

Ezra frowns at Lazarus, who's propped himself against the rear hall. "I'm on damage control," she says, and marches away toward the front of Lilly's house, making fast progress in a pair of needle-thin heels.

I see something reflecting light as she goes, in and out, in and out, beneath the overhead bulbs. There's something shiny on her arm.

"Ezra," I call out, but she doesn't stop.

"Let her go," Lazarus says. "We'll meet up again later, when she gets back."

I can't wait. Bolt down the hall after her. Ezra's fast. Already she's on the stairs leading up to Lilly's pantry. "Wait!" I shout.

"I don't have time for you now, Adams!" Ezra looks down between the rails. The outer door's already open. I can see the slightest hint of light behind her.

"Wait!" I take the stairs two at a time. Catch her just before she steps onto the landing.

"I don't have fucking time!" Ezra tries to buck me off and I grab at her elbow. Hold up my fingers.

They're shiny and red. She's touched Ben Dean. Accidentally marked herself with his blood.

I take off my T-shirt and she turns around, offers me her arm. I wipe until it's clean, then push her into the upstairs pantry. Ezra peeks back at me through the closing door, but doesn't say a thing.

apostasy

discriminate

ego

fossil

heresy

kindred

obstreperous

offline

veracity

ob-strep-er-ous: resisting control or restraint in a difficult manner; unruly.

HAPTER

TWENTY-TWO

There are twelve council members assembled at a long table made from other, shorter tables, all pushed together. They've been assembled to talk about the incident. The council is half women, half men, and mostly older. Lazarus sits in their center with Noam and Lilly on either side of him. Ben Dean's body has been cleaned and dressed, laid out in the main hall for something Lilly calls a wake. And a patched-up John Gage had to go back up top before I was able to speak to him. We've been assembled to discuss the fallout of Ben's capture and, to my surprise, the council is looking at me.

I smile back at the assembled faces and turn to Ezra, who's seated next to me. She's put on a new set of clothes since her return. Black stiletto heels. A black see-through blouse with the bra showing beneath. A sequined green skirt with a slit that opens to midthigh. I don't know how to begin this proceeding and Ezra can tell.

She holds up a hand but doesn't wait to be called on and stands up. "Ezra James asking for permission to speak."

Lazarus nods. "The council recognizes Ezra James."

"I found Jingo at 6:05 this morning at his residence. He was inebriated when I arrived." Ezra pulls out a cigarette. "There's not much to tell. He's not talking. Or anything else."

Lazarus taps his long fingers against the table and looks down at a woman named Casey who'll be our future Secretary of Defense. She's long and thin with flesh as orange as the wood used to make the library door. "Do we know when Skinner's debriefing is scheduled?" he asks her.

"Tomorrow at seven p.m. in Antioch."

Lazarus turns to an old man named Fitz who's sitting at the table's other end. In our new world, he'll be a Supreme Court Justice. "Fletcher can get her in."

Fitz pulls at his chin. "Yes, but we'll have to set it up immediately." He turns his worn eyes to me. One is completely white, the blue of the other almost gone. "Harper, we're going to have you attend this session. It's vital we know what he's discovered, if anything."

Involuntarily, I flex and the heel of one foot hits the leg of my chair. "Yes, sir." I know what a debriefing is and where it's usually done.

Lazarus nods. "Good. Harper, I need you to watch closely. What happens tomorrow is crucial."

Tomorrow afternoon, while everyone else is in the back field putting Ben Dean in the ground, I'll be heading out the front door. Getting into Lilly's car and driving to a cornfield ninety miles north of Bond, to the X on Lilly's map. Once there, I'll wait until my contact arrives. Then I'll bury my purse and Lilly's keys and ride with this stranger the final few miles to Antioch and Jingo Skinner's debriefing. Afterward, I'll make sure to gas up in Antioch before driving the ninety miles home. When I get back, I'll know if it's safe to go to war.

They're so sure I'll know just by watching. But that's not the way it works.

"I can't always tell when someone's lying," I say quickly before Lazarus can adjourn this meeting or move on to something else.

"What do you mean?" he asks.

I avoid the up-and-down eyes of the council. All of their attentions snapped to my face. "I'm just saying, it's not a sure thing."

A woman with bright red hair leans forward. She has nails that have been painted pink. I can't take my eyes off them as she folds together her hands. "Then how does it work?" she asks.

There's no way to describe it. "I don't know."

"You don't know?" The woman puts away her lacquered nails and looks at Lazarus. "Well?"

Lazarus frowns. At me, then at the woman. "She doesn't know how to *explain* it, Florence."

"What I'm hearing, *Lazarus*, is that she doesn't know how to *do* it. What I would like you to do is explain to us *why* we went to so much trouble to acquire her if she's of no use to our cause."

As much as I hate to agree with her, Florence is right to be worried. My sessions with Noam haven't been progressing my abilities as quickly as I'd hoped. Our new technique has become Noam repeating in soft, tender words the thing I'm to find or the place I'm to go. He does this over and over until that one thing erupts over the horizon of my consciousness, bright and beautiful like the sun. Noam's calm voice gets me there, but once I'm at my goal, maneuvering is difficult. I still don't know how to will myself from one point to another and for our purpose—finding the main redactor—this ability is vital. I need to be able to guide John to the master. To create for him a map. And while Lazarus still won't tell me how much longer I have, I feel it has to be soon. Maybe weeks, or even just days away.

Lazarus answers the question about my abilities deftly, steering the woman back to the task at hand. "The most Harper will be able to do is offer speculation about Jingo's knowledge, albeit speculation that profits from a gift for which there are no words. It will be an honest guess, and that's all. And we can't ask her for anything more. Harper can't explain how it happens any more than we can explain the atomic structure of love. For this, the empirical does not apply."

Florence nods. She's considered his argument and has turned to stare at my nervous, bouncing knees. "Lazarus, you seem to have more faith in this girl than she has in herself."

"That could have been said about all of us at one time or another."

Florence bobs her head and turns to me. "Thank you, Harper. Now, since you're going to be up top for a few hours, there's a little protocol we need to cover. Lilly has something to give you."

Lilly comes down from her seat and drops an amber-colored pill into my palm. "Cyanide. Instant death with a minimum of suffering. We call it a kill pill, as awful as that sounds." She curls up my fingers until the pill has disappeared. "If you get caught, use it. They'll torture you to get to us."

Lazarus stands. "We have a lot of work to get done. Is there anything else before we table this meeting?"

Elsbeth stands up. She's been sitting with her husband, Charles, at the edge of the room. "John Gage might be considered worth talking about," she says.

Despite myself, my legs flex. I kick my chair.

Lazarus rises up on his old spine. "You have our attention, Elsbeth."

"What we're wanting to know is this. How do you expect us to march into battle alongside a man who's spent well over a decade as a Blue Coat? How do we know he hasn't been compromised? It's strange, don't you think, him pulling Jingo Skinner off Ben during a punitive without reprimand from Internal Affairs—"

"It's just happened," Lazarus interrupts.

But Elsbeth doesn't pause. "And now he's gotten himself wounded. He was sent to Antioch General this morning, which means they've probably already begun an investigation. God knows what he'll have to tell them."

"Are we judging our members for being hurt now?" Lazarus demands. "What must you feel about Ben?"

"You know what I'm saying. Gage was clumsy and now we're more at risk than ever."

Lazarus is on a slow boil, trying not to speak too quickly. "We're not doing this now," he says.

"You've at least thought of it, haven't you? Considered the idea that maybe he's had to make a deal with the Confederation to keep himself alive?"

Solemn, Lazarus nods. "Of course we have. What I'm asking you to consider is John's loyalty. His sixteen years served as a member of this resistance, despite huge risk to himself."

Elsbeth doesn't want to hear such logic and looks at me. "Harper, I'd like to ask you one question."

"Okay."

"This question pertains to finding the main redactor. You're to find the master prior to our war effort in order to keep millions of people from dying when they try to follow our lead and speak Red Listed words. Yes?"

"Elsbeth," Lazarus says in a low voice. "If you have a legitimate question, I suggest you ask it."

The woman steps around the table and cocks her head my way. "Might this effort be affected by feelings you're harboring for John Gage? We all saw the way you reacted when he was shot."

The blood rushes into my cheeks and Ezra sees it. She laughs a little too loud, drawing Elsbeth's attention away from my burning face.

"Do we really have time for this?" Ezra asks, her eyes on Lazarus. "I've got about a thousand better things to do—"

Elsbeth isn't deterred. She keeps her eyes on mine while interrupting Ezra. "Wouldn't a strong emotional attachment to the man in charge of shutting down the main redactor put this effort at risk? If it was my husband who stood to be killed if I couldn't produce its identity, I can guarantee you it would never happen. The pressure would absolutely kill any abilities I might have had."

Elsbeth is referring to my private conversation with Lilly.

I want to tell the council that not only are Elsbeth's claims about my feelings for John false, they're gleaned from eavesdropping. I'm almost out of my seat to do so when the reality of this situation hits me. I can't. Lazarus would know better. He'd recognize the truth of Elsbeth's allegations by my red cheeks and dry lips. In how low my voice gets when John's name is on my tongue. And then Lazarus would be responsible not just for this truth, but for the next so doggedly following it—that these newfound feelings just might get in the way. Ruin everything.

The room has gone quiet. Everyone is looking at me, waiting for me to respond. For the second time this afternoon, Ezra comes to the rescue with a nod at Elsbeth's husband, Charles. "Sounds like you'd better watch your own ass on the field, Chuck. Old Elsbeth here won't have it covered."

Elsbeth ignores Ezra. "Harper?" she prompts.

I answer with my eyes on our leader. "Love only helps, if that's what you're asking."

Lazarus gives me a coy smile and I realize that he knows anyway.

"I don't think that is what I'm asking," Elsbeth growls, embarrassment turning her pink. She was looking for an easy argument with which to oust John.

"John Gage is not a threat to this mission," I say simply.

"John Gage is a Blue Coat. John Gage rapes and murders for a living—"

"John Gage is not a threat to this mission!" I repeat, surprised at the force in my voice.

Elsbeth is enraged. "Fine. Then let's talk about Ezra."

Composure slips past Lazarus, who bangs a finger against the table. "Ezra is the third highest ranking officer at this facility. If you have something to say, Elsbeth, say it to Lieutenant James!"

Elsbeth looks over to where Ezra's smoking. She's got her legs splayed out, giving Elsbeth a little peekaboo up her short skirt.

"I'm sorry, Ezra, but I don't feel comfortable bringing you into this war either, much less our new government." The woman turns her frown back on Lazarus. "And I am not alone in this. There are more than a few of us who feel this way."

"Why?" Lazarus asks.

Elsbeth squares her shoulders. "Her background. Her lack of experience."

"Who among us has any *experience* in the roles we've had to assume? None! And let's not discuss the Lieutenant's background as if it was something seedy and not the job we've *asked* her to do," Lazarus growls. "I welcome all questions rooted in honest concern, but not those stemming from prejudice. Is there any evidence you can bring before this council to validate these concerns?"

Elsbeth takes a heavy breath and says solemnly, almost sadly, "Only the evidence Ezra affords us every day through the things she does. And the people with whom she does them." She sits back down. Charles leans in to rub her shoulder.

Head shaking, Lazarus gets up from his seat. "You enjoy the protection these people provide but you don't want to acknowledge the enormous risks they take on your behalf, is that what I'm hearing? Would any one of you have the guts and the heart to do the unimaginable things we've required of both Ezra and John? Do you know what they give up on a daily basis to protect us?" He points at Elsbeth with a crooked finger. "What are you asking? That we stone the prostitute and string up the government assassin? Let's take a vote! All in favor of doing away with these two social and political liabilities, raise your hands!" He holds up a thick palm, inviting others to join him.

No one moves.

"You're all very lucky to be where you are," Lazarus says, both his voices thick. "God willing, there won't be much actual fighting here in the wastelands. But in the capital, in every large city in this country, *thousands* of your compatriots will be giving their lives for this cause!" Lazarus nods at our humbled faces. "We will *not* begin a new society with this kind of prejudice! And toward our own, for God's sake!" he shouts, wiping the perspiration from his brow. "Now, is there anything else before we finish this meeting? Good. Meeting adjourned."

I wait for the council members to leave before stepping into the hallway. Ezra follows. She tells me in a stream of quick, mumbled words that John will be all right. He's gone up top to have his wound treated and documented. To have Jingo's bullet extracted and cataloged. He'll be back in his car, handling backup duties by dinner, then the more physical ones within a week.

"Where'd you get this information?" I have to yell after Ezra, who's on a march toward the stairs. "I thought Jingo wasn't talking!"

She calls back over a shoulder, thick legs pumping on razor-thin heels. "Skinner's not my only client."

I am not one of the group standing like stones on the prairie. They go out in the early evening, when the sun is low on the horizon and a person has to squint against the sideways light. They gather around the hole someone dug under cover of night and pay homage to Ben Dean. For most, it's the first time spent aboveground in months. Just a few moments out of doors, not one of which they're permitted to enjoy. Then back inside they'll go, the warm sun a chafe on their faces. A rebuff.

While Lazarus and the others are tending to our fallen brother, I'm marching across the front lawn toward Lilly's car. Dressed in my cleaned-up blouse and one of Lilly's old skirts that's gray and smells of mothballs. It would be dull if it weren't so tight. But it's too short, reveals me almost entirely when I sit.

I'll be up top for the next few hours. What I should be feeling is ecstasy. But I'm terrified.

I'm to follow the map Lilly's drawn, memorizing the way as I go. At my destination, I'm to get rid of this guide, leaving no evidence that could trace me back to the bunker. I tap my breast pocket. The lump there is strangely soothing. It's my kill pill. Just in case.

After ninety miles of highway, the rocked country road I'm looking for appears. It curves behind a thicket of trees, then turns up a grassy hill heavily grooved by combine wheels. I burn the map, then dig a hole in the earth and tuck the black remains inside. Relinquishing this leaves a pit in my stomach. I don't know if I've memorized all the turns and exits correctly. It could be a burial of my sure way home.

I get back in the car and wait. A few minutes later, I hear the soft sound of another vehicle on damp weeds. It's a sedan, dark blue. I keep my right hand on the manual shift and my left foot on the clutch. If I need to run, my car's nose is pointed toward the road.

The car is parked and a man gets out. He's tall and wide, blots out the last of the day's sun. "Hey." He taps four times on my window. The way he's supposed to.

My hand shakes. It slips off the button as I lower the glass.

The man leans down so I can see his face. He's mid-forties, has dark blue eyes surrounded by a grid of lines from too much laughing. It would be a giveaway if it weren't for his skin mottled from too much drink and tobacco, and the trademark scars on his face. A trio of deep scratches one of his victims etched into his right cheek.

"When did Jefferson die?" he asks.

I swallow loudly. "July the fourth."

"Harper Adams, the name's Fletcher." He offers me a hand. I slide mine through the window and we shake. "I was hoping to tell you this trip was all for naught, but Skinner's not talking. Not to anyone. Now hold out your wrists. We have to make it look real."

I climb out and Fletcher snaps on the metal cuffs, then leads me to the back of his squad car. He tells me I'll be taken in through the lobby, head down, wrists cuffed.

"One of the most wanted women in the Confederation, right under their noses." He laughs.

I'm seated in the back of his squad. As soon as the door closes, the locks follow. This Blue Coat crawls behind the wheel and looks at me through the rearview mirror. He doesn't see me sweating through my blouse. About to puke all over his backseat.

"It's the only way to get you in," he says. "Don't say a word, do what I tell you, and you'll be fine."

"Uh-huh." I try to swallow but have no spit.

"Once we're through processing, it's all smooth sailing. We'll watch the debriefing from a remote monitoring station, then I'll take you out the rear exit." Fletcher puts the squad in gear and drives us away from Lilly's car. "It's okay, Harper. You're supposed to look scared."

The bullet-proof glass that separates us gives me a good look at the back of his neck and another set of scars. Three more scratches, horizontal beneath the hairline. "What if we get stopped on the way out?"

Fletcher turns the rearview mirror so I can better see his face. "Then we'll have to pretend you're with me, which wouldn't be unusual. Do you understand?"

"Yes."

"Good."

The next turn puts us on a road that has yellow stripes down its middle and tall streetlights along its side. They're just now starting to flicker. The sun I've missed so much is already setting.

"It's okay, Harper," Fletcher says. "People think what they're told to think. As far as they know, you're a hooker busted on an All Equals charge."

I look out the window. I'm terrified by the lights of a medium-size city coming into view. We're out in the thick of a six-lane road, the traffic coming over us like a wave. A tear slips down my face but my hands aren't free to wipe it away.

Fletcher sees. "I'm on your side, Harper. Can't you do your thing? Check out my colors or energy or whatever you call it. See for yourself."

I shrug. Laugh lightly, for his benefit. I don't tell him that, as has been my problem with John and, for good or for ill, it doesn't work like that. I can't so quickly get past the color of his suit.

I keep my head down as instructed. Take the steps carefully, Fletcher's hand on my back. Inside the foyer, other Blue Coats approach. I watch their shoes as they discuss my case, the points of their toes darting around mine like fish. They whisper awful things in my ear. Some call me *whore,* half in jest, whole in earnest. They pinch me. Reach across Fletcher to grab at my breasts while talking about their days. Who they've brought in. What their wives are making for dinner.

We skip the manual scans. Instead, I'm patted down vigorously by a man with bunions large enough to bend the leather of his sandals around them. He enjoys the intimacy that doesn't cost him any credits. Hums in my ear as his hands move. Then it's all high heels and polished wing tips as we walk the wide sweep of a laminate breezeway that leads to the interrogation rooms.

Fletcher opens a door near the hall's end and removes the cuffs from my wrists. "Lazarus tells me you've been in one of these before."

It's just like the office from which Mr. Weigland and I watched Lucille. Fletcher turns on the panel's instruments and the fuzzed window clears. Jingo and another man are already sitting in the far room. The interrogator is a small, thin man with prematurely gray hair. He's splayed out. Smiling and making jokes. Jingo looks pensive. Arms crossed, legs bouncing beneath the table.

"The interrogator's with us," Fletcher tells me. He taps against the glass and the man's gray head pivots. "He'll give us time if we need it."

The interrogator smiles at us from his casual seat. Legs up on the table, heels overlapping. He unravels his arms and flips a switch on the wall. "We good to go?"

Fletcher turns to me. "You ready?"

Here is Fletcher, waiting on me. And Jingo Skinner, from the other room. "Yeah."

Fletcher presses the intercom button. Tells the interrogator to start when he's ready, then turns to me, nodding at the bank of controls. "Move the cameras anywhere you like."

I put up three images. Close-ups of Jingo's head, hands, and feet.

In the other room, the interrogating Blue Coat scoots closer to Skinner. He opens two packets of sugar and taps them into a Styrofoam cup. "Officer Skinner, yesterday morning you were presented with an unregistered vehicle on Route 50 outside Bond. Is that correct?"

Jingo smiles into camera one. "Yes, sir." He likes talking about this. It relaxes him.

I settle in. Focus.

The interrogator is a naturally gregarious man and his sparkling cloud bank of light blue is all over the room. Jingo's tentative. He wears his aura closer to the body, like a suit made of burgundy-colored cotton candy.

"You called regulation numbers on a suspected member of the resistance named Benjamin Dean, is this correct?"

Skinner flares with the memory, producing sparks of red. "Yes, sir."

"Were you able to question Mr. Dean?"

"Briefly. Until Officer Gage showed up."

"Did you confirm a relationship between Ben Dean and the resistance?"

"Yes."

"Can you elaborate, please?"

Jingo shrugs. "He had a kill pill on him."

"On him or in his mouth?"

"On him. In a pouch in his right front trouser pocket. I threw it out, not that he was likely to take it."

"So he hadn't attempted to abort his run?"

"Nope."

Lazarus told Mary that Ben's pill had been lost in the melee before he could remove himself from the equation. I won't tell her anything different.

"What did you discover about this resistance?"

A mist of orange-brown floats up from Skinner's tightly reigned colors. It's the one I was hoping for, the hue of regret.

"It's not far, I can tell you that."

"And you know that how?"

"There was less than a quarter tank of gas in his car. And the lab found trace amounts of local soil embedded in the tread of his tires."

"He was driving through. Wouldn't that stand to reason?"

"Could, I guess."

"Did Mr. Dean tell you anything about the resistance?"

Jingo's right foot begins to tap. "No." His suit of energy expands. Bleeds into the interrogator's, who retreats to a corner of the room.

"Did Mr. Dean tell you what his purpose was or where he was going?"

"No."

"Do you have any idea where this local chapter of the resistance might be located?" The man is easy with his questions. His affiliation with our side completely opaque.

Jingo runs a hand through his hair. "He was on a fast clip toward Bond when I pulled him over, about four miles up from the interrogation site. If he was a runner, he was definitely on his way to the pickup and not heading home. There was nothing in that car. I'd say he was coming from Antioch. It would match the gas usage."

"So Antioch might be our target."

Skinner's face doesn't move but his colors spark, the energetic equivalent of a smile. "That's what I'm thinking."

Fletcher leans over, grinning in admiration. "God bless Ben. As soon as he knew Skinner had him, he dumped his goods. We found some of it alongside the highway. Thank God it was a medical run and just a few bags he could pitch into the culvert. If he'd been out for food, they'd have had everything between here and Bond dug up by now."

In the other room, our man retrieves a manila folder from the table. "Can you tell us what happened? Starting with the time you came upon Mr. Dean."

Jingo nods at the file in the man's hands. "It's just like my report says. I got a call from a Service Manager out at the Banger Petroleum Station. The suspect was able to enunciate one of the new Red Listed words without event, then fled when the Service Manager attempted to keep him in custody until I could get there."

"How did you intercept Mr. Dean?" the interrogator asks.

"Shot out one of his tires. Then followed until he lost control of his vehicle and put it in a ditch."

"Was the suspect hurt when you retrieved him from the vehicle?"

"He had a pretty good gash on his head. That's about it."

"So he was lucid?"

Jingo smiles. "Oh, yeah."

"Where did you take him for the interrogation?"

A shrug. "There's a shed the city keeps for vehicles." He keeps this response brief.

"And what happened at this interrogation?"

Jingo's face falls. His vibrant red aura dulls. "He refused to answer questions. And then fucking Gage walks in."

"We'll get to that in a minute, Officer Skinner." The interrogator taps his stylus against his notepad. "First, let's talk about what happened with the suspect."

"He wouldn't talk, so I cut him." Jingo's remorse is a surprise. It rises off him like mustard-yellow steam.

"That's it? He refused to answer and so you cut him?"

Jingo looks up at the interrogator. "We meet people in the field all the time that just aren't going to talk. Femoral artery was accidentally cut and that was pretty much it."

The interrogator clears his throat. "My report tells me that your partner, John Gage, encountered you delivering Dean's fatal wounds. That after you deployed one shot that struck Officer Gage in the side, he was forced to pull you away in order to try to preserve Mr. Dean for future interrogation. Can you tell me, in your words, how Officer Gage became involved?"

Again, Jingo's feet begin to bob. His energy flares red in time with his pulse. "Gage came onto the scene without having been called. I know that much."

"So you're saying you would have preferred it if he hadn't."

"I'm saying he wouldn't have gotten shot if he'd announced himself!"

"So it's Officer Gage's fault he was shot—"

"Hell, yes! And how come we're not talking about how Officer Gage just happened to show up when he did? You don't think it's strange? Him just *being there*?"

"Were you aware that Officer Gage had been assigned watchdog duty?"

Jingo pauses. Shifts in his seat. "Yes."

"Did you disclose to Officer Gage that you were . . . just a minute . . ." The interrogator flips through his folder. Holds up a page to the fluorescent lights. "Let me read this . . . 'I think about it all the time . . . I dream about it. I wake up and all I want to do is go out and bust somebody just so I can call a number on them.' Did you say these things to Officer Gage?"

Jingo's lips turn white. "You're telling me I'm being watched?"

"That's why we call it *watch*dogging."

"*Undercover?*" Jingo shouts. "*Twenty-four seven?*"

The interviewer nods sympathetically. "Rules is rules, Officer Skinner." He picks up a box of cigarettes from the table and shakes the pack toward Jingo, who quickly pulls one free. "What I do find odd is that you haven't asked how your partner's doing."

Skinner leans forward and looks the man in the eye. "'Bullet went clean through the distal right flank with no organ or significant tissue damage.' I saw the report."

"So you checked up on him?"

Skinner looks away. "Am I done?" he asks. "Can I get back to real work now?"

"Well, it's nice to know you care." The interrogator lights his cigarette and blows a smoke ring toward the camera. He shrugs. *We ready?*

Fletcher turns to me. "Well?

I nod. "Yeah."

Fletcher gives him the okay and the interrogator waves Skinner toward the door. "If you feel you're ready, get yourself back on patrol. We have what we need."

Jingo tucks his unlit cigarette behind one ear and responds on a quick beat out the door, "Goddamned right I'm ready."

Fletcher reaches past me to turn off the equipment. "You're absolutely sure Skinner was being honest?"

"Yes." Honesty is an eccentricity of pure rage. "He doesn't know a thing."

Fletcher hauls me along behind him too fast. I can't match his pace and keep stumbling. By the time we're to the car, I've bloodied my knees and torn Lilly's skirt. Fletcher tells me he's sorry but we had to make a hasty exit. And it didn't hurt either, my falling down. Looks normal that way. It would have been strange, him opening doors for me and the like.

Inside his squad car, Fletcher offers me moist towels from his first aid kit. I wipe the smeared blood off my legs and reassemble my face and hair in the rearview mirror. Fletcher tells me I'm to stick to the same route going back as I took coming in. Should keep it just a mile or two above the speed limit. Too slow and I'll draw attention. There's a gas station in Antioch, west side. I'm to fill up there.

I can't stop thinking about Jingo. He's already out on the roads, patrolling. I may pass him on my way back home. We may pass him on the way to Lilly's car. Everything Fletcher's told me has already spilled out of my head.

I don't remember digging up Lilly's keys or sliding them into the ignition or saying good-bye to Fletcher. Or leaving the soft earth for the paved road. I keep having to check for my final turn. It's dark and I'm worried I've missed it. I can't remember the number of my exit, so I watch for the cluster of trees I've memorized. Three of them. Tall, thick firs in front of a row of deciduous. In the dark of night, they all look the same.

My turn comes up fast. I'm in the wrong lane and have to jog over quickly. No traffic, but still I'm sweating. A Blue Coat would have pulled me over for the offense. I drive for an hour, fighting to stay lucid under this moonless night. It's a giddy rush of relief when a sign for Bond erupts into view. At the same time, a light the size of a thumb goes on beneath my left sleeve. I sit forward, nearly knocking my head on the windshield.

Sweet Jesus Christ.

I forgot to fill up in Antioch.

There are two bays. I choose the one nearest the road. The pump is a relic with old-style gauges that turn over, numbers clicking into place on black wheels. There's no outside slot for the pay card Lilly gave me. Not out here, six miles north of Bond.

I can see someone watching from the office. A man wearing the white shirt and black tie of a Service Manager. I wave and smile. Put in ten credits' worth of gas, a third of a tank. Walk easily to the door.

"Evening," he says.

"Evening," I return, social and even. Head toward the back wall, toward coolers full of cold drinks.

I remove a soda and wipe the moisture from the bottle. It feels good in my hot hand. As the door closes, I see the man looking. He's watching me with drawn eyes. Wondering why I'm coming in so late, so close to his quitting time. Why I look so rumpled in my torn skirt and wrinkled blouse. Like I've been run over.

Keep it together, Harper. The walls are beginning to shake some. Time to check out and leave.

"All set?" the man asks as I approach.

"Yes, thank you." I set my soda on the counter and pull out the pay card Lilly gave me.

He swipes the orange card through his machine. "Where you from?"

"Out east."

"Out east?"

I let my eyes wander, as if I'm considering a snack. "Wernthal."

"Long way from home, aren't you? Out here for family?"

"Business."

"What business might that be?"

He's trying to pull something out of me. *Remember the list, Harper.* I try. But can't. So we stare at each other over the small counter. Wait for the approval code together while I debate the answer.

"It's pretty boring stuff."

"Bore me." The Manager picks at his teeth with a pinky. They're nice and shiny white. Probably caps. Unusual for out here, where there's a paucity of rural dentists.

"I'm an accountant."

He pushes off the back wall. Catches me looking down at the reader now flashing the word *Approved.* "Really? Who you work for?"

I hold out my hand. "I'm sorry, but I'm in a bit of a hurry. Could I have my card back?"

The man holds it just beyond my reach. "I asked who you work for." His voice has dropped. It's a trap.

There's a word I shouldn't say somewhere in my response. A word I should no longer be able to squeeze out of my mouth without seizing up. It's new, one I won't know. Maybe released this evening, when I wasn't watching. And he's not going to give me back my card without an answer.

Who do you work for?

"For the people," I answer with a smile, spreading wide my collar. All cleverness and cleavage.

It does the trick. The man relaxes. Even smiles with me. It creeps up onto his stiff, pale face and forces his hand to drop the orange card into my palm. "I'm sorry about all this. We get these notices from the Department of Transportation telling us there's been some activity and you can guess the rest."

"It's okay."

The man sighs. "It's just, if we don't ask these questions, it's our asses on the line. You know?"

"Don't worry about it."

The man scratches his head. "These people they're looking for are on the move. They'll have to stop and get . . . *petroleum*." He laughs lightly. "I'm supposed to be watching . . ."

I offer him an out while backing through the front door. "That's the way it is when you're a government manager. I know."

The man's eyes narrow. I've said something wrong.

Who do you work for?

I work for the government.

Government.

I turn and run through the front door to the car, hurry to hit the locks, get the damned key in the ignition. The Manager chases after me. He grabs my door handle as I tear away. In the mirror, I see him tumbling to the ground. He leaps up, cursing, and races back to his office. To his phone, where he'll be calling a Blue Coat.

There's no choice about where to go. Anywhere that isn't a series of red arrows on the map leading back to the bunker will lead me too far away and get me lost. There's only one even playing field upon which to fight.

I head toward the farm slowly, without my lights on. I don't turn down the rocked drive as it's too quiet. Not even the cicadas are singing their night song, so I go on around, turn up the grass from a planed spot behind the bend, and pull into the deep cover of the field. Gently, I open the door, then press it closed even more gently. For the second time tonight, I bury Lilly's keys next to the front wheel and, keeping low, make my way to the crest of the hill. The thought strikes me that I might die here yet, in the farmhouse where I broke my slate.

It's pitch-black. Despite the stars, it's a moonless night and the knob leading from the porch to the kitchen doesn't move easily in my sweating palm. I bump into a chair on my way to the sink. Stand, shaking, at the basin. I look out the window and watch the tall grass along the drive wave in the wind. Far away, in some obscure place over the hill and the hill thereafter is a light that's reflecting this long, long way. It allows me a backward view of the kitchen, the top of the doorway leading to the porch, a nail driven into a wall on which some picture used to hang, a pair of eyes.

"You're home late, Harper." Jingo Skinner steps out of the darkness. "Got a call from Karl over at the petrol station. He thought you might be headed this way." I see his face reflected in the glass like the half-moon that's on its other side. The things he wants to do to me are in his eyes. "You came in like you knew I was waiting for you. Strange, you being out today. Just an hour earlier, and I would have missed you."

He's already behind me. Has a hand trailing up my skirt. With a flick of his wrist, my panty hose are torn, opened from crotch to knee, and his fingers are digging against that soft flesh. They're leaving pink trails that should hurt but don't. It's like I'm not here.

This whole thing could happen without me. I could evacuate my body, do it the painless way. But then I wouldn't be able to carry out my orders. Survive to bring back the information that Skinner knows nothing. To fight in the war.

"Do you want to hear the numbers?" he asks, working to give himself more space. I can feel the hard-worn fibers of his trousers on my leg. "I've been waiting for this too fucking long." His hands rip my blouse, the one I ran in. It parts easily, reveals my shoulders, my back, my waist above the skirt. "You fucking Monitors . . ." He's saying other things. How we live in ivory towers. How we like to do the easy part of keeping order and leave the muck and the dirt to people like him. "Fucking cunt." He kicks out my ankles so I'll buckle. And I do so beautifully. I imagine what Jingo Skinner must be seeing as I fall. My hips thrust out, my hands grappling for a better hold on the countertop, my chin hitting its edge, the skin there splitting over bone. They are actions of reluctant submission I perform for him. And my patron is pleased.

This isn't supposed to be the way it goes. Ezra's been training me. I'm supposed to know what to do. My daughter isn't supposed to find out later that I was raped and murdered. I gave up too much for this.

No. *No more.*

Skinner unzips his trousers, leaving them belted. He's going to pull himself free through the fly without lowering his pants. It's smart. He won't be encumbered by the material bunched around his knees, making him susceptible to a shove. It's obvious he's done this a thousand times before. He begins toward me. I don't wait for him to get here.

I grab one of Skinner's hands and spin, yanking him off balance. Infuriated, he comes back at me with a punch, his fist crossing my midsection on its way to my face. Centered the way Ezra taught me, and with all my weight sunk into my heels, I whip up my left elbow while twisting my body quick. It catches him in the upper arm, diverts the thrown punch. And the bone. *Snap.* The sound of it breaking is awful.

"Jesus Christ!" Jingo falls to the floor, screaming. He pulls out his pistol and fires.

The bullet rips my sleeve. Grazes the mounded rise of muscle beneath, but it's nothing. A scratch. Instead of pushing Skinner away, I pull him in, toward my open mouth. I find the meat of his hand and bite as hard as I can. The gun falls to the floor as Skinner screams. He tries to yank free, but I won't let go. I'm like a dog with a bone. Bite harder until something solid snaps and Jingo falls to his knees.

I spit him out. Make it all the way to the outer door before being stopped.

Jingo uses his good elbow to catch me in the side of the head. The world is doubled. Becomes loud, a clap of thunder. I crumble to the floor. Vaguely, I'm aware of being hefted onto his shoulder, then dumped down a basement stairwell and locked behind its door. I'm left lying on the steps as Jingo pulls out his phone and starts punching in numbers.

On the other side of the closed door, Skinner is breathing heavy, his speech gritted by pain. "Finally caught the bitch." It's a glib bit of boasting but he doesn't sound pleased. He sounds like someone about to pass out. He's talking to John Gage, asking for help. For "goddamned backup," he says. "I'm bleeding pretty good, partner. They tell me down at Antioch you're following me pretty close . . . good goddamned thing. Might need a ride to the hospital. Better get here fast." The phone is dropped and Jingo sits down. Not that much later, the front door squeaks open and is slammed shut. John couldn't have been more than five miles away.

"Skinner!" he shouts, stomping into the house.

"Jesus Christ, it took you long enough!" Jingo replies. He's close. Just beyond the basement door. "She tried to bite my fucking hand off! And she broke my goddamned arm!"

John sighs. "You need to get to the hospital." The door swings open and I see him there. A huge black form. "I thought you'd already finished her?" Except he says it as a question. *You didn't finish her?*

Jingo is standing behind him, drained and pale. His arm wrapped in a beehive of bloodied sheets. "I haven't even carried out her punitives yet!"

John crouches down so my face is obscured from Jingo's vision.

Skinner's voice comes round from behind him. "I'm not leaving," he wheedles. "Not until I get my due, man. And that Monitor is my fucking due! She's not going to get away from me twice!"

John reaches out a hand and turns my head from side to side. He's being too gentle. I duck my head further beneath the prow of his head so Jingo won't see.

"Come on, man," Skinner wheedles, his voice dimming. "Let me get to it before I bleed to fucking death over here . . ."

"Harper . . ." John whispers low, beneath Skinner's voice. His finger trails along the abrasions on my face.

"Christ, I feel weird, man . . ."

"Shut up, Jingo!" John barks suddenly, making me jump. He's angry about what Skinner's done to me.

I hold a finger over my lips. *Sssshhh.* Don't give us away.

"What's up your ass . . . just saying . . ." but Jingo doesn't finish his thought.

We both jump as his body hits the floor.

John moves and there is Skinner, laid out on the wooden slats of the old floor, head lolling to the side. For a few seconds, John holds two fingers around the Blue Coat's wrist, then nods down at me, still crouched in the darkness of the stairs.

"His pulse is pretty slow. I'm going to call in an ambulance for him while I get you back to the bunker."

The look on my face gives me away.

John takes me by the hands and gently pulls me up. "I'll

say you ran and I had to go after you. But we can't kill him, Harper. They'd tear this whole county apart."

I make it through the living room and out into the kitchen with only the slightest bit of help from John. Once we push through the door leading to the covered porch, I hear the rain. It stops me. My legs are unsteady enough on solid ground. Out in the muddy, heavily pebbled drive, I don't know how they'll do.

"You okay?" John asks.

I nod. "I didn't realize it was raining."

John opens the outer door and I go through. I make it all the way to the broken walkway, and then to the drive. Each drop of rain is like a little weight. All of them together are slowly driving me into the soft ground.

"You okay?" John puts an arm around my shoulders.

"Thank you," I say. I'm crying now. And not really sure why. "Thank you, John."

I don't want him to see and try to walk more quickly. *One, two, three, four . . .* Counting each step. I reach the car and bend down to pick up the key. But I never make it back up. Somehow the ground has come to rest on my chest, and the mud against my cheek. I can feel the rain on my back for only a few seconds. Then nothing.

Twelve, thirteen, fourteen . . . What am I counting? Just a minute ago, it was footsteps. But now it's something else. *Fifteen, sixteen, seventeen.* Pills. I'm sitting at my kitchen table, counting yellow and black Occlusia. I'm dreaming about before. About bees in my stomach, retching until my sides ache. I don't force myself to remember leaving Veracity. I've gone straight to the part where death snatches me up for just a few straight-line moments before rudely dropping me back in my body.

"Harper?" a woman is asking.

I look up and see a red-haired nurse leaning over me. I'm back in Chalmers. In a hospital bed with the rails put up.

The red-haired nurse is angry with me. She clucks her tongue while squirting a needle full of something into my IV tube. "I couldn't have children," she says, and gives the clear tube a flick to get it dripping. "Some people never learn to be grateful for what they already have, I guess." She's talking about me leaving my daughter. Trying to kill myself when there's a child to be cared for.

I'd be angry with her, but she doesn't know what's really going on here. I had to give my baby away like this. I had to swallow seventeen Occlusia in order to prove myself unfit. Have the Confederation take her away and put her with someone else so she wouldn't be used as bait, like Hannah.

"Harper!" someone screams.

The red-haired nurse is no longer here. Or the IV. Someone else bobs into view. Lilly.

She's shaking me. "Wake up!" Her glasses magnify the edges of an earthen room.

We might still be in the bunker. I drift away thinking about it when someone else comes along shouting.

"Wake her up!" And, "Don't let her fall asleep!" This time it's Ezra.

She and Lilly begin a discussion about my body. I have a concussion. Cracked ribs. Several gashes and a fever. Lilly thinks I need to be dropped into a bucket of ice. Other people I can't see make soft, agreeable sounds. "Good idea. We'll prepare the wash basin."

"Harper!" It's John. His face hovers above mine. "Wake up!"

For some reason, I'm wondering if he knows about my suicide, though I know he must. For all I know, he might have been there. I wonder if John hates me for it. I don't want him to hate me. For what I had to do to Veracity. For my prejudice. He's got to understand, trust isn't something

I can afford anymore. One more time losing it and I might lose all faith.

"I had to," I say, straining to make the words airborne, no longer even sure to what I'm referring.

John shushes me. He picks me up and carries me down the hospital's long halls. I focus on the white acoustic tiles above us. Between each one is a bead of black, packed-in dirt. I don't remember them like that at Chalmers. Their ceilings were all white, even the seams.

"We're taking you to get a bath," Lilly is whispering in my ear.

Now it's not just John holding me. I'm lying in a cot made of arms, somewhere near the kitchen. I know only by the odors of meals previously prepared.

Around me, people are talking.

"We didn't salvage any antibiotics from Ben's run, did we?"

"Not enough."

"We've arranged a drop off in Kern, between here and Springfield."

"Where?" This is Lazarus. "Skinner is still on patrol . . ."

"I'm handling Skinner."

"No one's handling anything until . . ."

"Until what?" It's Ezra. I can feel her bangled wrist as it reaches over my face. The cool wood of her bracelet touches me on the forehead and I open my eyes. I'm in a room with dirt walls. Our kitchen in the bunker.

"Hold her still now."

I look down. See Lilly with a syringe set level with my shoulder. Ezra holds my arm still as the needle is depressed. It doesn't hurt. I don't struggle until someone tries to take off my shirt. I bat at their hands until John comes over. He slides the material down instead of up, so I won't have to lift my arms and suffer the cotton scraping over my swollen face and split chin. My trousers are pulled off and I'm left in my underwear and bra, all the while airborne and juggled by a dozen arms.

"Get her in the tub." This is Lazarus, both voices warped with worry.

Down I go, into a vat of ice. I'm shocked out of my reverie. Forced back into my body by the pain. The water burns like it's dissolving skin and muscle. I shout and twist. No one lets go.

HAPTER

TWENTY-THREE

Sepsis. Lilly calls it. A mild case of poison in the blood. Had I chosen to die, I would have. That simple, she says. Good thing I decided to fight. *Though the days lost tending to me . . .* She clucks her tongue. *It was the worst possible timing. So much to be done.* And me lying around. Requiring too much water.

Lilly tells me that Skinner lost a bag of blood and a fair portion of his good wrist. Parts of it turned black. Some of the muscle and a strip of tendon had to be removed. Jingo took a week off for new weapons training, as he now has to hold a gun in his weak left hand. Best of all, he knows nothing of us. She then tells me John reported to his superiors I was killed that night. His explanation—I wouldn't confess. So far, his superiors seem to be willing to accept the word of a highly respected Blue Coat. But sooner or later, someone's going to want to see my body. Hopefully, we'll have gone to war by then.

Lilly tells me before I can ask, "John is fine."

A wound I somehow got in my right thigh has left a scar the size of a fist. It looks like a mouth grown into the meat of my outer leg. The skin there is ruffled in places. Curled around Lilly's stitches, lavender where it's just started to heal.

"It's not going to get much better-looking," Lilly says. She's retrieving a tube that's been inserted into my wound. A drainpipe for the pus, one of our drinking straws.

It doesn't move easily. My skin's tried to bond with it and

tears some as the straw comes out. It's two weeks before I'm cleared to resume my training with Ezra. Then another few days before she lets me go rounds.

I've tried talking to Lazarus about my concerns that one of our own is a traitor. Someone gave up Ben Dean, and perhaps me as well. I feel it, even if I can't prove it. It's in my mind night and day, but Lazarus doesn't feel the same way. He's committed to his idea that down here we're all family, and it's made him blind. I sit outside his room at night when the feeling gets bad. Nod at anyone walking by. I want them to know I'll be here until we go up top. Reading library books under the single bulb that hangs conveniently over his door.

My training sessions with Noam go nowhere. I can't tell a man from a woman anymore. Or navigate hallways or walls. Unfamiliar spaces become traps. I can get myself inside them but, once there, don't know a redactor from a computer screen. When this happens, Amy has to hurry up and pull me out again. She turns up the lights, dips my hands in cold water and I'm thrown backward, into my body. Crashing into failure, throwing up more than I used to.

I've done everything I know to produce the identity of the main redactor, but it eludes me. Lazarus says he's not worried and I believe him. But he doesn't know the whole story. Since my illness, I've stopped seeing colors. And I don't know how to fix it.

Helen Rumney is on the television. She's standing at a podium on the National House lawn, the same one President uses for the early morning national talks. She's wearing a bright pink suit, an extraordinary color for a Manager, very nearly taboo. She's smiling jubilantly at the camera. Mr. Weigland isn't there.

I grab a notepad and sharpened pencil. It's midnight in the middle of the week. *Something's wrong.*

"Good evening." Her smile is huge. "We have some

unexpected news. We've successfully lobbied the Tracking and Data group to have one of our new programs implemented immediately. Ladies and gentlemen, get ready to enter a new era of security. The first true satellite surveillance program in the Confederation's history has been cleared for operation. I'm happy to announce that SKEYE is officially a go!"

Oh, Christ.

Manager Rumney explains how this technology will prevent resisters from banding together. There will be no way for them to run. Or, once grouped, to move. *Anything bigger than a bison gets tracked. Too many vehicles driving in the same direction get checked. No questions asked.*

"Starting at five a.m. eastern standard time this morning, it will be a maximum of five people per vehicle. No more caravans. No more unchecked travel. Admittedly, in the past, there has been a lack of coverage in our skies. The Pandemic took out our flying forces, our ability to adequately patrol the vast and barren wastelands where the socially inept have been wont to travel. With the SKEYE program, our satellites will fill this gap. There will be nowhere we cannot see. No way for errant souls to band together beyond the easy reach of well-secured society . . ."

I race out of the library toward the sleeping quarters. Try not to think about what might have happened to the man who, in his own way, saved me—my friend Mr. Weigland.

I come upon Lazarus making laps around his room. Despite the gravity of my message, he doesn't stop walking.

"Lazarus! Did you hear me?"

Lilly and Noam are already here. Still in their nightclothes.

"You're sure?" Lilly asks.

I nod. "I'm sure."

Noam is almost in tears. "We had twenty-six T-Units lined up." These large manned vehicles were our sure ride to war.

Lilly turns to Lazarus. It's strange, how beautiful her eyes are without the thick, cloudy lenses to obscure them. She's holding them in her hands, has forgotten to put them on. "What are we going to do?"

"We have a backup."

"We waited too long!" Noam is wearing an expression I've not seen before. Resentment. He means they waited too long for me. "And now we don't have transport and we still don't have the identity of the main redactor!" He peeks over and catches my wide eyes. "I'm sorry, Harper. It's just . . . this is an unimaginable situation."

"That's enough, Noam," Lazarus scolds.

"We've spent most of our lives waiting for this!"

"Noam . . ."

"How are we going to tell everyone?" he shouts. Next to him, Lilly jumps. "There's no transport to our production site! No way to announce the war!"

Lazarus marches over. "That's enough! Regional bunkers have enough time to mobilize to their nearest hubs before SKEYE goes live. Let's go let them know."

Noam's face falls. Rage becomes despondence.

"We've always known this was a possibility," Lazarus says, looking wistfully at Lilly's white face.

"It's too dangerous," Noam says quietly.

Lazarus nods my way. "Harper, would you excuse us?"

I get up and leave, listening to them all the way down the hall.

"We'll have to take a vote."

"No vote to be taken."

"It's supposed to rain. Too much, I think."

"Then we'll gather tonight and go to war the day after, when it's had some time to dry."

"Are we still bringing in the bard for this?"

"Wouldn't have our last night here any other way."

Not a minute past one, it rains like the sky is coming down. I know by the darts of dark earth forming in the ceiling. The moisture worries Noam. He has three of the younger people make a late-night run out to the river that separates the barren fields behind us. They chop down a tree of the right size. Bring it in through the back entrance and prop it up in the center of the main room. I hear from multiple people that in all the time they've been down here, there's never been such a rain. It's brought eight or ten inches in only two hours. *Must be a sign.*

I don't sleep. I lie in my cot watching my own dirt ceiling. Any sign of black fingers coming down through the beams and I'll go sleep in the library, where there are steel girders and joists and tall, heavy bookcases that would support a collapse. Getting rest is a wasted effort, especially with the clatter of exuberant, nontired voices outside my door.

I step out into the hall and find it full of new people that have been packed in tight. They're wet and chattering. Smell like mildew. Despite the rain that's soaked them to the marrow, there's an excitement coming off them that makes our bunker glow. They've been up top, if just for a few hours. They've heard the good news. *Tonight, there's to be a party. Assuming it quits raining soon enough, we'll have our war.*

I walk to the back entrance and watch them come in like waves. Every few minutes the door opens and six or seven new people come tripping in, all of them brought over from surrounding bunkers. Soaked and confused, their shoes muddy, they stumble to where we point. Hours ago at their bunkers, someone shook them out of a sleep and bundled them into whatever transit they could find at such late notice. Cars, trucks, even field machines like tractors have hustled them to the pass, a spot far behind the field that shields our emergency entrance. They walked the final two miles with a few of our crew out making birdcalls to guide them.

Amy is one of the welcoming team. She stands just inside the mouth of the rear passage handing out brown bananas as people filter through. "This way to the restroom. If you'd like to change, if you brought your own clothes, we have a room set up. Sorry we don't have any extra blankets or towels. This is the last of our fruit. If you'd like some tea, we have sassafras and pine needle, someone will show you to the kitchen."

I tap her on the shoulder between groups. Ask her where they're coming from.

Amy's not so friendly now that I've slipped off my pedestal. "Everywhere within five hours of here," she answers without the courtesy of her attention. She's smiling at a pair of girls fresh out of the rain. Hands them each a blackened piece of fruit.

The two girls are drenched. Their clothes wrinkled against their bodies. They don't have coats like most of the others. Just wool hats and leather boots.

"Do you know where we can sleep?" one of them asks.

I look down the hall. All the floor space is gone, covered with other damp, rumpled bodies.

"Sure. Follow me."

I take the girls to my room. Pull the thin mattress from my bed and open up the poorly sewn bag. The batting is comprised of old, worn-out clothing, feathers, and straw. I spread it on the floor and place the old cover on top, tucking the corners beneath.

"Go ahead," I say.

Immediately, they climb in.

When I get to the library, it turns out I'm not the only one whose given up her room. Every single one of us is here, lying in various stages of sleep on the floor. We're head to toe a woven mat. No bit of concrete or carpet left uncovered.

I come into this dream halfway dreamt. A mercy.

Veracity is already to the point where she's thanking me for what I've done and is just about to use her first Red Listed word as an act of trust.

"I understand now," she says, just like always. Her new mother's hand reaches in to give her a tissue. My daughter takes it, uses it. Looks up at where I'm always watching from my clear cell. "I know you were just trying to keep what happened to Hannah from happening to me."

God, not tonight. Not this dream. I look down at my see-through hands. Try to will one of them to pinch the other, but they're against me and won't leave my lap.

My daughter leans back and puts her head against the metal bar of the light. "You were just trying to give me back my name . . ."

"No! Please!" I must say it out loud. I can feel my lips move. Am aware of a subtle shift in my waking world. Of someone over me.

"Vera . . ."

I hear the electricity before I see it behind her, blackening her long hair. Binding her to the ugly lamp with the swing-arm head. She can't move. Can't stop the metallic buzz issuing from her mouth that's traveled up from her slate. All the while, she's looking at me, not able to change her expression. Then her eyes roll up into her head so all I see are the whites and the thin veins there becoming wide. Then all the rest of it that's too horrible even to contemplate. It ends only when Veracity's new mother rushes in with a pillow at the end of her hands and knocks her free from the pole. But it's too late.

"Harper."

End this, Mommy. Finish this.

"Harper!"

See, Mom. See.

"Harper!" It's Lilly above me. She's using both arms to shake me awake.

"Lilly?"

"*Ssshhhhh.* You're yelling!" She points at the sleeping forms who're stirring around us. "Only one more hour to dawn. Let them rest."

She starts to leave and I put out a staying hand. "When are we going to war?"

"What?"

"Tomorrow morning. What time are we going to war?"

"Six o'clock we set out. We rendezvous with the rest of our troops at seven. We'll find out then if we've successfully taken the hub. If so, we'll broadcast our mission to the rest of the country and invite them to join us."

Thirty hours from now, if I don't have the identity of the main redactor, my baby will die. Lazarus will broadcast his plea, and in their zeal to join us, she and hundreds of thousands of others will try to speak a Red Listed word. If the redactor isn't taken down . . . I can't imagine. I have almost no time left to find it. The thought sucks all the moisture from my mouth.

Overnight, we've grown from a bunker of forty-eight to a small town of over two hundred. We have enough food to feed our original group for a few weeks but won't be down here that long. So the council decides to plunder the next month's reserves. Most of us have known nothing but the frugality of poor supplies and spotty contacts. The bucketfuls of food going by have drawn everyone out.

"Excuse me," says our cook, pushing by with a plastic tub full of vegetables between her pink arms. Inside the tub are white bulbs of onions, gray-brown heads of garlic, orange-red tomatoes, and tan, unshelled ears of corn with their tassels hanging out. Someone's brought fresh produce. Behind the cook, two men follow with meat. Brown paper packages closed with twine. What's inside we can only imagine. Everyone parts for the procession and sticks their head into the resulting wake to watch tonight's dinner as it's laid out on the kitchen's round table. Some people will stay here for the rest of the day. Eyes glazed over. Lips moist.

I retrieve a mug of hot water and a packet of green tea.

When I turn to leave, Rita Ramirez is watching me. The seventeen-year-old girl who was beat up by her boyfriend and brought to the bunker against her will.

"Hungry?" she asks, a carrot dangling from her mouth like a cigarette. "They've opened the vegetable pantry."

Rita is luminous today. Perhaps nerves about tomorrow have colored her skin. Or maybe it's excitement. War or no, the last time this girl saw the up top, she was only eleven years old, and it's obvious how much she's missed it.

"No." I hold up my mug. "Just wanted something to drink."

Rita follows me out of the kitchen and through the main hall. "You have something to wear for tonight?"

"No. Do you?"

We have to step delicately around people who're sitting on the floor, staked out on their bedrolls.

"No." Rita jumps over a woman still snoring beneath her covers. "I don't give a shit about that party."

"So you're not going." I try not to turn it into a question.

"Just long enough to find a date. I hear a whole busload of boys are coming from Springfield."

Rita moves ahead of me. She walks backward, stepping on unoccupied blankets and vagrant limbs as we move toward the hall. "Too bad you can't shake off that problem you're having with your *sight,* or whatever you call it."

People around us stop milling about and plummet into silence.

"It will come in time," I lie, ignoring my concern about how she knows.

Rita stops under the hall's threshold and asks loudly, "Without that main redactor, we're screwed, right?"

I step closer. Lift my hand and she reflexively pulls away. "What are you so worried about?" I laugh easily, as if I'm anything but worried. Remove a cobweb from her hair and hold it up to the overhead light. "You might want to clean up before the party."

Rita grits her teeth and marches away. Everyone else lies back down again, eager to be soothed.

It's my last session with Noam. We're in the only room not crowded with dozens of sitting or sleeping bodies.

"We're going to do some exercises today that might help us narrow down the field," Noam says. "You already know our ultimate goal. The number, letter, or name of the master. Whatever will provide us its exact location. We know it's in the Geddard Building, sitting in a room with a few thousand other redactors just like it." He nods at Amy, who's holding a large rolled-up piece of paper in her hands. She comes over and tosses it on the floor. We watch together as it unfurls. "This is an accurate schematic of the basement. We'd like you to simply try and choose a quadrant. See if you can't get a feel for direction."

I nod. *I know the drill.*

Noam pulls me away from the wall and centers me in front of the map. "Now close your eyes and try to relax. This is just the first try. Nothing life or death hinges on today's efforts. Okay?"

Life and death do hang on today's efforts, but I agree anyway and close my eyes. "Okay."

"Now, try to imagine a room full of boxes. And, in it, the main redactor, the master that will turn off all the others. The master that will turn off all the others . . . the master . . . that will turn off all the others . . . the master . . . the master . . . the master . . ."

I'm fatigued, and today it's a help, fading out and listening to Noam's undulating voice. As he talks me into a trance-like state, I float away into that basement room. Come back quickly with a solid direction.

"It's in the northeast quadrant."

"You sure?" Noam smiles.

"Yeah."

He takes Amy's clipboard. Stabs at the page with the tip of his finger. "As you know, they have the redactors set up in a master-slave configuration. If we accidentally take down a redactor that's *not* the master, the room, the building, the whole city gets locked down."

I knew about the alarm that would be sounded, but not this. John will get trapped. Any headway made by the first exercise has just been lost. I begin to sweat.

Noam puts a hand on my head, like my father used to do when he had something bad to tell me. "Lazarus didn't want you to know because he didn't want you to feel pressured."

"Well, I do, Noam. I feel pressured."

He shrugs. "This is our last shot. I'd like to try blindfolding you and giving you directions down into the basement as they've been provided to us."

"It doesn't work like that . . ."

"Please."

I nod. "Okay." I'll try anything at this point.

Amy wraps a black piece of cloth around my head as Noam begins to talk.

"West central Wernthal," he begins slowly. "A hundred feet below the Geddard Building. Encased in layers of lead and concrete. Try and travel in through the piping. Through a vent off the corner of State and Wellesley. Follow the heat backward home to the fields of turbines and air conditioners as big as cars . . ."

This isn't how it works. I travel only as I'm pulled. The journey begins at its end. Not the other way around.

"Noam, this isn't working." It's hard to explain to him why.

Poor Noam looks as if I've just popped his last balloon, although he already understands these basic truths. It's a trick of the mind, thinking we're all separate. Walking around disconnected from one another, without the same access to all there is to know. All one needs to do is shift focus. Sounds easy enough.

"Okay," Noam says, impatient. "We'll do it the old way."

He begins the chant to which I've become so familiar. I close my eyes and let his soft voice become a picture of the master. I imagine it as tall and wide, big as a room with a million flickering lights. I envision what it does, feel the heat coming off it like an oven.

Harper, do you think you can do this? Noam's worry has reached out and caught me. I'm pulled away from the redactors too fast, before I can mark my way back to them, or get a glimpse of the right one.

When I open my eyes, Amy sees I've come up short and starts to cry. Noam walks over and pats me on the shoulder.

"We'll try again later," he says, adding in a broken voice, "No worrying. It's counterproductive."

By midafternoon, there's an hour-long line for the shower. Bars of soap have been set out next to a gallon jug of shampoo. Someone's put out a mirror.

It's been weeks since I've seen my reflection. Even so, I have to look. *"Jesus."*

There's a trail of raised skin just under my hairline from some old wound I don't remember. The cut on my chin has been sewn shut, but Lilly's needle could only do so much. The deepest parts are still raw and look like day-old meat.

I walk back to my room and find Ezra putting on her makeup at my table.

"Come here," she says.

I sit down and she drops some folded fabric into my lap. They're clothes for tonight's party. A short black skirt and a sheer yellow blouse.

"These are on loan for tonight only," she says, straight-faced. It takes me a few seconds to understand she's joking.

I pull off my trousers. Work the skirt slowly up each thigh. It's snug. I don't want it to tear. "Thank you."

Ezra waves at me with the wand from her mascara. "Shut

your eyes." She applies my new face tenderly, taking care around the wounds that are still healing.

I pucker my lips like she instructs. Pout so she can draw me a fuller set.

"Just so you know. Everyone is on lockdown tonight. That means no getting drunk and no going up top. You see anyone stumbling around or starting toward the back exit, you let someone know." Ezra drops the pink tube back in her makeup bag. "You're welcome, by the way. You look halfway decent."

Lazarus is wearing a long orange tunic and, on his head, a brown and orange cap. He leads me past couples lined up in the hall, giggling around pockets of spilled beer, and to the front hall, which has become nearly impassable. New people are standing around in clusters speaking loudly and in animated voices about what they saw last night on their way over. Lightning. Rain. A few frightened deer on the country roads caught in the flame of their headlights. Women are wearing too much makeup. Men are close-shaven. Everyone is smoking and drinking, filling up the air with clouds and cologne.

Most of the people near the stage have been born underground. I know by their age and their slate-free necks. They are largely teenagers, some in their early twenties. Their paper-white skin shows no moles or freckles, holdovers of sunburns or windburns, exposure to the topside elements. Without slates, their undisrupted necks look romantically long.

Some of these bunker-born people appear underdeveloped. Even with the required supplements they receive from birth, there are a handful of young men and women markedly shorter than the others. This lost height is in their legs. There beneath the hemline of the women's dresses and pressed against the outer line of the men's trousers, their legs have an unnatural, outward bow to them, leaving a large space where their knees should be.

Lazarus leads me toward the makeshift stage beyond them. It's a series of cardboard boxes that have been pushed together to form a ten- or twelve-foot-long rectangle. An old man is already standing in its center, his arms waving to calm down the crowd.

"Who is that?" I ask. ·

"He's a storyteller." Lazarus answers with his head turning from one end of the room to the other.

"Looking for someone?"

"Yes." Lazarus turns back to me. "John. He'll only be here for a few hours before he has to get back to Antioch. They're flying him out to Wernthal tonight."

My face must lose all its color. Lazarus smiles and turns to the crowd, a finger held to his mouth. Immediately, they're quieted.

I lean in quickly and whisper into his ear. "You're sure John's coming?"

He nods yes. "Quiet now. You'll want to hear this."

"Why is he coming?"

Lazarus leans down, amusement and frustration compressing his lips. "To see you. Now, *ssssshhhh*." He pushes on my shoulders until they're parallel to the stage. "Listen."

"Anna! Anna!" the storyteller yells. "Come on now, daughter." He beckons one of these pale young women with a puckered finger. "Move along! We have an audience to entertain!" His words are coming out strange, like they're getting caught on his tongue and tripping out of his mouth. I wonder if this is what I've heard Lazarus call an *accent*. "These fine people haven't risked life and limb to watch your old father tell tales."

Arms go up in protest. "Tell us about the beforetime," the audience begs. Their hunger is all over them. They long for stories about lives lived anywhere and anytime other than here and now.

The old man nods and holds up a hand. "Sovereignty!" he shouts.

"Sovereignty!" the crowd responds loudly.

On the stage, the old man bows his head slightly. "My home is across the sea. In a faraway country where God walks freely through the land. Through mountains made soft by snow and fields the color of the sun. All of it is a church. There, when you speak to God, you get answers. Clear as my voice, they come, and you understand them.

"In the land of my mother and father, we coveted sustenance for our souls as much as sustenance for our bodies. And, thusly, we kept our words as if they were made of gold." Such a voice this man has. The way he sounds isn't a sound at all. It's a river into which words are thrown.

"We knew the difference between that which cannot be expressed and that which *must*. We understood that while words are a path taking us only so far, they are requisite to the journey. They are like road maps that show us which way to go.

"Tonight's entertainment will be short and sweet, as tomorrow we go to war. This final tale will be the story of our landing. 'The Fallen Queen.'"

The storyteller holds up his hands and the room is hushed. Heads are bowed for the benediction. "God be with us on the field. Grant us pardon from the belly of this good earth. Let our numbers be sufficient. Let our hearts be valiant. Give us strength over whatever might try to stop us. Above all, let us move into our new world with what we've tried to bring over from the old. Give us ears to hear and eyes to see that we may never lose so much again. Amen."

A couple hundred voices: "Amen."

The old man is standing with hands down, his body diminutive in opposition to his voice. "Many years ago, we heard the cries of this country's people. We heard the rolling-back silence that is a soul being starved. So we came, a young man with a young wife. We came as missionaries to do what we could. My wife and I and a boatload of others came across the Atlantic, our voices strong, our stories sheathed like weapons at our sides. We were willing to die for the cause. To free a few kindred souls, should we make it through the harbor and the line of men with guns.

"We were an hour off the coast when a boy came sliding down from the crow's nest, his shaky finger pointing toward the land, eyes wide." The old man smiles big, providing the crowd a view of his rotting teeth. "We ran to the bow, prepared to see an army of ships, boats with guns aimed our way. But it wasn't any such patrol coming after us, a small group of well-storied missionaries. It was a woman. A woman tall as the sky! A hundred feet toe to crown and made of greened copper! In the highest hand, she held a torch to guide us safely in. In the other, she held a tablet. A book, it's said, inscribed with the date of their independence. Around her feet lay chains unbound—the remains of her former enslavement. She was still as a stone. We thought her a statue. Until she moved."

A few people gasp. Most go stock-still even though they've probably heard this story before.

The old man walks slowly along the edge of the stage, his eyes bright as stars. "She bowed down to us. To a small boat filled up with small people who'd sailed halfway round the world to help her. She bent at the waist, her brittle gown screeching. The torch came arcing down, like a seaplane landing. When it breached the surface of the water, there was a moment of luminescence. The nighttime harbor was set alight. It was as if the sun had fallen into the sea. Then it went out and she toppled forward. The chains that had been loosed began to move. Like a serpent, they slithered up her torso and wrapped themselves around her waist. They pulled her off the island's mantle and dragged her body down and away, down and away, until the only thing left was a circle of white marking a hole in the sea.

"Our queen was swallowed up right there before our eyes. And the boats that might have been set out toward us were swallowed up with her. We were pushed away from that shore and set on another hundreds of miles away. This mighty queen had drowned herself so that we might live. And each and every one of us knew it. We understood her sacrifice as if she'd whispered it in our ears." The man breaks off, one trembling hand held aloft in the air. Eyes squeezed shut, face pinched in sad remembrance, as if it had been real. "Long live the queen of America!"

Long live the queen of America!

"May we, on the morrow, do her proud."

Applause follows. But the clapping hands and whistles are tempered by sadness. There is no tall green woman standing off the eastern shore, holding a torch and welcoming strangers. Just a string of militia that runs the whole length of the seaboard to keep us in and others out. I don't understand the story. But I understand the sacrifice.

I look around me as the storyteller abdicates the stage to his daughter, Anna. John's still not here. Or at least nowhere I can see. I watch as the white-skinned woman takes her position in the center of the stage and begins stretching out liquid words of her own.

Summertime, and the livin' is easy
Fish are jumpin' and the cotton is high . . .

Goddamn the Confederation, I think. Had I heard music before, I would have joined up years earlier. There's something about the vibration in the woman's voice that feels familiar. I close my eyes and let Anna's song play behind my memory.

I think of Veracity as a newborn. She had a mass of curly hair and inky brown eyes. We spent my two weeks of maternity leave together in a gliding chair Mr. Weigland bought me. We rocked back and forth for days, her impossibly warm head on my chest, me making similar sounds. Like exhalations with tone. Nothing like Anna's song. Nothing with words. But the peace those expressions brought . . . I'd forgotten.

"Harper." John is standing behind me.

I turn and look at him. Encourage him with a smile.

"I know I'm presuming a lot by coming . . ."

"No," I say. "You're not." I reach out and curl one of his hands into my own.

"I only have until midnight."

I nod. "Lazarus told me."

We're so close, I can see the fine details of John's face. He has a scar just beneath his hairline and a mole above his left eyebrow. There are telling lines in his forehead and at the outer corners of his eyes that show me a lifetime of worry and concern.

Who are you? I blink. *Are you safe? Are you someone I'll be able to know? To love? To trust?* God, how I want to.

"Is this okay, Harper?" John asks.

I close my eyes and lean into him. *Can I trust you? Can I trust you?* "Can I trust you?" I finally ask. But it doesn't matter what he says. My heart's going to have its way, whatever his response.

"Yes." John leans down and kisses me on the lips, the neck, the line of my jaw. "I had a son," he says, his mouth moving between words. "He was six years old. They killed him for speaking a Red List word." He stops and looks into my eyes. His are pink, yet dry. Long-run-out tears nowhere to be seen. "I don't even know which one."

I resolve to let go of everything and make a deal with God. *Give me a few moments of intimacy, a memory to carry with me into war and I'll give up the safety of isolation and let my heart love what it loves. Whom.*

I follow as John leads me away from the stage, down the main hall, and into the one leading to the library. A light emanating from the handle reads his identity as his free hand holds mine. The door opens and warm air rushes past.

I follow him up the stairs toward the far corner of the library. Only there do we take off our shoes. Kissing and touching, we make quick work of each other's clothes. Our hands are nimble. There isn't much time to catalog John's scarred body or the flecks of gold in the center of his brown eyes. The feel of his hands tangled in the back of my hair.

"You're safe here." He kisses me, repeating, *"Safe. Safe."*

We lie down together on the carpeted floor under the stars of a painting someone has only recently placed on the wall. John's hands guide me gently to him, stroking the flesh of my arms and face. He understands the history I can't forget and is giving me control. Whatever the spigot that will guide this love, my hands are on it. I tighten the valve, and John pauses, kisses my mouth, wipes away tears started in the corners of my eyes. I loosen the valve and he's free to remove my clothes and explore me. I turn my head into his shoulder and inhale. *God, the smell of him.* Just like that day in the alley.

Everything about this is bittersweet. Every feeling, movement, scent, and taste is tinged with our unfortunate past and the unknown future that begins nearly as soon as we've finished. He's going away. I am not.

"Harper." John is saying my name. Repeating it into my hair and neck. "Tell me what you want. Tell me."

I take hold of John's head and look into his eyes. Invite him in.

After, we hold each other for longer than we should. Until we have to hurry and put on our clothes and our shoes and walk back down to the first level and then out to the rear hall, where he'll leave, exiting the bunker via the emergency door. He's going up into the world, where, in the early hours of the morning, he'll find himself in the Geddard Building. It will be a suicide mission if I can't get him the identity of the main redactor. The thought pierces me. For a few seconds, I forget to breathe.

It's a struggle not to tarnish this experience with all the things I want to say. *I'm sorry. I promise to get you to the master.*

Don't go. We stand at the mouth of the rear exit, holding each other until it's fifteen minutes past midnight. Then John keys in some coded number on a pad next to the door. Like the library's, it springs open with a pop, this time letting in cold air.

John smiles down at my face and kisses my mouth. Then steps out into the earthen tunnel that will deposit him in some barren field. "You know how I feel about you," he says.

I take one step toward him. "John . . ." I begin.

But he's already pressed a button that closes and locks the door between us. I stand there for a whole moment. Blinking at the place John just was. I didn't get to return my answer that would have sounded more like a question.

Do you know how I feel about you?

apostasy

discriminate

ego

fossil

heresy

kindred

obstreperous

offline

veracity

off-line: operating independently of, or disconnected from, an associated and master source.

HAPTER

TWENTY-FOUR

Lilly is standing at the side of my cot, holding out a small pile of new clothes. They are the color of the dormant, midwestern earth. Utilitarian garb, like I'd imagined. But they're new and clean and signify an end to living beneath the soil.

"Get dressed," she says. "You can use the loft area behind the O'Keeffe paintings." She steps away, indicating she means now. "You still have your pill?" She's talking about the cyanide. The kill pill.

"Yes."

"And your drive?"

It's on a chain around my neck. Only a few of us got one. A bullet-size map to the new government. The DNA for our new country on a flash drive worn around our necks.

"Yes." I feel for the short tube. If caught, I'm to swallow it, too. Before the kill pill, not after.

"When you're dressed, let me know. We have one last thing to do before we head out, seeing as you're the carrier."

I go up to the library's art section and put on my uniform. It's loose in the legs and tight across the shoulders. Itchy canvas, unwashed and unyielding.

When I come back down, the council is assembling. They come in through the open library door and gather behind Lazarus, Lilly, Noam, and Ezra, who've formed a front row. The group is standing before a table that's been pulled into the center of the room. Lazarus motions me over. On the table is a medium-size box with golden brown sides and an engraved cover.

"Harper, despite the stress of the situation"—by which, he means my recent loss of abilities—"we believe you'll be able to help us keep safe the most important document this country has yet to see. Therefore, we're asking you to be the carrier for our most precious possession, *The Book of Noah*."

The box's cover is etched from a dark reddish wood. Mahogany. Adorned in a pattern of vines below, a cluster of redwood trees above. The slim trunks set in copper, the arms in gold. Redwoods are the oldest known trees in existence. Older than Christ himself. I know from a presentation given by our Pastor, complete with slides.

"As far as we know, this is the only copy that survived. You'll have to be careful with it." Lazarus runs a bony finger over the tree. "Do you know what a metaphor is?"

"No."

"A metaphor is an expression that uses seemingly unrelated imagery to convey its meaning. For example, this tree represents the individual. What you see below . . ." He taps on the bottom, on an endless coil of roots where each tree has become hopelessly entangled with the others. "This is what keeps them standing. This is the resistance."

A redwood can grow to a height of almost four hundred feet. Looking at them in Pastor's pictures, I was amazed these skinny giants could withstand a high wind. Or even a good stiff breeze. So disproportionate to their base, they should have been easily toppled.

Pastor explained it this way. "They hold hands beneath the earth." It was the one thing he ever said that I liked.

Lazarus's explanation is more literal. "They intertwine their roots." His finger follows a tendril. "Alone, a tree of that stature would never survive. United, they live almost forever." He motions me over next to him. Nods at the box. "Open it up."

I push the top aside slowly, holding my breath. Beneath the

revealed seam, I can see the book's pickled leather binding, gold letters that have turned mostly brown or been scratched off. The book itself isn't pretty or ornate. It's old. Heavily used.

"Many people have paid the ultimate price to keep this book safe, Harper," Lazarus whispers.

"I'll be careful."

"Go ahead."

I reach in carefully and lift out the precious cargo as if it were a newborn. It's as thick as my balled-up fist. Fifty or sixty years old, its spine is bent with age. It sits askance on my flat palms, revealing a diagonal row of finger-size holes cut into the long side. I look down at the title, then up at Lazarus.

"This isn't *The Book of Noah*."

"*The Book of Noah* was never its real name."

I let it slide gently off the slope of my fingers and onto the table. It yawns upon impact, its spine twisting and stretching, happy to be out of its box. "I don't understand." I try not to sound disappointed. It's a textbook. Hardly the key to our survival or the mythic book I'd heard so much about in Monitoring.

"Samuel Johnson completed the first English dictionary in 1755. Noah Webster adapted that version in 1828 to better reflect American usage of the English language. Somewhere along the way, people began calling it *Noah's Book*. And then, *The Book of Noah*."

I turn it open with a finger. "How many are there?"

"Words? The first edition contained forty-two thousand. Later versions, a half million."

A half million. Five hundred thousand words, and so many things to know about each one. Language of origin. Definition. Variations of usage. The hairs on the back of my neck rise as I begin to understand. I can look words up. Know them. Talk to others who've done the same. It's a way of passing along the contents of not just the world and the way we experience it, but maybe of our souls. How we feel about God. How and where we find him. Most important, this book is how, together, we can show our fellow citizens all the freedoms they've been missing. Things, and words, taken away by the Confederation.

Lazarus pats me on the shoulder. "That's the greatest power in the world, young lady. Your history, your weapons of mass destruction, your cures. They're all there. You read that book, cover to cover, and I won't have to teach you a thing."

I read the title out loud. *"Webster's Unabridged Dictionary. Third Edition."*

"This is the last known dictionary in the country. The testable, visible, incontrovertible proof of a freedom citizens of the Confederation of the Willing haven't had for decades."

I slide the book back in the box. Ceremonially, two of our council members wrap it in a dark green piece of velvet, taking synchronized turns around the table. They move until the box has disappeared, then bind it with a dull, tan cord, one end left loose to serve as a handle.

I take hold of the tasseled rope and lift. It's heavy. Maybe twenty pounds, and bulky. I position the book at my waist, elbows bent, wrists locked, the handle wrapped over both palms to divide the load. Proceed third in line out of the library and down the corridor to the main hall.

The room is filled far past capacity. The tables have been put up and people are standing shoulder to shoulder. They have short-billed hats pulled down low to cover their eyes and wear clothes the same as mine. They in no way resemble the travelers from last night. This morning they're quiet and attentive. All eyes on the head of the room.

"Coming through!" someone shouts as Ezra leads us in.

I watch the others as we go. Some of the crowd, like Elsbeth and Charles, disapprove of Ezra as anything other than a whore. They dismiss her with turned heads. Let their eyes float away. She has crawled free of their pigeonhole and they refuse to bear her out. They've deemed her one thing and can't afford to let her be another.

Mary, Ben's widow, has her shirt untucked, the last two buttons undone to make room for their child. Our eyes meet but she doesn't see me. She hasn't yet come up from the depths of her grief. Standing next to her is Rita, her skin still colored with excitement or anxiety. She comes out from beneath long bangs as we pass, looks at me briefly. Stares at Ezra. It's understandable. In her uniform with three stripes on each sleeve and no makeup, Ezra looks formidable. With no black lines drawn around her eyes or silver flecks in her lashes, no lipstick, and no red sash, she looks normal, like the rest of us.

We march down a forming center aisle, Ezra at our head. She steps onto the stage that, last night, was used for stories and singing. The rest of us fan out on either side and fill up the front row.

"Listen up!" she shouts. "Everyone, listen up! We head out in twenty minutes. Look under your right sleeve. Whatever color you see there is the group you've been assigned to. Under your left sleeve is your identification patch. Take a moment. Read what it says. If your information is wrong, hold up a hand."

Inside my right sleeve I find a dull yellow band of cloth, the color of old butter. I roll back my left sleeve until a label slips into view. It's attached by a few easy-to-break stitches, should I fall or be caught and need to remove it quickly. If I yank too hard, it will come off in my hand, so I hold it lightly apart from my shirt. Read what they've deemed as my critical information.

Harper Abigail Adams, Monitor, Field Dispatch #89, one daughter—Veracity Adams. Tracking Advisory Board, Head of. And, *Reacquisition of Language, Advisor.* Once at the capital, I'll be in charge of dismembering the Monitoring Department and burying its remains so deep, no one will be able to resuscitate such informational sabotage ever again. In addition, I'll be helping people learn the difference between opinion and fact. Currently, they have no idea what's one and what's the other. I'll be assisting as an Instructor and Advisor, teaching and developing courses such as Critical Thinking and Informed Participation in Government. I've already created an outline for each.

"Now listen up!" Ezra steps onto a chair someone's brought in from the library. She's too short to be seen in full without it. "The person heading up your platoon is called a point guard. Green and blue, you'll be subdivided into squads once we take the field. Yellow, your point guard is Aaron. Aaron, hold up your hand."

Our point guard is the tallest man in the room. He's young, with dark hair shaved close around his scalp.

Ezra claps to get our attention. "If your point guard holds up an arm, that means get down immediately! Drop to your bellies. Not your knees. Got it?"

We are divided. The blue group is sent off to stand in front of a tall woman with a heavy brow and deeply recessed eyes named Kerry. I can tell by the people heading toward her waving arm that this is the industrious group. People possessing strength, courage, and agile minds who'll be good at scouting and setting up perimeters. Those with a green patch are directed to stand with a red-haired, round-bellied man named Mercer. This group is older, less dexterous, and the largest number of us by far.

Those of us with a swatch of yellow up our sleeves are the dignitaries. We're to make up the new administration. Ezra explains that we'll have the most guards. The most guns. Will walk sandwiched between the other groups.

"Yes, people!" Ezra shouts. "I said *walking*. You were called up early for a reason. Some of you know why, some don't."

A few people fall out of their lines and wander into neighboring groups.

Lazarus whistles and puts up both hands. "Attention! Attention!"

The lines reform. Voices dim.

Lazarus steps onto the platform. He waits for the room to still before providing the explanation. "The satellite program we know of as SKEYE was initiated early yesterday morning. That was why all of you had to be brought here so quickly. It also means we no longer have a motorized way to reach our former broadcast site."

Protests go up. Loud, rebellious roars of indignation stipple the room. Even though it was a logical conclusion given the quick exodus from outlying bunkers to ours, we weren't prepared for this. *Walking into war?* It is a collective cry. *And walking to where? Bond?*

Lazarus has to shout. "Listen to me! *Listen to me!*" Ezra jumps down from the podium and starts yanking people back into place as he continues. "Once we get to Bond, our operatives in Wernthal should have taken the main conduit for all media dissemination in the Confederation, a portal to every television in the country called the Hub. Then we'll be free to broadcast our message. We've moved our broadcast location from Antioch to Bond so we won't have far to walk . . ."

"*Walking,* Lazarus?" Elsbeth shouts from her group. She's a part of the blue team. Will be one of those going out first. "There's no cover from here to Bond! It's suicide!"

Her husband, Charles, chimes in. "It's extermination! . . . *Walking across the prairie.* And to a shit-hole town like Bond! You think *Bond* is going to communicate *freedom*? You're telling us the world's gonna see that little pissant square, and us, a bunch of ragtag people lined up around it, and think to themselves, 'Gee, I'd better put on my walking shoes! This is a resistance I want to join!'"

"We don't have the slates down, Lazarus!" Elsbeth jumps back in. "And Charles is right! If the Confederation's first look at freedom is a run-down town like that, *no one* will join us!"

Ezra marches over and pushes the two apart, back into their groups. Greens and blues.

"Listen to me!" Lazarus commands, and the room calms. "This country lives and breathes technology. So much so, they've forgotten anything else. It is their vulnerability and why we chose the wastelands for our base. We've rerouted our sister and brother units to Bond from any location within a hundred-and-fifty-mile radius. When we reach the square at Bond, there will be more than ten thousand troops waiting for us. Your knowledge regarding the scope of this movement has been limited, and for good reason. I realize our great numbers may come as a shock to you, but it should reveal the strength of our resistance and the reason we needed to mobilize so quickly. Already, the capital you know of as Wernthal has passed into the hands of our sisters and brothers. Already, President and his Ministry are being held until we can bring them to a legal, honorable justice. Once we take the square at Bond, we plan to broadcast our message to the people of this nation. Once armed with truth, we are confident they'll accept our invitation to be a part of this new nation."

Elsbeth juts out her chin. "How do we know we haven't been compromised?"

"We don't. And we won't know until we're either dead or have made it to the square. There are no guarantees, Elsbeth. There never were." Lazarus sighs and looks out over the crowd. "My friends. My family. Last night, SKEYE went live and we moved a few hundred thousand troops into our nation's lost capital. Many lost their lives to secure for us a seat of power. Now it's our turn to rise to this challenge. The gauntlet has been thrown. There is no more waiting. This war happens now or it doesn't happen at all."

"What about the main redactor?" Elsbeth asks in her coarse, venomous voice.

The question makes the blood rise in my cheeks and draws all eyes to where I stand.

But Lazrarus doesn't miss a beat. "We'll have it down by the time we broadcast." He says this as if he truly believes it, which makes me all the more nervous.

My heart skips a beat and the room tilts some. I have to steady myself against Noam.

Ezra steps back onto the stage, providing me cover with her instructions. "Making it to the square is paramount. When those cameras roll, every face counts. Every expression counts. Got it?"

We're told that our new country depends on not just making it, but making it on time. And as many of us getting there as possible. It's quantity as well as quality, which means, *Nobody fall down. Nobody get hurt.* The crowd wags their heads in agreement. It's a good plan. *Walk. Follow orders. Don't get killed.*

Ezra talks for another few minutes. Mostly about us, the yellow group that, among others, includes Lazarus, Ezra, Noam, and Lilly. We'll be surrounded by eight guards, half of them with weapons, half without. We're transporting *Noah.* She nods my way and I step forward. Lift up our most precious possession.

"Security for the yellow squad takes precedence over all others."

Should anything happen to compromise our group, should any of our guards be shot, key members of the others will be called upon to replace them.

"It's currently 6:02 a.m.," Ezra barks. "We're to be at the square and ready to broadcast by seven."

The captains of each group take a moment. Bend over their wristwatches and fiddle with the knobs. Ezra takes the pause to lean over and whisper in my ear, "You see anyone you think looks off, in any way, you give me the sign." She holds up the first two fingers and thumb of one hand. Points. "Got it?"

"Do you have anyone in mind?"

Ezra turns and looks out over the crowd. "No."

On the stage, Lazarus holds up his hands. "Take a moment and say your good-byes. As of the last person out, this bunker's officially closed."

Some people bow their heads and study their coupled hands, praying. Most stare straight ahead. There are no good-byes to be said. These people would rather die walking toward their freedom than live another moment down here.

"Move out," Ezra says, and the whole room pushes forward.

We sweep along as one body. Move in formation to the front of the room, then up the stairs, where we bow our way out of the pantry. The pale blue of an overcast sky is on the kitchen boards. Sadly, there's no sun to greet us. Someone yanks down the old curtain covering the living room window and the place is bleached white. We wait until our eyes adjust. For most of us, the first thing we see is the squalor of Lilly's front room and the dead gray air beyond. A few people start to cry. It isn't pretty. Not the decaying couch or the crumbling porch or the flatland we see through the door. It isn't at all pretty, and we needed it to be beautiful.

We slide together off the porch, a long line of uniformed troops already extending out fifty or sixty feet. We're blinded by the wide white sky and our heads fill with shooting stars. When my vision returns, I look around. Nothing to see for miles but dull earth.

Our team is moving surprisingly fast, considering Lazarus is near our tail. We've been told to keep an undulating line as we go. To regard ourselves as the individual vertebrae of a very long snake.

Ahead and behind us, the other squads and platoons travel in this same back-and-forth manner, keeping us in their middle. What Ezra calls a *traveling-over watch*. If we're ambushed, if bombs drop out of the sky, there is one way to go. Not back to the house that's been locked up tight, or sideways to the electrified tree line, or across the road to the wide-open fields. The only direction we're to go, even if the enemy comes marching up from that way, is east. Forward, always forward. If need be, into the barrels of their guns.

I think of last night's music, of the bard's young daughter

and her voice. That was sweet music, what Lazarus called a love song. The music we're making with the *swoosh, swoosh* of our legs is its opposite. There won't be any cover at all. We're as exposed as caged birds. Anyone driving down this road would find a few hundred soldiers single-filing it along. It wasn't real when I had forty feet of earth between me and the Confederation. Up here, there's literally nowhere to run.

Ezra is marching along as if she hasn't noticed the saturated earth. Most of the rain has been soaked up by the dry fields. But in places, our footfalls are like cups. They fill with standing water as soon as they're made and become potholes that threaten to trap us. Lazarus, most of all. He's behind me, his legs blackened up to the calves with mud. He suffers to make each step. The two guards behind him have begun to close the gap between them. They come to stand on either side of him and each takes an arm. I imagine there was a plan to somehow carry Lazarus to the square, but with the rain, even two men's combined weight would set them a foot deep into the soggy earth.

"Adams! Eyes forward!" Ezra whispers harshly. She's two people up on our chain, waits for me to turn around. Then goes back to a discussion with a guard who's pointing to the moist earth with his gun.

Ezra marches farther up the line to discuss the perimeter with another guard. He hands her a set of tubular eyes that allow her to see long distances. She points them toward the far horizon, where there's nothing but the cleft between sky and earth. Bond is still not in sight.

I divert my attention by watching our group. We are a sorry bunch of marchers. The only ones holding a staggered V formation are the guards who comprise a good third of us. There is the point guard and three others with him at the front, a few more sprinkled between, another three or four guards pulling up the rear. We are in some semblance of a serpentine line for the first mile. Then the moist, sucking earth wins out and we become a wounded snake.

Sidewinding left, then right, wearing Ezra out with our lousy footing. It doesn't help that I'm having a hard time keeping hold of my package. Twenty pounds wasn't much weight for the first mile, but every step since, *Noah* seems to have grown in girth and bulk.

Most of our guards carry their weapons waist-high with their index fingers resting ever so lightly on the trigger. All save for Rita, whose gun is dangling next to her thigh. They walk in a half crouch, with their eyes in constant motion all over the landscape. Not Rita. She turns, and shows me her mouth, curled up on both sides.

There's something different about Rita. Is it that I've never seen her smile? It worries me, gets into my feet.

We trek along another quarter mile with Ezra at the head of the line. She turns and frowns at someone behind me. Comes back down the chain and tells the guards we're slowing down for Lazarus. He's having a hard time keeping up. The words aren't out of Ezra's mouth when we hear gunfire.

Our point guard, Aaron, has a line of black hair down the center of his head and massive shoulders built disproportionately to his thin waist and stick legs. He stops and holds up one arm, his hand made into a fist, and we drop to our bellies as directed. As if tripped by our sudden weight, a bomb goes off somewhere to the east.

I hear movement all around me. Think it's someone come to shoot us while we're sprawled out on the ground, but it's our people. Ezra and another guard from the rear have begun a forward march on their elbows. They shoot past me, nearly as fast as if they were walking. Behind us, the guards have made themselves into a shell covering Lazarus. He won't be able to move but he'll also have a hard time getting shot.

Ahead of me, Lilly is the only one standing. Noam vaults past the others between them to push her down. The couple makes it to the ground as a second bomb goes off. This one is stronger. It shakes the ground. There is a brief silence, then the sound of small-arms fire off in the distance, toward Bond.

"Ezra?" Lilly asks from beneath Noam's protective arm. Raw fear has smoothed out the pleats of her face.

Ezra doesn't reply. She holds up a finger and makes a circle in the air. Immediately, the front guards begin walking the perimeter. All save for Rita, who remains sitting, her gun still put away.

"Harper?" It's Lilly's voice. When I turn back around, she and Noam are next to me, hunched into a clump of Queen Anne's lace a few feet away. "They'd be in Bond by now, wouldn't they?" She means the first group out. Given our status, and the fact that we have *The Book of Noah* in tow, our group is positioned in the middle.

I nod slowly. "Probably." Truth is, Lazarus has slowed us down. If it weren't for his disability, we'd probably be in Bond right now, too.

Ezra's put her phone back in her trouser pocket and is walking quickly up the line. She gives me a look as she goes, doesn't plan to stop.

"Hey!" I shout.

Ezra doubles back to where we're standing. "Shut up and move out, now!" she whispers hotly, then turns to Noam and Lilly. "I can't reach the blue team by phone." She pauses, something else on her mind to say. Then turns and marches to the front guards. She huddles up with them. Points at the road leading east and comes back down the line again.

"We're to proceed as planned," she repeats slowly and calmly until she's at the end of the line. Standing in front of Lazarus, her weapon cocked. Again, the guards lead us out. No one refuses to go.

Lazarus is in pain. His knees won't punch and push. Don't accede to the uneven ground as well as ours. Were it anyone else, Ezra would have left them behind. She motions to his guards, who provide him one arm each to be used as rails.

"What's so interesting?" Ezra asks, stopping next to me.

"Nothing."

She looks at me, her head turned while her body moves

straight ahead. "What's on your mind, Adams? You have something to say, say it."

"Where was Rita last night?"

"Why?"

"Something's different."

"What's different?"

I shrug. "Look how she's carrying her weapon. And she wasn't spooked by those explosions."

"What are you trying to say? You think she's a spy?"

"Yeah. I do."

Ezra shakes her head, but I can tell she's thinking about it. She's watching Rita. Noticing how the girl's eyes don't follow the curve of the field, like the other guards'. How easily she walks across the earth. As if it's neither new nor dangerous.

"Keep your eyes open," Ezra says, heading off toward the easternmost part of the line, where the final clouds of night are beginning to disperse.

We march the next mile without event, the yellow group bowed out ahead of us. Rita has her own pair of binoculars. She holds them up as she walks, looking at the land that will eventually plane right up to the houses on Bond's west side. Ezra's noticed Rita's diverted attention. She lifts her own pair of eyes and begins watching the windows for flashes or people. Anyone that might be signaling to Rita, or anyone else in our crew.

As often as I can, I check on Lazarus. Despite the pain, he's looking everywhere, at everything. At the yellow sun low on the horizon, and higher up where the clouds are taunting us. His eyes follow a red bird with black wings to something new in our path. It's a fence stretching the length of the field.

The prairie beyond this wooden boundary is shrouded in twilight. The browns and blacks and shiny hollows of gray there change as the clouds disperse. I hear the small rupture of sun before I see it. People are sucking in their breath, trying not to shout. A finger of light is spilling onto the grass. This beam grows eastward toward Bond and lights up everyone in its path. People stop and gape. Hold up their hands into the bright, dust-specked air like children.

The guards at our helm are smiling. They shake their fists in the air. Rita, who's been six years without the sun, doesn't even notice. Her eyes are set on something small and silver. A bullet she's preparing to slip into her open gun.

I march ahead, pushing past a guard, then Lilly and Noam. I march toward Rita until I can see her face clearly. And there, on her nose, is what I've been noticing all day without understanding. The clue I didn't need my sentient abilities to see. *Freckles.* Fresh, light brown remnants of yesterday's rosy-red skin. *She's been up top.*

"You sold us out," I say.

Rita's eyes narrow but she says nothing.

"You made a trade. Us for your freedom. Isn't that right, Rita?"

"Adams." Ezra is talking in my ear. "What are you talking about?"

"Rita's our spy."

"How do you know?" Ezra gets closer. I can feel her breath on my neck. "I thought you couldn't see colors anymore."

Before I can explain, the crackle of filtered voices starts coming out of the field phone Ezra carries around her waist. She puts it against her ear despite the terrific whine. I watch her face whiten as she listens. It's news from the blue team, nothing good.

"Ezra?" I ask.

She turns and looks back at Lazarus.

"Ezra!"

"Not now, Adams!" She's already running toward him.

Lazarus understands whatever is happening and like our Lieutenant, has gone pale. Someone's coming for us. And there's no place to put our leader. Without him we'll lose our binding and scatter like so many pages.

Ahead of us, Rita has her open gun on one hip. Is sliding bullets into her magazine when one of the guards alongside her drops into the grass. He motions forward with two fingers, then sweeps the straightened hand to the left. The other guards follow and disappear into the high weeds. Rita is the last.

Behind me, Ezra is running. She skids to a stop next to Lazarus. Drops to her knees and pushes him backward, into the wet earth.

"Harper!" Ezra is stretched out above him, her body covering Lazarus's exposed head and shoulders. "Get down!"

There is a cold wind, like a bird diving. It bursts into the ground just beyond me. Throws up a bit of dirt.

"Get down, goddamnit!"

I fall onto my belly. Look up just in time to see Rita and the other guards pointing their weapons at something across the fence. I follow Rita's outstretched finger and see shadows in the grass, like fish beneath muddy water.

A line of cars has begun down the country road from the direction of Bond. I recognize the clipped hum of older-model Confederation engines. They're squad cars, used ones from the city that have been redistributed to the wastelands. As they get close, I'm able to see their locations of origin plastered across the driver's-side doors. Dover. Chesterfield. Whitt. Laconda. Greene. Shelby.

Ezra calls out to the guards busy hustling up from the rear. "Bury the package! Bury the package!" She turns her head to the front of the line. Tries to push those of us there away from the road with her palm. "Fall back!"

The squads are getting closer. I can see a head behind the first wheel. Behind him, another head atop the long barrel of a gun that's sticking out of the rolled-down window.

Aaron runs toward Ezra. He pulls a small black box from his trouser pocket, his head turned toward the procession of cars. Each thumb is over the single button in the small square's center and all eight fingers are being used to hold it in both hands.

"Now?" he asks Ezra, not quite to her.

"Not yet!"

Ezra stands and begins running toward the road. Aaron angles off to follow. They run in tandem, their legs throwing up mud as they sprint toward the cars.

We can now see all six squads and their drivers. The men in the backseats are aiming at us with guns. They've opened fire, but are too far off and miss Ezra and the guard. They settle their sticklike barrels against the half panes of their windows and wait for closer ground.

Ezra and our guard stop running. He holds up the box, depresses the button, and all hell breaks loose.

With an intensity that knocks some of us from our feet, the road explodes. Chunks of asphalt and dirt burst skyward and all six squads throw on their brakes. The first five vehicles begin racing backward, away from the line of explosions chasing them. The last car in their procession is the only one that pulls off the road. It finds safety off the asphalt just as the first car's tires explode over the rippling pavement. The steel frame jumps off the ground as if on springs and the tank explodes, sending up a bright yellow-orange plume. When it comes back down, the car is nothing, just particles held together by cracked atoms. The man who'd been preparing to shoot us from the backseat has gone limp. The heat has started his bullets firing, so we flatten ourselves against the grass. The same thing happens four more times, taking out the next four cars. The last squad is parked on the grass. Ruined, but still in one piece. Its tires have been blown out, the hood is smashed down into the cab, and its undercarriage is on fire. But behind the darkened windows, hands are pressing against the hot glass. Three men from what I can tell. Trying to pound their way out.

"Take them out!" Ezra motions to the lone vehicle.

Two of our guards rush toward it. The first turns and shrugs at Ezra. "They're trapped in there." He smiles. *Why waste the bullets?*

Ezra gets up and stalks toward the road, unholstering her

gun. The three Blue Coats are yelling now. Banging on their windows. One is behind the wheel, the other two in the backseat. Ezra lifts her gun and dispenses five or six bullets into the wrecked car. They go cleanly through the windows, drop two of them immediately. The last man, still sitting in the far side of the backseat, crawls over. He pushes his dead partner out of the way and presses his chest against the window. He's giving Ezra a better target.

"Let him burn!" Aaron is laughing.

Ezra sets her eye behind the rifle's sights and shoots. The man falls away from the burning window. She then turns to the guard, her rifle aimed at his feet.

"You do what I tell you to do, goddamnit! Or you get left behind! Got it?"

Aaron swallows. "Yes, ma'am."

Ezra reholsters her gun and storms back to where Lazarus is still lying in the grass. "Harper, bring me *Noah*. Time to bury the package."

I run over and pass our dictionary to a young guard named David. I'm surprised at what a relief it is to unload the weight of it. David accepts *The Book of Noah* with both hands and holds it tight against his belly while another guard digs a hole in the soft earth. Then, eyes big, fingers careful not to smudge any dirt onto its green velvet wrap, David extracts a piece of something bright and silver from a pocket. He and the second guard work together to wrap our dictionary in a swaddling of moisture-proof aluminum. Then down it goes, into the hole.

"Harper," Lazarus says. "We were hoping you'd be able to use your sight to find it again after it had been buried. Will you remember where we put it?"

"Absolutely."

"Good." Lazarus turns to Ezra, who's made the short trip over and is reloading her gun. "Where's Skinner?"

"Blue squad estimates he's a quarter mile off the main route, east down 2070."

"How will he be coming?"

"How do you think?" Ezra grumbles. "On foot. Straight down the middle."

"Why?" I ask.

Ezra looks at me as if I'm an idiot. "You just stay the fuck out of the way and let me handle it."

"Don't do anything stupid," I say, but Ezra doesn't hear me. She's already off. Making her way up the line to confer with her guards.

I run over to a clump of Queen Anne's lace. Choose one with a dappled, dying plate of yellowish flowers for a head, then watch as *The Book of Noah* disappears. The earth where it's been put looks exactly the same. I lean down and put the flowers in the center of *Noah*'s grave. My powers of perception have been well honed over the years. Despite my inability to find *Noah* by its vast glow, I'll be able to recognize its burial place from the fence.

Something buzzes across the tops of our heads. It hums as it splits the air and sends down a slight breeze.

Ezra pushes Lazarus onto his back and me onto my belly. She crawls around and lies down sideways at our front.

"Lieutenant!" Aaron calls. He's standing with his back to us, legs planted. His weapon ready to fire at something over the fence. He's saying something we can't hear.

"Repeat!" Ezra shouts.

The boy shoots, stepping back to absorb the recoil. "Four on the ground! Twelve o'clock!" he yells, eyes swinging to Ezra. Before he can turn back to the front line, he takes a quick, surprised step toward us, as if shoved.

"Aaron?" Ezra asks.

"Four." Aaron takes another involuntary step our way. He inhales sharply. A look of surprise sprouts on his face as he looks down at his chest. A small hole appears equidistant from each breast pocket. The boy blinks. Gurgles for a moment on his own blood, then spits a little of it onto his chin. "Four," he repeats, and the field around him explodes.

Rita's put her long-barreled gun on a short tripod. It swings from one side to the other, emitting shells and small thunderclouds of smoke. She's shooting at the Blue Coats just across the fence. Taking down no one while spraying away our ammunition. *Goddamn her.* She's putting our bullets in the ground.

"Harper!" Lilly shouts from her spot in a clump of overgrowth. She's alone, as Noam's gone back to help Lazarus.

She holds out her drive for me to see. It's housed in a sleek black casing the size of a large tablet. If we're caught like this, we're to swallow them, those of us who were chosen to carry them.

"Aaron!" Lilly points. "Is he wearing his?" The young guard is still sitting up. I can see a chain around his neck, the drive a weight at its end.

Aaron died too fast. Didn't get the chance to swallow his.

Christ, help me. I barely have enough spit to swallow my own.

I elbow my way across the pockmarked ground. Have to feel around on Aaron's torso before the flash drive comes into contact with my hand. I snatch it loose and begin crawling back to my higher bit of weeds when I see his gun shining a surprising distance away. It's half hidden beneath a patch of high grass close to the fence. Too far for an attempt at retrieval. I'll come back for it if given the opportunity.

Beyond the fence, tall grass is parting. A man is standing up, his face deep brown, eyes black. He has no fear of us. Waves at me and then at Ezra with the small hole at the end of his gun, deciding casually which one of us to shoot first.

"There!" I shout at Ezra, but she's already seen him.

I hear the loud popping of weapons being fired but my twisting head can't see from which way it comes. Then the sickening, hard-soft sound of a bullet ripping flesh and the falling spray of blood. Like a sprinkler passing a large-leaved shrub.

Someone is dead. I don't want to look.

It's the Blue Coat. He's collapsed into a small, neat circle as if his knees have been cut out from beneath him. Rita's taken him down. She looks back, searching for my face. When she finds me, she smiles as if it's been enough to make me think I was wrong. That she's on our side.

"Three!" she says.

"Adams!" Ezra is motioning toward another man who catapults across the fence on a direct course toward me. He hits the ground and raises his gun. I won't be able to get out of the way fast enough. I just start to move when he's made to step sideways and falls heavily into a cross-legged seat. The man looks at me with big eyes. *What just happened?* Then dies where he sits. He never shows a drop of blood. I'll never know where Ezra's hit him.

"Two," she shouts. "Watch your ass, Adams!"

Ezra grabs hold of my shirt and tugs me along to behind the fallen Blue Coat. We use his body as a shield.

"Where's Skinner?" she asks.

"Didn't you see him?"

"No." Ezra pops a new clip into her gun. "That cocky son of a bitch is going to come straight down the middle. You let me know when he does."

I scan the horizon. Stop where Rita is hanging on to her weapon. She's got both arms up and the muzzle lifted, but no finger on the trigger. Fifty feet beyond her, just over the fence, I see Skinner. He's right in the center of the far field. Coming straight down the middle like Ezra said he would.

I point. "There!"

He's with another man. They begin to run. Vault over the fence with long, fast-shooting guns, Jingo first, then the other. Jingo shouts something to his partner. He's to collect our weapons, and us, in whatever order is easiest. There are only three people Skinner wants to keep alive—Ezra James, Harper Adams, and Lazarus Cobb. The rest are to be given one chance to lay down their weapons.

Jingo disappears into the high grass. I can see his shoulders flexing over a lump of green and brown canvas that's been heavily splattered with blood. It's Aaron, our dead guard. Skinner has removed the boy's boot laces and is using them to tether our guard to his shoulders. When Skinner comes up again, it's with two heads and four arms. Skinner is using Aaron as a shield. Wearing him vestlike on his way to me. As Skinner runs, it's our comrade's body that absorbs the bullets.

It happens fast. I'm putting up my hand to shield myself from his approach, then I'm up in the air as Aaron falls past. His stubbled head soaked with blood and face peppered with shot, the dead guard falls into the space I'd just occupied.

"Come on," Skinner says, grabbing one arm and twisting me painfully off the ground. "You're better cover."

Jingo's wearing a cast on his right arm, from elbow to palm. It pushes painfully against my ribs as I'm yanked in front of him, my arms bound behind me with his belt. He walks us together toward Ezra, who's scrambled away. He sucks in quick breaths as we move. Each step hurts his damaged wrist.

Ezra is standing ten yards away. Her long-barreled gun is in her hand and pointed at Skinner.

"Put down the gun, baby," Jingo says.

"Put down the Monitor."

"Let's not do this. I happen to know you need Harper here as much as you need Lazarus."

Ezra lowers her barrel so it's pointed at one of my legs. She's going to shoot me to prove how little I'm worth. She glances up at my face and I nod. *Okay.*

"Shoot out both kneecaps." Jingo kicks at my shins. Splays me out so both legs are offered up as easy targets. "Long as you keep it below the jugular. We need her alive, don't we?"

I close my eyes. It's a lifetime of waiting before I hear Ezra's gun being tossed into the grass. Skinner doesn't immediately kill her, but it's no surprise. He loves her. Doesn't want to shoot her if he doesn't have to.

"What do you want, Skinner?"

"I think that's my question to you, darling. You have any preference for what numbers I call on you?"

I open my eyes. Ezra's pulled a package of cigarettes from one of her many pockets. "I'll take an eight-aught-five, if you have the energy for it."

"Don't fuck with me, Ezra. Not today."

"Oh. Okay, then how about a straight-up nine-sixteen?" She puts the lit cigarette in her mouth. Offers Skinner one from the held-out box. "Smoke?"

Her nonchalance enrages him. Skinner lifts his gun and sets it atop my shoulder for support. Shoots the offered cigarette away, taking a bit of her finger with it.

Ezra wasn't ready for this. For a terrible second, her facade of calm slips and I see a fear that tells me she knows what's coming. Then she seals herself off. Flips Skinner the bird with what remains of the digit and smiles.

"Put her down, Skinner." Ezra is trying to sound bored and unharmed. But her face betrays her. White cheeks and gray lips are the colors of too much lost blood. She needs to sit down before she falls there.

Skinner reholsters his gun. Behind me comes the sliding friction of a knife being unsheathed, then the cold tip pressed against my neck. "This is what you girls came to do, right? Get rid of your slates? How about we start with this one."

Ezra has retrieved a cloth bandage from a pocket. She uses it to tie off her finger's bleeding stump. "I thought Helen Rumney needed her."

"Maybe not." Jingo looks at the side of my face. Turns it in his hand. "We've got other Sentients coming. Rumney has 'em lined up around the block for that BodySpeak program of hers."

Ezra looks at him as if he was slow. "If you want to kill someone, kill her. But if you want to fight someone, fight me."

"You're about to fall over, darling."

"Then we should be about even." Ezra pulls her shirt over her head and drops it to the ground. Beneath her sports bra, she's damp and white, and even more muscular than last I saw her.

Our remaining guards march forward slowly. We are greater in number, but Jingo and his partner have better weapons, automatics capable of spraying out hundreds of bullets before their clips run dry. And Jingo has me.

He unleashes my arms and pushes me ahead of him, the hot muzzle of his gun pressed between my shoulder blades. "Hold it there," he says, and our group stops. "Throw 'em down."

The other Blue Coat collects our weapons as Jingo pushes me onto the grass. I'm kicked forward. Yanked up by the other cop and corralled along with the rest of us. Next to me, Rita's hands are empty. Her gun is lying on the wet ground along with the others. I glance quickly at the fence. Aaron's weapon is still there, ten feet behind Jingo's partner.

Jingo points his weapon at us. "I'm going to be needing that book now." The muzzle skips up and down our faces, marking our foreheads with the red sights of his gun.

"Fight me," Ezra says.

Jingo answers with his gun pointed away from her, the muzzle trained on us. "When we're done killing all your friends here, then I'll get to—"

Before the last word is out of his mouth, Ezra crosses the short space. *Snap.* Jingo's head shoots back as she punches him in the face with her good hand. "Are you going to shut up or are you going to fucking fight me?"

Jingo is furious. He catches Ezra with the heft of his cast, the one I all but put on him at the farm, then looks down at where she's fallen into a rumpled pile. Mouth bleeding. "Fine."

He waves over his compatriot and hands the man a second weapon, his own. "Watch the others." Jingo begins to turn away, then stops, his eyes stuck on something beyond us. "Missed one." He points.

No.

Both weapons in hand, the other Blue Coat walks over to Aaron's gun. He bends down and, with the tip of Jingo's rifle, pitches it into the pile containing ours.

"Good eye," he says to Jingo, then plants his feet wide on the ground before us, cocking the barrels of both guns.

I could die from the loss of hope.

Jingo's knife flashes under the rising sun. He circles Ezra, who's pulled herself to her feet. "So this is what you do during the day. And here I thought you were sleeping."

"Now you know."

Jingo moves closer, keeping his knife at the level of her throat. "We're not that different. If you'd been born a man, you'd be a Blue Coat, too. Hell, you might have been my partner. Damned shame, Ezra."

"Damned shame," she agrees, widening her feet and taking the sideways posture to which I've become so accustomed.

The Blue Coat guarding us has become intrigued. We've already become heaps of former things. Discarded bits of waste. He's bored with the lot of us. Would prefer to see the fight.

I catch Lilly watching him, too. We nod at each other. We'll wait for an opportunity. If it doesn't come, we'll make one.

"So Lazarus Cobb is right here in my little corner of the world." Skinner looks at Lazarus, who's glaring back at him from his station on the ground. "And *The Book of Noah*."

Lazarus pushes himself clumsily to his feet. "You want me, Jingo, you can have me. Leave Ezra alone."

"I don't want you, Mr. Cobb. It would be best for everyone if you'd sit back down." Skinner points the tip of his knife at the ground. Before Lazarus can bend his knees, Skinner starts toward him, *The Book of Noah* not ten feet away.

Lazarus holds up his hands. "Fine. Fine. It just takes me awhile." With a sound like snapping twigs, his hips hit the earth. Ruined shoes go up in the air.

Skinner marches back to Ezra. *"Where is it?"* he snarls.

"It?"

The thought of killing her has affected Jingo. His eyes are pink and unbalanced. He's developed a taste for retribution that has him constantly licking his lips. "Come on now. Where's your book?"

"Fight me and I'll tell you." Ezra glances my way briefly. *Watch now, Harper.* Then looks back at Skinner. "Who sold us out? Was it one of my team?"

Skinner smiles. "You don't trust your own people very much."

"They haven't seen the sun for years."

He points at Ezra with his knife while nodding at his compatriot. "You want a little of that before I gut her?"

The other man shakes his head, missing Ezra's eyes, which are on mine. "Hell, no. I know where that's been."

Ezra blinks. *Go.* It's all the opening I need.

Three quick strides and then I dive toward Skinner's partner. His gun fires as he falls. The bullets fly over my head and into our people. I don't think about who might have been shot or who's dead. I do it exactly as Ezra's taught me. Use the force of my stride to grab the earth with my hands and swing my outstretched legs into the side of his knees. There's the muted snap of a bone breaking and the man goes down with a scream. He loses his grip on the guns and one bounces toward me.

I pick it up and turn it round. Point it at the Blue Coat. His eyes grow large as I squeeze the trigger. The man's head recoils before I hear the sound.

Jesus, forgive me. It's the worst feeling of my life.

He was someone's son. Someone's father maybe. Someone.

"Throw it down, Adams!" Somehow, Skinner has found Ezra's gun in the grass. He has it in his left hand, pointed at her head. His knife dangles awkwardly from his right hand. The tendons there no longer pull correctly on the fingers protruding from his cast and he has a hard time keeping up the blade. "I said, throw it down!"

Ezra's not going to wait for me to decide. She and Jingo are only ten feet apart. She starts walking straight toward him. Is there before I can tell her no.

"Ezra!" Jingo lifts his gun. "Stop!"

But she doesn't.

The first bullet catches her in the top of the shoulder. It turns her sideways, like an invisible hand pushing. Does nothing to stop her progress. The second catches her beneath the ribs and she steps backward, then forward. By the time I have my gun trained on Jingo's head, she's already to him.

"No, Harper!" she shouts. "He's mine."

Ezra makes it look so simple. The knife comes easily away from Jingo's bad hand. With a simple swipe of the blade, she's drawn him a second mouth. It forms in the skin above his slate, smiles big. Jingo falls to his knees. His hands are up, trying to catch the blood that's pouring out of him, unsure of what to do with it. He blinks at Ezra, then falls back.

Ezra walks over so easily that for a precious moment, I allow myself the idea that she's not mortally wounded. But then she turns and the sun catches her clothes and the fresh holes made there. Her blood shining on the grass.

"Rita?" she asks.

"I'll handle Rita," I say, and Ezra nods her head.

"Good, then." Her words collapse in the air. Never really get out of her mouth.

HAPTER

TWENTY-FIVE

Ezra is resting at my feet. Her gun is in my right hand. She's bled out and blue, and in no time at all. Lazarus has come forward and is standing next to me. The rest of us have made a semicircle around Rita, who's been set directly in our center.

"Why?" I ask her.

Rita's face is closed. She isn't giving me anything, least of all an answer.

"Was it Lazarus?"

Lazarus watches her with a look of incredulity. Betrayal shows as a set of two white circles on his cheeks.

I step closer. My gun raised. "Was it because he brought you into the bunker?"

Rita's eyes float over to our leader, then back to me. "I was just a kid," she says, pulling out her gun. "Six years beneath the earth! Six years without—"

Our weapons fire simultaneously.

I feel the bullet graze the side of my head, but there's no pain. It feels like someone running their fingers too close, pulling hairs. I have no idea if I've hit Rita.

Suddenly, I'm lying in the mud. Lilly's face is above me, blotting out the sky. Noam is over her shoulder.

"Harper!" She dabs a wad of cloth against my head where something warm and pulpy is leaking out. It's soaking my collar and running down my shirt to pool at the apex of my abdomen.

"Lazarus?"

Lilly pulls the towel away. The material is soaked in my blood. "He's fine. Rita didn't get the chance to shoot him."

I'm on the field. I can feel Lilly shaking my shoulders, but I've evacuated the premises. My body's grown tired of fighting me. Always in control. Pressing on when I was supposed to just stop. I never did, so my body's doing it for me.

I sigh and the breath takes me away from the field and Lilly's voice. The backs of my eyes go bright, then Veracity is there. Sitting in the same old chair, in front of the same yellow wall.

"Mom . . ." she begins. "I understand now."

This time I can see the whole room, including the woman who's now her mother. She's petite with black hair and a kind face. I can see their dog, a little brown terrier they call Scout who sleeps with Veracity at night. I can even see Veracity's room with its four-poster bed and blue and white comforter. Here, everything flows together. I dip my toe in this river and seem to be able to find any answer I seek.

What you did, you did for me. You were just trying to give me back my name.

I have no eyes here, no limits to my perception, so I focus on the ubiquitous. The worn floor tiles beneath her chair. The side table and its picture of Scout in an ornate silver frame. A clock and its red, boxy numbers flashing the time, just past seven in the morning.

I hear the electricity that begins the worst part of this dream. Then the sound of my daughter being electrocuted stops and the room becomes silent. I drag my attention back to her seat and, to my surprise, Veracity is still there. Staring calmly back at me.

"Mom, it's time."

Mom . . . Her voice sends me traveling down a tunnel. Then

I'm dumped out on a floor and left lying in a closet, Veracity's picture taped to the ceiling above me.

You can do this, she says. Then, just like before, she reaches down and cradles my face in her small hands. *Finish this.* Veracity looks me in the eyes and there it is, the answer reflected back to me. So simple and ever present. As most answers are.

Do this, Mom. Finish this.

Okay.

I watch from above as floating bits of me are deposited on the shore of my body below. Watch as my chest rises and falls and the cool air enters my lungs. Immediately and with great force, I'm slammed back into myself. I lie gasping for air, blinking at the bright morning light like a fish just thrown out of the ocean. It is both painful and wondrous.

"Harper!" It's Noam. He's standing above me, wiping blood out of my eyes.

All around him, the sky has caught on fire. *Thank you, God.*

I push myself upright and stare at the sparkling banks of salmon pink and daffodil yellow disappearing against the dark horizon. It's the aura of night, a set of colors I've never before noticed, or maybe never before had the ability to see. Beneath this sky, a cobalt blue floats over the dutifully breathing grass. The color comes up from each stem with a burst. Combined, these millions of blue exhalations make the earth look like the starriest of twilights. And then there are the colors of my compatriots. Beneath the war-worn colors of puce and ash, each and every one has retained a core of the most magnificent magenta. It is their literal spark of passion, still intact.

My sight is back. And maybe even more than that.

"I know how to find it . . ." I mumble.

"Sssshhhh. Quiet now." Noam dabs at my wound with the sleeve of someone else's shirt. "You're going to be fine. She got you right above the ear. It's just a flesh wound."

"Listen to me, Noam!" I grab his arm. "I know how to find the main redactor. You just have to get me there."

His eyes widen in understanding. "You're sure?"

I nod. *Yes.*

"Okay, then. I'll get it set up."

As Noam prepares for our impromptu session, I retrieve *The Book of Noah* from its temporary resting place. It's glowing so brightly beneath the soil, I have to hold a hand over my eyes and direct our guard, Daniel, from a few steps back. It's a good thing my abilities have returned. The sprig of yellow flowers I'd used as a marker was lost in the scuffle. Probably knocked away and trampled under someone's boot.

Daniel digs up the dictionary and, with great reverence, wipes off as much of the moist dirt as he can. When I again accept my twenty-pound parcel, the silver jacket is still caked in brown mud. It's a long moment before I can bring myself to put the book back in its velvet binding. To me, this now represents the loss of Ezra. What she gave her life for.

I walk back toward the fence where the guards are meting out our dead. They're putting our fallen troops on this side of the fence and the Blue Coats on the other. Lilly is waiting to wrap a length of cheesecloth around my head. She agrees to hold my precious package for me while Noam and I go to work. Noam has collected one of the guard's backpacks, and from it pulls a perspiring silver canister and a large black tarp. Unfurled and held vertically to the earth, the material becomes a six-by-six-foot wall behind which I'll find some uninterrupted space.

"Come on, Harper." Noam beckons me with a hand.

I pray as I walk over. *God, make your truth mine.* This is our last chance.

Noam has taken off his jacket and laid it on the wet earth, making a place for me to sit without the distraction of sticky, seeping cold. The two guards holding the tarp stand on the side nearest the fence. They've formed themselves into poles with only their fingertips visible over the cloth. Noam kneels down next to me and leans in close.

"Ready?" he asks.

I nod and close my eyes.

"The main redactor will look like the others. But it will pulse, as if it has a heartbeat. All the lives touched by it, John's nearness to it as he wanders the halls looking for it . . . they bind themselves to it. Make it into a sentient thing that calls to you, Harper. Find the life in it . . . the master . . . the master . . . the master . . ." Immediately, I am pulled out of my body and spirited away on the sled of Noam's voice.

Things are different this time. There is no light inside this dark tunnel, though I can see scant traces of it as I fly past. I appear to be high up in the sky, above the radiance of earth, and it's unnerving. The effort of looking for something familiar is affecting my body. The sensation of my eyes working hard beneath fluttering lids threatens to pull me back. I breathe it away. Think of Veracity's calm voice and of John and am rejoined to my course. The sky is rising or I'm falling and the barest bit of sun floods this hollow space.

I blink and am in the basement of the Geddard Building.

Usually, I see a place as a product of the energy within it. But the room is as clear as if I was actually standing on the white tile floor. It's huge, a football field with a nine-foot ceiling. There are six-foot-tall redactors organized around three main aisles that run the length of the building. I'm at the room's center and need to walk or run or think myself forward to a brown-red glow shining in the room's northeast corner.

Go. A handful of steps and I've covered hundreds of yards. I'm now in the correct quadrant of the building with my head near the ceiling tiles and my lower half warm and tingling. I look down and find a redactor where my legs should be.

This refrigerator-size metal box is humming with active

machinery. I know each part's purpose and name. Even intimate details of the men and women who sparked it into life and fed it the colostrum of bios, making it thrive. Through this redactor flows more lives than I can stand to consider. Information is this creature's sustenance, received from the many and returned to the one. Then the flow reverses and information comes from the one and returns to the many. Red Lists and infractions and biographical data. Everything, about everyone. I sense it all.

I follow the collected information as it flows out of this machine and is swept, along with the others', into a rising tide. With the gentlest shift in perception, I'm able to see this ghostlike river of green data flowing around and through me. It surges toward the one redactor near the corner of the room, then disappears into it. The humming black box throbs a toxic brown-gray with the consumption of each incoming wave. Then it switches colors, becoming an incandescent red, and the flow is reversed. The river comes back. I watch as its glowing waters approach and take a deep breath just before it rushes through me.

Abjure, abolition, abominable, aboriginal, abrogate, abscond, accent, accretion, accustom, affluent, aggrandize, agnostic, alliance, ambition, amend, amok, anarchy, ancestor, ancient, angst, anguish, annihilate, anomalous, antiquity, aspire, assault, assert, assertion, assimilate, atheism, authentic, awe . . .

I sputter to the surface. This Red List is thousands of words long. It's an attempt by the Confederation not just to drown the resistance but to starve the wanting soul with silence—the ultimate isolation. It's a last-ditch effort in which they're trying to turn us all mute. They're betting everything on me not getting the right redactor. Helen Rumney. President and his Cabinet. They knew something, maybe not about the war. Certainly not about John's job here, but they knew about us and how close we were—how close we *are*—to retrieving our lost vocabulary and all the ideas and freedoms therein.

I look around for John and find his blue light a few hundred feet away. Hurry toward him before Noam can call me back.

John is kneeling between two redactors. His head is bent over a black machine tucked in the palm of his hand. I touch him gently on the arm and the contact throws up a pearlescent spark. He turns toward the aisle and frowns at the place where I'm standing. I back away so as not to distract him.

"Noam? Is she here?" John speaks into the device, his other hand held like a cup just beyond it to keep his voice from traveling.

"She's there." Noam's voice comes back softly, but I can't tell from where. Either the black machine in his hand or the small round receiver inside the whorl of John's ear. "I'm calling her back now and we'll have the identity for you right away."

John reaches out across the aisle and puts his fingers where my thigh would be, were I here in body. The pink of my aura there is turned violet as he passes through me. *John . . .*

He looks up, right where my face would be.

Harper? It's Noam speaking but his voice is no longer coming from John's receiver. *Harper?*

My right hand suddenly hurts. I look down and see the tips of my fingers disappearing.

Harper!

Quickly, I kneel down next to John and lean in until the rose-colored aura floating off his face is a warmth on my own. *I love you,* I say.

"Harper?" John asks.

Harper!

It's like being shot from a cannon backward. I land in my body with a grunt. Open my eyes to see Noam right in front of me, frowning.

"Goddamned time!" he shouts, reaching down to remove

my hand from the cup of ice into which it's been thrust. "Now, where is it?"

I give Noam the counts. From where John sits, he's to walk east to the second, then third aisle. Next, he's to turn north and go one, two, three, four, five redactors down. It's the one on the right side with a small silver triangle hidden on its base. He'll have to look hard. The emblem is no larger than the tip of my pinky.

Noam repeats these directions into his transmitter, talking John to the main redactor, then waiting nervously as the deed is done. It is two minutes—120 seconds—before John's voice comes back over the line, informing us that the task is completed. And with no alarms having been tripped. We wait until John is safely out of the basement before signing off. He gives us the one word that means he's alive and well out of harm's way—*Clear*—then the line goes dead and it's just me and Noam sitting behind a tarp in the middle of a field. Smiling.

When I go to stand, my forehead becomes moist and the horizon dips. I barely get to a clump of weeds before throwing up last night's dinner.

Noam helps me up and leads me to Ezra's body, where Lazarus and Lilly are saying their good-byes. I kneel down next to her. After sliding my hands beneath Ezra's shoulders, I pull her body into a sitting position.

"Harper," Lazarus says from behind me. "We have to leave her here."

"No." I yank Ezra with all my strength, but she's heavier than I'd anticipated. Doesn't come along so easily on the uneven turf.

"We'll come back for her after—"

"*I said no!*"

But I can't move her an inch. Sobbing, I lower her back to the ground.

"Harper, Harper . . ." Lazarus whispers softly. He takes one of my arms and pulls me away. "We'll come back for her. If we're going to win this war, we have to go now."

Bond is a half mile ahead. We see it as a normal line of brick houses with open windows showing the slightest bit of curtain. From here, there is no sign of damage.

We walk alongside the road, not daring to put our weight on the asphalt that's grown warm in the early sun. Lazarus doesn't know how far up our people have seeded it with bombs. I stay close to Lazarus as Noam and Lilly and the others rush ahead. There are preparations for our broadcast needing to be handled. We only have seven or eight minutes to verify the larger things that should have already happened. By now, a comrade in Wernthal has already climbed out onto a hill high atop the city's outer perimeter and taken over a station. When Lazarus takes the stage, we'll have wrestled away control of the airwaves so people will be able to watch and listen. We've taken down the slates so people can follow.

Ahead of us, Lilly has rounded the corner that opens up to the square. She puts her hands to her face. Even without her glasses, she can see something awful. "Lazarus!" she shouts. "They've ruined it! *They've ruined it!*"

Lazarus and I walk faster up the slight rise. The square that will be our theater is a hundred yards off. The path between us is covered with bodies. There's been serious fighting here. Our dead have been laid out on their backs and stare up at the blue morning sky. Those that are Blue Coats have been turned facedown, their noses ground into the road.

This has just happened. A few of our people are making the rounds. Identifying the dead, collecting ID patches and any items people might have tucked into their pockets or the underlining of their caps.

A woman just ahead is flipping over a Blue Coat. She looks up and sees us collected on the hill. Points with a shaking finger. "They're here! They're here!" she shouts to the others, who stop what they're doing and look.

Dozens of people begin to shout. Some run toward us, others run back to a group of people sitting heavily around the concrete center of the square. They're revived by the news. Jump up and hug one another. Run into the surrounding buildings and gather up others who've taken cover. Out comes a line of our fellow resisters that doesn't end. There are thousands of us here. They flow out into the roads and spill onto the side street we're using to approach. A young woman with jet-black hair and topaz skin bursts through the crowd's perimeter. Her uniform is striped like Ezra's.

She motions to Lazarus with a flattened hand. "Lieutenant Emerson reporting, sir!"

Lazarus repeats the movement and the woman puts both hands behind her back. "What's happened here?" he asks.

The woman can't wipe the smile from her face. "Forgive me, sir. We didn't think you'd survived."

Lazarus looks around. The damage is tremendous. "We have to begin broadcasting in five minutes, Lieutenant. Tell me, what's happened?"

The Lieutenant's face dims. "We lost approximately six hundred troops. But we're nine thousand strong. And we're ready, sir."

"What's the report from Wernthal?"

"We have over twenty thousand troops just in Wernthal proper alone, sir. Thirteen thousand of those are in National House Square, and at the Geddard Building, another ten. Thousand, that is, sir. We've taken seventy-eight percent of our targets . . ."

"How clear is the path between here and Wernthal?"

"We've secured all but Danville up in Kibner, sir, but we have a workaround that won't take the teams more than two hundred miles out of their way. The transport vans will be here tomorrow morning, sir. And Air Force One will be here in two hours, sir."

I lean in to ask Lazarus, "What's Air Force One?"

"My ride to the capital. President's plane. You, Noam, and Lilly are taking the slow road to Washington, as you'll be stopping to assess conditions in a few key locales between here and there. You, darling, will be taking a van." He turns his attention again to the officer. "Did we take the Hub?" he asks her. Lazarus is referring to the center from which all media in the Confederation flows. If we've acquired access, we'll be able to project our message into the homes of every man, woman, and child in the country. It's critical.

The woman takes a deep breath. "We think so, but we don't know for sure. We won't know, sir, until it's time to broadcast."

The woman and Lazarus discuss the details of our efforts all the way to the edge of the square, where we stop to observe the destruction. Main street, the two side streets, the west side avenue, they all look like what they are: a war zone. And this from only three T-Units. These black hulking beasts, the most elite of Blue Coat transports, have been stopped with armor-piercing artillery, their bellies emptied onto the bloodied cement. Hundreds of dead Blue Coats ring each one. The State must not have known about us for very long or they would have mobilized a vastly larger assault.

"What are we going to do?" Lilly is whimpering into Lazarus's ear and pointing at the square. "Look at it!"

The buildings' facades have crumbled or fallen off. Tree limbs litter the cracked roads. The grass has been trampled by the dragging away of bodies. The square itself has received the most damage. Grenades and the hammer of heavy artillery have pockmarked the cement, the exact place where Lazarus was going to stand and say, *Come out of your homes, we've already done the fighting. See how easy it will be.* People were to have been given a pristine look at war. We were going to produce for them a safe, easy passage to freedom. Play down the associated costs.

Lazarus nods at a tall metal structure standing on the far side of the square, shouts, "Follow me!" and begins through the growing crowd toward it.

People part for Lazarus as he makes his way toward a tall seat at the structure's tip, now occupied by a man in a short-billed hat. Noam runs ahead, climbing the lower rungs of the metal contraption to shout up at the man. "Lyle?"

"Hello, Noam!" He turns and nods at a woman standing on the sidewalk beneath him. In her arms is the largest camera I've ever seen off a tripod. "We're ready when you are." He looks back over at Lazarus, who's pulling thoughtfully at his white beard. "I know it's not what we expected."

"Our director, ladies and gentlemen," Lazarus says, stopping a few feet out so he won't have to tilt up his neck. "I think it's better. What do you think, Lyle?"

"Do we have the book?"

"Yes." Lazarus motions to me and I hold up the velvet pouch.

"Then I'd say we have four minutes." Our director smiles.

Lazarus has already begun across the broken asphalt toward the square.

Lyle has to yell after him, "Anywhere you don't want us to shoot?"

Lazarus shakes his head. "Nope. Shoot it all."

The crowd has been grouped into equal quarters around the square. Lazarus has been cleaned up and is positioned in its broken center. Noam is holding *The Book of Noah* and Lilly is in charge of the radio. In just a couple of moments, we'll learn if our troops in Wernthal have taken over the airwaves. I'm the only one without something left to do.

"Lazarus?" Lyle's assistant calls.

"Yes?"

"We have two minutes, sir."

"We'll be ready."

The woman turns and runs back to our director, who's mumbling to a half dozen people. Things about lighting and shots he wants to make sure they get in.

Lilly is up on the square with Lazarus. She fiddles with the dial on our transistor radio as Lazarus raises up his arms. Everyone goes still.

"My friends! We're going to do what we came here to do!" he shouts. "We're going to show the citizens of the Confederation of the Willing the true face of courage! The Blue Coats knew we were coming. And even so . . . *we won!*"

A roar goes up from the crowd. Lazarus waves his arms again and they're silenced.

"In one moment, we're going to find out if our men and women in Wernthal have been successful. If our people have indeed taken over the Confederation media, we'll be receiving a transmission." He motions to the black box that's been placed next to him. Lilly is working the dial, running it up and down the numbers until a bit of static sounds. She leaves the knob where the feedback is loudest, then steps off the cement podium.

"When we receive the go-ahead from Wernthal, we'll immediately begin broadcasting an invitation to our sisters and brothers in the Confederation. For the first time in three decades, they'll have a voice uniquely and inviolably their own. And a choice to make. Freedom or false security. Pursue their own happiness, express their own beliefs, live according to the mandates of their own hearts, or continue on with that which they currently know. Our people stationed in the Geddard Building have been successful. The slates have been taken down."

Again, the crowd roars.

The director's assistant pushes onto the stage and attaches a small microphone to Lazarus's lapel. She sets another in front of the small black receiver so we'll hear when the transmission comes. "Ten seconds . . ." she whispers, and Lazarus holds up his hands. Everyone stills.

Lilly comes over and takes my hand. "God be with us."

The assistant flashes us a countdown with her hand. *Five, four, three* . . . Then slips silently away. We're all leaning forward, watching Lilly's receiver.

Nothing. Too many seconds pass and our faces drain of color. A woman on my other side slides her hand into mine. It's slick. Hot with fear.

Lazarus looks down at Lilly. "The frequency?" he asks.

Lilly is terrified. I can barely make out her words. "It's tuned correctly."

It's 7:00 for only a few seconds more. Then it's 7:01, then 7:02, then 7:03, and the world has collapsed. I watch the second hand on my new friend's watch.

7:04.

"Patience," Lazarus whispers. We've become restless. All popping joints and moving feet.

"Oh, God!" a woman somewhere behind me cries. It kicks off a chain reaction of murmured prayers and sobs.

"Quiet!" Lazarus shouts. He points to the black box.

". . . *sshh-shhhhhhhhh . . . crrrrrr . . .*" It's begun to crack and whistle. ". . . *shhhhhh-k-k-k-k- . . . crrrkr-k-k-k-k . . .*"

These hissing snippets of sound come through the small black face of the receiver like sun coming through storm clouds. "*Heeeeelllllllllloooooooooooo . . .*" I can see it reflecting on people's faces. Lighting them up.

"Hello! They're saying *hello*!" Lilly shouts and a few people clap.

The box makes a deep popping sound and out comes a fully formed voice, "Group . . . Fiiiive . . . aught . . . niiiiner . . . We have secured the primary!"

There is a flurry of activity. The director's other crew members jump to attention. A woman races up onto the platform and presses a cloth to Lazarus's sweating head. Another scrambles onto the landing to take a reading of the suddenly breaking, early morning light.

"People!" The director has a large white tube held to the end of his mouth. He shouts repeatedly for us to quiet down. Says we're going to be live in *eight, seven, six, five, four, three* . . . The final two numbers are mouthed by the assistant on the ground. She rolls two fingers toward the square and

Lazarus, cool as the day I met him, smiles at the rest of the world.

"My name is Lazarus Cobb. I've come into your homes and offices to tell you that the resistance has taken over the Confederation's networks, and earlier this morning, your slates were turned off. The former Confederation Cabinet is, at this moment, being held by members of this resistance until we can organize a trial presided over by you, the people. You have been robbed. Of your families, your voices, and your lives. This government has lied to you. Starting with one big lie that necessitated a million others." Lazarus takes a deep breath. Looks directly into the camera and tells the world as gently as possible, "Fellow citizens, there was no Pandemic. They euthanized hundreds of thousands of innocent people just to lay claim to the country! To begin anew with as many helpless orphans as possible, shackled victims of a holocaust made to run their new world for them!"

I look around at our group. We've pressed into one circular body, have grown drastically in number, even since Lazarus began speaking. There's no more empty space between his concrete podium and the surrounding buildings. The camera will see only faces and heads, nine thousand of us, still as statues.

"Those of you old enough to remember the beforetime are hereby charged with dispensing the truth to your fellow citizens. And those of you too young to know the truth will very shortly be provided documented proof of it. We will provide as much information as you need once more immediate concerns have been handled." Lazarus motions toward Noam, who climbs up onto the square with *Noah* in tow. "Let me tell you something, my brothers and sisters. *Freedom*—the concept of doing what is in your soul to do, of not being bound to the ideologies of others—is not just a state of being. Freedom is also a word. One of many that have been kept from you."

Noam holds the leather tome gently by its spine so Lazarus is free to flip through its pages. "There is a book that's been kept from you. You know it as *The Book of Noah*. But in truth, it's something called a dictionary. This collection of words and ideas has been hidden from you for over three decades because the best way to enslave a people is to *censor* truth. To censor ideas that would otherwise set you free. What does the word *censor* mean? Let me tell you."

Tenderly, Lazarus flips through the thin, yellowed pages. People around us who don't know about *The Book of Noah* are standing on tippy-toe, trying to see.

Lazarus finds the page and reads with his head bent, "*Censorship*. To suppress or delete anything considered objectionable. Censorship. Exclusion from consciousness."

Suddenly, the portent of this book is on everyone's faces. They watch Lazarus's hands as they move to another word. Nodding him along, *hurry up, hurry up*.

He reads from another page. "*Democracy*. A government in which the supreme power is vested in and exercised by the people."

Hands are going up all over the crowd. People have begun to shout out words they've heard and don't know. Or those whose meanings they've forgotten.

Lazarus can't keep the smile from his face. He tells the crowd that there's no time to look up too many of them. But, if he points to them, he'd like to hear their requested words. A few hundred arms wave in the air.

There. *Lyrical*.

And you. *Destiny*.

Sir? *Ethical*.

Yes, ma'am? *Independence*.

This goes on awhile until the director signals to Lazarus, *Time to wrap it up*, and our leader waves their arms back down to their sides.

"There is one more definition I'd like to read before we move on. It's for the word *veracity*." Lazarus pauses to find me where I stand. "Veracity means the power of conveying or perceiving the truth. It means a *devotion to truth*. The kind of quality that will serve as a benchmark for our new government and remind us of the need for a diligence we lost many years ago."

I nod my thanks and turn my moist eyes down. Lazarus's voice continues overhead.

"My sisters and brothers, you have a language and a truth of which you know nothing! You have a *history* of which you know nothing. People—ancestors—who've fought for our freedom with words instead of guns.

"Freedom is not an option. It is not a *want*. It is a need. Freedom to live according to the truth of one's own heart is as necessary as fire. As water. As food. As air. As you can see, we lost women and men here today. What further evidence could you require as to the timeliness and importance of this cause? As well as our commitment to it? Take note of these fallen heroes and understand that the price they've paid is worth the prize. Just as it shall be again, and again, and again, until we lay honest claim to honest lives."

The audience is transfixed, their attention rapt on our leader's face.

"Here, around this square, you see the price of freedom. But now you also see the reward. Come and be counted alongside us! There is a far worse fate than living in unsure times and that is the death of the soul. That is the true Pandemic!"

Lazarus is as tall as a tree on that small cracked square. I try to imagine what the rest of the country must see. What they must look like, staring openmouthed at their televisions, or at the wall-mounted screens posted at their places of work.

Lazarus says his good-bye and the camera pans away from us. It's replaced by a board marked up with crude instructions about what to do next. Where to go. How to get there. What will happen. The pirated stations will immediately begin broadcasting excerpts from *Noah*. Electronic copies will be sent out to every city. A library will be established in each county seat and will serve as the home base for lessons the resistance has prepared. We'll be providing them classes in history, literature, and a dozen other topics. And in return, we ask for their involvement in government. To learn about American policy and be active in election processes.

The camera stops rolling and we wander around for a while, not knowing quite what to do next. We won't know right away if Lazarus's words have been sufficient to have saved us from apathy. The world is on the other end of the camera and, for the moment, silent.

apostasy

discriminate

ego

fossil

heresy

kindred

obstreperous

offline

veracity

ve-rac-i-ty: habitual observance of truth in speech or statement; truthfulness; conformity to truth or fact.

HAPTER
TWENTY-SIX

"So. How are things going today? The last couple of weeks?"

Mr. Weigland is sitting on top of his desk, short legs bouncing off the side. He's grown a goatee. A piping of orange hair on his chin that points down like an arrow and draws attention to his wattle. It makes his enormous smile look all the more ridiculous. He's trying to appear languid and carefree. But carefree isn't a moist face and high-pitched voice. That's *nervous*.

Oh, God. What now?

"Sit down, sit down." Mr. Weigland jumps off the side of his desk and his new glasses fall off his nose. "Oopsy daisy." He squats down to find them, patting the floor for the flashy gray metal and rectangular panes. He's sweet like this, flustered and fumbling. I pick up the glasses and hold them out. Let him feel his way to them, starting at my hand.

"What can I do for you, sir?"

Mr. Weigland leans against his desk, staying within reach of the tissues. Never a good sign. "You've had a hard couple of months." He stops. Is assessing my reaction to the mention of my lost daughter and attempted suicide.

"Yes, sir."

He smiles. "I have a little something set up for you. Something I think you might just really need." Mr. Weigland is giddy with himself. He pushes off the desk, nearly skipping around its edge. He presents me his phone, numbers-side out. "We all thought it might be good if you could call Sarah."

I panic. *He knows where she is.* Mr. Weigland knows the whereabouts of my baby.

The chair slips out from under me. Or maybe I fall out of it. Either way, I'm suddenly on the floor with Mr. Weigland's hands hauling me up, tucking me back in.

He points up at the circular grate on the ceiling, at the recording disk through which we're being monitored, and holds a finger to his mouth. *Sssshhhh.*

"You okay?" he asks, pulling a sheet of paper from the top drawer of his desk. "You want some water?"

"Uh . . . yes. Please." I stumble over my response as Mr. Weigland jots down quick, sloppy words. "I would."

He finishes the note and slides it quietly across the table. I read as Mr. Weigland retrieves the pitcher of ice water always perspiring on his bookcase. *We've put my office cameras on a fifteen-minute hiatus. It's as much as we could get without drawing notice. All that's being recorded right now is what we say, so respond carefully.*

"Here you go." Mr. Weigland presses the cold glass into my hands. He kneels down in front of me and looks directly into my eyes. "No need to worry, Harper. Your daughter is in safe hands."

"Thank you," I mumble.

He's with the resistance. God bless Mr. Weigland. There were so many signs over the years. If I'd wanted to, I would have known.

"If you don't want to call Sarah, I understand." Mr. Weigland goes back to his seat. "It was just a thought."

I take the pen and write one question. *Will it put her in jeopardy?*

He shakes his head no. "It would be perfectly okay for you two to talk. And that's straight from the company's grief counselor."

Do I want to call my daughter? *No.* Veracity has become a

girl named Sarah who might not want me. And if I do talk to her, I'll want to see her, touch her, hold her until this nightmare world folds back and reveals the blue sky of normalcy. A few moments of awkward dialogue won't ever be enough. But saying no isn't really an option. This could be my only chance.

I put down the glass. "Would you dial for me? Please?"

The receiver in the crook of his neck, Mr. Weigland punches in numbers from a card. He then comes back around to the front of his desk, where he can offer me comfort if things go bad.

"Yes . . . hello?" He sits upright. "Yes, this is Mr. Weigland. I have Harper Adams here. Yes. Yes, thank you. That's very nice. Thank you. Well, uh . . . she's a little nervous. Uh-huh. How about I put her on?"

This is my introduction. A few fumbling "um"s and "well"s and I'm handed the receiver, still warm from Mr. Weigland's grasp.

I put it up to my ear. "Hello?"

"Yes. Hello." It's not my daughter. It's a woman around my age with a softer voice. Lighter, as if she has no lost freedoms to miss. "It's nice to finally meet you. Talk to you, anyway." She's too immediately friendly. Too pert, like those women who form themselves into circles, pray for the sins of their neighbors, obsess together over their gardens, all that crap.

"Harper Adams," I say. "And you are?" She won't answer because she's not supposed to and because she never does a goddamned thing to break the rules. I'd wager my pay card on it. "You are?" I repeat, not caring if it comes out sounding rude. She can't expect me not to ask.

"Harper!" Mr. Weigland leans forward.

I turn in my seat so he can't snatch the phone out of my hand.

"I would feel exactly the same way you do, Miss Adams. But you know I can't give you my information." A pause. She's lost her voice. It comes back cracked, like a poor transmission. "This is hard for all of us."

Christ. She isn't so docile, doesn't sit around in noxious church circles, maybe. *Maybe* is nice.

"I'm sorry." I have to push it out.

Her niceness should comfort me. This woman is taking care of my child, after all. But I'm selfish. I need something to tell me that my daughter won't love her more. Not now. Not later when she grows a woman's body, loves a boy who doesn't love her back, falls into the real world and loses some of her faith.

"I don't know how to start this," I say, needing to dig my way out of this bitterness and prepare myself for Veracity. I need to be happy when she gets on the line. I need her to be listening when I warn her.

"Harper." The woman says my name too carefully. Immediately, I know what's coming. "I don't know how to say this any other way. We can't get Sarah to come to the phone."

The blood falls from my face. Mr. Weigland sees it. He reaches around my turned body and puts his hand on the phone. "You need me to talk to her? Let me talk to her . . ."

"No," I say.

My daughter's new mother thinks I was talking to her. "Both my husband and I feel it's not right to pressure her," she says beautifully. In that tone that means, *I will not let you harm my child.*

"I was talking to my boss."

"I'm sorry . . ."

"No." I clear my throat. "Let's not use that word anymore. Okay?" I'll start crying. *Sorry* is the best descriptor of this situation. It doesn't need any further evidence. "What's your name?" I whisper, begging. "Just so I know . . ." *Whatever I can know from a first name.* Which will be mostly about this woman's parents: were they conservative or liberal; romantic or stoic; did they have her prior to the Pandemic or after. The name they chose for her will answer these things.

Mr. Weigland stands up. Erect, disapproving. "They're not supposed to give names."

I nod into the phone. "Never mind. It's okay . . ."

"Sophia." She's almost crying.

Sophia. It's a good name. Unconventional, which means she went through the Pandemic. Has probably suffered some and grown past needing the hard lessons. These are all good things pointing to normal. Telling me she'll know how to love Veracity. How quickly my needs turn. Now I want her to be a saint, a warrior, a safety net. My cardboard cutout.

Mr. Weigland presses a tissue into my hand and it baits the tide. I start to cry. "Is she okay?" My voice wobbles over the question.

"Fine." Sophia is nodding. Dabbing at her eyes. I can hear the movement, the creasing tissues. "Happy as she could be, considering."

Happy. I'll be glad she's told me this later. But not now. "Why won't she get on the phone?"

The husband is listening. I hear the low drone of his voice behind hers, suggesting, comforting. They're deciding together what to say. I hear the woman call him by name. *Jeremy.* Perhaps she's done this for me.

"Sophia?"

She puts her lips right up next to the mouthpiece. Cups a hand over the answer. "She just . . . doesn't understand." Sophia breaks for a moment to take a breath. "There's just never going to be a good enough answer. Do you understand?"

I sob. Don't try to hide it. "Listen to me . . ."

"I'm listening."

"Work with her on her Red Words."

"We will. We already do."

"It's important!" I say it with more force than I'd wanted. "Please. She could get hurt if she says one accidentally. I mean, she *will* get hurt if she tries to say even one. Do you understand? I've dreamt it," I say. "I know it."

There is a pause on the other end of the line.

Sophia comes back softly. "Okay." Then stronger, with understanding. "Absolutely. I promise. We promise."

"Thank you," I say, though I don't think she hears me.

Or maybe I haven't said it.

All I can think about is getting off the phone. Running down the long main hall and lying down in the women's restroom. I want to rest my head on the cool tile.

"Will you tell her that I love her?" My mouth is wobbling. My words come out so warped, I don't know how Sophia understands.

But she does. "Yes. We will . . ."

I give the phone to Mr. Weigland and turn away. I can hear Sophia's voice assuring me, "We love her, too." It's in the air. Floating down like a feather. Landing like a lead weight.

Mr. Weigland takes my place. He tells them not to be too upset. It's natural. We'll try again in a year, maybe two. Then puts the receiver back in its cradle.

"Harper," he says.

I don't answer.

"Harper." He leans forward. Puts his hands over mine. "She's safe."

I interlace my fingers with his. "Thank you."

Mr. Weigland's voice is the barest whisper, more a thought than spoken words. "No, Harper. Thank you."

HAPTER

TWENTY-SEVEN

Winter is shoring up in the western sky. We feel it behind us like an invisible hand. It's the third week of October and we've made frustrating progress. We stop for week-long periods of time to secure towns between Bond and Wernthal, now referred to as Washington. Our group consists of roughly one hundred members of the resistance. Some of us are newly organized Armed Forces. These new troops carry weapons as we move, flanking the rest of us and acting as our armor. The majority of our group is soon to be inducted into a governmental body called *Congress*. We've taken the slow way to our new capital in order to talk to members of the communities through which we pass. We're getting to know our *constituents*—the people who will be represented by these Congressional Members in a new administration. We are one of many groups marching across the country toward Washington, providing outreach and collecting data.

Our group started small with strictly members of the resistance, but grows with every new town. We come into a place like a snowball, or maybe more like a swarm of locusts, descending in vast numbers, needing shelter, food, and drink. When we leave, refurbishing trucks have to follow to keep the town stocks full. Despite our consumption, most are more than happy to have us. Often, they're waiting for us at the new county lines, eager to set up a library and get what we've started calling our catch-'em-up courses, provided free to schools. We've even been thrown something called a *parade*—an embarrassing show of gratitude that has us sitting on top of cars. Waving to the others who're relegated to the sidewalks that line the streets. When we leave, we've collected a new cadre of cadets—women and men who want to be a part of things and a better world for their children.

People are hungry for copies of *Noah*, handed out on portable drives. They get a taste of what they've been missing, freedom of speech, a language that maps to all the things they've been feeling and needing, and they're hooked. And they're angry. They are learning the extent of their bondage via the things from which they've been kept.

In each county hub, a group of government liaisons has been set up. These liaisons have been put on, for lack of a better term, Media Watch. As changes pour in, they call meetings that a representative from each town must attend. Representatives then take these updates to their communities, passing on the status of such things as the development of money institutions called Banks, the free health clinics being set up, when the gasoline trucks will arrive, how to register for reassignment to all the new positions that are about to be opened up, and so on.

Until we get to our new capital and take on our administrative duties, Lilly and Noam are in charge of setting up digital libraries in former administrative buildings. My job has been to go into a town ahead of our group and use my abilities to search out potential threats. There are always a few Confederation loyalists hiding in somebody's basement. Or die-hard Blue Coats holed up in the admin building's safe zones. There is an awful resemblance between this job and BodySpeak. I stretch out my hand and point to people whose colors are suspicious and they're taken into custody. Held for questioning by a jury of their peers. As long as that second part happens, I'll have to choke it down. I can only imagine what John would think if he was around. I've become a cop of sorts. Doing the dirty work myself so other, worse people won't get the chance. It is my prejudice come full circle. And my understanding.

Only Lazarus and a few other key members have been picked up and flown out early. These acting members of our administration are overseeing and implementing changes too numerous to list. It will be four or five weeks before Lilly, Noam, and I get there. A month or a little over before I get to see John again, and how everything in my former home has changed.

I think of John every day. Wonder what he's seeing and doing and where he is. On the worst days, I pick a point on the road coming into whatever town we're in and imagine him appearing over the horizon. Running or walking, sometimes on a horse, behind the wheel of a car, his face lit up. I think of John every day but won't let myself think of Veracity. I don't know what's happened to her. There are too many possibilities. I need us to get to the capital before it snows and we're stuck in one of these small towns with poor reception and no connection to the online lists being constantly updated. Lists that tell us who's still living by the inverse information of who's dead.

In this rural portion of the former Confederation, news of the war travels slowly. Men and women donning the couriers' signature red cross stitched onto one sleeve come into town on foot, horseback, T-Unit, or car. They bear huge stacks of printed records of those who've been killed and those who are missing. Sometimes Lilly's receiver begins spitting up names of the dead, lost, or wounded and people come running, bleary-eyed. Some already crying.

The third week in, Lilly finds her niece on the Casualties List. The next week, her nephew. After that, she stops looking and listening. Begins running the other way every time a courier is seen making haste into town or when her receiver starts crackling.

The fifth week in, I hear names coming out of Lilly's radio I hadn't anticipated: *Sophia Williams* and *Jeremy Williams.*

Sophia and Jeremy, the names of my daughter's new parents. Then following them—*Sarah*, my daughter's new name. The announcer explains that their home has been bombed, but no bodies have been found. They're being presumed *lost*, not *dead*. It could be some other group of people, the three names a fluke. The waiting to see is intolerable.

Lazarus has written to tell me he's made it a special job of his to find my daughter. In a handwritten note, he advises me I'm not to lose my focus and start worrying. He's put the best of the best on the case. As soon as they find Veracity, I'll know. And this special dispatch will find Veracity alive and well. *Even if I'm not a Sentient,* he writes, *I feel that Veracity is very much alive and well. I feel it in these worn-out old bones.*

Lilly, Noam, and I are in a town named Chester, sleeping in a tavern during our stay. This morning, as soon as the light comes through the main hall's shuttered windows, Lilly shakes me awake. She tells me something came for her last night by pony mail. Something I'm supposed to see.

I roll out of my sleeping bag, already dressed. Tuck my hair under a hat someone gave me two towns back and follow Lilly into the cold, empty street. I'm too tired to ask her where we're going. Mostly, I don't want to know.

We sludge along a few blocks, then take a turn into what must have been a police station. Two guards are standing just inside. They recognize Lilly and wave us in. We walk down a long corridor studded with offices and stop at what I recognize as an old interrogation room.

"Hello, Lilly." A man with white hair and wild gray brows greets her with a big, gap-toothed grin. He's sitting at the only desk and stands as we enter. "So good to see you again."

"You just saw me yesterday," Lilly says roughly.

"I did!" the man replies, unfazed. "And hopefully I'll see you again tomorrow!" He smiles even larger, picking at his teeth with the tip of a long fingernail. He turns to me and offers his hand. "Reginald Parker. I used to teach at the University of Illinois with Lilly here."

"Nice to meet you." We shake.

Lilly is exhausted. She waves a hand at the man who so obviously adores her. "Where are we doing this?"

Reginald motions us into two chairs. "Right here."

Lilly sticks a hand into her satchel. It's wide and deep. Bulging with all the things we have to carry with us, as there are no more walk-in restaurants or corner pharmacies. Lilly's anxious to find something that's not coming easily into her hand.

"What is it, Lilly?" I ask.

She puts her whole face at the purse's mouth. "A disk."

"What's on the disk?"

"I don't know," she says. "John sent it to me. I'm supposed to show it to you first thing this morning."

I look down at my chair. There are the same brown armrests from my nightmare. And my legs, wearing the same corduroy pants. If I'd known we were coming here to see this, I'd have changed clothes.

Please God, I pray. *Don't let it be bad.*

Lilly retrieves the disk and hands it to her friend. Reginald takes it to a screen posted on the wall and pops it into the reader. Immediately, an image appears. It's the room I've dreamt of. A living room holding a chair, a tall brass floor lamp with a neck that extends, a small side table with curved legs. Soft light is coming through the window, turning the room yellow just like in my nightmare.

John walks in and comes to stand in front of the camera. He gets down on one knee so I'm staring at his face. "Hello, Harper." He smiles and I put a hand over my mouth. *It's a good sign.* "I wish there was time for me to tell you everything that's happened . . ." He pauses to look down at some spot on the floor. "And how much I'm looking forward to seeing you when you arrive in Washington. But I have to go back almost this minute, and there's someone I've had the luck to find who'll be coming back with me." John looks to his right, smiles back at me, and ducks out of the picture.

"Oh, Harper!" Lilly puts a hand on my thigh.

There is my daughter. Taking the same seat as in my dream. Her hair is long, now darker and thicker. Her face less round. More like a woman's.

"Mom." Her eyes go slowly to the camera. She's shy, not sure how to talk to me from so far away. "I'm sorry I didn't visit you in Chalmers. And I'm sorry I didn't take your call." She pauses to wipe away a few quick tears. "I know you were just trying to keep what happened to Hannah from happening to me."

Veracity sits back to pull a tissue from her hip pocket. "I understand what you're doing. I don't have to go by Sarah anymore," she says. "You were trying to give me back my name . . ."

I put a hand out and touch the screen as my daughter's voice fills the room.

". . . Veracity."